Elven Blood

Debra Dunbar

Copyright © 2013 Debra Dunbar All rights reserved. No part of this book may be used or reproduced in any manner whatsoever without written permission except in the case of brief quotations embodied in critical articles and reviews.

Anessa Books, Bethesda, Maryland

ISBN:1484001354
ISBN-13:9781484001356

DEDICATION

To Dr. Hadley Tremaine (1939-2001), Chairman of the Department of English, Hood College, Frederick, Maryland, who taught me that there is great treasure to be found in what others consign to Hell.

Special thanks to Mount Olivet Cemetery and Keeney and Basford Funeral Home for their friendly and enthusiastic help in my research for this book.

~1~

I heaved the decapitated demon head through the gate to Hel and turned to look at the guardian. The way her shoulders slumped and she kicked at the floor, gave me the impression she was not happy to be supervising.

"Third one this week," I told her, as if she didn't know.

I had a bounty on my head, but the demons Haagenti was sending after me were the dregs of the hierarchy, desperate beings looking to get lucky and boost their fame by taking me down. Idiots. I kept killing them and tossing their heads through the gate that connected the realm of the humans with Hel. I wasn't sure if the powerful demon, Haagenti, was more pissed at the fact that I'd shielded my foster brother, Dar, from his wrath this fall, or that I'd kept the Iblis sword instead of turning it over to him.

Not that I really wanted the thing. I was stuck with it, and all the paperwork and responsibility that seemed to come with holding the empty title of leader of the demons. Iblis. Ha-Satan. The Devil. No one had held that title since our split with the angels two and a half million years ago. Why had this sword, this artifact that came with the title, chosen me? I was nothing but an imp. I wasn't qualified to be the Iblis.

"Can you do lunch?" the guardian asked, checking her cell phone for the time. "Or we can try on shoes at Nordstrom's. They have these amazing suede pumps. Royal-blue."

I glared at her. Gate guardians were tasked with ensuring demons stayed in Hel, keeping us from darting through and messing with the humans, starting wars, spawning plagues, stealing souls. High level demons could evade the guardians, but not the rubbish I'd been killing the past few months. Maybe one or two Low in a decade or so could evade her grasp, but not dozens in a month. I had a sneaky suspicion the bitch had been letting them through.

"I don't want to take you away from your duties," I said. "Clearly you're swamped with all these crappy demons making it through the gate and overwhelming you."

She grinned, confirming my suspicions. I wondered if she was acting solo, yanking my chain, or if it was her boss, Gregory, playing some game. That angel scared me. And turned me on. But mostly scared me.

"Maybe next time," she said as I turned to leave the posh mall that had sprung up over the ages around the gate in Columbia, Maryland.

Thoughts filled my head on the drive down I-70. My life revolved around killing the demons that Haagenti kept sending my way. It had become part of my daily routine. Wake up, brush teeth, go to the gym, kill a demon, stuff its head in my car then drive to Columbia and send it back to Hel. How long was this going to go on? When would Haagenti give up and leave me alone? I had a bad feeling the answer was "never".

It was putting a serious cramp in my lifestyle. And my relationship. Wyatt was my human boyfriend, my neighbor, my best friend. I'd had to cancel plans and move dinner reservations in order to deal with these stupid demons that showed up all hours of the day and night and tried to kill me. What happened to the cushy routine I had as Samantha Martin? I wanted to go back to it, back to my pre-Iblis life— the one where I'd hang out with my friends, eat hot wings, have sex with Wyatt and then let the air out of all the car tires on Market Street. Those were the days.

There seemed no end in sight. Haagenti would continue to send people to kill me, and I'd spend millennia fighting them off until my luck ran out and one managed to take me out. I knew I'd eventually have to face him. I'd lose. Haagenti was a good ten levels above me, with far more power and clout. He had an enormous household and practically owned a major section of Hel. If I went back to face him, he'd defeat me and drag me off for centuries of torture, "punishment" for my defiance. Haagenti was pretty creative when it came to torture, and by the time he finished with me, every human I ever cared about would be long dead. Wyatt would be long dead. I'd never see him again.

As I turned down the long road to my house, gunshots rang out. I hit the accelerator and squealed into Wyatt's driveway. My heart pounded as my mind raced through all the possibilities, none of them good. I cursed under my breath. I should have waited to take that last demon's head to the gate, just to make sure there weren't any more. Lately they'd only shown up one at a time, usually a day or two apart, but I ought to never have assumed the pattern would continue. If another demon had appeared while I was gone and attacked Wyatt, he'd be in real trouble. These Lows might be pretty weak, but Wyatt was only a human and would be easy to kill.

I ran in to find Wyatt standing over a mangled heap of flesh. Blood. Everywhere. Wyatt's eyes met mine and I felt the room spin. Relief that he wasn't the mangled heap of flesh on the floor collided head on with fear that the demon may have seriously injured him.

"Got him," he told me with satisfaction before he slid to sit on the floor. It was hard to tell what blood was his and what belonged to the demon. The relief disappeared, and adrenaline nearly drowned me in a rush.

"Where are you hurt?" I asked, feeling a sharp stab of panic. Humans were fragile and I lived in constant fear that Wyatt was going to die before his time. Human life expectancies were brief enough as it was.

"He raked my leg pretty good," Wyatt said. His voice was breathy and light. His hands shook as he tried to take off his belt to tie a makeshift tourniquet.

"Let me," I told him.

It looked deep. Three lacerations across his thigh. I tightened the belt and he applied pressure with a dishtowel that had been conveniently lying on the floor. Wyatt shook his head and mumbled something, sliding further onto the blood-slick floor. Blood. He was losing too much blood, and I wasn't sure how quickly an ambulance could get here, out in the country. Making a snap decision, I dove my spirit self, my personal energy into his leg and repaired the blood vessels. It would stop the bleeding, and give us enough time for the human doctors to fix the rest.

"We need to get you to the hospital for stitches," I told him. He was breathing better, but his eyes were unfocused. I knew he was going in to shock, that I should go get a blanket or something.

Wyatt shook his head. "Can't. Cops will show up. They'll think I got knifed or something. You do it."

No way. I could fix myself, could probably do a decent job fixing another demon or a hybrid, but humans and other beings didn't allow much room for error. I'd had some spectacular fails in the past. Things went horribly wrong right away, or they went horribly wrong in weeks or months. He knew this. He knew better than to ask this of me.

"No Wyatt. I won't," I told him as I stood up and searched the room in vain for something to use as a blanket. It was bad enough that I'd done the blood vessel repair. That had been an emergency, and I hoped the doctors at the hospital could check, and re-do anything I'd fucked up.

"You have to," he insisted weakly. "Heal me."

Demons don't heal. They fix. It's a different process with very different results. I couldn't heal Wyatt, but I knew someone who had that skill. I had him on angelic speed dial.

Gregory. He wasn't normally very cooperative and he particularly disliked Wyatt, but I'd been reading his stupid reports and papers for months now. I figured he owed me a favor. Besides, the worst he could do was say "no". I was pretty much out of options, and as much as I dreaded this, it was my only real choice. Reluctantly, I reached into the red purple of his spirit that ran like a network of fibers throughout my being and pulled, feeling rather foolish as I summoned the angel forth. He appeared instantly, less than an inch from me, practically smashing my nose into his chest.

All the other angel's I'd met had been somewhat androgynous, but not Gregory. He was well over six feet and build like an Olympic weightlifter. His face was unequivocally masculine with sharp cheekbones and black eyes. Coppery curls dropped across his forehead.

Demons and angels are beings of spirit, and physical forms, including gender, can be altered at will. Yes, I really liked this attractive male shape he'd chosen, but much more than the physical attracted me. He was so very old. Older than the planet I stood on, older than the sun that graced its sky. His power overwhelmed his corporeal self and poured from him, burning me like the heat from a hot oven. He was amazing, awe-inspiring, and when his spirit self reached out beyond the flesh to caress mine, I could think of nothing but him. I stepped back, trying to put some distance between us, and he grabbed my arm.

"You wanted me?" Gregory asked, although it seemed more of a statement than a question. His voice was deep and seductive, the word 'want' full of innuendo. Yes, I did want him. And that scared me because I kind of hated him too.

"Wyatt is hurt and can't turn to the human doctors for help. Can you please heal him? As a favor to me?"

Gregory looked amused. "No. Fix your own toy."

"I *can't*. I'll make it worse. It will only take you a second. Come on, please?" Fuck. I was begging an angel to heal my human boyfriend. Was I even a demon anymore?

"Sam, you. You do it." Wyatt muttered. His color was starting to come back and his voice seemed stronger.

"The human has spoken." Gregory shrugged then turned and walked over to the dining room table laden with piles of stuff.

I knelt down and picked up Wyatt's hand. It wasn't cold. He wasn't bleeding anymore. And most of the blood on the floor *did* appear to be the demon's. He'd probably only lost a pint or two before I'd stopped the bleeding. I'd get him some water, grab a blanket from the bedroom and drive him in. At this point, he just needed a whole lot of stitches.

"Wyatt, be reasonable." I begged him. "I'm not good at this. We'll make something up at the hospital. You're not hurt as bad as we thought. Let the human doctors stitch you up."

"You need to work on these things, little cockroach," Gregory said, picking up a half empty bag of chips and peering inside. "Healing, fighting, controlling the elements. You will need to be much more powerful if you're going to survive more than a year as the Iblis"

"You're letting these demons through on purpose. How does it help me to be a more powerful Iblis lopping heads off these puny worms?" I motioned angrily at the dead demon on the floor.

Gregory dug a chip out of the bag and frowned at it. "You need to smash the one who sends these worms to kill you. That is what you must accomplish. Deal with this demon who threatens you; establish your authority."

Haagenti. I shuddered thinking of the likely outcome of that confrontation. He'd be the one doing the smashing, and I'd be spending a few centuries dipped in acid or pulled apart limb by limb.

"It's your fault Wyatt is hurt," I protested, shaking off the disturbing thoughts of my torture. "Innocents are being injured and could be killed because you want me to learn a lesson? What kind of angel are you?"

"A greater good always requires sacrifice," he said, rubbing the chip between his fingers. "And to be quite honest, I really wouldn't mind if your toy died. He holds you back from redemption, and his soul is lost anyway."

"Sam, just fix me," Wyatt interjected. "I trust you. You can do it."

Redemption? What was he talking about? I felt cold at the thought of redemption. And at the thought of fixing Wyatt. I'd never successfully fixed a human before. I watched Gregory for a moment, wondering what bargain I could strike that would tempt him. The angel took a bite of the chip and made a face.

"What is this orange stuff?" Gregory said, dropping the half eaten chip back into the bag and scrutinizing the powdery spice on his fingers.

Did he just eat something? Eating and drinking were infractions of angelic purity standards. I'd seen several angels violate it, so it must be a minor infraction, but never Gregory. He was a stickler for the rules.

"Umm, it's a spice." I took the bag from his hand and read the ingredients. "Old Bay. It's common in the Maryland area. Humans put it on crabs and other shellfish mostly, but I've seen it on burgers, chips, fries, lots of things."

"Sam, I'm injured here and you're discussing snack foods. Get over here and fix me," Wyatt ordered. Well, that didn't sound too injured to me. Evidently the shock of the sudden blood loss was wearing off.

I went back to him and checked the wound. Three gashes. The skin was split wide, but they didn't go all the way through to the bone. It didn't seem as if there were any nerves damaged. Muscle and skin repair, then check the blood vessels I'd fixed on the fly. It shouldn't be hard, but this wasn't a strong skill of mine. I looked up at Wyatt in dismay. I didn't want to do this.

"Now, Sam," he insisted, his voice firm in spite of his pallor.

I knelt down beside him, put my hands on his leg, and sent in tendrils of my spirit self. Wyatt gasped as I carefully explored the wound. There. Skin, blood vessels, torn muscle, but no nerve damage. I could do this. He groaned softly at the caress of my energy inside him. He wouldn't enjoy it as much once I started fixing things, but right now my energy was lighting off all sorts of pleasant nerve endings throughout his body.

"Feels incredible when she does that, doesn't it?" the angel asked, his voice smooth as silk.

Wyatt jerked and I felt my energy rip along his cells. Fuck! I tried to align my energy tendrils with his movements, so I wouldn't tear him to bits.

"Hold still," I told him tersely. "I almost killed you."

"Sam, have you done this with him too?" Wyatt asked, his euphoria turning to anger.

"It's even better when you do it back to her," Gregory said. "Oh, but you can't do that can you? You can't return the favor. Because you're a human."

"Sam?"

"He's just fucking with you Wyatt. Don't pay any attention to him. And hold still."

"I believe she said it was 'epic' when we did it." The angel smiled slightly, as if at a fond memory.

"Sam, answer me right now!"

I had done this with Gregory. More actually. Our entire spirit selves hurtling together outside corporeal form, joining in a flash of light. It *was* epic. It wasn't anything like the physical sex that Wyatt and I had. That was awesome too, just different. I was pretty sure Wyatt wouldn't see the difference. Plus Gregory was an asshole. I loved Wyatt.

"I did not have sexual intercourse with that angel," I lied. Sort of lied. It wasn't *really* sex, by the textbook human definition anyway.

"I didn't say sexual intercourse, Sam," Wyatt said sternly. "I asked if you did this. Put yourself into him, joined with him beyond the physical self."

Damn. Wyatt knew me too well.

"Absolutely not. Never." I lied again.

Gregory made a disapproving tsk tsk noise and dumped the contents of the chip bag on the table to examine further.

"Sam, you're lying," Wyatt thundered.

"Yes. Yes she is," Gregory agreed.

"Wyatt, he is trying to get you worked up. Just hold still, so I don't kill you. We'll talk about this later. In private. Please, sweetie?" I begged him.

Wyatt took a deep breath. "Ok. But we will discuss this."

Again I edged the tendrils of myself deeper, to re-check the wounded area and ensure there was nothing beyond what I originally sensed I needed to fix. Slowly, I repaired muscles, skin and checked my previous work on the blood vessels. Wyatt stiffened and clenched his teeth, but couldn't help vocalizing his pain. I knew it hurt to fix him this slowly, but I was trying to be as thorough as possible.

"Will you at least check this for me, make sure I've done it right?" I asked Gregory when I'd completed and pulled my energy back. Wyatt panted with glazed eyes, still sprawled on the floor.

"No. You'll find out soon enough, won't you?" the angel said cheerfully.

Asshole. I looked down at Wyatt and thought of all that could go wrong, imagined all the horrible ways he could die because of my attempts to fix his wounds. Fear of his mortality mixed with feelings of love for him. I don't know what I'd do without Wyatt. He was a part of me, he was everything to me. . ..

"Oh all *right*!" The angel slammed his fist on the empty chip bag and glared at me. "Fine. But not because I like him or care about him in any way. I'm doing this as a personal favor to you."

I stared at him in surprise. Where had that come from? Why had he changed his mind, and why was he so pissed at me about it? I moved aside as he approached Wyatt.

"Sam, I don't want him to touch me," Wyatt snapped.

Great. The one being that actually could heal Wyatt, that could ensure any mistakes I made were corrected, and Wyatt didn't want him to do it. Gregory paused and waited for my verdict, eyebrow raised.

"Wyatt, this is important. You didn't want to go to the hospital? Fine. But I need you to let him check my work."

Wyatt frowned at Gregory. "I'll only allow this as a personal favor to you, Sam," he said, echoing the angel's words.

Gregory knelt down, his physical form blurring slightly with an intense glow. Placing his hands on Wyatt's leg, he murmured a word. There was an explosion of light. Spots swam before me as I saw the angel rise and walk back toward the table.

"You okay?" I asked Wyatt, who looked rather stunned.

"Yeah. It doesn't hurt when he does it," he replied, distracted.

Great. One more thing the angel did better.

"Thank you," I said, walking over to him. He was examining the various cables on the table.

"Don't mention it." He didn't meet my eyes, his tone distant and flat.

"How'd I do? Was it a decent job?" I asked, wondering if I'd actually managed to properly fix the wound.

He shot me a quick glance before returning his gaze to the cables. "I believe the humans would tell you not to quit your day job."

Crap. I wondered what I'd done wrong, how quickly Wyatt would have died. Would he have been in terrible pain? Would he have just dropped dead one night as we slept? Panic crept back up my chest.

"Stop. I took care of it. He's fine now. Healed and better than ever." He still didn't look at me, but Gregory's voice was soft, with a reassuring note. I saw a faint tint of blue around him, felt his spirit self reach out to mine in a quick caress. How could he be such a cruel asshole, then change to this one moment later?

"We don't have to go out to dinner tonight," I told Wyatt, turning away from the angel. "You can rest and I'll cook something."

Outside of the gashes he hadn't been wounded, and he'd helped me take out a fair number of demons lately, but I wanted to be sensitive. Wyatt was my boyfriend, after all, and I did love him, in a demon sort of way.

"No, I'll be fine. I really want to get out and have a normal evening with you. An evening without some monster trying to take us out."

I felt a twinge of guilt. For forty years I'd lived as a human, under the radar, but now I was the Iblis. I didn't think we'd ever have a normal evening again.

"Can you even stand?" I asked, bending down to help him up. He rested his weight on me and gingerly got to his feet, testing the leg.

"I'm still a bit light headed, but the leg feels fine. I think I'm good to ride with you up to Columbia to dispose of this demon, but maybe we should just get take-out instead."

I helped Wyatt into the other room, sweeping various game controllers and magazines off a couch so he could lie down. "You relax here a bit, and I'll clean up. No hurry. Wait until you're less dizzy, and we can leave then."

Gregory was still in the room, crushing the chips with a fist when I returned. I ignored him and began sopping up the blood with paper towels, kicking the dead demon out of the way. Whoever it was, he hadn't even bothered with a human form, or maybe he didn't have the skill to manage it. There was some fur, long curved claws, a reptilian snout, and a whole mess of stuff that I'm thinking should have been on the inside of him. It was like he'd exploded from Wyatt's bullets.

"I need to talk with you about the upcoming Council meeting, and go over a few key things," Gregory told me as I stuffed the dead demon, along with the bloody towels, into a garbage bag. "You'll meet with me tonight and you can eat with your toy some other time."

That was another downfall of being the Iblis. I now had a seat on the Ruling Council of angels. It seems when we were exiled long ago, a spot had been designated to give a voice to the demons on matters of mutual significance. It had been vacant for two and a half million years, and I wasn't thrilled to be filling it. Gregory, on the other hand, seemed perversely amused by the prospect and eager to see me in a room full of bureaucratic angels. I'd have to meet with him to go over things, but not tonight.

"No," I told him. "I've got a dead body to take care of. Wyatt has bullet holes in his house. I'm hungry, and tired, and I want to get freaky naked with my man. You can come back some other time."

Suddenly, I had an idea. "Unless you'd like to put a gate in my backyard for me. Then I'll stay and spend the evening listening to you. Just a little gate to Hel, so I don't have to keep trekking to Columbia with these bodies every day or so."

"If you'd take care of the root cause, then you wouldn't have to worry about any of this," the angel said. "You can continue to shirk your duties, to avoid responsibility all you want, but eventually you are going to be forced to face this demon. It will be far more painful the longer you drag things out."

"One little gate. Just one little gate, and you can have me for the whole evening."

I regretted it the moment it was out of my mouth. A slow smile crept across his face, and the power he leaked grew, practically blistering me with its intensity. I'd always been partial to the sin of lust. I routinely said all kinds of nasty things to everyone else. Smutty propositions, innuendo, downright porn talk were all a major part of my vocabulary, but I'd been trying to keep things clean with this angel. I got the feeling he was a hair's breadth from dragging me off to be his private, captive pet. Still, it was unlike me to be this nervous. Maybe if I acted bold he'd back off. Call his bluff, play a game of sexual chicken with him. I was a demon, after all, and he spent his existence avoiding sin.

"All yours," I told him, moving closer and trying to feel less like a rabbit toying with a panther. "This council stuff can't take long. You can make my gate and we'll spend the evening together. I'm sure there are all sorts of things you can teach me. And I'm *very* sure there are things I can teach you."

To make my point, I took his hand and lightly bit his thumb, looking up at him from under my eyelashes. Something flashed across his eyes, and he snatched his hand back.

"Tempting, but I don't indulge in pleasures of the flesh. And I'm not putting a gate to Hel in your backyard. I'll come by tomorrow. Early."

His words were sharp, and the power he emitted had decreased significantly. Success. I might not get my gate, but at least I knew I could make him turn off the seductive angel routine.

I nodded, biting back a smile, and he vanished.

"Sam, we will talk right now," Wyatt said behind me, his voice full of cold fury. He'd heard me proposition the angel. I was so fucked.

"Wyatt, I didn't mean it."

But I wasn't sure whether I meant it or not. If Gregory had assented, I doubt I would have stopped with a handshake and a peck on the cheek. I saw Wyatt's face, sadness mixed in with the anger, and I felt guilty. I was the worst girlfriend ever. I just couldn't do this. I couldn't keep pretending to be a human. I wasn't. I was a demon. An imp.

"I was just trying to get him to back down from that creepy, predator thing he's got going on. He's all about purity of the spirit and virtue. I don't even think he has sexual organs as a part of his physical form."

"The sin is sex with humans. You're not a human; you're a type of angel. He wants you in every way shape and form, Sam. And you clearly want him too."

"No, physical sex is a sin," I insisted, ignoring the last part of his statement. "You heard him say he didn't indulge in pleasures of the flesh? Angels risk their level of vibration, their purity, by assuming corporeal form. That's why their physical form sucks so badly, they refuse to commit deeply to it, refuse to experience anything beyond a miniscule sensory input. He's really old. There is no way he'd risk his path to enlightenment on a sweaty fuck with me, or anyone else."

"He'd risk everything for you, Sam," Wyatt said. "He'd trade heaven for an eternity in the depths of hell to possess you."

Okay, that was way over the top. Wyatt was getting overly dramatic. Gregory liked to annoy me, irritate me, and this was just his way of doing it.

"That's ridiculous. He's bound me. I'm already his. You heard him; he's trying to redeem me or rehabilitate me, or something. I knew he'd back down, otherwise I wouldn't have come on to him like that."

Now that was a lie. I'd gambled, and I wasn't sure which outcome I'd really wanted. Wyatt knew, and he knew I was trying to divert him from our original subject.

"Physical intercourse aside, you've been having some angel equivalent with him. You're cheating on me with him." His voice was raw and filled with pain. I knew this was important to humans, but things were different with my kind.

"I'm a demon, Wyatt," I protested. "We don't do monogamous relationships."

I *had* been unusually committed to him though. Some hanky panky with a guy I'd Owned up in Atlantic City this fall, but nothing else. For a demon, that made me practically a nun.

"Remember that jockey this fall?" I asked. "He wanted to fuck me and I ripped up his number. I've never contacted him."

I could see Wyatt was considering that statement.

"Wyatt, I don't mind if you have sex with others. You're my boyfriend, my best friend. I would resent anyone interfering with that part of our relationship, but I don't care about exclusivity in sex."

"Seriously?" Wyatt shook his head in disbelief. "You wouldn't mind if I had sex with one of our friends, someone we see regularly? Like Candy or Michelle?"

I squirmed. A one night stand with a stranger was one thing, but it did bother me to think of Wyatt with one of our friends. It would be more than sex, it would be sex and friendship. That would be dangerously close to infringing on what we shared.

"If he were just some random guy, I wouldn't care as much," Wyatt continued. "But I see how you are with him. The angel equivalent of sex, the time he spends teaching you things, how you gravitate right to him to discuss chip spices: all this interferes with what we share. He's edging me out, and soon, he'll be the one you spend time with. He'll be your best friend. He'll be your partner in crime."

"No, Wyatt. He'll never edge you out. There's no competition here."

I understood what he meant, but he and Gregory weren't at all the same. How could I convince him that my feelings for Gregory were poles apart from the things I felt for him? I did my best to honor his human need for exclusivity in physical intercourse, but this thing with Gregory was different.

"You're not jealous of my brother, Dar," I added. "I'm friends with Michelle and Candy. I don't have sex with them, but I do things with them that I don't do with you. This angel doesn't mean the same to me as you do. Yes, I care about him. I enjoy spending time with him. And I've done things with him that you and I can't do together. That doesn't make me love you less. It doesn't make you less of my best friend."

Wyatt searched my face, looking for signs of deception. "I can't help but be jealous of him, Sam."

"I'll try not to angel-fuck him again."

Wyatt winced. I saw him consider my sort-of promise. "I can't hold you to that, Sam. You're a demon. I'll try and wrap my head around the fact that what you do with him doesn't have anything to do with what we share. Just let me know if you do, so that jerk doesn't surprise me with it at a really bad moment."

I held him close, burying my hands in his blond hair and rubbing my face against his stubble. I was so relieved that I'd somehow managed to get through this horrible incident without the heartbreak of losing him forever. This was unfamiliar ground. I was trying to balance a relationship with a human and my own demon nature. This thing I shared with Wyatt was like constantly teetering on a knife's edge, and I kept tumbling down.

"I will, Wyatt," I vowed.

I took the demon corpse in the Hefty bag and pitched it though the gate in Columbia, while Wyatt waited in the car. Then we picked up take-out and went back to his house, where he relaxed on the couch. He protested as I scrubbed blood and gore off his walls and floor, insisting he'd do it later. I knew better. Left to his own devices, the mess would be there for years. Wyatt's housekeeping style was kind of "early demolition".

For the first time in the two and a half years we'd known each other, I spent the night at his house instead of him coming to mine. We'd had gentle make-up sex, and Wyatt promptly dropped off to sleep, encasing me in a straitjacket of arms and legs, crushing me against his chest. I was sweaty and hot in his embrace, unable to shift even a fraction of an inch. He always slept like this. At first, I hated being confined in the uncomfortable grip of a human, but now it felt intimate. It felt like he never wanted to let me go. Random moments throughout my day, I'd find myself longing for him to hold me immobile and breathe into my hair. Nights never were quite right without the kind of bondage spooning Wyatt practiced in his sleep. I'd grown to enjoy it, to need it.

I lay there all night, thinking of the differences between us. He was a human, physically weak, and I was immeasurably stronger. I could crush him with so little effort. Instead, I'd always held back, let him call the shots and set most of the parameters in our relationship. We had sex without my hurting him, without broken bones or torn flesh. He made compromises too. I knew he deliberately overlooked my more disturbing actions, that he emphasized everything about me that seemed more human. This was what he needed to do to come to terms with having a demon girlfriend. We both knew I wasn't human, and to pretend so was a lie, but we lived with it.

I should have used this argument to break things off, to set him free. He'd be hurt, but he could live a normal life with a human woman. Have children. Not worry about the demons Haagenti was sending ripping him to bits, torturing him in order to pressure me to return to Hel. He'd probably live a lot longer. Bounce grandkids on his knee.

But I couldn't. I couldn't give him up.

~2~

It was after lunchtime when Gregory arrived for our meeting. So much for "early".

He usually appeared in my house, unannounced, but this time he strode in the front door holding a head by the hair. He plopped it down on my dining room table and waved a hand, causing a depressing amount of paperwork to cover the table surface. I ignored the paperwork and focused my attention on the more interesting item.

"Is this a present?" I asked in delight.

I picked up the head and sat it like a hat on top of my own head, modeling it with a flourish.

"How did you know? I've always wanted one of these. And it fits perfectly."

The angel was not amused. "We've got a lot to review today, and as often as you get sidetracked, we're liable to be at it for a week. Put the head down and focus."

Why the fuck did he bring a head if he didn't want me to mess with it?

"Should I put it in a vase? Display it as a centerpiece on the table? How can you expect me to focus on stupid, boring paperwork when I've got this amazing, decomposing flesh tempting me with its beauty?"

"Fine. We'll address this matter first, and then I'll get rid of the thing so it won't continue to distract you."

He took the head from my hands and stuck it back on the table. It made an entertaining squelch sound.

"Do you know him?" the angel asked, pointing at the head.

"Uhhh, no?" Was he serious? Just because I lived among humans didn't mean I knew every single one of them. There were billions, after all.

Gregory threw up his hands in frustration. "Check his energy signature. You might recognize him."

Now I was confused. "He's human. He doesn't have an energy signature. Do you mean check his DNA? The structure of his brain? Is there something specific I should be looking for?"

"He's not human. He's a demon."

I was pretty certain the head was human. I always scanned stuff. It was a habit. Still, I checked again. When a demon committed suicide, they exploded their entire form out and nothing remained. Sometimes we died by another's hands. Although our personal energy, our spirit-self, scattered, a signature remained, burned into the flesh. This head held nothing.

"Nope. It's human. There's nothing."

Gregory frowned. "This human died in 1922 at the hands of a demon. He was Owned. Since I'm clearly not looking at a ninety year old corpse, it must be the remains of a demon form."

Demons Own. We rip the souls from human bodies and hold them within ourselves as long as we exist. We absorb the human's memories, and can then create a replica of their shape and form. We kill too, but Owning is fun—messy, but fun. Gregory clearly thought this was the remains of a demon who'd been in an Owned human's form at the time of his death, but I couldn't find any trace of a demon whatsoever.

"There's nothing there," I protested. "I believe you. I really do, but there's no energy signature at all in this head."

I felt his suspicion hang in the air. "Honestly. I'm not even a thousand years old. I've never seen anything like this. Why would you think I'd know anything about it if you didn't?"

"You're a demon, I'm not," Gregory said. "And you know elves," he added reluctantly.

Ah. Elves. So he wasn't as blind to their little extracurricular activities as I'd thought. He suspected sorcery.

The elves snared human adults in their traps to use as servants, training talented ones in the arts, but all the truly skilled sorcerers were changelings—human infants taken away and dead elf babies left in their place. The elves had magic of their own, but humans had qualities that made them especially powerful. I'd had dealings with the elves. I'd retrieved a couple of their sorcerers that had gone rogue. Reaching for the head again, I did a more thorough search.

"I can't feel any residual magic," I confessed. "I strongly doubt this head belonged to a sorcerer."

"Could this death be a result of a sorcerer's magic?" he asked. "Maybe he killed the demon and stripped his flesh of any remaining energy signature to cover up his deed or the demon's presence?"

"Possibly. I really don't know if they can do that sort of thing or not."

"Aren't you friendly with some elves?" he asked. "Can you inquire? Investigate a bit."

Fuck. One more thing I needed to remember to do. I had Haagenti trying to kill me. I had a stack of breeding petitions that I needed to deal with sooner or later. I had my human businesses to run, a boyfriend to spend quality time with, impish pranks to pull. I had a pile of boring bullshit on my table I needed to wade though. And there was something else too. I couldn't recall what.

"Yeah, I'll add it to my list." I said. Maybe in a couple of centuries. If I remembered, that is.

He picked up the head and paused. "Perhaps you'd like to keep it."

What did he expect me to do with it? I hadn't killed it. The demon, or human, had been no threat to me. It wouldn't be of any interest as a trophy, and after all my time living as a human, I wasn't as fascinated by dead flesh as I'd once been.

"As a snack for your pet, maybe?" he asked.

For a second I thought he meant Wyatt. Then I realized he was referring to Boomer, my Plott hound hybrid, my hellhound. There was nothing Boomer loved more than feasting on corpses, but I hadn't expected an angel to offer one up to him, like a Milkbone. It was a touching gesture.

"Oh yes, thank you," I said, taking the head and putting it by the back door. I'd run it out to Boomer later. He usually wasn't up and about until nightfall anyway.

"Well, let's get to the rest of this," Gregory said, rubbing his hands in anticipation. I looked at the paperwork in despair. This was going to be the most boring day of my life. Outside the actual council meeting, that is.

"There are four hundred and twenty eight items on the agenda, but we'll only cover three hundred and thirty three because that is the number deemed most auspicious for this particular council session."

Angels were fucking crazy, but anything that reduced the workload was okay with me.

"Quite a few of the agenda items deal with matters internal to Aaru. You won't be expected to weigh in on those, so, in the interests of time, we won't review them. I brought the summaries though, so you can bring yourself up to speed if you'd like to educate yourself further."

"Where in Aaru do you hold the meetings?" I was envisioning a big fluffy cloud with a huge conference table and PowerPoint presentations. That would be funny.

"We'll be meeting here. On Earth. In a conference center."

I laughed. "Do you guys usually hold Ruling Council meetings in a Marriott? I thought with your distaste for corporeal existence you'd want to hold them in Aaru where you could float around without bodies."

"We normally do," he confessed. "But there is strong resistance to your presence in Aaru. Many don't believe you truly are the Iblis. And there are those who feel the demons have forfeited their seat on the council since they haven't had an Iblis since the exile."

Great. The angels didn't recognize me as the Iblis. The demons didn't acknowledge me as the Iblis either; they treated me the same as they always had. There was no rise in my status, no fanfare, nothing. No wonder the title had been unclaimed for two and a half million years. It wasn't worth shit. It didn't bring anything but boring meetings and endless fucking paperwork.

"So you guys are seriously all going to manifest physical form and sit around a big table with flip charts and nasty hotel coffee?"

"Yes." He didn't sound happy about the prospect.

I reached for the nearest stack of papers, but Gregory halted me with an outstretched hand.

"There's a demon at your door," he said right as a knock sounded.

My foster-brother, Dar? Hopefully not another one of those Low hit men. I went to the door and was surprised to see Leethu.

"Ni-ni," she said in a delightful sing-song voice. She kissed me on the forehead. Leethu was a Succubus, and thus was too fragile for the traditional types of demon greeting.

"Leethu, what's up?"

"I'm hoping you can put me up for a couple of days," she said, with a flick of her long, black hair. "I'm in a little trouble back home. I've popped over to let things cool off a bit."

She was putting out pheromones like crazy, trying to convince me to let her stay. I wondered what she'd done to want to hide out with me. I liked Leethu, though, and wouldn't mind having her around for a bit. Hmmm, maybe the monogamy Wyatt expected didn't extend to Succubi? Because those pheromones she was coating me with were mighty nice.

"Sure, come on in," I told her, opening the door and standing aside.

Harpy noises were more pleasant than what suddenly assaulted my ears. Leethu let out a piercing scream that went on and on. I grabbed the sides of my head, certain my brains were exploding out my ears, and realized that she'd seen Gregory.

No demon ever survived meeting an angel, especially this angel. Except me, that is. I'd forgotten how alarming it was to see one, how threatening his presence in my house would normally be. Leethu was terrified, convinced her death was at hand.

"Take her, take her," Leethu wailed, thrusting me in front of her as a kind of demon shield. Her pheromones became erratic and tinged with fear. She cowered, trying to edge back out the door while screaming her fool head off.

"Shut up," Gregory thundered.

I could have told him that was not the way to deal with a frightened Succubus. Leethu began the high pitched scream again, when it suddenly ended.

"That is the most offensive noise I've ever heard," Gregory said, rubbing a faint trace of blood from an ear. I was surprised mine weren't bleeding.

I looked back at Leethu, who was still holding me in front of her with an unusually strong grip. She was like a fish out of water, her mouth gaping open and snapping shut without sound, her eyes huge in her lovely face.

"It's okay," I told her. "I know this angel. He's not going to kill you."

"I might," Gregory growled. "I really want to."

I wrestled free from the demon and dragged her by her clothing over to the sofa. She struggled with all her might, taking the angel's threat seriously.

"I'm the Iblis. I have duties I must perform that involve my meeting with angels. He's here to go over some of them. He's here a lot." I glanced over at Gregory. He was here an awful lot lately. "I'm happy to have you stay here with me, but you'll need to be okay with him hanging around."

The Succubus made a slashing motion across her throat and pointed over the edge of the sofa at the angel.

"You're safe here. It's sort of like an embassy. I won't let him kill you." I looked over at Gregory to confirm. I wasn't sure if that was true or not.

"I'll try to restrain myself." He glared at Leethu, which wasn't helping me calm her down at all.

I faced him and crossed my arms in front of my chest, frowned and tapped my foot. I'd seen humans do this before with great results. It was worth a try.

"Oh, all right." He turned to face Leethu. "I promise I won't harm you as long as you are under the protection of your Iblis, but you need to abide by behavioral standards to keep your immunity. Is that understood?"

Leethu nodded and held her throat with both hands in a choking gesture. A smile flickered across the angel's face.

"I'm assuming you're not asking me to throttle you? No? Okay, I'll allow you sound once more, but if you make that horrible noise in my presence ever again, all deals are off."

The Succubus nodded frantically, and she made a soft whimper as Gregory released her from her silence.

"You really are the Iblis, Ni-ni?" she whispered, darting nervous glances at my angelic guest.

"Yeah. Wanna trade?" I asked hopefully.

"Never."

I didn't think so. Nobody wanted to be the Iblis. I didn't want to be the Iblis.

"Go upstairs and pick out a bedroom. Not mine," I added. She pouted, clearly disappointed. "Just stay out of the way and I'll come get you when we're done here."

Gregory watched her scurry up the stairs and turned to me with his eyebrows raised.

"She's an older foster sister," I confessed. "I was really young when she hit puberty and went off for training, so I don't know her that well. She seems nice enough though."

Gregory's eyebrows rose further.

"Aside from the screaming, that is. She is a Succubus too," I added, feeling the pull, even from upstairs. I needed to ask Wyatt for a hall pass. Or maybe she wouldn't count? Or maybe he could join in? She wouldn't be rough with him during sex like other demons would.

"*She's* a Succubus?" Gregory asked in confusion. "That's got to be the most disgusting demon I've ever encountered."

"Well, she really wasn't at her best right now. She's actually very strong. She's probably got a determined suitor shoving his or her breeding proposal down her throat. It's the pheromones. She's right to let them cool off a bit, put some distance between them."

He shook his head.

"Didn't you feel it? Wow. I just want to bury myself in her when she turns it on. It's hard to say no when she's like that."

"I find her terribly unappealing, even with the chemicals, the aura, and the power leak. I can't imagine who would want to be in the same dimension as such a creature."

Maybe angels were immune? "You've surely been around Succubi before? Killed them? Is it just Leethu that's revolting to you, or are others?"

"She's the first Succubus I've met. They have very little power, so other angels take them out on their own without turning to me for assistance. Other angels have told me they are very seductive, but . . ." he paused, frowning. "I guess I imagined something different."

Huh. To each his own. I walked back over to the table with the depressing stacks of paper.

"We should get to these. Before I chicken out and run away, that is."

We spent the day going over agenda items. I don't remember a thing. I was especially distracted when a noise began upstairs. It sounded like a weed whacker. Leethu had found the toys. Great.

Gregory looked at the ceiling, then at me.

"You don't want to know," I told him.

"Is this similar to that vibrating bed in the hotel?" he asked.

"Same idea. Only a little more up close and personal."

"Does this one actually have the desired effect?"

"Yep. Sure does. Are we done with these papers? What else do we need to go over?" I would have loved to demonstrate, but I was pretty sure the angel wouldn't be turned on by watching me masturbate. Still, it was difficult not getting worked up with Leethu's delighted noises joining the deafening buzzing sound.

"You'll quickly learn who leans which way on all the issues. I don't want to influence you, so you'll need to make your own judgments."

"Can you at least tell me who is on this Ruling Council? You said seven, including me. Let me know their names and levels so I'm not walking in there blind."

"No. It's important you make independent decisions."

"They all probably know who I am. It's only fair."

"No."

"It's not like I'm going to summon them or anything. You don't need to give me their sigils or all of their names. Just their common names and main responsibility."

"No."

"Fuck you." I threw a stack of papers on the floor. He didn't seem to care. "How am I supposed to prepare if I don't know who I'm on this stupid council with?"

"Research it. Ask other demons, elves, werewolves. Make that worthless human of yours do some digging. Stop being childish and start acting like the Iblis."

I glared at him. I felt a serious tantrum coming on.

"There's a human at your door," he said.

My mind went blank. Was that a riddle? And then my doorbell rang.

Gregory looked thoughtful. "The human has magic."

Well I guess it wasn't the pizza delivery guy then. I went to the door, lamenting the days when no one came to visit, when even the cable installation dude was afraid to come down my lane. There was a neatly dressed man at my door with short brown hair and intelligent blue eyes. He looked vaguely familiar. Maybe he was the pizza delivery guy. Except I didn't see any pizza.

"Iblis, I hope I am not inconveniencing you in any way."

The man walked in the door, obviously confident that his visit was, in fact, convenient, and halted as he saw Gregory. Interesting. A human who recognized me as a demon, as the Iblis, and clearly recognized Gregory as non-human. He didn't have that adoring, worshipful look that everyone else got when they saw the angel. He looked wary.

"Uh, I can come back. I see this is a bad time."

"Nope, it's a perfect time. We were just wrapping up here." I looked pointedly at Gregory who smiled, folding his arms in front of him. Great.

"Uh, I just wanted to remind you of our request we made this past fall, when you were in Atlantic City," the human prodded, shooting uncomfortable glances at the angel.

Now I recognized him. One of the elf high lords sent him. I couldn't remember his name; either the high lord or the human. Actually I didn't think the human ever told me his name, but I remembered the high lord was from the area where I'd spent my childhood.

"Yes. I'm glad you came because your request did slip my mind," I admitted. "I've been really busy, and I'm not sure I'll have time to attend to his lordliness anytime in the near future."

The human shot another wary look at Gregory. "His Lordship recognizes the many demands on your time, and offers to help alleviate the situation by taking care of a particularly vexing problem for you. He will gladly ensure that your schedule is free and that you have all the resources you need to assist him. He begs this as a boon from you, the Iblis, and he will be most grateful for your assistance."

Wow. That had to have been the most flowery speech I had ever heard. I was pretty sure he was offering to help me with my Haagenti problem, but I wasn't sure what he planned to do to free up the rest of my schedule. Be my proxy at the Ruling Council meeting, perhaps? That would totally rock. Besides, he was kissing my ass, and I'll admit it was working. Elves and their human servants never kissed my ass. They never kissed any demon ass. If this guy was going to start begging boons from me and being most grateful, I was in.

"Okay. I can probably pop over sometime this week, but I'll need to be vague about the date and time due to my vexing problem. Can your lord be flexible?"

He glanced again at Gregory. "Yes, definitely. Will you do me the honor of walking me to my car, Iblis?" he asked.

I expected him to extend a bent arm so I could delicately take his elbow and stroll from the room. He didn't go that far though. I followed him out my front door and down the driveway where, as I expected, there was no car.

"Didn't come in through the gate?" I asked. Servants did sometimes use the big gates, but they also used the wild gates. An elf would activate it to let them out, then they just walked right on in through the trap to come back. The closest gate I knew of was on the C&O Canal towpath, which was not exactly walking distance, so I wasn't surprised when he held up a palm-sized disk. An elf button; a portable gate. They were expensive and difficult to make. This high lord really wanted my assistance if he went to all this trouble to give me a reminder.

"Lord Taullian requests your presence as soon as possible. He has a proposal that is in line with your particular skills, and in return he offers to take care of the demon that has a price on your head."

I felt as if a load were lifted from my back. Things with Haagenti had escalated, he'd begun targeting Wyatt. This human was proposing the perfect out. No doubt the elf lord wanted me to track someone down and kill them. I'd take on the job and never have to face Haagenti. This just moved to the top of my list.

"I'm interested. I'll pop over as soon as I have a free moment."

"Lord Taullian of Cyelle will anticipate your arrival sometime this week," he said. "In the Western Red Forest by the Maugan Swamp."

Smart servant. As happy as I was to be reminded of the guy's name, I'd probably forget it within the hour. Elf names were really weird, and they all sounded the same. I swear they picked baby names by grabbing a handful of Scrabble tiles and putting them in a random order.

"I'll be there," I assured him. He activated the gate and vanished.

Haagenti finally off my back. That would be glorious. Plus, I was really curious what this guy had in mind. Screw the boring Iblis stuff, this elf had a far more interesting activity for me.

"Playing with elves?" Gregory asked as I came back in.

I grinned. "Every chance I get."

"This high lord is very foolish."

"They never contact us unless they're desperate. They know the risks, and they've carefully weighed out their options. I've done stuff for other elves, but not this particular guy. I've never met him. He probably wants something dead and doesn't care about the mess, or collateral damage"

"As I said—very foolish."

I nodded. I didn't care. It would get Haagenti off my back, and it would be more interesting than these horrible stacks of papers on my table.

"Are we done here," I asked, indicating the paperwork. "It's getting late and I've got other things to do."

Gregory looked disappointed. "I guess we can call it a night. We've covered the major issues. I'll leave the rest for you to peruse at your leisure. I trust that you'll review it all before the meeting?"

Now who was foolish? "Oh, of course. I'll have it all read by the end of the evening," I lied.

He sighed and stacked the papers neatly, putting them on my kitchen counter. "Then unless some pressing matter arises, I'll meet you here to bring you to the council meeting."

He vanished and I stood in my dining room, with a noisy houseguest, paperwork I had no intention of reading, and a head at my back door. Crap. The head. I walked over and looked at it. It looked back at me, the eyes glazed with decomposition, the skin grey and papery. Guess I better get rid of it before it leaked even more on my floor.

I glanced up and saw Boomer standing outside the huge French doors leading to my pool. At the moment he looked like a regular dog, a tall brindle Plot hound with floppy ears and golden green eyes. At will he could switch to his hellhound form, which was significantly larger with two massive heads. Boomer stared at the head through the glass with that peculiar fixation a dog gets when he really, really wants something. I picked up the head to toss it out to him and was amused to see his eyes track the movement.

It felt just like a human head, I wondered again. Nothing at all to indicate it had ever housed a demon. An odd thought struck me. Nothing at all to indicate it had ever housed a demon. How had Gregory known? Did someone alert the angels to this oddity? Humans wouldn't have been able to tell. As a demon, I couldn't tell. Humans died all the time; did angels examine each one of them? Maybe a werewolf had reported it?

Werewolves. I texted Candy. Might as well have her take a smell before Boomer ate the evidence.

Can you come by? I need you to sniff a head.

A few seconds passed before I heard the beep of a message.

Do u have autocorrect on? You wrote "sniff a head".

I wrote back: *Seriously. Sniff a head.*

She replied: *Intrigued. But not surprised. B there soon.*

Candy arrived, a cream cashmere car coat over her gold and brown tweed pants suit. The werewolf shook her head and a light dust of white fell from her blond hair.

"Oh, is it snowing?" I asked in delight.

She ignored my question and stared at the top of my head. "You have road kill in your hair."

I reached up a hand. The goo had dried into a stiff mess. "I put the head on top of mine, like a hat. I guess it leaked a bit."

Candy curled her lip. "Why in the world would you put a severed head on your hair?"

"It was funny."

Candy shook her head and sniffed.

"The head is over by the back door," I directed helpfully.

"It smells like an orgy at a chocolate factory in here," she accused.

Leethu.

"Uh, yeah. Don't pay any attention to that. My foster sister is crashing here for a few days and she's a Succubus."

Candy wrinkled her nose.

"Is that going to affect your ability to smell the head? Should we take it outside?"

"Probably. It's going to take me a few moments to get your sister's smell out of my nose. Someone needs to do an intervention and get her to turn it down. She reminds me of those people that douse themselves with a gallon of perfume. Gives me a headache."

We walked toward the back door with Candy pinching her nostrils. I pointed at the head.

"I'm not picking it up. You're going to have to carry it and hold it for me. I better not get one speck on my clothes either."

I grabbed the thing by the hair and yanked the door open, amused to see Candy carefully avoiding the wet spot on the maple floors. Once outside, she breathed deep, shaking her head to clear Leethu's smell.

It *was* snowing. We never had snow back home in Hel. It was something I truly enjoyed about living here with the humans. A light dusting of it covered the pool furniture, heavy and wet. The ground was too warm to allow it to accumulate much, but my stone patio was coated with a grey slushy sheen. I felt the bite of the flakes on my bare arms and stuck out my tongue to taste it. I loved snow.

Candy scraped some off a lounge chair and held it up against her nostrils.

"There. I think I can finally smell again." She turned to the head in disgust. "So what do you want me to sniff for here?"

"I think it feels like a normal human head, but Gregory is convinced it's a dead demon. I wanted your take on it."

The werewolf leaned in, as close as she could without risking her cashmere coat, and inhaled. Pulling back a fraction, she scrutinized the head, closed her eyes and inhaled again.

"It's human, but it doesn't smell right. It's right on the edge of my memory, but I can't place it."

"Demon?" I prompted.

"Nope. Absolutely not. Not the slightest bit."

I had an idea. "Does it smell like those elf guys? The ones who were going to fill you full of arrows when you went through their trap this fall?"

She looked at me in surprise. "I don't think so, let me check again."

She inhaled deeply, shaking her head. "No. They smell like alfalfa and wild cucumber. This guy smells like a human and something else." Her eyes popped open.

"Snow," she said.

"Well yeah, we've been standing out here and he's got snow on him. I'd expect him to smell like snow."

"Not real snow. When I describe scents to you, I'm comparing them to things you'd be able to smell. When I say you smell like burnt chocolate, that's the closest equivalent. You smell like you, but that's the best way I can describe it. Yes, this corpse smells like the snow that's on his head, but he smells like something else. And it's sort of like snow."

"Have you ever smelled anything similar? Vampires? Angels? Water sprites?"

"There are water sprites?" she asked, surprised.

"Not here. Unless they come in through one of the wild gates, that is. So there probably are some here." I waved my hand. I needed to hurry this up: Boomer was standing at a respectful distance, drool stretched in long strands from his jowls to the slick pavement, patiently waiting for his treat. "Is it like anything you've smelled before?"

She thought carefully and shook her head. "No. It's a clean, cold smell. It's even stripped away some of the human smell. Like there is nothing left but raw flesh."

Damn. I was hoping Candy would have the answer. She usually had the answer to everything. Normally, I'd just forget about the whole thing—a mystery that would never be solved. But Gregory wouldn't have asked unless it was important. There were things he wasn't telling me. How had this head come to his notice? Who had realized there was something wrong with it? Why did a powerful angel give a shit about a dead demon in the form of a human Owned long ago?

~3~

I met Wyatt outside, coming up the driveway as I tried to make a snowman. There wasn't enough snow yet, so it was a really tiny snowman. At least it was the right consistency for packing together, and hopefully we'd have more. Maryland usually saw several decent snowfalls each winter, although they quickly melted with the mild temperatures. I'd be lucky if my creation lasted more than a day or two.

"Aren't you freezing?" Wyatt asked. I was in jeans and a t-shirt.

"Totally. The skin on my arms is numb, and I can barely move my fingers." I looked at them, white and shriveled at the end of my palm. "I think at least three are frost bitten."

Wyatt grimaced. "They're going to hurt like crazy when you go inside and they begin to warm up."

"I know." I smiled. "Especially if I put them in warm water. Last year I even got some skin to peel off."

"Let's save that for another day and get you inside." Wyatt helped me stand, and I stumbled on barely responsive legs up to the house.

Inside was warm and welcoming, a big contrast from the cold, wet, January evening lurking outside the door. My hands tingled and cramped with pain, and I spread them before me to admire the chapped, white and red skin.

"I'd make you some coffee" I told Wyatt., "But my fingers don't work yet. I don't want to fix them and miss the thawing frostbite agony. Can you put on a pot?"

Wyatt didn't respond. His head swiveled as though he were looking for something, his eyes slightly unfocused.

"I was hoping you could do some research for me. I need. . .."

Wyatt grabbed me, cutting off my sentence as his lips claimed mine. He snaked cold hands under my shirt, quickly unhooking my bra as he kissed me. Wow, where had this come from? Frostbite could wait, I thought as I fixed my fingers. I wanted all my nervous system intact for this kind of activity.

My legs were still numb, and I stumbled backward from Wyatt's onslaught, stopping abruptly as my rear hit the dining room table. Wyatt didn't break stride. He picked me up by my waist and sat me on the table, pushing me onto my back and unbuttoning my jeans. I helped by kicking off my shoes and wiggling my shirt and bra off.

Wyatt was all over me. Hands. Mouth. He was frantic. As much as I enjoyed his crazed lust, I couldn't manage to get his clothes off with him sprawled all over me. He wasn't helping move the situation along either. He'd completely ignored his clothing after removing mine and was apparently attempting to penetrate me through his jeans. I'd seen demons do this, but creating an erection strong enough to break through denim required a skill beyond human capabilities.

"Hold on, you porn star. Let me at least unzip your pants and get your cock out."

A wrestling match ensued as I tried to navigate the tangle of Wyatt's arms, slide a bit from under the press of his chest, and reach his pants. Finally I grabbed him by the hair and yanked his head out of the way. He adapted, running his tongue down my side, nipping sensitive spots with his teeth. Oh, wow. This felt so darned good. But I had a mission to accomplish here, and must not be distracted. I reached my hand forward and stretched as far as I could toward the crotch of his jeans. Just a little bit further.

A delighted squeal filled the room. "Oh Ni-ni! I thought I heard you talking to someone. You are the best sister ever, providing me with my favorite entertainment! I'll watch."

I glanced around the side of Wyatt's breathtaking abdomen and saw Leethu, with an enraptured look on her face. Now I understood why Wyatt was so sex crazed. Well, more sex crazed than usual.

"Leethu, turn it off!" I wasn't sure I wanted her to turn it off though. It all felt so good, Wyatt's hands caressing me, his mouth against my waist, the pheromones filling the air. My mind blurred with the intensity of it.

"But Ni-ni, you are having so much fun. And this human likes you, *wants* to have sex with you. He is so attractive. And virile too. Can I join in?"

Oh, that would be lovely. And I got the feeling Wyatt thought so, too. The atmosphere shifted again and Wyatt paused, his mouth leaving my skin as he glanced over his shoulder at the Succubus, considering her request with whatever brain function remained. I envisioned the three of us, a tangle of legs and arms. It wouldn't be a problem if Leethu joined in, although she'd upstage me as always. I didn't want Wyatt doing this under the influence though. I didn't want him to regret it, feel like he'd been forced against his will. Reluctantly, I tried to shake off my desire.

"Leethu, turn it off now. Wyatt is my boyfriend. This isn't okay."

She looked confused.

"He's my toy, my pet human," I said, trying to think of something she could relate to. "I won't share him, and I don't want him having sex with me or anyone else unless he is in full control of his actions."

Leethu sulked. "You are so selfish. So greedy. Same as when you were a child."

True. But I wasn't about to break that habit with Wyatt. I looked up at him and saw the lust. Real lust. Not just the lust brought about by the presence of a Succubus. I smiled at him. It was nice to be wanted.

"Sam, who is this woman and why hasn't someone bottled her and sold her?" His voice was husky, full of desire.

"Her name is Leethu. She's one of my foster sisters. She'll be staying here a few days."

He hadn't moved. He was still pressing me flat against the table with his hands, holding me in place with his hips.

"I don't care if she joins us. Or if she watches," Wyatt said, dropping his head to my breast.

I lost all mental capability for a few moments, consumed by the feel of his fingers and his tongue. I was so turned-on, but suddenly I didn't want Leethu to join in or even watch. Yes, I was worried that Wyatt would regret having a threesome once he was of out of reach of the Succubi pheromones, but it was more than that. I wanted this intimate sharing with Wyatt to remain between the pair of us. At what point had it become more than sex? Pleasing each other in this way confirmed an emotional bond beyond the physical one, and I didn't want to share it with another. I didn't want an outsider to soil what had become an act of love.

I grabbed Wyatt's hair and yanked him up again. "You have no idea how much I want you to finish me off, here on this table, but I think we should confine our sex to your house for the next couple of days, until Leethu goes home."

I glared at her, and the pheromone level in the room dropped significantly.

"How fast can you make it to my house?" Wyatt asked, still torturing my breast with his skillful fingers.

"Faster than you," I told him.

I beat him there, running naked through the snow with Wyatt hot on my heels. We did it on his dining room table, amid the stale chips and computer cables. Then we did it again on his couch. Then again in his bed. Maybe Leethu could stay a few extra days.

By three in the morning I was sprawled on the bed in a sex coma. Wyatt was still awake and energetic.

"Wasn't there something you wanted to ask me to do?" he asked. "Besides put on a pot of coffee?"

I was surprised he remembered. I certainly hadn't remembered.

"Research." I tried to focus. "I'm trying to figure out what angels are on the Ruling Council. Names, strengths, areas of responsibility. Anything to help me. I need to be better informed going into these meetings."

"Would human stories be of any help? I can't imagine they'd be accurate."

"There is probably some truth to the human stories. I've got to start somewhere. I'll see what the older demons know, although our knowledge is going to be from before the war. Things have probably changed."

Wyatt looked thoughtful. "I'm assuming it's probably seven."

"Six," I corrected. "I make seven."

"I'm remembering seven from when I went to church."

"Cool," I pivoted on the mattress to face him. "What are their names?"

Wyatt grimaced. "I didn't go to church *that* much. I remember there was a Gabriel one. A bunch of them looked like fat babies."

I stared at him in amazement. *Babies*? Why would an angel ever want to manifest as a baby? They would have terrible fine motor skills. I couldn't see any advantage at all in assuming an infant form.

"I'll see what I can find," he said. "Starting tomorrow."

He reached out and pulled me toward him, wrapping his legs around mine. Yeah, Leethu definitely needed to stay a while.

~4~

The hiss of Wyatt's shower penetrated through the fog of my pre-caffeinated brain. I was still sprawled on the bed, hidden under a heap of covers, wondering whether I could sneak in a few more minutes of sleep. It was rent day, and I was already late in making my collection rounds. Stretching, I poked my head from under the blanket and watched a small lizard cross the floor. It had a scorpion tail, pointed ears and crimson eyes that darted intelligently across the room. Those red eyes locked onto the bed just as I realized this wasn't a lizard. It was a demon—and not the usual Low one either.

There was a flash, and I rolled across the bed and onto the floor just before the mattress sliced into two smoking sections. Unfortunately I was trapped in a tangle of sheets. Instinctively I converted my form, deconstructing my usual human one into basic atoms and re-assembling into a creature that was small and hard to kill.

I heard a muffled curse, and felt the sheets snatched from above me. The demon was no longer a lizard; he was bipedal with furry, clawed legs and a scaled torso. Arms hung down past his knees, ending in sharp hooks. His head twisted and turned, forked tongue tasting the air as he searched for me.

I held my energy tight inside and scuttled into a dusty refuge under the bed. He stomped around the room, kicking a chair and sweeping the alarm clock from the dresser. It clattered to the floor and bounced, coming within inches of my hiding place. I was safe. He'd never find me. Eventually he'd just give up and go away.

We heard it at the same time. The hiss of Wyatt's shower, the thump of a dropped shampoo bottle. The demon's head turned. No. Not Wyatt. No!

Two steps and I was on him—transformed from cockroach back to human as I emerged from under the bed. Hooked hands dug into my thighs and our momentum smacked his head into the drywall.

"Sam?" Wyatt called from the shower. "What are you doing in there?"

His voice galvanized me into action. I drove a stream of energy through the demon as I grabbed his head in an attempt to break his neck. Smoke rose from his skin, and he spun around, slamming my back repeatedly into the wall in an effort to shake me off.

"Sam?"

I didn't respond, all my attention on a formidable foe who was ripping chunks from my thighs. I couldn't feel my legs. The only thing holding me onto his back were my hands gripped tight around his neck: his thick, solid, unbreakable neck.

The shower noise stopped. "Sam?"

Any minute Wyatt would come out half-naked to investigate. One blast, one rake of a clawed foot and he'd be dead. My head spun from repeated violent contact with the wall behind it. I had one last chance. One shot. A blast of energy burst from every pore of my body into the demon. He froze with a gasp then exploded, sending me crashing to the floor in a spray of flesh and blood.

"Sam?" I heard the bathroom door open, the pad of bare feet on the hardwood floor.

"I'm okay. I'm okay."

I quickly fixed my injuries, but there was nothing I could do about Wyatt's ruined bed and the gore decorating his walls, floor, and ceiling.

"Sam!" Wyatt halted at the doorway, his face pale.

"I'm okay," I repeated. "It was another demon, but I got him."

I was torn between wanting to reassure Wyatt that all was fine, and being honest with him that it most definitely was not fine. This wasn't a Low. This demon had been fairly close to my level. He'd been able to easily change form, manipulate energy for offense and defense. He knew how to fight. This was really worrying me. What if I hadn't been here? The demon would have easily gotten to Wyatt before he could get from the bathroom to one of his guns.

He moved towards me and I held my hand up. "Stay there. You're all clean from your shower. I'll take care of it."

I stood and looked around at the wreckage. I needed to buy Wyatt a new bed, and do some serious cleaning. So much for rent day. I rubbed my hands through my hair, frustrated at the turn the morning had taken and wondering what Haagenti would be sending my way next.

"It's not that bad, Sam—few hefty bags and a good douse of Clorox should fix it. I needed a new mattress anyway."

I shook my head, depressed and worried. A hand caressed my shoulder and I looked up to see Wyatt beside me, ignoring my edict and standing in a pool of blood as he comforted me. His hair was damp, tousled about his head, and he was naked except for a towel around his waist. Drops of water beaded on his skin in places where his rushed drying efforts had missed. I should be licking the water from his neck, feeling his naked body against mine. Instead I was standing amid a pile of demon guts in a destroyed bedroom.

Wyatt continued to rub my shoulder. "Sam, it's fine. Really. We'll take care of this problem. We'll figure it out together. We've killed a lot of demons. We can handle anything this guy throws at us."

Maybe. Or maybe not.

"I better get started cleaning this up. You finish your shower, maybe put on a pot of coffee, and I'll meet you in the kitchen."

"You're really gonna scrape all this up and run it down to Columbia? Didn't you have something you were supposed to do this morning?"

"It's rent day." I gave a largish chunk of flesh an angry kick. "I'm tired of having these idiots fuck with my schedule, with my life. I'll never get to rents if I have to haul this carcass down to Columbia. I should just let Boomer eat it, but he's fat enough as it is."

"Stick it in your freezer," Wyatt suggested, shifting his towel. "Haul a bunch down at one time and save yourself a trip."

That was a good idea. I hated the thought of this mess in with my pork chops though. Perhaps I should get a second freezer, just for demon guts.

"Let me grab some of your trash bags, and I'll put this guy on ice." I eyed his towel. "Hurry up and get dressed. We're late and I've got fifteen houses to collect from."

Wyatt's eyebrows rose. "That may be your idea of fun, but it's not mine. I'm playing Call of Duty with some friends this afternoon. Why would I go with you to collect rents?"

"Because this guy snuck in through your locked door and blew your bed in half. I was barely able to kill him. And the last time I left after a demon attack, there was a second one and you nearly bled to death." A vision of Wyatt, slumped on the floor in a pool of blood sprang from my memories. What if I hadn't come back in time? What if he'd hit an artery? Worry gnawed at me.

"I have my gun. I have lots of guns, actually. I'm not going to collect rent with you; I've got plans, and I can take care of myself. I killed that one last time, all on my own, remember?"

"I remember you almost bleeding out," I retorted. "Fine. I'll put off rents until tomorrow and stay here with you." Ugh. Spending an entire day watching Wyatt play a video game would be worse than being boiled in oil. Although it was a small price to pay for his safety.

"Sam, I don't need a babysitter. Get out of here. I'll take care of this mess. I'll even order a new mattress. Go collect your rents. Then go hang out with Candy or Michelle. I'm serious. I don't want you popping in here every ten minutes fussing over me. I'll be fine."

I hesitated. What if he was wrong? What if I went out and had a great day, only to come home and find him dead, clutching one of those little plastic controllers?

Wyatt whipped off the towel and began smacking me with it. "Get. Go. Now."

"Sure I can't stay?" I teased, admiring his magnificent nakedness as I tried to avoid the snap of the towel.

"Later," he promised. "After ten tonight. Bring some hot wings."

"I will," I shouted, halfway out the door.

I walked back to my house, hoping Wyatt remembered to have one of his guns handy. Or two. I was worried our luck was running out. The last two demons had come straight to his house. Haagenti had obviously discovered how much I cared about Wyatt and was now targeting him. I needed to find a way to make Wyatt safe, a way that hopefully didn't involve me returning to Hel and accepting my punishment. This elf deal was looking like my best alternative at a long-term solution. I just needed to somehow squeeze it in between the Ruling Council meeting and everything else on my agenda.

Leethu was on my sofa with a bottle of vodka in one hand and a carton of milk in the other, alternating swigs of the beverages as she watched the morning news. I put on a pot of coffee, because I knew she hadn't the foggiest idea how to work the machine, then went up to shower. My room was trashed. Despite my edict, the succubus had slept in my bed, gone through every drawer, dumped out half the contents of my bathroom toiletries. I was beginning to rethink my hospitality.

"Are you heading out somewhere today," I asked her before I left. "Dance club? Biker bar? Grocery store?" She was going to destroy my house from boredom if she didn't get out and incite orgies somewhere soon.

"The angels will get me if I leave. I'll just hang here and watch porn. Don't worry about me at all."

I did worry about her; and my house. I made a mental note to pick up more booze on my way home, and see if I could grab some smutty magazines. Maybe I'd hook her up with an Internet chat room later. That might entertain her for a while.

Leaving Leethu to her pay-per-view porn, I headed in to Frederick to lose myself in the joy of rent collecting. On the way my phone rang. It was Candy.

"Wyatt has informed me that I am to keep you occupied until ten tonight, then send you back to him with hot wings," she informed me. "Oh, and he says to stop texting him."

It had only been three texts. And that one phone call before I'd left my house. Just to check on him.

"I'll be busy until late afternoon," I told her. "Rent day, you know."

"How about a run then? We should be able to get a quick one in before sunset."

Candy was my jogging buddy. We usually did a trail run at least once a week, regardless of the weather, but we'd both been so busy lately that it had been almost a month since we'd been out together.

"I don't have any running clothes with me," I told her. "Unless you want to run four legged? We could run after dark that way too."

"Can't." Her voice was full of regret. "Full moon was last night, and we had our sanctioned hunt. I can't risk losing control and getting caught without a permit."

Werewolf life was strictly monitored by the angels under an existence contract. The penalty for being in wolf form without permission was death. Candy sometimes took the risk, but the chance of discovery this close to the full moon was high, especially if Candy succumbed to her instincts and made a kill.

"The Eastside Tavern then?" I asked. "I can get Wyatt's hot wings there too."

"I'm in town today showing some commercial properties out by the mall. Let's do that new Korean place."

"Text me when and where," I told her as I pulled into a parking spot. "I'll be there."

There were three apartments I needed to visit on this street full of row houses. They were all over two hundred years old and had been converted into apartments decades ago. A good number of my slum rental properties required a monthly cash pick up, and there were always the one or two deadbeats where I needed to make a personal, threatening collection visit. These three would be fun. Two drug dealers and a violent ex-con. The other twelve were just routine cash collection from people who didn't trust the banks or postal system.

I hopped out of my Corvette, placed my hands on the parking meter and ran a stream of energy through it that melted the electronics and blackened the screen. This month I was melting them. Last month I'd broken a dozen off at the base then dragged them around the city behind my SUV like a string of huge tin cans. Done with my vandalizing, I locked my car and pulled my coat tightly around me as I made my way to the first apartment.

Last night's snow had melted into a wet mess that slopped around my shoes. The chill wind whipped my hair against my cheeks and the damp air made the temperature seem far colder than it was. I hugged my coat tight and shivered. Even with the bad weather, I enjoyed this part of my business. There were a few interesting tenants that I liked to chat with and the delinquents gave me an opportunity to take out my frustrations on their skulls. This day, I'd begun later than usual, delayed by my insane night of fucking and my demon-killing breakfast. Still, I only had to break into two of the houses and threaten people with mutilation. That was a big improvement from five last month. People were learning.

Michelle had already left the office by the time I wrapped up, so I headed over to her house to drop off her cut. She'd want it before the weekend, and with all the craziness in my life lately, I wasn't sure I'd be able to meet up with her before then.

Michelle lived in one of the subdivisions just outside the city limits. The development had been planned during the sixties and been through several developers who had all been unable to complete the original vision due to financial issues. The modern, cedar-sided houses were nestled deep within wooded areas, hugging a man-made lake and perched on steep rocky slopes. It was beautiful, but the roads were a mess, cracked and sunken from poor drainage. Michelle's contemporary was three stories with layers of decks and a switchback of stairs leading down from the road to the front door. I wondered how she managed to lug groceries down these steps every time she shopped. No wonder she was thin.

I trudged from the parking area down to the landing. Halfway down the stairs I stopped. Seriously. I stopped. I couldn't go any further forward. It was like I was pressed against an invisible wall. Hopping over the railing, I navigated the rocky slope along the front of the house and down the side. The invisible wall continued. I circled the house, but couldn't get in anywhere. An impenetrable barrier surrounded the entire house. Back on the landing, I hollered for Michelle.

I knew she was home. Her car was parked up top, next to mine.

I called a few more times before I came to my senses and dialed her cell phone.

"Hey," she answered. "What's up?"

"I've got rents," I told her. "I'm outside, halfway down your stairs on the landing but I can't get in. There is a weird invisible wall around your house. You might be trapped inside forever. Should I arrange for PeaPod to deliver food or something? Fuck, I'm not even sure they can throw the food through this thing. You might just starve to death."

"Oh, Sam! I'm sorry about that." She opened the door and walked up the steps, through the invisible wall to where I stood.

"When you said you were having problems with demons attacking you, I had this put in. I was worried they might come after me, especially since Wyatt's been attacked too."

"You put in an invisible wall?" I was astonished. I didn't know humans could do this. I didn't know anyone could do this. It wasn't like that hex Gregory had done this summer that melted my arm practically off my body. This was a barrier—an impenetrable barrier.

"It just blocks demons," she said apologetically. "Everyone else can get through."

"Did you do it yourself? How?"

Michelle looked a bit embarrassed. "My Aunt did it. I wouldn't have the foggiest idea how to do something like this."

"Is your Aunt a sorcerer? " I asked, knocking on the wall to reassure myself of its continued presence.

"No, a priestess. You have no idea the trouble I'm in with my mother over this though."

A priestess? I'd never known any religious organization whose gods or goddesses actually responded to their clergy. I needed to meet this woman.

"Your mother is upset you didn't turn to her for assistance first?" There was a protocol to follow in human families that went along relationship and gender lines. It's very complex and I never have been able to understand it.

"No, my family thinks my Aunt is crazy, and they're upset that I'm encouraging her by having her do this. Honestly, I wasn't sure it would work. I always thought she was crazy too, but after finding out I know a demon and a werewolf, and that vampires own my favorite nightclub, I figured I'd give her a chance."

"It worked." I tapped the invisible wall in admiration. "Your mother should give her more respect now."

"Oh, she'd never believe me. You're the only one so far that's not been able to pass. And I'm thankful for that. I really don't want a bunch of demons hammering at my door. No offense," she added hastily.

"None taken." I had an idea.

"Could you have your Aunt do this at Wyatt's house? Haagenti is really starting to focus on him and I'd at least like him to be safe inside his own home."

"But that means you couldn't get in either, Sam," she protested. "There's no exception, and it's not an easy ritual. I couldn't exactly call my Aunt to dispel it each night and re-do it in the morning. The wall would need to stay in place until you were confident that Wyatt was safe."

Sheesh. Gregory was right. I really needed to take care of this problem once and for all. I'd eventually need to pay the piper. I was hoping that would be later. Like after-Wyatt-had-died-of-old-age later.

"I've got something in the works that will put this whole thing to rest once and for all," I told her, thinking that this elf better come through for me. "Until then, I really need something to protect Wyatt when I'm not around. This wall would be awesome. I'll deal with the bother for now. It will only be temporary."

"Okay." Michelle was skeptical. "I'll have to arrange for my aunt to come down."

"Can you fly her in from Jamaica? Maybe get her here first thing tomorrow?"

Michelle sighed. "We're Haitian, Sam. I keep telling you this. And my aunt lives in Ellicott City. She immigrated thirty years ago."

"Even better! She can drive down early, and we can have an invisible wall around Wyatt's house by lunchtime. I'll even pick up hot wings for us to eat." I frowned, wondering if Haitian people ate hot wings. I think I saw Michelle eat them once.

"Normally I doubt I could get her here with so little notice, but if I tell her she's doing a favor for Satan, she'll probably drop everything."

Uh,oh. Favor? She'd expect one in return. And I wasn't sure what kind of favor a Haitian priestess would want.

"What will I owe her for this invisible wall?" I asked suspiciously.

Michelle looked surprised. "She didn't charge *me* anything, but I am her niece. I can ask her how much. Is there a certain amount you don't want to go over? I mean, you've got a lot of money, Sam, and this does seem kind of important. Especially if the demons are focusing on Wyatt now."

"It's not money I'm worried about."

"Umm," Michelle nodded knowingly. "I'll ask. Who knows with her. Maybe she'll want you to help her with something?"

Or get something for her. I left for home with Michelle's assurances that she'd call me later tonight to finalize arrangements. It would be such a relief to have Wyatt somewhat protected, especially if I was going to be away meeting with an elf lord and then at a Ruling Council meeting. This way he could hole up in his house and wait out any demon attack until I returned. Or shoot at them from the safety of his home. It would be a real pain, being effectively banned from his house, but with any luck I'd take care of this elf job and have Haagenti off our backs in a week, tops.

I walked in my front door to see Leethu still sprawled on the couch, with several empty vodka bottles on the floor. She'd managed to find my secret stash of good stuff too. Between booze and entertainment, Leethu was proving to be a rather expensive houseguest.

"Ni-ni, you're home." She jumped up from the couch and ran to me. I felt a moment of guilt. She was truly glad to see me after being stuck in my house alone all day. I could hardly begrudge her my best vodka. Poor thing.

"Look what I brought you." I handed Leethu a stack of naughty magazines. They weren't the cheap ones either. I told her to not trash them because I'd like to peruse them myself at a later date. I was sure Wyatt would be interested too. Then I set up my laptop and found a hard core S&M chat room and banished her to the upstairs to entertain herself while I made my call to Dar. Leethu seemed clueless, but I got the feeling she was shrewder than she let on. I wasn't sure how much I wanted her to know of my business at this point, how much to trust her. I'm sure she knew Haagenti was after me, and she knew I was the Iblis, but it was better to keep the details away from her until I could gauge whether or not she'd be likely to betray me. I waited a few moments to make sure she was engrossed in her activities then called Dar.

"So am I still deep in shit?" I asked him as soon as he picked up.

"Oh yeah. Haagenti is not going to give up on this one. You really should come back here and let him beat the holy fuck out of you for a few centuries. The longer you stay away, the worse he gets."

"I can't Dar," I protested. "I've got these stupid Iblis duties, and while I'd be happy to shirk them, I won't be happy to never see my human friends again. They'd all be dead by the time Haagenti is finished with me."

"They're going to be dead soon anyway," Dar warned. "If you come back, at least they'll live out their normal life expectancies. I can't imagine why, but I know you care about that sort of thing. I'm guessing you'd rather they live happily to a ripe old age and never see you again, than watch them be eviscerated right in front of you."

I winced. He was right. But I still wasn't going to let Haagenti get his hands on me if I could help it.

"I need you to do some research for me," I asked, changing to a less violent topic. "First, I need to know if sorcerers or anyone can remove a demon energy signature from a corpse. Like a kind of cleansing."

"Why in the world would someone do that?"

"I have no idea. Can you just see if anyone has ever heard of it before?"

"Sure. Anything else?"

"Do you know any old ones? I need to find out anything on the angel's Ruling Council that I can. Anything is helpful, but specifically the names, titles, responsibilities, and strengths of the members."

Dar laughed. "Mal, I know everyone. How dare you doubt my social reach?"

Dar called me "Mal Cogita," which he claims means "bad fuck" in Spanish. I'd been hoping to ask someone if that was true, because Dar often inflated his knowledge, but I hadn't had time.

"Of course I can find that out, but even so, any information I get is going to be really old. Like almost three million years old. I'm sure the original angels are dead by now."

"I don't think so. They don't die like we do. The one I deal with was in the war, and I know he's got brothers just as old who are probably on the council too."

"Still, they may rotate members. Or maybe they vote on them. I really can't see how dated information is going to be helpful."

"It will better than nothing, which is what I've got now. Besides, knowing who they were during the wars, what their titles were, will help. Even if they've swapped out council members, they're probably similar in power and skills."

"Okay. I'll do what I can," Dar replied.

"But don't ask Ahriman," I added as an afterthought. I'd not responded to his breeding petition. Although I intended to decline, I was hoping to keep him warm on the back burner as a kind of emergency, desperation, get-out-of-jail-free card. Under the protection of Ahriman's wing, no one would fuck with me. But the price would be high.

Dar snorted. "Ahriman? He wouldn't give me the time of day!" Dar paused then continued, his tone thoughtful. "Although I do think he is a bit obsessed with you, Mal. There is a rumor he presented a breeding contract to you, and he does seem to keep close tabs on your situation."

"He has petitioned me.. I wonder if I hint that I may accept, if he'd pressure Haagenti to back off."

A shout of laughter filled the room. "Mal, you idiot. You've been hanging out with humans too long. I'm willing to bet that Ahriman is spurring Haagenti on. Just think for a moment, Haagenti grabs you, tortures you mercilessly, and Ahriman swoops in to save the day. If you didn't jump at his proposal right away, he knows you're reluctant. What better way to overcome reluctance than to orchestrate a kidnapping. Desperate and in pain, you'd leap at the chance to take him up on his offer. In fact, he could substantially change the terms in his favor and you'd probably still accept at that point. Ahriman isn't one to take rejection lightly. Or stalling. He gets what he wants."

Shit. I'd never even thought about that. Maybe Ahriman was behind this whole thing with Haagenti. It would explain Haagenti's over-the-top reaction, and his persistence, as well as his deep pockets in trying to haul me back. Now I was even more reluctant to return. Torture from Haagenti I might be able to face, Ahriman I couldn't. He was too strong, and I wouldn't put it past him to force me unwilling.

"Crap, that puts a wrinkle in something else," I told Dar. "I need to meet with an elf lord. Taullian in Cyelle. It's by the Western Red Forest over where we grew up. The Columbia gate puts me near, but it's west of Cyelle."

"Yeah, from that gate you'd either need to go through the Elven kingdom of Li and into Cyelle, or skirt the edge of Li in the demon lands to the Maugan swamp, and the Cyelle border. But the problem is going to be the gate. Haagenti knows you're partial to that gate and he has it watched constantly. Your only chance would be to dash through and into Li before they nab you."

"That high lord hates my guts."

"You could come in by Klee," Dar suggested. "I don't think Haagenti has anyone watching that gate."

"Uh, no. That's through four different elf kingdoms, and every single one of them would be happy to see me dead. Haagenti's torture would be like a spa day by comparison." Besides, to get to that gate, I'd need to fly to Mogadishu, and I didn't think there was quick and easy air travel there right now.

"There's no way you'll make it past the Seattle gate either, the one that comes out in Dis. No way. That gate is wall-to-wall demons. You'll just need to find another entrance."

I sighed. There was another gate: the elf gate on the C&O canal towpath. But that came out into another high lord's lands, and even though we were on decent terms, elves didn't take kindly to trespass. There was always a cost if you were caught on their lands. I was going to have to risk it though. Just as soon as I was sure Wyatt was safe.

Mulling over the best way to go through three elven kingdoms without offending anyone or being snatched up by demons, I ended my call and headed out to meet Candy. Korean food and the company of a good friend would put everything in perspective. And if that didn't do it, hot wings and a night curled up in Wyatt's arms would.

~5~

Michelle's aunt appeared to be in her sixties, a voluminous woman in a voluminous bright-blue dress. She glared at me, clearly disappointed.

"This is no Satan," she announced. I felt rather ashamed, as if I'd defrauded her. "This is not even a Loa. She is a minor servant of Eshu of the Yoruba. She is of no use to me."

She'd insisted that her wall needed to be constructed at night, and had raced up from Ellicott City in her sporty little BMW convertible. I'd had to interrupt my girlfriend time with Candy and hot-foot it back to meet her at Wyatt's house. I probably didn't look too impressive, standing beside Wyatt's old truck holding a bag of hot wings.

"I am the Ha-satan, the Iblis," I assured her weakly. "I can show you the sword."

She scowled. "I care not for your weapons. That horse you have mounted is not even an initiate. Why would you choose her?"

I glanced over at Michelle, silently beseeching her for clarification. I wasn't on a horse at the moment, and I wasn't sure exactly who this initiate was that the woman referred to. Did she mean Piper or Diablo? And who was this "her"? All my horses were male.

"She means the human whose form you are in. Your "horse". She is wondering why you would possess someone who is not a worshipper. Normally a spirit only possesses those who are initiated into the religion and who are willing vessels."

I turned back to the aunt. "I can Own anyone I choose. Anyone I find interesting. I don't need their permission, and they don't need to worship me." Although that would be really cool. I'd never had anyone worship me before.

Her dark eyes were uncomfortably intense. "But you do not Own this horse you ride. A symbiosis such as this is only possible with permission."

"Can you build this wall, or not?" I asked. I wasn't about to get into a discussion of the terms and conditions surrounding my Owning the human known as Samantha Martin. It was complicated, and strange, not something I discussed with anyone, let alone some unknown priestess.

Wyatt had come out at this point, and the aunt turned her attention to him, her face clearly approving.

"Is this the young man seeking protection?" she asked. Without waiting for an answer, she turned to Michelle. "I will do this for you and your young man. Not for this servant of Eshu."

Michelle shot me an uncomfortable glance. "He's not my young man, Auntie. He's Sam's boyfriend."

The piercing eyes returned to me. "Greedy," she pronounced. Yep, that was an understatement. "I will not do this thing for you."

"I'll pay you," I pleaded.

"Please?" Michelle intervened. "Wyatt is my friend, and I want him to be safe."

"All right," the aunt muttered. "But that little crossroads demon has to go away and leave me to work in peace."

Wyatt walked closer, while the aunt slandered me.

"I really don't want this thing," he told me. "I can take care of myself. You don't need to do this."

"Weak, paltry spirits who cannot even protect their own against the lowest of demons. . ." the aunt raised her voice.

"You do need this, Wyatt," I assured him. "What if one comes after you when you're in the shower, or taking a shit? You can't have your gun loaded and ready at every moment. This will give you a safe place, and buy you some time if one attacks."

"If she stopped cowering under a rock, like vermin, and actually confronted those who would threaten her. . ." the aunt shouted to be heard over our conversation.

"Okay," Wyatt conceded. "But I hate the idea that you can't come inside my house. Leethu is in yours, and now you can't come into mine. Where can we be together?"

"The barn," I suggested. "The Eastside Tavern?"

"Coward. Miserable, worthless coward, undeserving of the attention of the god she serves."

"Fine!" I shouted back. "I got it. The neighbors two miles away don't need to hear this."

"Come on," Wyatt urged. "Let's go hide out in your barn while this horrible woman does her thing."

"No," the horrible woman proclaimed. "The worshiper of this cowardly spirit must remain here while I secure his house."

Wyatt, my worshiper? I nearly choked in amusement.

Wyatt gave me a pained look. "Go on," I told him, still grinning at the aunt's comment. "It won't take long, then she'll leave and we can go curl up in my barn among the saddle pads and feed sacks."

It took forever. There was a lot of swaying, chanting, humming and depositing of dust at various spots around Wyatt's house. Michelle had told me that originally the protection was just on the dwelling, the dust placed in the corners of the building, but she'd asked her aunt to place the barrier further out, for added protection. I kept creeping close, trying to see what was going on. Finally Michelle came out to me and told me I needed to go away, that her aunt had instructed she was to "beat me off with a stick" if I came any closer. So I went back to my house and watched fetish porn with Leethu, waiting for Michelle to call me and have me come out to test the barrier.

It was almost dawn, and Leethu and I were dozing on the couch when the call finally came. The Succubus had been trapped in my house for far too long, so I coaxed her out to see Wyatt's wall, promising she could try to seduce the aunt. I had my doubts that she'd be successful.

"Now *that* is a spirit worth knowing," Michelle's aunt said in admiration upon seeing Leethu. "A minor in the hierarchy of Erzulie Freida, but still powerful."

Leethu looked up coyly from downcast eyes and graciously thanked the horrible woman for her flattery while I tested Wyatt's new barrier. I pounded it with my fists, kicked it, and threw myself against it all around the perimeter, and it held admirably. The woman was a real bitch, but she did know how to make an invisible wall.

By the time I'd made my way around the other side of Wyatt's house, Leethu was in close conversation with her, hanging on the woman's every word and looking up at her respectfully. I watched as she took her hand and ran her fingers caressingly down the aunt's arm. The woman smiled. It was an alarming sight to see; the smile was absolutely out of place on what I'd assumed was a permanently scowling face.

"All right, Leethu," I told her. "Let's get back before Gregory shows up and lops your head off."

The succubus shot over to my side for protection, looking nervously around at the dark shadows cast by the trees.

"The barrier will protect against servants of Rada as well as Petro," the aunt assured me. I looked to Michelle for translation.

"Angels as well as demons," Michelle helpfully chimed in. "I didn't have her do mine against angels, but with Wyatt as your boyfriend, I thought protection against angels might be a good idea."

I hadn't thought of that. I knew Gregory didn't particularly like him, that he often claimed to wish Wyatt dead, but I didn't honestly think he'd take any action against him. In fact, I kind of got the impression he would protect Wyatt, even though he disliked him. Still, it was a good idea.

"Thanks," I told her. "And thank you," I said to the aunt.

The aunt waved her hand dismissively. "I like this boy," she said. "I think my niece should date him."

Michelle looked horrified. "Auntie, I'm already dating someone. And Wyatt is Sam's boyfriend. I mentioned that before."

I kissed Wyatt, just to emphasize the "my boyfriend" part. Demons wouldn't care, but I was starting to have very un-demonic, rather possessive feelings toward Wyatt. Michelle was my friend, and if Wyatt wished to be with her, I wouldn't stand in his way, but it would bother me. I was beginning to want him all to myself. Mine. In every way shape and form.

"Lock up your place and meet me in the barn in ten," I whispered to him. "I'll bring breakfast and we'll watch the sunrise together."

He cupped my face with one hand, brushing his thumb across my cheekbone. His eyes were warm with passion and a kind of gentle emotion. "I'd like that," he said, and those words set every nerve in my body alight.

"She said I could mount her," Leethu confided to me as we walked back toward my house. "She is so soft and round. I find her irresistibly attractive. I can't wait to fuck her."

"She doesn't mean 'fuck'," I explained. "She's talking about something entirely different."

I quickly told her about horses. She sighed with regret.

"That does not sound as much fun as fucking," the Succubus whined. "I am so disappointed. I'll bet I could change her mind though."

Yes, I'm sure you could, I thought as the pheromones flowed in a velvety caress over me. They soothed me and added to my rather satisfied mood. Wyatt was safe, rents were in, and I was confident that I'd soon have Haagenti off my back. At the moment, I was relaxed and sleepy from the late hour and Leethu's presence. I couldn't wait to see Wyatt, to glory in both the sunrise and the feel of his skin against mine, then fall asleep wrapped in the tight embrace of his limbs, but as I poured coffee into a thermos, my doubts returned. Wyatt was safe, but for how long? What if the barrier failed? What if he was ambushed while grocery shopping or pumping gas one day? This last demon was smart and strong. Wyatt wouldn't stand a chance. I needed to resolve this issue with Haagenti, and resolve it fast. Before it was too late.

~6~

I'd hauled the trailer with the Surburban to Dargan's Landing early afternoon. Wyatt and I had eaten microwaved bacon and mini donuts in the barn, then slowly explored each other as pink lit the morning sky. I hadn't wanted it to end, but with a defensible barrier around Wyatt's house, it was time for me to see about a more permanent solution to my Haagenti problem. So here I was, hauling my horse to the safest gate to Hel that I could think of.

It wasn't unusual to see various trailers at this particular access point to the C&O Canal. There was a boat launch; but not just the rafters, kayakers, and fishers put in here. Cycling groups, joggers, and those who longed for a nice easy trail ride with their horses also used this spot. Of course, there weren't as many horses on the towpath as there used to be. With all the joggers and cyclists, it took a placid horse to handle the chaos without bolting. My huge draft gelding, Piper, was such a horse, but he wasn't the one I'd brought today. I had Diablo.

Diablo was a thoroughbred cross, and I don't just mean in equine breed terms. Some demon had gotten his freak on with a mare and sired this horse. Breeding is an intentional act for our kind, and we can exercise great creativity in the traits we endow our offspring. I was surprised to find Diablo in the hands of humans because his breeding had clearly been given some thought. I could only assume his sire meant to return to collect him and sell him at a later date but had either been killed or was unable to successfully cross the gates again. I'd bought the horse for practically nothing from humans who found him so dangerous and unpredictable that he was seconds away from finding himself in a dog food can.

I didn't find him much easier to handle than his human owners had. He was smart. He had skills. And he obeyed . . . sometimes. He was crazy and skittish, terrified of plastic grocery store bags, blowing leaves, even his own damned shadow. Which was really ridiculous since he had the ability to store enough raw energy to explode any killer plastic bag that threatened his being. Horses.

He wasn't any happier about the elf gate we stood in front of. Or the cyclists. Or the joggers. Or that insane guy kayaking the Potomac River in January. He danced around with his ears pinned flat, snorting at the elf trap and its bait; an illusion of a dirty, tear stained toddler sitting at the bottom of the ravine.

"It's an illusion, you worthless horse," I told him. "It's a gate. You just walk right on through the damned thing."

Piper would have plodded through without a second thought, but once I was on the other side, I needed a horse with a good bit of demon in him. We'd need to move fast though the elf kingdom, dash across a tiny swath of demon lands, then head deep into the Western Red Forest where I should be safe. I needed a fast horse, one that could defend himself and me, one that could teleport. Although there was no guarantee he'd be able, or willing, to teleport me along with him. Stupid, unreliable horses.

Diablo pranced, and I was getting tired of kicking him in the sides and jolting him with energy. I needed to change tactics.

"You'll get to see the horses back home. Mmm-mmm. Other hybrids like you." His ears twitched. "And the Elven mares. You have no idea, my friend. Elegant and leggy. They always think they are better than us, so you need to chase them down and pin them against the fence before you fuck them."

Not that I'd ever fucked a horse, Elven or otherwise. Clearly the idea of a challenge intrigued Diablo, because he cautiously made his way down the canal embankment and extended his nose toward the gate.

"We need to go through fast, and then run like crazy. They always have a couple of scouts near the gates to scoop up the humans, so they'll be on us quickly. They won't have horses though, so we'll get a good head start before they alert the cavalry. If we hustle, we'll be out of their territory and safe before they even saddle up."

I hoped so anyway. Elves were a tricky bunch. This was trespass, and if they caught me, there would be repercussions. I'd done work with this elf lord before, so hopefully I could negotiate a service or some favor in exchange for passage. If not, I'd be spending some quality time in their dungeon.

Then there was the narrow strip of demon land I needed to cross. For all I knew, Haagenti had his own people patrolling the area. And there was always the chance that this was a trap, that Taullian was luring me in to turn me over to Haagenti for a bounty. I hesitated, reconsidering, but then I remembered the demon in Wyatt's house, and urged Diablo forward. I had to take the chance.

Diablo tensed then leapt through the gate in a standing jump that would have done a mule proud. I had to duck so the top of the gate didn't take my head off.

As soon as we hit the soft ground, he bolted. I got one glance of a shocked elf, his mouth wide open, then huddled as close to Diablo's neck as I could to avoid the branches that were smacking me on the legs and arms like a series of whips. There was one problem. I needed to look up and see where we were going, so I could give Diablo direction, but I didn't want my head decapitated by an overhanging tree limb. I compromised by hanging slightly sideways off the saddle and gluing my cheek to the horse's neck.

Now I could see, but I was constantly shifting my body left to right to avoid tree trunks. Diablo had a great sense of personal space, but that personal space didn't include my body. I wacked my knee on several trees and nearly dislocated my shoulder on another.

"Slow down a bit," I shouted. "And don't cut it so close. You're going to rip the legs right off my body."

He paid no attention to me whatsoever. He wasn't afraid, wasn't racing terrified through the forest. He was exhilarated. He'd never been in Hel before, and the energy that flowed thick through the air filled him with an adrenaline burst. He was faster, stronger, and he could draw power right from the air. He didn't have to wait for me to give it to him. He wasn't limited by the small amount he was able to store. The world was at his hooves and he was ecstatic.

I knew how he felt. I hadn't been home in so long, and I felt the same godlike feeling of power. It soared through me, making me giddy. I missed this.

Thankfully, we made it through Wythyn without any trouble. We darted across the three-mile stretch of demon land separating the elven kingdoms and were safely in the borderlands of the Western Red Forest, which connected the demon lands with Cyelle. Hopefully safe.

I slowed Diablo to a walk, which wasn't easy given his current state of excitement. The forest evoked all sorts of memories from my childhood. Technically the woods were part of Cyelle, but a treaty allowed demons access. Besides that, they'd always been tolerant of demon children encroaching on their lands—as long as we didn't come too far. We'd chased each other through the trees, blasting woodland creatures, carving patterns in bark, boulders, and even dirt with claws and spikes. Sometimes the young elves would try to trap us, or ambush us with their special arrows. Sometimes they caught us and poked as they whooped and hollered with triumph. It was fun. Adult elves were not as much fun.

We were only a few miles into the forest when Diablo snorted and tossed his head. He didn't have to warn me, I could feel them nearby. Elves. I stopped the horse and kept my posture relaxed and open.

"I'm the Iblis, here at the invitation of your Lord Taullian. He should be expecting me. I'm not sure where to meet him and would appreciate an escort."

Elves materialized from the forest, weapons at the ready. I understood. It was always prudent to be cautious around demons. Diablo had never seen an elf before, and he totally lost it as they appeared from the shadows. It was a little embarrassing having him leap all around the narrow path, smashing me into trees as I tried to control him. At first the elves were alarmed, but they relaxed, realizing I was not a threat at the moment. Their attitude quickly shifted to amusement as Diablo bashed me against a large oak. Normally they would have stepped in and calmed the horse down, but with a demon hybrid, they knew to keep their distance. Finally, with no help from me, Diablo settled down enough to stand frothing and shivering, rolling his eyes at the elves.

"Can you get him through a gate?" one asked me.

"He's been through one already. I'm hoping he'll go through another, but I'm not promising anything."

These elves had clearly mastered an inter-realm gate, as the angels had. I'd never even heard of this before I'd met Gregory. Another little secret the elves kept all to themselves. I hoped I could get Diablo to go through since I wasn't sure where in the kingdom this lord would be and didn't want to be gone for weeks. The longer I was here, the more likely I'd be handed over by some bounty-hungry elf. And there was that stupid Ruling Council meeting hanging over my head. Actually, it was nice to know if I was held here against my will, Gregory would summon my ass back for the meeting.

Two elves walked forward and made a downward motion, as if they were unzipping the air. There was a crackle of power and the gate shimmered before us. Diablo rolled his eyes and hopped backward like a rabbit.

"Come on boy, these guys have some really nice mares you want to meet," I encouraged him as four of our party walked through the gate.

I managed to get him right up to it, but he refused to go further. He danced back and forth, skipping sideways as I urged him forward. The elves snickered patiently behind me. This went on for what seemed like hours before I finally nudged Diablo up, nose to the gate. He sniffed at it tentatively, almost ready. As I encouraged him to go through, I heard a laugh behind me, then Diablo rocketed through the gate and took off through the woods. One of those asshole elves had jabbed him with a sword.

My horse raced out of the tree line, practically mowing down the surprised elves that had preceded us through the gate, and shot across the meadow. Trying to slow him, I braced on his neck with one hand and pulled back on the other rein. In theory, Diablo would circle, and I would spiral him in tighter and tighter until he was forced to slow down. That was the idea anyway. In reality, I had his nose crammed solidly against my knee, his head bent nearly backward as I tried to turn and slow him. It didn't work. He charged ahead. This was rather alarming because it meant he was running blind, absolutely unable to see where the fuck he was going. I finally gave him his head, figuring it was better to let him run it out then plow into the city gate, or throw me by stumbling over an unseen durft hole. I rethought my logic as he tore through the open city gates and down a well-populated street, scattering screaming shoppers and merchants.

He did finally stop. Slamming on the breaks right in front of a troop of guards, and launching me over his head to skid across the flagstone pavement. An entrance fitting for the mighty Iblis. I lay on the pavement and looked up at their astonished faces, while Diablo nudged me apologetically. Bastard.

My breathless escorts eventually managed to catch up with me while I was flat on the ground with a troop of guards pointing arrows at my chest. Luckily it didn't take the scouts too long to arrive behind me. Elves were fast. Very fast. I really had no idea why they bothered with horses.

"This is the Iblis. To see his Lordship," one gasped to the guards. The guards looked back and forth between us in shock.

"*This* is the Iblis?"

"Yeah, that's me," I informed him, standing and dusting my jeans off as they lowered their arrows. "Wanna see my sword?" I figured it was kind of like an ID card. I always carried the Sword of the Iblis—the artifact that symbolized the title I held—but in the more portable form of a barrette.

"No, there's no need to display your sword," the guard assured me. He motioned me to follow, parting the crowd before us. Diablo was subdued behind me. I think he knew he'd behaved badly. I should punish him, but it really wasn't his fault. He'd never experienced any of this before, and he *was* a horse, after all. This had to be far scarier than a plastic bag.

Diablo was more than happy to abandon me once we got to the stables and he saw all the other horses. I left him in a groom's capable hands and followed my huge entourage into what, for want of a better term, was the palace. I'd been in elf palaces before, invited for various social events with my demon peers, or summoned to hear requests for services. They were all organic, merging in with the natural surroundings and complimenting the beauty of the woods and meadows around them. The other buildings in their cities were the same. Still, the palaces had a kind of ostentation to them, a false modesty. They seemed to bow in deference to the nature they mimicked, but with a deeper look, they had a faint superiority. As if the elves felt they engineered a better nature than the very goddess they worshipped.

This palace was the same: lofty spires resembled the oaks, granite floors as moss-covered stones, windows that shot beams of light down through the cathedral ceilings like sunshine through a forest canopy—beauty with an unflinching eye to detail and cold perfection.

I expected I'd be led straight to his lordship, but instead my huge group of guards and scouts herded me up a set of winding stairs to a suite of rooms. Halfway up, another elf emerged from an adjacent hallway and joined our procession. He was wearing the same uniform as the other guards, but with chains of gold leaves draped across the front. I assumed the jewelry indicated a higher status than the others.

"Please feel free to relax and freshen up," the one with the bling told me. "You will be our guest tonight at a banquet and festival to celebrate the birth of the snow king."

Snow king? It didn't snow in Hel. And if they meant Jesus, they were about a month too late for that one.

"As I mentioned to your messenger, I have a very full schedule. Would it be possible to see his Lordliness right now, so I can begin my return journey?"

The elf smiled sympathetically. "I'm afraid not. This festival is a much-anticipated event in our kingdom. We were given the impression you would be here much later in the week, so we're a bit thrown by your arrival. We would be honored by your presence at tonight's festivities though. You needn't feel out of place; other demons will be in attendance."

I'd hoped to avoid other demons. Once they knew of my presence, they'd gleefully alert Haagenti. He may not risk coming onto elf land to get me, but he'd be laying in wait the moment I stepped a foot across the borders. And there was always the possibility he'd bribe an elf to turn me over.

"Will his Lordship be able to see me after the party?" I asked hopefully. Maybe I could meet the guy and bolt for the border before the other demons ratted me out.

The elf shook his head. "He'll see you first thing in the morning. You'll want to be rested and refreshed when you meet him."

He turned and left, along with the dozen other guards and scouts that had been tagging along after me. I stood in my lavish gold and silk draped suite and thought. How long was this whole thing going to take, and how in the hell was I going to make it home in once piece?

~7~

I stared at my reflection in the ornate mirror, and at the jeans and t-shirt in a heap on the floor behind me. My brown hair was in a simple braid; the dress was one of several I'd found in the closet. I had no idea whose they were. Hopefully they were left specifically for my use; otherwise I'd probably be accosted by an angry elf for clothing theft. The dress was one of those complicated wrap designs; it could have fit a variety of figures. It had taken me an hour to figure out how to get it on, and I wasn't sure I had it right. I hoped so.

Normally I went to these parties in a typical demon form. Scales, feathers, beaks, fangs, wings, claws. That had been my first thought. My second to just go as Samantha Martin, in the jeans and t-shirt I'd traveled in. Then I'd had an idea. It was a long shot, but if I could masquerade as a slave human, and avoid the demons, maybe I could remain undetected. I didn't leak energy. I'd been living with the humans for over forty years. If I kept my distance, the demons shouldn't suspect anything. The big challenge would be fooling any humans who were here, and ensuring the elves didn't blow my cover.

Of course, if this was a trap, and Taullian was intending on turning me over to his demon guests, then my appearance would be moot. But if they were just some invited guests, I might be able to squeak by this evening without detection.

There was a knock on my door, and the elf guard that entered stopped abruptly, his eyes wide at my appearance. He wasn't as ornately accessorized as the earlier one, but clearly not far below him in rank. A gilt oak leaf decorated his forearm, and his berry shaped buttons were equally shiny.

"Iblis," he stammered. "I am here to escort you and announce you at the banquet."

"Yeah, about that," I grinned. "I don't want you to announce me, or usher me in as the Iblis. Can I just blend in as one of your humans instead? I'm sure you understand that in my particular situation, I really do not want other demons to know I'm here. Even if they are friendly."

Comprehension dawned in his eyes. He looked me over carefully. "Not a human servant, but an apprentice, or a mage maybe? Not one of ours, though. You could be visiting from another kingdom, sent on business and attending the festival as a guest."

"Are there sorcerers here? Other mages? I'd be up shit creek if any of them approached me to talk shop." I didn't know much about their magic, beyond what it took to summon a demon.

"An apprentice then. One newly brought over, so you would be somewhat ignorant of elf customs and our sorcery teachings."

"But would an apprentice be out and about on her own after being newly kidnapped?" I asked. Adult humans were snared through the elf traps and usually spent a lot of their first decade trying to escape. They weren't allowed much freedom early on.

The elf looked affronted. "Not all of our humans are unwilling. We do have some, those who are strong in witchcraft and other magic, who jump at the chance to come here and learn from us. They find us far more accepting of their talents than their human brethren."

"Ok, so I'm a human witch, newly arrived, who is still learning the basics of sorcery and elf society. Shouldn't I be studying or something? Why would my master send me to another kingdom so soon?"

"Gaial, up north, sometimes sends people down to swap scrolls and magical items. It wouldn't be unusual for them to send a new apprentice to experience southern culture."

I nodded. "Is there anything I'd need to know?"

"Not that I could tell you in the next two minutes, no. This dress is in our style, but you could have easily borrowed it for the festival. Of course, you have it on backwards."

I looked in the mirror. The light green silk draped in folds over my shoulders and my breasts, to cross and wrap around the waist before opening up into a full skirt that barely came to my knees.

"You're going to have to help me with it then, because I have no idea," I told him, removing the long strip of fabric to stand naked before him.

Elves have no problems with nudity, so the guy didn't bat an eyelid. He walked over and began to wrap the fabric around me, casually brushing against my breasts and rear as he worked.

He stood back to look at me with a critical eye. "If I may say so, Iblis, your form is nicely done. I honestly would take you for a human if I didn't know differently."

I'd heard that compliment before, but it was particularly gratifying coming from an elf. Their standards were high and they didn't express approval lightly, especially toward demons. I looked once again at my appearance in the mirror. Yikes. If I'd been at a party with Wyatt dressed like this, I would have been arrested. The silk wrapped around my neck, then over my shoulders to run along the outer edges of my breasts, looping under them to cross and wind around to my back. My boobage was totally exposed, pushed up and together by the strips of fabric. Somehow, the rest of it wound around my hips to hang in the front and back like a sort of loincloth drape, leaving my legs uncovered. I would be flashing my crotch and ass with every step. I'd seen elves, male and female, in lesser states of dress, so I was confident that the guard knew what he was doing and wasn't playing a prank on me. If the elves didn't care about seeing all my naughty bits, then I didn't care either.

"Let's go," I told the guard and followed him out of the suite and down the stairs.

The banquet hall was cavernous. A marble fountain complete with stone swans spraying a fan of water towards the heavens stood in the middle of the room. A carved marble tree emerged from the center of the fountain showering the swans with a gentle cascade of water from stone branches. At the far end of the hall was a fire pit that could easily fit a grove, and a series of long tables filled with food. Fresh fruit of all shapes and colors, loaves of hearty bread, and a cornucopia of vegetables loaded down one table. Roasted meats with dishes of savory sauces and gravies were spread across another. There was more food here than the attendees could possibly eat and I rolled my eyes at the overabundance. Elves were always excessive when it came to food. High metabolism had its benefits.

Most elven events I'd attended featured flowers: tons of colorful bouquets and greenery artfully woven around tables, chairs, ceiling and walls. There were none here, just some stick-looking grapevine things, and rocks. I really wanted to check out the composition of the rocks, but it wouldn't do to have my energy out and about right now.

"The Iblis would be at the head table," the guard indicated in a hushed voice. "An apprentice would eat from the buffet, over there."

That actually worked to my advantage. If I had to sit next to other humans, or elves, and make polite dinner conversation, I'd be discovered in less time than it took an elf to drain a goblet.

"Good luck," the guard told me before leaving my side. A human apprentice would hardly be entering the banquet with an elven guard.

I stepped into the hall and it hit me immediately. Cold. Temperatures in Hel ranged from hot to hotter. The elves did some temperature control of their areas to provide greater variation in support of their beloved foliage, but this was far outside the range I'd ever experienced. It was below freezing in the place. My skin rose in goosebumps and my nipples became like rocks. I was amused to see the humans shivering around the fire, some cupping hands around a steaming beverage. Elves and demons would be reasonably at ease, but humans had a narrow window of comfort when it came to atmospheric parameters. They'd be cold, especially in these ridiculous scraps of clothing the elves considered fashionable. I had an urge to grab the tablecloths and pass them around.

"Here. This helps." Something warm and hard nudged my arm. I looked down and saw a hot steaming mug.

I followed the mug to an arm and upward to a smiling, male, human face. Shit. Not two seconds over the threshold and one was accosting me. This game would be over real quick.

"Uh thanks." I took the mug and sipped. It tasted of green and berries, but there was something else in it beyond the leaves swirling in pretty patterns at the bottom. Immediately I felt more comfortable.

Sipping my tea in silence, I pointedly ignored the man who'd brought it. The human shifted his weight awkwardly, but didn't leave. He tried to keep his eyes above my neck, but couldn't keep his gaze from drifting to my headlights. I wanted to laugh, but I really wanted him to go away more.

"I've not seen you around. Are you from Cyelle, or another kingdom?"

"Gaiaia," I mumbled into my tea. I really wished he'd go away.

"Gaial? I've always wanted to go there. They say the volcanic rock formations are pleasingly symmetrical and rise up to ten meters in clusters."

Damn, he sounded like a guide book. He knew more about my supposed home than I did.

"I've just come here," I told him hastily. "I haven't seen or done much."

He laughed. "Nor will you. I've spent the last ten years either with my nose in a book or my body in a circle. We do make an effort to get to these events though, so we don't become crazed recluses. Are you a level four or five?"

Fuck. "I just came across the gates," I repeated. "I really don't know much about anything yet."

He peered at me, a kind of excitement in his eyes. "Seriously? I thought I misheard you. Your Elvish: your accent is amazing for someone recently arrived. You must be a willing apprentice. They'd never let a new human stroll around a festival otherwise. I haven't been home in fifteen years. What's it like? What's going on?"

I kicked myself for not remembering the language issue then made some generalized comments about military conflicts, areas of drought and famine, and any notable epidemics that had occurred in the last decade. We demons tended to keep our eyes on those sorts of things so we can jump in and contribute whenever we feel the urge.

"I was twelve when I fell through the trap to this side," he reminisced. "My whole world changed."

I was curious if he'd go back given the chance. Probably not. He was a mage. He seemed to be enjoying his life. It's not like the elves had grabbed him and made him shovel shit, after all. I kept silent though, hoping with the lack of conversation, my new friend would go away.

No such luck. "I'm Kirby," he said, extending an awkward hand. It was a touching gesture. Elves didn't shake hands. He clearly remembered the human custom and was performing it with me, to make me feel welcome, or perhaps to connect with his old memories of a past life.

"Samantha Martin," I told him automatically. I shook his hand. There, now maybe he'd go away.

Instead he launched into a lengthy lecture about the kingdom, the beneficent lord who ruled it, the festival at hand and how unusual and creative it was. This was just as good as going away. As he spoke, I glanced around and looked to see if there was anyone I wished to avoid.

There were elves and humans throughout the hall, laughing and enjoying themselves. They tended to socialize separately, but there were some rare occurrences of an elf and human in the same group. I counted five demons in attendance. Not a lot, given the size of the party, but five demons would still be hard to handle. They seemed relaxed and playful. They didn't appear to know I was in the kingdom from what I could see. Still, I unobtrusively checked their energy signatures, which was easy since they all leaked like bad plumbing.

Every one of them was a heavy hitter. None of them were Low. It wasn't likely that a Low would be invited to an elf banquet, but I had hoped they wouldn't be this powerful. I recognized Assalbi and hoped he didn't recognize me. He'd be thrilled to see me under Haagenti's thumb, after he'd extracted his own pound of flesh. He was a treasure hoarder. I'd helped myself to compensation from his stash a few centuries back, and he hadn't seen the situation the same way I did.

Chamoriel was there, an ooze of slime and leaf mold covering both his serpent body and human head. He was actually a decent guy, smell and appearance aside. He blew a lot of stuff up, but he had always been polite and friendly during the process. I had a feeling he might turn a blind eye if he were aware of my presence.

I didn't recognize one, but I think he may have been one of Gediel's household. And then there was Zalanes, who had been a buddy back in our school days. He was another imp; a troublemaker. I can't believe the elves invited him. Imps weren't often included in festivals. I didn't think he'd rat me out though. So basically, Assalbi was my problem. Unless that big demon over behind the fountain was who I thought he was.

My heart sank as I saw a bull with the hind end of a lion and griffin wings. Even before I checked the energy signature I knew. Haagenti. The demon swiveled his bovine head, obviously searching the room for something. I'm sure that something was me. That fucking double-crossing elf must mean to turn me over to him. All that rhetoric about helping me with my "vexing problem" was bullshit. Two-timing jerk. Once my initial wave of anger equalized, I puzzled over why the elf lord would have brought us together at a banquet. The elves I knew would never risk disruption to their festivities by setting things in motion that would lead to a potentially lethal brawl with inevitable civilian casualties. It was dicey enough just having demons at a party without throwing a feud into the mix. What was this elf lord scheming? I'd expected the elves to hand me over behind closed doors, or arrange an ambush once I'd left their lands. I looked around for the elf lord, Taullian, to see if I could better assess his motives.

He was at the huge head table, populated solely by elves. No humans. No demons, although one seat remained conspicuously vacant. The guard had meant to announce me, and said I was to be at the head table. Haagenti would have been on me within seconds and probably have pronounced a feud with the elf lord who dared to seat his despised rival above him in status. Who the fuck was this elf lord, and why was he so eager for a fight? If he truly meant to turn me over for the bounty, why would he risk offending Haagenti by having me at the head table?

I watched Taullian politely conversing with a female. Something looked odd about him and it took me a moment to realize it was his hair. He'd draped the wavy locks over his ears in a strange kind of comb over. Elves loved displaying the points of their ears and often arranged their long hair to draw the eye to them. Ears to an elf were like wings to an angel. They were sensitive, personal, individual, considered both an ornament and an appendage of great spiritual significance. Ears to hear the Word of the goddess as she whispered in the wind. Why would a lord cover his ears in such a fashion? Perhaps it had something to do with the theme of the festival? Outside of the weird hairdo, he seemed pretty much like the other elf lords I'd met. Relaxed, arrogantly surveying his surroundings, entitlement in every fiber of his being. He wasn't particularly watching Haagenti, or looking at the door waiting for me to come in.

I felt a hand slide tentatively up my arm. Kirby seemed to be making a move. He was relaying gossip on how the high lord of Wythyn had lost yet *another* sorcerer. "If he'd treat his humans better, they wouldn't be constantly running away," he told me, his voice full of sympathy and superiority about his own kingdom. "A sorcerer. That's one of the highest social levels a human can hold. It's got to be pretty bad for one of them to take their chances and bolt. Especially in Wythyn. Did you hear what happened to the last sorcerer he lost? The lord sent a demon out after him and he came back barely alive. He'd been tortured for weeks, used as a play thing."

That was a gross exaggeration. At least I hadn't brought him back dead in a bag. I quickly bit back defensive words and pulled my attention back to Haagenti. I needed to concentrate on the powder keg ready to explode in my face and not on runaway sorcerers or randy apprentices. How could I sneak out of here without bringing notice to myself? I looked down at the hand on my arm and had an idea.

"Kirby? Would you like to fu. . . I mean go somewhere more-" I wasn't able to finish my proposition, which would hopefully get me out of the room pronto. There was a ringing noise and we all turned to the head table, wine glasses or hot mugs in hand. Silence fell and everyone looked toward the elf lord with rapt attention. Damn, I could hardly drag Kirby off now. Such rudeness would draw everyone's attention.

The lord began a long, dull speech about winter, death and rebirth, so fresh new growth could occur, rejuvenating the land, or some shit like that. I was bored. The humans were bored. The other demons were especially bored. Bored demons are never a good thing. They wandered among the attendees, shoving food items into inappropriate places and laughing loudly while the elves swatted them away. The demon I didn't know crawled under the tables, bumping them with his horned back and spilling food and drink off the sides. With a leap, Zalanes jumped into the fountain, unaffected by the cold water. He shoved his hands into the gentle spray from the tree-like column, re-directing it onto any unfortunate nearby humans and elves. Now that was funny. I wished I hadn't needed to be incognito, because I would have loved to join in on that one. Haagenti suddenly frowned and looked around the room while I held my breath and tightened my energy even further inside. What had he noticed? I never leaked. He can't have sensed me. Suddenly he jumped into the fountain with Zalanes and kicked the center column with front hooves. With a flash of light, the marble column broke in half, and the pipe supplying the fountain snapped in two, shooting a stream of water toward the ceiling like a fire hose.

Everyone screamed, the lord's speech forgotten, and ducked for cover. Instinctively I shot out a net of energy and grabbed the water molecules, every last one of them, changing their surface temperature and structure in a show of power that no other demon could. Gregory had taught me, and I'd spent months practicing this angelic art. The stream of water burst into white, and snow fell light and powdery from the ceiling in a gentle swirl.

The elves abandoned their usual decorum and shrieked in joy, racing about catching snowflakes with their hands and tongues. His lordship looked startled, but quickly recovered, proclaiming the snow as a symbol of the death of the old god, preparing the world for a fresh start. The demons froze, and not from the cold of the snow either. Eyes narrowing, they looked around, searching. I tried to hide behind Kirby as I saw Haagenti smile and reach for my net of energy. Fuck.

Time slowed to a crawl and I felt a snowflake on my finger. Its geometry was delicate and irregular. I looked up and noticed Kirby carefully examining a snowflake. His eyes slowly rose to meet mine and they held awe, uncertainty, and fear.

"That snowflake is not symmetrical, not balanced," he said, comprehension dawning. "You … you. I saw...."

I shook my head at him, in a gentle warning. Elves strived for perfection, for balance, just as the angels did. Their magic, the magic they taught to the humans was the same. The snowflakes were clearly a demon creation, obvious to anyone who examined them closely. But demons didn't do this sort of thing, angels did. And only one demon had contact with angels and lived to tell the tale.

The other demons were beginning to take their cue from Haagenti, reaching out with their own energy to trace the source. Their movements became purposeful, predatory. Shit. I needed to break off my snow-making before they followed the unusual energy stream back to me. I needed to break it off and resume my guise as a human with not a hint of demon energy at all. Then I needed to get the fuck out of here, although that would be near impossible with his stupid lordship droning on and on.

"Can someone shut off the water?" I whispered at Kirby.

He nodded toward a group of elves, who were trying to shoo the demons aside and climb into the fountain basin. The demons ignored them, their eyes scanning the room. Fuck. I had no time. Abruptly I cut off my energy, pulling it tightly back inside with a snap. The water shot out of the broken pipe in a wild, rotating spray, knocking an elf through the air and across a buffet table full of food. Everyone screamed and ran, frantically ducking under the tables. This was clearly the cover I needed to get out of the hall. Ironically I now found it impossible with the hordes stampeding the exits, slipping and falling on the slush-covered floor. A blast of water smacked into Kirby and I, sending us to the ground in a heap. The demons continued to search for me, looking for the slightest energy leak. Haagenti tried a different tactic. He began directing the spray of water and systematically blasting down any standing biped he saw, planning on forcing me to reveal myself.

I did what I do best. Hid. I scrambled into a crouched position and tried to blend with the crowd frantically racing for the door and trampling anyone who impeded their rushed exodus. Kirby ducked in after me, trying to keep up by holding on to a scrap of my miniscule dress. There was a blockade at the huge doorway as Haagenti directed his stream there, knocking people against the walls and pushing them across the floor. He knew. Knew I'd be trying to sneak out the door like the cockroach I was.

"Hang on," Kirby shouted, pushing me to the side away from the door and getting in a solid grope of my breasts. Evidently his libido didn't care that I was a demon. "Give the sorcerers a second to lock them in a circle and then we can safely get out."

"There's five of them," I shouted back. "*Five*. One sorcerer can't contain five demons of that level." Sorcerers were not thrilled about attending these kinds of events. Usually they took turns making obligatory appearances. There wouldn't be more than one sorcerer here. The others would be far away, at their studies.

Kirby grimaced as he realized the truth behind my words. "Others will be here soon," he assured me.

We didn't have time. Haagenti turned the stream our way, and suddenly elves and humans were being blasted into us. They thudded against each other, shrieking and gasping as the terrible force of the water drove the air from their lungs and smashed us all together against the wall. I could let them crush us, pull away from my flesh as Gregory had instructed and live inside a dying form. Wait out Haagenti. I could do it, hide in my form and play dead. Dead along with Kirby and all the humans and elves piled on top of each other.

I couldn't do it. Couldn't play possum and let them all die.

Instead I shot out a blast of energy, sending it between the bodies on top of me and altering the energy as it passed through the stream of water. It raced against the current to the source. In a deafening sound, the marble fountain exploded, knocking Haagenti backward where he slammed against a banquet table. The water, no longer under pressure, surged out, like the opening of a spring, to cover the floor. Humans and elves, fell to the ground gasping and crawling to safety.

"Get out of here," I told Kirby, shoving him toward the door. "Things are going to get really bloody in about two seconds."

No way was I going to fight a bunch of demons in the soft squishy form of a human. Especially a human with so much flesh exposed. In a snap I converted my entire form into the one I was most comfortable in. My birth form. The humans and elves renewed their frantic efforts to get out once they found themselves nose to scale with a huge orange serpent's leathery wings and three heads. I leapt over them and took flight, careful not to brush any of the humans with my poisonous spikes. The hall ceiling hung only thirty feet above, so my flight was more of an assisted hop before I was back on the ground and scrabbling on my stubby legs toward the crash of tables: and Haagenti.

A table flew through the air and Haagenti was on his feet in a charge, Assabli right behind him. I'd have a hard enough time taking on Haagenti solo. In a preemptive strike, I shot a bolt of lightning at Assabli, knocking him into the burbling fountain, and quickly glanced to see the reaction of the other demons.

The one I didn't recognize sat on a broken table, eating an apple and preparing to enjoy the show. Zalanes and Chamoriel held back, waiting. I didn't blame them. Normally they'd both probably support me, but the odds were not in my favor.

Haagenti plowed into me, his horns hooking around my lower body and pinning me against the floor. Luckily I was bendy in this form. I stretched one long neck out and bit him hard on the ass with one head, while the other two stretched underneath to tear at his belly. He roared and jerked his powerful neck send me skidding across the floor. At least I took a chunk of his lion butt with me.

I knew he wanted to keep this physical, to ensure he didn't accidently kill me quickly or knock me into blissful unconsciousness. Inflicting pain and backing me into a corner of desperate doom was his plan, and unfortunately for me, he was just as skilled at physical fighting as I. Folding his gryphon wings tight to his body, he jumped on me again, trampling my long, scaled length with hooves and tearing at me with his back paws. I squirmed, trying to wiggle out from under him, and by chance managed to impale a paw with one of my spikes. I heard him scream, and he jumped off me, tearing the spike from my body. He hopped around, frantically trying to pull it out with his teeth. I took advantage of the opportunity and shot him with a stream of raw energy.

The smell of burning flesh and hair filled the room. Haagenti roared, snatching the thorn from his paw and retaliating with a burst of energy. I converted as much of it as I could, storing it within me as raw energy, and had the satisfaction of seeing Haagenti's eyes widen in shock. *Yeah, fucker. I can hold more than you. I can probably hold more than anyone.* Undaunted, the demon blasted more energy at me, this time in a colossal, steady stream, pulled from our surroundings. The room felt like a vacuum had sucked the air out of it, and I struggled to convert and store such a great volume of energy. He planned to overwhelm me in a game of demon chicken. How close to our deaths were each of us willing to push this?

Haagenti continued his attack as he made his way toward me. I tried to retreat, but had to choose between defending myself from the stream of energy that would cook me from the inside or the demon's approaching horns. I chose to avoid the more lethal, and felt sharp points slide between my scales and into flesh. The pain broke my concentration and as I frantically clawed at Haagenti's sides to push him away I began to feel the burn of his energy attack along the edges of my spirit being. I was so fucked. This fight was just about over, and I was seconds away from a dungeon and torture.

"Yield," Haagenti commanded, his horns still slicing through my insides.

I began to say the words of submission when I felt an agonizing rip through my abdomen and stumbled as the demon's forward pressure abruptly ceased.

Zalanes. He'd decided to pick sides. Haagenti flew backwards, a shocked expression on his bovine face as the imp grabbed him by his lion tail and swung him around. Haagenti's head crashed into a table and he lay on the floor, momentarily stunned. I ran toward him, slipping and sliding on the two inches of slush covering the floor. I could hardly believe it. Thanks to Zalanes I'd gained the advantage and now had a snowball's chance of actually killing this fucker. With a leap I planted my front legs on him, preparing to drive a lethal stream of energy through his form, and felt the bottom of my foot hit something hard. There was something under his skin; round with a slight give. Instinctively, I recoiled; trying to pull my weight off the object, but my momentum was too much to overcome. I felt a click and heard a whisper from off to my left:

"*Glah ham, shoceacan.*"

"Fuck!" I screamed as my front legs hit the watery floor. Fucking elf buttons. But who had said the activation words? It hadn't been me. It hadn't been Haagenti.

A net ensnared me, holding me tight to the floor and immobile in a ring of light. Now. Now the stupid sorcerers arrive. And who did they hold? Me. I rolled my eyes to see if any other demons had been subjected to this indignity. Nope. Just me. Fucking elves.

I saw a beautiful pair of brocade slippers pause before one of my heads. I was so pissed I would have bit them if I could.

"Is the other one dead?" a voice above the slippers asked. It didn't seem a particularly caring voice.

"No, my lord. Just unconscious," a voice off to my left replied.

"Interesting. Dump him over the border. He'll find his way home once he comes too. The others are free to leave. Usual procedure."

They'd be 'escorted', to be sure they crossed the border.

The slippers shifted, moving out of my range of vision, even with the benefit of three heads. "The Iblis appears to be fatigued from her journey, and the festivities. Ensure she is comfortable in her suite and has a restful night."

Fuck. A chanting began and I felt myself hover on the edge of sleep. Fucking elves.

~8~

I woke up in a soft bed. Yes, I was well rested. I was also pissed. And I was still in my first form. The back four feet of my body spilled over the end of the bed and onto the floor, my rear legs dangling off the edge. One of my heads rested upside down on the floor, with a beautiful view under the bed. It was dust free. With a 'pop' I converted my shape back to Samantha Martin. They could have at least let me change forms before knocking me out and dumping me in a too-small bed. But that was the least of my grievances. I was lured through the gates, under false pretenses, nearly walked into a trap, somehow managed to get the upper hand on Haagenti only to have him yanked out from under me. Literally. Then I suffered the indignity of being circled, dropped, and carted off like a dead deer. The first elf I saw was going to be a dead elf.

The fates were smiling on me because as I rolled over, one walked right through my door. I sprang at him with a speed and agility that the human Samantha Martin would never have had outside of Hel, and pinned him against the wall.

"I'm going to rip your tongue out first, you lying sack of shit. Make an example of you."

"No, no," he choked. "Remember me? I helped you last night. Made sure you looked human. It's not my fault you blew your cover."

He was right. Reluctantly I let him go and he clutched at his throat, looking at me with a wary gaze.

"His Lordship will see you now. I am to escort you to him."

I glared at him then dressed in my jeans and t-shirt, which had been laundered and neatly placed on a table. Such a courtesy wasn't enough to outweigh all the outrages I'd suffered in the last twelve hours.

"I'll bet he fucking wants to see me. No doubt to stick a bow on my head and hand me over to Haagenti. Well, I want to see him too. I want to feel his blood run down my chin, taste the pulse of his heart on my tongue, hear his last screams ring in my ears."

The guard shivered, his eyes wide. "Iblis, hear him out. He was sincere in his offer to you. He would never risk his reputation and his people's safety with such an act. You have common enemies."

Fine. I still muttered explicit threats under my breath the whole way down. The guard looked ready to vomit by the time he announced me. I strode across the opulent expanse, radiating anger. His lordship walked calmly toward me—weird comb-over and all—as if nothing had happened, as if he were greeting a long-lost friend. I wouldn't be pacified.

"Iblis, I am so pleased you made the time to see me. I am Taullian, High Lord of Cyelle." He paused and looked at me expectantly, as if I was supposed to know him. I'd never met this guy before and was far too angry to play these games. I stood silent, burning a furious gaze into his eyes.

Finally he sighed. "I sincerely apologize for last night. Please believe me when I say I had no idea one of the demons in attendance was the one who has a price on your head."

"Bullshit," I shouted. "You brought me here under false pretenses to turn me over to him, to gain substantial favors in return."

"No," he replied, his voice calm. "I would never sabotage my own festival, appear a fool in front of my guests, a paltry lord who cannot protect his own people or control a pack of unruly demons. Someone made sure Haagenti was on the guest-list, let him know you would be here. Someone wanted me to look weak at my own festival."

He waited a moment while I struggled to gain control. He was right. Elves watched carefully for weakness like this. He'd face internal and external pressure as a result.

"Why do you feel the need for that guy, then," I asked, gesturing toward the sorcerer trying to be unobtrusive in the corner.

He smiled. "From what I could see last night, you are a formidable foe. And I knew you'd be very angry with me."

"Fuck yeah," I glared. But it was a halfhearted glare.

He backed away a slight step. "When I find out who orchestrated last night's events, there will be repercussions."

I moved closer, leaning in to where his ear would be under that mountain of hair. He jerked back, a flash of terror on his face quickly hidden. "You might want to look inside your own house first. Someone triggered that portable gate Haagenti had hidden on his person. It wasn't me, and it wasn't him. Someone close by knew he had it on him, knew I had accidently hit the trigger, and spoke the activation words."

He looked at me thoughtfully. "Thank you. I am grateful for that information. I'm certain you will be able to help me with my current problem, and in return, I offer to relieve this Haagenti from the burden of his existence. I believe it's a good trade."

"Well I don't know. That depends on your problem."

He looked at the sorcerer in the corner. "Leave us."

The human didn't question. Rising, he crossed to the door, his robes flying behind in his rush to leave. His Lordship motioned me over to a series of couches and seats. He waited until I sat, joined me and poured us each a glass of red liquid from an etched decanter. Ugh. Wine. And before breakfast too.

I took the obligatory sip while the elf nodded approvingly.

"I need you to locate a baby living among the humans and bring it back to me," he said, sipping from his goblet.

Well, that was a new one. Usually it was runaway humans. Demons were very good at retrieval, especially when you didn't care if your property came back alive.

"You want me to do a changeling exchange? Isn't it cheaper to have a trusted human do it, like always?"

He shook his head. "We have had an unfortunate and embarrassing incident here in Cyelle. It seems there is some doubt as to whether a changeling elf baby was actually deceased when it was exchanged. I want to make sure we have not inadvertently left one of our offspring among the humans. If alive, please bring the baby back. If dead, please return the corpse so we may put these ugly rumors to rest."

I smelled a rat. Never had a live elf baby been exchanged. The babies were kept in stasis for months, sometimes years, until a suitable human changeling was identified. A live baby would never have survived the wait. And no elf mother would have let her baby go without every test to ensure it was truly deceased. She would have had to be absolutely positive the baby was dead before even considering the exchange.

"No problem. I'll speak to the mother of the baby first."

"She is under confinement pending the outcome of this issue," he replied quickly. "We suspect she may have been complicit in the crime. That she may have knowingly sent over a live child to exchange."

Yep: definitely a rat. "Right. So this horrible mother willingly sent a live baby to the humans? Never. What was wrong with this baby? Deformed? Really ugly? Did its head spin around as it shouted profanities?"

His eyes flashed at the last one. No fucking way. "The baby is alleged to be only half elf," he admitted with clenched teeth. "The mother claims she was seduced by an Incubus and deliberately impregnated."

Holy crap. We'd been trying to seduce elves since the beginning of time. It never worked. Never. Even the most skilled Succubi and Incubi had failed. Seducing an elf would be a huge boost in status. But what fool would impregnate one? Sheesh that was really going too far.

"I'd like you primarily to find and bring back the baby, dead or alive." Yes, he'd clearly want a hybrid dead, either by my hand or his own. "I'd also reward you handsomely for bringing me the Incubus responsible."

"Okay, let's start with some information here. Who is the alleged Incubus?"

"He primarily appears in female form. Goes by Leethu."

Well, shit. I should have seen that one coming. No wonder she was hiding out at my house. She probably had a price on her head as big as the one on mine.

"And I'm assuming you've questioned the human who did the changeling exchange? Do you have a human family name and address?" This should be easy. Go grab a baby, drop it off here, get Haagenti off my back for good. But what to do with Leethu? Something inside me clenched at the thought of handing her over to this elf, sending her to a certain death.

He shook his head. "The woman says she killed the human who did the exchange, as a precaution. I had my people check, people I trust, and there has been no sign of him since the exchange. There was no bill of sale or transfer either—either inside Cyelle or to another kingdom. "

Great. This was getting harder. "So question the woman. Find out who the exchange family was."

"She claims not to know. Says she was so mortified and humiliated she never inquired. She just wanted to put it all behind her."

Something bothered me. Why hadn't she aborted the baby? True, the elves valued pregnancy, so they would not readily have abortion techniques available, but she still should have tried. She should have been desperate enough to go to the dwarves, her own mages, or even paid a demon to expel the fetus.

I wanted to speak to this woman, but I also was curious about something else. "Who started this rumor? The whole plan sounds fairly airtight. The one person who knew all and could blackmail her is dead. Why has this leaked?"

"That's the part of the mystery I'm working on. It has to be someone who certified the baby dead, or someone in attendance at the birth. All those records have conveniently vanished."

"How are you going to find out without the records?"

"I'm tracing it backwards. Someone wants to discredit me, to weaken my throne. They have paid for the information to leak the rumors. I suspect Wythyn. We have a rather uneasy truce at the moment."

"Okay. I really need to talk to the woman though. When did this changeling exchange happen? You must have the human baby from the exchange. Are there records of the gate they went through? The baby's gender? That might narrow it down a bit." Wow, an elf/demon hybrid, lost in the world and probably unaware of his or her power and skills. A little baby, confused and … different.

"Nineteen? Twenty years? Not long ago."

The hybrid wouldn't be a baby then. Twenty would still be an infant for an elf, but nearly a quarter of the way through a human's lifespan. Even with the longevity of an elf and near immortality of a demon, the hybrid would have adapted to its human surroundings and aged itself accordingly. If still alive, it would appear to be a young adult human.

"It's female," Taullian continued. "They used a gate we had in existence back then in what the humans call Virginia.

The changeling family was probably within a hundred miles of Leesburg, Virginia. That's one of the reasons I thought you could be of help. You know the human world better than any other demon, and you have a residence close to that area."

Well, that should narrow it down to fifty thousand or so, if I assumed the baby was alive. Maybe I'd start with deaths. It would be a smaller number. I could have Wyatt get me a list, and perhaps he'd have some ideas on how to go about finding this needle in a haystack.

"So where is the human baby? Did she have anything distinctive, anything that might help me identify the changeling family?" If I saw her, I could at least narrow it down by race. I assumed anyway.

Taullian smiled. "We have the human female right here, along with her owner. You can see them now, and then I'll allow you to speak to the accused elf woman."

I conveniently left my wine on the table as we strolled from the room to another nearby. Inside was an elf relaxing on a comfortable seat, admiring a sculpture. A human female stood to his left, in a sort of military at-ease pose. The elf jumped to his feet as we entered and greeted Taullian with great deference.

"Iblis, this is Aelswith. He is the one who purchased the changeling rights on the human we've been discussing."

Aelswith nodded at me politely and I waited for him to introduce the human. An awkward silence stretched out, and the elf looked at his lord questioningly.

"So you received this human female approximately twenty years ago after purchasing the changeling rights from….I turned to Taullian. "What is her name?"

"Tlia-Myea."

Aelswith nodded. "Yes. When I received the human female, she was approximately seven days old."

I walked to the woman, looking her over. She was blond, fair skinned, thin, average height. Nothing that would make her stand out from thousands of other humans in the Virginia area. I had hoped she would have been an unusual minority, or perhaps had a defect that would have been noted at birth. Of course, she would never have been chosen as a changeling with a defect.

"What's your name?" I asked.

She shot a surprised look at me, her eyes a deep, vivid blue, then glanced questioningly at Aelswith.

"Nyalla," Aelswith pronounced.

"Can I touch you?" Again she looked at Aelswith, who nodded.

I did a quick scan, but there was no genetic disorder, no inheritable flaw that might have identified her parents. By this point I'd gotten the idea that Nyalla wasn't allowed to so much as blink without her master's permission. It irked me.

"She did come to me with an item," Aelswith commented. "Normally in the exchange, clothing and all personal items are left behind, but a demon brought her through the gate and he missed something."

A demon? Demons were an odd choice for a changeling exchange, especially when this Tlia-Myea woman had sent her human servant. I wondered if the human had been killed here, in Hel, or if he'd died before returning from the swap.

Aelswith handed me a small metal object, careful not to touch my hand. It was a ring. A tiny gold ring with an "A" inscribed on it. "A", possibly the baby's first or last name. It might help narrow things down a bit.

"I believe it is a piece of human jewelry," Aelswith said. "Very poor quality, with little aesthetic merit at all. Of course, the human is of very poor quality too. A terrible waste of money. She failed even the most basic of mage tests, has exhibited no magical ability whatsoever. She can't even manage to boil water without a fire. Even has to have someone else start the fire for her. Her artistic skills are nonexistent, and there is no poetry in her speech. She's an idiot. An imbecile."

Taullian made a sympathetic noise. "You can never really tell what you'll get with a changeling, but it seems you received an especially poor one."

"Worthless," Aelswith agreed. "I can't even sell her. I've tried."

I looked at Nyalla in surprise. My scan had not revealed any particular mental defects. At Aelswith's words, her face flashed with anger and hatred, before hardening into stubborn resignation.

"So what do you have her do?" I wondered.

Aelswith shrugged. "Clean. By hand, as she has no magical ability. She ensures the waste disposal system is in order and is sanitary and occasionally assists in laundry."

Ugh. Not exactly a dream job for a young woman. I shook my head, unable to think of anything else that might help me track down this hybrid. Taullian thanked Aelswith for his time, and Aelswith went into a boring, flowery speech about his loyalty to the kingdom. Nyalla's eyes strayed from their downward position and met mine. Her lips twitched into a quick grin, and she winked, immediately returning to her previous submissive posture. There was no way a baby could have fudged the extensive magic tests, but this woman was clearly resisting the will of her master the only way she could. I was filled with admiration for her passive-aggressive ways. Clever. Not at all an idiot.

We left and proceeded to walk through a series of doors and up a spiral staircase to another room. It didn't seem to be a jail cell. It was small but comfortable—the elf woman inside, Tlia-Myea, clean and composed. Her scant silk clothing was intricately embroidered with silver thread, and gold chains draped across her bare skin. Golden hair in a series of braids rose from her high forehead to fall behind her ears and down her back to her waist. Her flawless complexion was the color of cream, and her eyes as she turned to meet my gaze were the deepest indigo. She didn't look like a deprived, tortured prisoner. She looked like a privileged noble relaxing and enjoying the view from the tower's narrow windows.

His lordship ushered me in through an open doorway. "I'll leave you two alone. Just come down when you're through. And try not to injure or kill her."

I waited for his footsteps to fade. "Doesn't seem much like a cell," I mentioned, walking to a window and looking out. "You could just walk right out of here."

"And go where?" Her voice was tired, defeated. "Cyelle is my home."

She didn't appear to be the type who would be seduced by an Incubus, even one as tempting as Leethu. Of course, none of the elves did. They were elegant, friendly but remote. I couldn't see any of them overcome by passion.

"Did the Incubus appear to be an elf—one from another kingdom, foreign and mysterious? Or in the form of a friend of yours that you've secretly longed for?"

Tlia-Myea turned her face from me and I couldn't tell if it was from embarrassment or an attempt to hide her expression. "I didn't recognize him. I had suffered a disappointment, one of many, and he offered me much-needed compassion. By the time I discovered he wasn't an elf, it was too late."

"He raped you?" I asked, alarmed. Leethu was in enough shit without adding this to her rap sheet.

"No. I mean I had let my guard down, and we were in the act. I was stunned. Mortified. I just let it continue in the hopes I could cover it up afterwards. Pretend it never happened."

"But you were pregnant."

She nodded, her face still turned away. "I thought about bringing death to the baby, but I just couldn't do it. I had been intimate with elves too, and if I had killed an elf child…." she choked on the last words and covered her face.

Many elves miscarried or remained barren. I could understand her hesitation. It was better to be cautious, since this could be her only pregnancy.

"The baby was born live?"

She nodded, pulling her hands away from her face. "The midwife and I knew it was demon spawn and we killed it. She signed the changeling form and took the body for preparations. I arranged for my human to handle the exchange, instructing him that I wanted to know nothing about it, that he should tell no one."

Her voice shook, and she covered her face again. Possibly her only live birth, and it was demon spawn. I was surprised she hadn't killed herself from the shame and depression.

"Who was the midwife?"

She turned to look at me, her jaw firm. "I will not disclose that. I've destroyed that paperwork. I don't care if it means my death. She helped me, kept my secret all these years."

"But if she can confirm the child is dead, His Lordship will call off the hunt." Of course that would mean I wouldn't have a job to do in return for getting Haagenti off my tail forever.

"He wouldn't believe her. He is furious I kept it hidden for so long, convinced that I've lied and the abomination is still alive. Plus she will be punished, and I refuse to have such loyalty rewarded with death."

"Why aren't *you* dead?" I wondered out loud.

"In case I need to be interrogated for further information. I'll be killed once the baby's body is found."

"You could jump," I mentioned, looking out the window. Suicide might be preferable than giving these elves the satisfaction of an execution.

She shot me a startled glance. "Demons," she said in disgust.

"And the human who did the exchange is dead. Convenient."

She glared at me. "I would hardly keep him alive to blackmail me. I'm not stupid."

"Stupid enough to be seduced by an Incubus."

"We're not immune to your charms. We have moments of weakness; longings. Some of us more than others."

I wondered at that statement. The only weakness I'd ever seen elves show was over their children. I couldn't see them swayed by the promise of sexual delights, and as good as Leethu was, she was a bit of a one trick pony.

"Why did a demon accompany your human servant on the exchange? The elf who bought the changeling rights said a demon delivered his purchase."

A kind of wariness flitted across her face. She paused. "I had the demon kill my human on the other side of the gates once he'd exchanged the babies. It was the best way to ensure his silence. The demon brought back the human infant."

"Awesome. Who is the demon? He can collaborate your story."

Her jaw clenched, her eyes hardened. "I have no idea. You all look the same, and you constantly change shapes. Half of you share the same name. It was just a onetime deal with some random demon."

It was believable. A demon wouldn't have really cared about the details of the job, or Elven politics. He would have waited for the human servant to return with an infant, off the guy, and then bring the infant back where directed. Easy job, easy money—certainly not worth bothering about motives or the reasoning behind it.

"What was your human's name? If he was killed among the humans, I might be able to find his burial site."

She started in surprise, her eyes wide with a sudden flash of fear. "I ... I don't remember. It was a long time ago, and he *was* just a human."

I frowned. That was odd. She should have said 'Bob something' or 'we called him Sticky'. He had been her human. Instead she floundered and denied remembering it, dismissing him abruptly as 'just a human'. This one had been loyal, entrusted with her secret—a secret he supposedly died for. Why hadn't the fierce devotion that made her withhold the midwife's name been extended to the human? Yes, humans were of no more value than animals, but they were *expensive* animals. Their ownership conveyed status to the elves. Why hadn't she remembered his name?

"Thank you for your time," I told her, as I turned and strode out of the room. Her anxiety filled the space behind me.

His Lordship was downstairs. Waiting.

"What's the human's name? The one she says she killed."

He frowned. "I'll get it to you. Why? There wouldn't be any records on your side beyond his childhood ones."

"I'm curious. He was killed on the other side of the gates, so maybe he was buried near where the exchange was made." Hopefully he wasn't buried as a John Doe, although even that might be a place to start. There couldn't be that many John Does in the area I'd be searching.

He shrugged and led me down toward the courtyard, where Diablo awaited me. "I'll get you the name. We keep records of these things, so it should be readily available."

"How easy is it for a human to cross a gate?" I asked, curious. "I know they can't activate them. Are the gates guarded? Do the humans need written permission or are they entrusted with some kind of activation device?"

"Those with trusted humans can send them to and fro as they wish. They are given an activation key. They own their humans, so any misdeeds would reflect on the owner. It would be a terrible waste of resources to have a continuous guard on our gates. Instead, they have a triggering mechanism that alerts area scouts to come collect any visitors."

"Do those scouts keep records of who comes through the gates? New humans? Currently owned humans who are returning from an errand?"

"Yes."

"If you could also find out when this human of Tlia-Myea's went through the gate to do the changeling swap, that would narrow down my window of time considerably."

He nodded then stopped abruptly and handed me a small, round object. "I have a transport button for you. When you find the demon spawn, you can use it to return here."

I appreciated the gift. I could hardly keep trespassing on Wythyn land, and the other gates would be watched by demons who were just waiting to hand me over to Haagenti. Clearly Taullian knew this and wanted to ensure I wasn't waylaid while delivering on his request.

If Tlia-Myea was telling the truth and there was a dead hybrid baby, and if I could narrow down the window of time, and perhaps tighten the search radius to where the human was killed, success would be a possibility. I'd probably only have five or six graves to search. I could bang that out in a couple of evenings with Boomer's help.

But if Taullian's hunch was right and there was a live hybrid roaming among the humans, then a lot would hinge on whether the human servant was dead or not. Dead servant—I'd be in Haagenti's hands before I managed to sort through tens of thousands of young females. A live servant would be better. I needed to find the human, get him to give up the info on the hybrid and find the young woman and drag her back dead or alive to collect my reward.

I was really, really hoping it was the former. The idea of having to grab a hybrid that had grown up considering herself a human girl wasn't appealing.

"I can't believe an elf was actually seduced by a demon. Seems totally out of character for you guys," I commented casually.

His shoulders tightened. "We have moments of weakness," he said, echoing the woman in the tower.

"And to carry the baby to term, only to kill it?" I shook my head. "Also seems out of character. How could she bring herself to kill a baby after a long pregnancy and holding the infant in her arms? I know how crazy you guys are about babies of all kinds. You're all like a fucking Disney movie."

"It was demon spawn," he said, his voice a little too offhand. "Killing it wouldn't involve an ethical dilemma. No more so than killing a rat that was soiling your grain."

Diablo awaited me in the courtyard, casting longing glances back at the stable. He wouldn't be thrilled to be back in the company of Piper and Vegas after hanging with such exalted equines. A groom held him while I climbed into the saddle.

"I would avoid that narrow strip of demon land," the lord cautioned. "I've been told it is wall to wall with assassins after last night."

Great. I'd need to go around which would put me through a kingdom I didn't know and through Wythyn with the lord who kept losing his sorcerers. Luckily I was on good terms with him.

"What's the scoop on the kingdom adjacent to you?" I asked. I hoped they were friendly.

"Tonlielle. Lady Moria's kingdom. We'll escort you to the border and she should allow you passage. You'll be on your own after you leave our lands though. You'll need to go through a short stretch of her kingdom, and then a really long stretch of Wythyn to get to the gate where you came in. We're not on good terms right now with them, so you might get a rather rude reception."

"Where is your gate?" I asked hopefully.

"Argentina." Shit. That was just too damned far. "The Tonlielle gate is currently in Indonesia."

Fuck. Even further. I guess it was the Wythyn gate then. I wished for a moment I could just cut through demon lands and use the gate not far from here. So close, but there was no way I could hack my way through a forest of assassins to get there. I nodded to his lordship and set out with my band of escorts.

~9~

I could feel them behind me, all around me. In the trees, hidden by deadfall, blending into the foliage like only elves could. Diablo's ears swiveled, quickly shifting between nervous and excited. There had been a river to cross on the Tonlielle and Wythyn border that had required I journey north, even further out of my way. I had a huge section of Wythyn land to traverse before I reached the gate; and they were watching. I was a demon, a trespasser, and I wasn't sure my past relationship with their lord would keep them from trying to haul me in. They might not even recognize me.

I bided my time, poised for action. Diablo felt my tension, and his mood weighed heavier on the nervous side. I hoped they'd call out, confront me so I could beg passage. It would cost me a favor, but I'd grant it. Instead, the forest was silent, the air still. Maybe they just intended to follow me, to make sure I didn't cause any problem and left their kingdom peacefully. I tried to look harmless. It wasn't easy for a demon.

I heard a faint sound, like a note on a guitar, and managed to duck as an arrow whispered by my head to thunk into a tree trunk. My heart raced at the near miss, and I dropped low over the horse's neck to try and present a smaller target. Diablo took off like a shot. I didn't discourage him. In fact, I dug my heels high into his flanks to drive him forward and held on tight.

With no more need for stealth, the woods erupted around me, elves materializing from everywhere. The elves on foot shot arrow after arrow. The air was thick with lethal barbs and I hugged close to Diablo's neck, no fucking idea where he was running. One arrow tore a groove on the edge of my shoulder, and another grazed my leg. My eyes blurred with pain, my shoulder burning and dripping blood down my arm, my leg feeling strangely numb. They were shooting enhanced arrows. A few more and I'd fall right off the horse. I held on as best I could with the numbness spreading up my leg and urged Diablo onward.

Elves are fast, but Diablo was faster. We outpaced the ones on foot and I glanced behind to see what I was up against. I counted seven, moving at speed on their finest horses. The few with bows were able to use them while tearing full-tilt through the forest on a horse. I was barely able to hold on at this point, my leg useless and my shoulder screaming in pain. I turned to face forward, hoping to guide Diablo back onto a path toward the gate. It was gamble, but as a demon hybrid, he had stamina and there was a chance he could outlast them: unless they continued to shoot me. A solid shot with those enhanced arrows would more than knock me off my horse. It would drop me into unconsciousness for a few seconds, which would be long enough for one of them to put a more substantial restraint on me.

Branches raked at my skin as Diablo went off the trail and plowed through thick brush and clusters of trees. I smacked my numb knee on a sapling and heard an unpleasant crack. Good thing I was a demon and could fix it on the fly.

"Hit the horse," I heard one shout.

"No! Spare the horse. He's demon spawn," another shouted back.

Another arrow seared my shoulder and I slumped, numb, over Diablo's neck. Somehow I managed to stay on and shake off the effects. Another arrow whizzed past my ear. Even with Diablo's speed, they were closing in. Their knowledge of the forest allowed them to accelerate where Diablo needed to look ahead and plan his path. Another arrow shot by. I wasn't going to make it. I could easily take them out with a burst of energy, but then it would be war. Even though they were shooting at me, I was a trespasser on their land and their attack was far from lethal. They were clearly trying to capture me without harm, and without harm to Diablo.

I glanced up and saw the tree trunk right before my face hit. Everything went black for a second. It was long enough. Flying off the back of Diablo, I slid along the rocks and branches, hooves dangerously close to my face. The elves couldn't slow in time. They yelled as they tried to weave their horses around my tumbling form. I managed to not get kicked, but hitting a tree at top speed had done plenty of damage. Two arrows thudded into my leg, and then I felt a net holding me immobile as the elves in the lead turned their horses back and dismounted.

"Grab her horse," one said.

"He's gone. By the Lady above, I've never seen an animal move that fast. He vanished right before my eyes."

"He teleports!" another elf said, in admiration.

"We'll get him later, once he calms down. We'll bring out a couple of mares to help bring him in."

I felt myself dragged along the forest floor, like a deer carcass, and through a gate to a cool marble floor. Restrained and blind, I was unable to use my stored energy. I knew from experience that anything I tried to shoot would just bounce off the net and back to me or dissipate.

"You could have let her fix herself first," a voice complained.

The elves released me from their net, and I stood. I was seriously fucked up. I'd fixed the knee earlier, only to have it smashed again from my tree impact. That wasn't all. Dislocated shoulder, abrasions on my chest and arm, and bruises forming all down my leg combined with the arrow wounds. The whole left side of my body was battered. My face was worse—having taken the primary impact, and my nose and cheekbone were full of jagged bits of bone. My forehead throbbed with what I'm sure was a hideous purple lump and concussion. I wondered how bad the tree looked.

"I'm sorry, Lord Feille. We didn't want to risk allowing her to use her magic. She can fix herself now," one of the scouts said.

Instead I spat a mouthful of blood and teeth onto the floor. "I'm sorry for the trespass, your lordship. I was trying to get to your gate and was in a bit of a hurry."

He nodded, looking completely uninterested in my apology or my excuse. "You planned to use our gate twice, ride two times through our kingdom without even a by-your-leave? That's beyond trespass, that's rudeness."

"As I said, I'm in a hurry. I'm not able go through our lands right at the moment, and your gate is the closest to my earth home. I didn't intend to be rude. Is there something I can do to make up for my lack of manners?"

Because it all boiled down to favors. I'd owe him one, and he'd let me go. That's the way it worked. That's the way it had always worked.

He smiled. "Actually, there is a small service you could perform for me."

I waited patiently, my shoulder screaming, and the lump on my head beginning to take on a life of its own. I truly expected my skull to erupt at any moment and another being to spring forth—kind of like Athena. My mind wandered for a while, envisioning a Xena-looking warrior woman popping out of my head, scantily clad in leather armor and grasping a sword. I was startled from my daydreams of a choreographed fight scene by the high lord's voice.

"A sorcerer, one we call Gareth, has left without permission, taking valuable texts and objects with him. His apprentice has been foolish enough to accompany him. I would be very grateful if you retrieved them for me."

I could have guessed that one. "It seems an awful high value you place on two uses of your gate and passage through your lands. And capturing a sorcerer, especially one that is not alone, is a very difficult task."

I hoped he hadn't recognized me. Maybe he and the other elves thought I was just some random demon they could press into service. We changed forms constantly, and it was very difficult to identify us. Without a way to read our energy we kind of all looked the same. Of course, the elves had special skills.

Feille smiled. "You have proven yourself capable in the past, Az. I am sure this sorcerer will not be beyond your abilities. I'm prepared to offer you permission to use our gate to travel through our lands for an extended period of time. Given the bounty on your head, that should be of great value to you."

It was of great value to me. Normally I'd jump at it, especially since I didn't know how long it would take to find this darned baby, but my schedule was getting full. I still wanted to hear the details though, just in case this was a better offer.

"So where do you think this sorcerer is?"

"We have been told he is in Eresh."

Crap, that was way north of the elf lands, beyond the mountains. This wasn't a quick job.

"His human apprentice met with demons in Dis and is alleged to have paid one for gate passage. We suspect he has left and is gathering information and supplies for his master. It would be a perfect time to capture Gareth while he waits in Eresh for his apprentice's return."

Why the heck were they so far apart? Eresh was north, in between two mountain ranges. Dis was due south. They were separated by several Elven kingdoms and tough terrain.

They could have been at opposite ends of the world and they wouldn't have been farther apart. Why? It would be an easier job with them both in one place. Time and distance weren't the only issues though. Eresh was demon land and Dis was Haagenti's homeland. I wasn't about to stroll around in demon territory given my current circumstances, even if I did have time for it.

"Very tempting offer. I've got quite a lot on my plate right now, so let me put you on the list and I'll get back to you when I have a better idea of when I can work on this project."

"No. I need your services now. These other things will need to wait."

"They can't wait. And I'm not strolling around Eresh with a price on my head looking for your runaway. I need to take care of a few things, and then I'll go find this guy for you."

"You will go now."

"Yeah, I'm going *home* now. I'll go to Eresh sometime in the future, but not now."

"The price on your head is very high, Az. Very tempting. Tempting enough that I could pay another demon to find my runaway *and* purchase a replacement sorcerer from another kingdom. You and I communicate well, so I would like to work with you on this, but if you refuse, I'll turn you over and collect the bounty."

"Okay, I'll move a few things around on my schedule and make some time next month or so. But I cannot do it now."

"Now," he thundered, and I felt the net hover over me again.

"Fuck you," I told him and pulled on the red purple deep within, summoning Gregory to me. Let's see how much of a prick this elf was with an angel standing in front of him.

Nothing happened. Well, nothing besides the net closing around me and two guards grabbing my arms to drag me off.

Again I pulled desperately at the network branching throughout me. *I need you right now, asshole.*

There was a disorienting flash, and I was standing with my nose buried in the cotton of a polo shirt—strong arms wrapped around me. I looked up at Gregory, astonished, then peeked around him to see busy shoppers outside a Yankee Candle store.

I gaped at the angel.

"Well, here I am. As you commanded." He sounded amused.

"No, this is not as I commanded." I tried to pull away, but he held me tight. "I commanded you to come to me."

He laughed. "I'm *not* going to Hel. This seemed like an acceptable alternative."

"It's not acceptable," I insisted. "I summoned you. You are supposed to come to me."

"You're not strong enough to make me go somewhere against my will, little cockroach," he said, amusement still in his voice.

Against his will? So what good was this two way binding if I wasn't strong enough to even use it to my advantage?

"Fine. Send me back then."

"No, that would involve my going with you, and as I said before, I'm not going to Hel."

"But I left my horse there," I shouted at him. Shoppers glanced at us in mild curiosity. "You were supposed to come to me, and threaten an elf so he'd let me go. Then I could find my horse and come back the way I went in."

"Well, I'm glad I didn't come to you. This is a much better plan all around."

"Except that I left my horse there, at the mercy of those shithead elves."

"They'll treat him well. Elves cherish horses."

"That's not the point. He's my horse, and I want him back." I suddenly had an idea. "Wait. Can you gate the horse here? Bring him to me?"

He sighed. "No, the horse is not bound to me. I have no way of knowing its whereabouts. And even if I did, I wouldn't gate a horse into the middle of a shopping mall. That's far too impish an action for me to even contemplate."

"But I've marked the horse, and I'm bound to you, so can't you just follow the trail to him and bring him back?"

He was amused again. "It doesn't work like that little cockroach. I thought you were on good terms with the elves. Just go through the gate here, stroll right on in and ask for your horse back."

"Elves don't take 'no' for an answer. Evidently they don't take 'later' for an answer either. And I can't go through this gate. It puts me in demon lands. Haagenti will grab me the moment I step through."

"It's past time for you to deal with this problem. Do it now." There was an edge of command in his voice.

"I'm trying to deal with it in a way that doesn't involve me dead or tortured for centuries. I've got some plans in the works that are better than strolling through a gate and trying to chop my way through a few hundred demons."

He released me and raised his hands in exasperation. "You don't need to kill them all. Just go in with a mighty show of power. They will all switch sides in an instant. Demons have no loyalty. Be the Iblis and they'll drop this other guy and rush to your side."

What did he mean? Demons had plenty of loyalty.

I needed to figure out some other way to get Diablo back. I'm sure he headed toward the elf gate, but they'd be watching that like hawks now. It was only a matter of time before they caught him. If I didn't get him back within a day or so, I'd need to plan on retrieving him directly from Feille. And I wasn't sure how well that would go over after I cursed at him and vanished before his eyes. Even if I did retrieve his sorcerer, he probably wouldn't be willing to return Diablo. Anger burned inside me at the thought of losing my horse, and as cushy as Diablo probably would find the elf world, he'd become bored with their restrictions. Elves weren't appropriate owners for a demon hybrid. Clearly they weren't appropriate mothers for demon hybrids, either.

"Fine. Can you gate me back to my house? I have a project I'm working on that's kind of time sensitive." I also needed to have word with Leethu and see what Dar managed to find out for me. And see if Wyatt would help me with yet another project. Wyatt. I'd been gone only a day and I missed him terribly.

The angel looked as though he was about to say 'no', then paused. "Okay, but you will owe me a favor."

I was astonished. That's the sort of thing a demon would ask for, not an angel.

"Done. As long as the favor does not contradict any vow I've made." Standard language, just to clarify the terms.

He smiled down at me. It was a very naughty smile for an angel, and I began to wonder what exactly this favor would entail. His arms went around me, crushing the breath out of my lungs with an unnecessary firmness, and in an instant we were in my living room.

"And now you owe me a favor," he murmured against my ear. His voice had that dangerous tone to it and I imagined all the favors I really wanted him to request of me. But I had a lot to do and no time right now to play hide the sausage, or the angel equivalent.

"And the favor is that I stand here and let you pulverize my ribs?" I asked.

"No." He released me and stepped away. "See you in two days, little cockroach."

Shit. The council meeting. And I had so much to do.

~10~

"Leethu," I shouted the moment Gregory was gone. I knew she was here. She wouldn't risk being nabbed by an angel, and she could hardly go home with an elf lord waiting to end her life.

A face peeked down from the stairwell. A beautiful Thai face with a waterfall of dark hair.

"Ni-ni, I'm so glad you're home. I've been bored."

Uh oh. That didn't sound good. She crept down the stairs.

"Is that angel gone? I don't like him. He wants to kill me."

"Of course he does, Leethu. You're a demon."

"He doesn't want to kill you." She looked slyly at me as she crossed the room. "He wants to do other things to you."

"Yes, I'm pretty sure he does. But he probably wants to kill me too."

The pheromones were flying. Leethu had been bored, and her seductive self was very tempting. She reached up and ran fingers through my hair.

"You are covered in blood, Ni-ni. And many of your teeth are missing."

Crap, I'd forgotten. I wondered for a moment why all the shoppers at the mall hadn't been aghast at my battered appearance. It must have been Gregory's influence. Humans were blind to a lot of things around an angel.

Leethu trailed a finger across my jaw and down my neck. "I'm so lonely, Ni-ni. Trapped in this house for days with only the Internet and your toys. Can you be with me?"

I was so hot for her I was ready to throw her on the couch and go for it, but I had a lot to do before that stupid council meeting, and once sucked into Leethu's embrace, it would take far more willpower than I possessed to break free.

"You fucked an elf, Leethu."

It was better than a bucket of ice water. She yanked her hand from my neck with a gasp. "Oh no, Ni-ni; not at all. The elves, they don't find their pleasure with demons. I've tried, but they always refuse me." She said the last with a little pout, but I wasn't fooled.

"Cyelle, about nineteen or twenty years ago. You seduced her. She didn't even know you were a demon. And then you had the stupidity to impregnate her. What the fuck were you thinking?"

Leethu made a gurgling noise.

"She carried the baby to term, in case it was an elf, but when a hybrid was born, she killed it and sent it over as a changeling. Now some rumor has gotten out and the elf lord, Taullian, wants your head on a platter and the baby's body as proof. But you already know that, don't you? That's why you're hiding out here, at my place."

"That fucking elf," Leethu gasped. "The bitch set me up."

"Well, what do you expect? You're lucky she didn't accuse you of rape. It's borderline. And impregnation? What the fuck, Leethu?"

"It was a deal, a contract," Leethu said, her voice quivering with rage. "I assumed a form she would find pleasing and gave her the child she so badly wanted. In return, I got to fuck an elf."

Now it was my turn to make that gurgling noise.

"She approached me. At one of their parties. It was her idea."

Demons lie. But something about Leethu's story rang true.

"She didn't totally blame you, Leethu. She said she thought you were an elf from another kingdom, that she was distraught from some event and sought solace. She didn't know you were a demon until you were actually doing the deed, and she was too ashamed of her foolishness to stop you. She hoped to deny everything and just pretend it didn't happen."

"Ni-ni, I vow on every soul I Own that she lies. She knew the whole time. She let me fuck her in return for a child."

I snorted. "Oh right, because every elf wants a demon hybrid in their womb. Yes, they all desperately want a child, but an *elf* child, not a despised demon spawn."

"She had lost two babies early in pregnancy. She'd discovered there was no hope of her ever having an elf child. Only a demon could give her a child. She could have aborted, but she carried to full term, knowing that she carried a demon hybrid."

"She had the faint hope that it was an elf child. Leethu, she couldn't have possibly thought she could carry off bearing a hybrid child and raising it as an elf."

"I was careful," Leethu insisted. "I formed the child so that it would appear to be an elf. It was one of my best works. Only a very subtle part was demon, a hidden part. I'm positive the baby could pass."

No one was that good. Yes, humans are fooled all the time, but no one else. We can all sense even the faintest hint of demon in a being. Even as good as I was at keeping my energy deep inside, I couldn't pull it off with regular, repeated contact. Eventually something would show. A baby would have no control. Her demon self would have peeked out constantly, no matter how carefully she was formed or how much of an elf she looked like on the outside.

"She was desperate, Ni-ni. I swear to you. She wanted this baby, didn't care that it was half demon. She'd thought this out carefully, had made provisions to ensure the baby wouldn't be exposed as a hybrid. She would foster it somewhere until it reached an age where it could control and hide the demon half, then she'd bring her child back to her."

If Leethu was telling the truth, then the baby most definitely was alive. Loved, protected in a foster home. The human might be alive too. Plus, there would be more reason to hide the identity of the midwife, who under torture could reveal the fact that a live hybrid baby had been hidden away. I knew human mothers would readily die to protect their children; perhaps elf mothers were no different.

"Did she say anything about where she planned to foster the baby? Any clue about where the baby might be?" It was a long shot.

Leethu shook her head. "She had every intention of keeping it when we made our deal. I'm assuming she'd made arrangements with a dwarven foster home. They normally don't care for hybrids, but I'm sure if the price was right, one would consent and agree to keep their mouths shut. I never heard from her after we fucked. It's not like I cared what she did with it."

Dwarves, or a human foster home? I'd met the human changeling: Nyalla. All her paperwork had been in order. A human and a demon had gone through a gate, made an exchange and returned with a human baby. So either the hybrid was alive in a human foster home, or she was dead at the time of the exchange.

"Leethu, you are so fucked," I told her.

Suddenly that shrewd look was back in Leethu's eyes. "You are my Iblis. I request sanctuary. I request that you negotiate with the elves on my behalf as a matter of diplomacy."

What the heck? I was the Department of State now? Should I send out regular alerts? The Iblis advises all demons not to fuck any elves. The Iblis advises all demons that the elf lord in Wythyn is a total asshole.

"Leethu, I'm an imp, I don't negotiate. And I definitely don't negotiate on someone else's behalf. You've got to deal with this issue. Do you plan on hiding out here in my house for the next ten thousand years or so? Can't go out, angels will get you. Can't go home, elves will get you." *Can't sleep, clowns will eat you,* I thought randomly. "You'll go insane within the next few days. You're already going nuts."

"They'll kill me, Ni-ni. If you can't work out some terms of immunity, they'll kill me."

"It's a good possibility, but that was the risk you accepted when you *fucked an elf,* when you *impregnated* an elf. Even a willing one. That was our first lesson in school; remember? Evaluate risks, weigh the benefits, be willing to accept consequences." I assumed she learned that too. Succubi and Incubi went to different schools than the other demons. It was good to keep them away from us at that young age so we didn't kill them in our enthusiasm.

"Please, Ni-ni, as my sister, as my Iblis, I ask this of you. I will owe you many favors—put myself and my household under yours—anything."

I sighed. This was getting to be a regular thing with me. "You are now part of my household, you and all your associates, possessions, and assets. In return, I will protect you from both the elves and angels and negotiate with the elves on your behalf."

She launched herself at me, rubbing her glorious silky skin against mine as her mouth trailed down my neck. Mmmm, little bites, a pinch of nails on the inside of my thighs. Mmmm, I was soooo tempted.

I grabbed her hair and pulled her up for a kiss, tasting the copper of her blood as her tongue tore on my broken teeth. Reluctantly, I held her away.

"I've got to go see Wyatt." Was that my voice, all husky and choked?

"Bring him back, Ni-ni," she said, pushing herself into my arms and nuzzling my neck again. "I'll express my gratitude."

The short walk over to Wyatt's house did nothing to cool my raging libido. I needed to resolve this fast and get Leethu back home or all I'd be doing was fucking all the time. Which would not be very productive.

Wyatt's house always looked the same. An ancient Cape Cod style that he'd done nothing to fix up since he'd bought it almost three years ago. The elderly couple that owned it before him hadn't been able to keep up with even basic maintenance, and Wyatt was continuing their tradition. I went to walk up to the front door and hit an invisible wall. Michelle was right; this really *was* going to suck.

"Wyatt!" I shouted. My cell phone was still in the house and I was reluctant to go back, especially with Leethu waiting, full of bored frustration. "Wyatt!"

I picked up some rocks and began throwing them at his door, careful to avoid the windows. Wyatt wouldn't bother to get them fixed and there were enough bits of plywood nailed over openings. One more and the county would probably condemn the place. I threw some bigger rocks. I really needed to talk to Michelle about this loophole. Even if demons couldn't get in, they clearly could pitch physical objects at the house. Wyatt wouldn't be very safe if demons demolished his house by lobbing construction equipment at it.

Finally he answered the door. "Sam, why are you out there? Just come on in. Oh, yeah."

He padded out on the cold walkway with bare feet to meet me, halting ten feet away and staring at me in shock.

"You've got to come out further," I told him. "The wall is right here." I really wanted to feel his arms around me. And more, since Leethu had stirred up a whole lot of lust.

"Sam, what happened to you?" He came all the way to me, his eyes getting big. "You're covered in blood, and your forehead looks like someone surgically implanted a grapefruit in it."

Oh crap. "I got knocked off Diablo coming back and forgot to fix myself."

I quickly fixed everything, although my shirt and jeans were still torn and bloody. Then I grabbed Wyatt tight, burying my face in his chest and telling him all about elf high lords, my narrow escape, and Diablo's plight. Everything felt right in Wyatt's arms. His shirt rubbed against my cheek, and I breathed him in, relishing the feel of his hands stroking my back. Suddenly my situation didn't seem so hopeless, or insurmountable. We were partners in crime; together we could accomplish anything. We'd find this demon hybrid, whether it was dead or alive, and get Haagenti off of our backs for good.

"I was worried about you, Sam," he said, rubbing his face in my hair. "I actually went into your house to try and get your mirror when you didn't come back last night. Leethu was on me like a shot. I barely made it out the door with my virtue intact."

"Have you had any more run-ins with demons?" I asked, looking him over carefully for any damage.

"I hit one with my truck last night coming home from The Eastside Tavern. I think there are still bits of him inside my wheel well. I put the body in a bag and stuck it behind my shed, but it was gone this morning."

Boomer.

"I may have a way to get us out of this mess," I told him. "This elf lord, Taullian, wants me to find a hybrid for him, and in return he'll kill Haagenti."

"Sam, that's great. What kind of hybrid does he want? Horse? Dog? Or is he more of a cat person?"

Wyatt thought Taullian was pet shopping. How funny.

"Uh, no. Seems Leethu knocked up an elf woman and he wants me to retrieve the offspring."

Wyatt looked confused. "I didn't think elves did that sort of thing. Nice that he wants to bring the child back into the fold though."

"Uh, no. He wants it dead."

I felt Wyatt tense against me. He adored Boomer, and although he wasn't particularly fond of Diablo, he wouldn't want to see him killed.

"I spoke to the mother, and she assured me that when she realized the baby was a hybrid, she killed it and sent the body over as a changeling. So I'm probably looking to dig up a corpse and return it for proof."

The likelihood that the offspring was alive had increased in probability after my discussion with Leethu, but I figured Wyatt would be more accepting of corpse retrieval than finding and killing a hybrid.

"She *killed* it?" Wyatt was outraged. "She killed her own child? Because it was different? It wasn't elven enough? What kind of sick person does that?"

Wyatt let go of me and began to pace, his anger building. I wasn't sure where all this was coming from, why he was suddenly so upset. What was the big deal?

"I hate these elves. Setting traps for humans to fall through, and then making them slaves. Stealing human babies. I know they're treated reasonably well, that they don't lack for basic needs and are educated. I know that human children and adults here are often worse off, but it's still *wrong*! And now this? A mother casually ends her child's life, just because it's a hybrid? That's not the child's fault."

"I have my doubts that she actually killed the baby," I told him, uncertain he'd find this alternative any more palatable. "Leethu seems to think she had every intention of fostering the child out. So she may have hid the hybrid over here, intending to keep it safe until it had enough control to pass as a full elf."

"So are you looking for a corpse, or a live baby?" Wyatt frowned, and I suddenly felt backed into a very uncomfortable corner.

"I'm not sure. She may have panicked once the baby was born and killed it, regardless of her original intentions. Or it could be here, being raised among humans."

Wyatt's eyes bore into mine. "But the mother isn't paying you to bring the baby back to her loving arms, some Lord is, and he wants it dead. So you're going to snatch a poor, innocent baby away from unsuspecting parents, kill it, and then hand it over to the this monster of an elf?"

It didn't sound very good when Wyatt said it. "The hybrid isn't really a baby," I protested. "She's around nineteen or twenty years old."

"You're going to murder a young woman then. She's walking around, has no idea who she is. She thinks she's a human, and you're going to just walk up and kill her?"

"Wyatt, she's a hybrid. She's not human. You don't have any problem killing demons. Why is this bothering you? It's the same thing."

"No, it's not," he insisted. "Those demons are attacking me; it's self-defense. What you're proposing is murder."

"She's not human!" I was feeling really frustrated with him. "You kill innocent groundhogs. I've seen you kill deer. They're not attacking you. She's a hybrid. It's no different than shooting a raccoon."

Wyatt looked very uncomfortable with my comparison. "But she looks like a human, doesn't she? And she probably thinks she's a human. I can't condone this, Sam."

"But I need your help! How am I going to find the hybrid without your help? There were probably tens of thousands of live female births in the window of time and area I'm checking. If I do it myself, it will take me forever."

Wyatt ran a hand through his blond hair, clearly conflicted. "I'll help you with corpses. But I'm not helping with any live beings. I just can't do that, Sam."

I wasn't happy. I understood. After all, Wyatt was a human and they had strange, complicated notions of acceptable behavior. But I still wasn't happy.

"Okay. I have no idea if I'm looking for a live baby, a dead baby, a human servant here in hiding, or what, so I might as well assume the hybrid is dead."

"No killing," Wyatt insisted. "If the baby is already dead, then fine, but if we discover the baby is still alive, I don't want you to kill it."

Great. That meant I'd have to catch a live young woman and turn her over to the elves. It would be easier to kill her; and kinder too. I was just going to have to lie. And somehow keep it all from Wyatt.

"We'll only look for corpses," I promised. We. I'd look for a live one on my own. "And what the fuck am I going to do about Diablo? The elves will have him soon. How am I going to get him back?"

He gathered me close and I felt him smile in my hair—he thought I was consenting to his wishes. "I guess you'll have to catch a runaway sorcerer and trade him for your horse."

"When?" I snapped. "I need to fend off the never-ending stream of deadbeat demons sent to kill me, find this needle-in-a-haystack hybrid corpse so I can hopefully get Haagenti off my back permanently, all while doing bullshit Iblis duties that asshole angel thinks up for me. I have no time for my human business, no time for you, no time to do the things I love."

Wyatt made soothing noises against my hair and rubbed a hand down my back. "What can I do to help? Let me take something off your plate so you have more time."

I pulled back and looked at him. "You're already helping me with angel research. And now I've asked you to research infant deaths. Anything else and you won't have any time left for your own stuff. No zombies, no hacker work."

"No hot wings, no snowboarding with my psychotic girlfriend." He was smiling. "Sam, anything I can do to help get this Haagenti guy off our backs so we can hopefully return to a reasonably normal life is good for me. You need some time freed up to do the things only you can do; that way I can get back to my zombies and having fun with my demon lover."

I hugged him tight. "How do you feel about sleeping in my barn with me tonight?"

"Let me get some shoes and blankets, and I'll meet you there."

~11~

I got up early, untangled myself from Wyatt's bondage embrace and ran out for coffee and donuts. It was cold in the barn when I returned, in spite of the little heater I'd brought, so we snuggled under blankets as we sat propped against the wall of one of the stalls, enjoying our breakfast.

"Think you can withstand Leethu for a few moments? I need to call Dar, and I'd really like you to hear anything he's found out about the Ruling Council."

"As long as we can have hot, monkey sex right after; I think I can keep her at arm's length."

"We've had a lot of hot, monkey sex last night and this morning. Not that I'm complaining," I added. "I'm just thinking you might be more resistant than usual."

He laughed and pulled me onto his lap, sloshing my coffee over the lip of the cup and onto my hand. "Are you doubting my prowess? My stamina? My amazingly short recovery time."

"Not at all, you stud, you. Let's go inside and see if you can restrain yourself long enough for me to call Dar."

No sooner were we in the door, than Leethu was down the stairs looking at Wyatt with an expression resembling the way Boomer had looked at the decapitated head. Pheromones were thick, and Wyatt's breathing was ragged. Fuck, my breathing was ragged.

"Leethu, we've got some business stuff we need to do. Can you possibly go upstairs for a bit and tone it down. I really don't have time for an orgy right now."

"Later?" she asked. "I'm so lonely. I am always gentle with humans, Ni-ni. Not like the other demons at all. You can supervise and direct me. I'll obey, as a member of your household should."

Oh wow, that was so tempting. Images flashed through my mind of watching Leethu and Wyatt, telling her what to do. I know the same kinds of images were going through Wyatt's mind too. I knew where all his favorite spots were, his most sensitive areas, what really drove him over the edge. Part of me wanted to keep that experience just between Wyatt and me, but demon habits die hard, and Leethu's pheromones were very convincing. I struggled to keep control.

"Obey by turning it down right now," I said with a voice more stern than I thought possible given the circumstances. The level immediately dropped to zero. Leethu was proving to be very compliant. "I'll discuss your offer with Wyatt later, when he's not so addled."

She smiled and skipped up the stairs. "You okay?" I asked Wyatt.

"Ummm," he replied. "Dead puppies, dead puppies, dead puppies."

What? That might be something a demon would think about when turned on, but I hadn't realized corpses of young canines had any attraction for humans.

"Should I slap you?" I offered. Sometimes that helped. Sometimes it just made it worse.

"No." He shook his head. "Guys get woodies at really inopportune moments, so we think about non-sexy things to make everything behave. Usually it's stuff like Uncle Phil in a Speedo, the woman down the street with really bad breath, or that nun from third grade."

Confident that Wyatt's mantra would help him resist Leethu's seductive overtures; I walked over to my mirror and touched the button to call Dar. He picked up straight away, as I thought he would. Dar had a small mirror he carried around with him so he never missed a call.

"Did you find anything out?" I asked.

Dar gave a bark of laughter. "Mal, a room full of angels is the least of your worries right now. What the fuck went down between you and Haagenti?"

Oh yeah. A bunch of elves, humans and four demons were witnesses to our fight. I'll bet that was all over Hel within seconds.

"I ran into him at one of those elf festivals, and we kind of got into it. I fucking kicked his ass, Dar. You should have been there!"

"That's not what he's saying," Dar warned. "Although Zalanes has a very amusing tale about you *biting* his ass. Either way, Haagenti is furious and humiliated. He now wants you dead. Dead, Mal. And his bounty on you has doubled. No more 'torture for centuries' stuff; he won't rest until you're a pile of gore on the ground."

Crap. That really upped the stakes. Between the huge reward and the ability to use any force, more than Low would be after me now. I really needed to find this hybrid for the elves. Now. I glanced over at Wyatt, who stood listening. He looked worried. He should be. If Haagenti wanted me dead, he would probably extend that edict to every one of my household, earthly or otherwise.

"So I'm assuming Ahriman is no longer behind this. It wouldn't do his breeding petition any good to have me dead."

"Who knows?" Dar said. "Maybe he's tired of waiting for you, or angry that you're not jumping to accept?"

The whole thing was depressing. I wanted to crawl back under a rock and hide, just Wyatt and I. But I was the Iblis.

And that thought reminded me of the original reason for my call.

"So what did you find out about the angels?" Time to shake off this feeling of defeat and get on with it. Haagenti wasn't going to go away, and there were no more rocks to hide under, at least according to Gregory.

"Seven angels were part of the Ruling Council back when we were in Aaru," he said triumphantly.

"Six," I corrected. "I make seven."

"Seven," he insisted. "There might be six now, but there were seven back then. Maybe one of them got fired and you got their job?"

Hmmm. Could be. "Do you know their names?" A few leapt to mind, but I doubted the Ruling Council was made up of Dopey, Sneezy, Sleepy, Bashful, Doc, Grumpy, and Happy.

"There's a lot of overlap here," he warned. "It's a wonder any of them knows who's in charge of what, honestly. One is Truth, sometimes called Justice."

Ah. No names then, but more like job titles. No doubt this would be very convoluted and confusing.

"Another is Balance, or Right Order."

Yep, that sounded like the angels I'd met to date.

"Obedience."

"I certainly hope that's not the position they expect me to take." Those angels would be in for a rude surprise. Of course, I'm sure Gregory had already told them I was a lost cause when it came to obedience.

"Prosperity."

Oh, I totally wanted that one! Maybe I could put a bounty on Haagenti's head for a change.

"Wisdom."

Now that would be funny.

"Immortality."

"That's six. What's the seventh?" I asked.

"I don't have any information on the seventh. Everyone agrees that there were seven, but no one seems to remember the other one."

"Any more detail?" This would help, even without the info on that last angel. I could glean some personality traits from the titles, but more would be better. After all, an angel's idea of wisdom was probably very different from mine.

"The Immortality one is also said to be the one who weighs souls. He is the beginning and the end—the first one born, and the last to die. Kind of like the guy who cleans up after the party, from what I gather."

Could be Gregory. He was old as dirt. Older. I could see him ushering everyone out the door after last call.

"The Wisdom one also sings."

I chuckled at that. I knew angels sang, that they loved music, but I just couldn't see any I'd met belting out a Carpenters' tune in the shower.

"The Truth one kind of walks a fine line between mercy and vengeance. I guess that's the whole Justice angle. I just don't get that one at all. I think the Obedience one is his buddy or something."

I laughed, my mood lightening. Angel BFFs, walking hand in hand, texting each other late at night.

"Nothing on the others, or on the mysterious seventh one. Oh, except the Balance one has something to do with duality. I don't know what the fuck that means either."

Yeah, well he wouldn't be any more enlightened after hearing Gregory go on about it for hours either. Right order. Angels got all wet just thinking about it, but I could never figure out what the fuck it meant.

"Let me know if you find out anything else." Dar was thorough. I doubted he'd have missed anything.

"I also have a message for you from the High Lord Taullian, Ruler of Cyelle. I'll never understand why elves need to use so many 'L's. It's just absurd."

I agreed.

"He says the human you wanted information on was named Joseph Barakel. He was forty-five years old when he did the changeling swap, and that was about nineteen years ago."

I shot a quick glance at Wyatt, who didn't appear to be paying attention. He was clenching his fists and staring hard at a spot on the wall, resisting Leethu's pheromones that had crept back up. He said he would help me with the research on dead infants, but there was an increasing probability the hybrid wasn't dead. With Haagenti upping the ante, I fully intended to follow up on my hunch that the hybrid remained alive over here, and that the human was also alive keeping tabs on her. I was desperate. I needed to find this hybrid now, before Haagenti made good on his promise. But the human servant was middle-aged when he'd done the changeling swap. He might be dead of natural causes by now, even if the elf woman hadn't killed him as she claimed.

"He never returned," Dar added.

That jived with Tlia-Myea's claim that he was killed over here. Or possibly that he remained here alive, watching over a fostered hybrid. I glanced at Wyatt again. It was looking more and more like I'd be committing what in his eyes would be a murder.

"Never returned?" I asked Dar, just to confirm. "Who brought the human baby back after the swap?"

"A demon, evidently, but their records don't show specifically who. There clearly was a human baby. There's a bill of sale and everything. Taullian's people traced it down, and her owner confirmed the purchase and the date."

I'd met the human, and her odious owner, but had hoped something would identify the demon who'd brought the baby back. He'd at least be able to confirm or deny the human's death. I wondered again who had leaked the story. It wasn't the sort of gossip a demon would spread around. It had to have been an elf. The midwife that Tlia-Myea was so fiercely protecting? Or was there someone besides the midwife who knew this little secret?

"Oh, and Joseph Barakel came into his mistress' service as an infant." Dar added.

I was stunned. An infant? And he had risen only to the level of a servant?

"Was he addled? Mentally lacking?" I thought about the human changeling, Nyalla. Changeling babies usually became magic users, sorcerers. I'd expected this guy to have come into elf hands as an adult if he was a mere servant.

"Noooo. His scores were pretty average, for a human. I'm not sure why she didn't put him in the mage apprenticeship program. He certainly qualified. With intensive training he probably could have been skilled."

The training *was* intensive. I'd found out about it from the runaways I'd tracked for asshole-elf, otherwise known as Lord Feille of Wythyn. The babies went in right away and remained at the school full time. There was no family life for them. No normal human childhood. They spent decades in training then served their owners, often while still residing at the academy.

"Who did the elf woman in the tower, Tlia-Myea, buy him from?" Maybe he'd had behavior issues and been sold from out of kingdom. Maybe his original elf homeland had more exacting standards and he hadn't made the cut.

"She had him as an infant. She purchased changeling rights from another elf, and he came straight to her when the swap was made."

It was like a lightning bolt had hit me in the forehead. She bought a human baby, never turned him over to the academy of magic, raised him herself. It was an absurd, sentimental waste of money. To spend a fortune to get the rights to a changeling then not allow him to be trained as a valuable magic user was insane. She could have ended up with a mage, but instead she wasted her money and wound up with a servant. The only reason for her to do that would be because she wanted to raise him herself, as her own child.

Elves lived for tens of thousands of years. Humans didn't. And suddenly her human baby was a grown, middle-aged man. He'd die. She needed an elf baby to love. One who would outlive her. She knew the baby she bore wouldn't pass for an elf, so she sent her two children off together. One to watch over the other. One tasked with keeping an eye on the infant. One so concerned with watching over the baby that he couldn't even return with the human changeling. One who was probably sending occasional reports to her. It was all just a hunch, a long shot, but my instincts had seldom failed me before, and they were screaming at me about this one.

I shot one more quick look at Wyatt, who was thankfully oblivious to our conversation. "Dar? Would you dig around and see if you can discover who the demon was that brought back the human baby? And also if there is a demon who has been sending fairly regular correspondence to this elf woman? Maybe once a year or every other year? It may be the same demon, but don't rule out that it could be two different ones. Is there a way you can do that without involving Lord Taullian, or him knowing what you're doing?"

Dar snorted. "Of course, Mal. How dare you doubt my competence."

Now that's the Dar I know and love. And I told him so. "Dar, you arrogant, worthless cow. Day-old shit is more competent than you. Still, you're all I've got. Try not to fuck it up."

"Fuck you, Mal," he said affectionately before disconnecting the line.

"The net closes in on this elf hybrid," I murmured to myself before turning to Wyatt, who was in the process of closing in on me.

I had been engrossed in Dar's information, so I hadn't felt the dramatic increase of sex in the air. Leethu leaked like crazy, and evidently she was pouring it out like a geyser right now. Wyatt wrapped himself around me, pushing me backwards to slam against the wall, the sharp edges of my mirror digging in to my back.

"Now, Sam," he said, his voice husky with need. "I don't care if she hears, watches, joins in. Right now I wouldn't even care if that angel joined in. I need you now."

"Barn," I told him, trying to negotiate the path to the door as he unhooked buttons and snaps with great skill and speed, once again ignoring his own clothing in his frenzy to remove mine. I swatted his hands away and yanked open the French doors leading out to the pool and patio. It was January, so my pool was snugly tucked under a huge foam cover, patio furniture stacked neatly in the corner. Otherwise I may have taken advantage of a handy chaise lounge or done it in the water. Instead I moved as quickly as I could with Wyatt pawing me all over, leaving a trail of my clothing on our way to the barn.

I'd barely managed to throw a few blankets down in the tack room before Wyatt shoved me onto my hands and knees. Clearly he'd taken those moments to get his own clothing off, because instead of bulging jeans against my rear, I felt hard, naked flesh. Digging a fist into my hair, he yanked my head backward and plunged full length into me. A human woman would have been pissed by the complete absence of foreplay. I wasn't human though, and I was really loving this side of Wyatt—the Leethu-influenced side.

"Yeah, go!" I laughed. It felt like he was going to rip right through into my abdomen. I wished he was bigger.

In response Wyatt let go of my hair and gripped my shoulders, shoving my face down into a saddle pad. He braced against my shoulders, pulling and pushing against me to force his thrusts even deeper. He was lucky, because all this rough stuff was testing my control. Humans weren't sturdy enough to handle what I was longing to do, though, so I let Wyatt call the shots and just enjoyed myself.

It was over quickly, and Wyatt collapsed in a heap on top of me. After a few moments of listening to his panting while I struggled to get even minimal oxygen from my squashed lungs, he rolled off me and gathered me tenderly to his chest in the spooning move he preferred during sleep.

"Sam, I am so sorry," he gasped.

"Are you kidding?" I laughed. "That fucking rocked."

"I'm serious." He buried his face in my hair. "

"I'd be happy to let you apologize in a slow and gentle fashion," I said turning to face him.

I felt him wince. "That was fast and crazy. I think I'm going to be out of commission for a while."

"Can I reciprocate?" I teased. "You just roll over face down on the saddle pads and I'll take care of the rest."

He flinched, even though he could see my smile. "Uhh, no. I let you get away with all sorts of things, Sam. You've always rocked my world, but there are some things I draw the line at."

I sighed as though he'd broken my heart. "Fine. I'll cross that off my list. I've got lots of other ideas though. I'm hoping Leethu stays. She brings out your wild, unconventional side."

He laughed. "*You* bring out my wild, unconventional side. I kind of like your sister Leethu though. I like her a lot. A whole lot."

"Yes, that's part of her evil plan," I teased him. "Draw you in with her beauty and promises of ecstasy then leave you a useless quivering mess for months."

"Kind of like you do?" Wyatt teased back. "Have you noticed how she only has an Asian accent when she wants something? It seems to get really thick when she's trying to seduce me."

"That's her favorite form right now. She attracts humans with a tiny, helpless demeanor. They never know what hits them. She's the absolute master of topping from the bottom. Works even with us demons."

"She has a male form too, the Incubus?"

"Oh more than one, although Leethu has always preferred female, both in form and in sexual partners. She has over fifty Owned beings to choose from, and most of them are human. That's pretty good for a Succubus, even at her age."

Wyatt looked astonished. "Fifty? She's killed fifty people and kept their souls?"

I shrugged. "More like thirty-five, give or take a few, the rest are animals. It doesn't sound like a lot, but Succubi can't manage a whole lot of Owned spirits. They don't multi-task as well as other demons do."

He looked at me. Oh no. I knew where this was going.

"How many beings do you Own? How many are humans?"

"Four hundred and thirty six. Two-hundred-and-twenty-eight are human." I knew exactly how many. It's important to keep track of these things.

Wyatt caught his breath. "You have two hundred and twenty eight souls inside you? Are they in some kind of coma until you need them?"

"No, they are active and aware, every last one of them. I provide environment, sensory input, experience. It wouldn't be any fun if they were all like folders in a file cabinet. They need to be active, otherwise why bother to Own them?"

"How do you manage all that?" Wyatt asked, astounded.

"I don't really think about it. It's kind of like breathing to you. You can concentrate on it, or you can set a standard for a default breathing pattern and just do it. Not unconsciously, but semi-consciously. You feel it; you know you're breathing, but you don't need to divert brain power every time you take a breath."

"Seriously?" He sometimes had a hard time thinking what it meant for me to be a demon, a totally different creature, a being of spirit. I think he sometimes thought of me as just a weird human.

"Yep. We all do this. Well except for angels. They don't Own, but they do similar types of multi-tasking. Gregory really rocks. He can do this aspect thing where he assumes multiple corporeal forms. I have no idea at all how he manages to do that. I've never seen it, but I hope he shows me some time. Can you imagine?" I was awestruck at the thought. His power was so unbelievable.

Wyatt scowled. Oh yeah, not a good time to be talking about an angel when you're wrapped up in your lover's arms. Especially an angel I admired so much.

"Are they happy? What is it like for your Owned humans?"

"A few are happy, but happy really isn't much fun. I get really creative with the environments, but the best ones are pulled from a human's own mind—their fears, their sins in life, whatever they dread the most. That's what elicits the greatest reaction."

Wyatt hesitated. "So it's like hell, only it's inside you."

"No, Hel is a place. It wouldn't work to duplicate Hel as an environment; none of the humans I Own have ever been there."

"I don't mean your home Hel. I mean hell as in how the humans perceive it. A place where the damned spend eternity in torturous punishment."

"Kind of," I wasn't really sure where he was going with this. "I'm not punishing them though; it's all in good fun"

Wyatt shuddered. "Not for them. So they are evil people? Suffering because of their misdeeds during life?"

"It's not like prison. I don't judge them and deliver punishment."

Wyatt frowned. "So you just grab someone, take their soul and do whatever you want to them, regardless of whether they deserved it or not? You snatch people, unwilling, then give them pain and suffering even if they've been good people during their lives."

I squirmed. Demons never really thought about humans as anything worthy of judgment or fair treatment. We didn't even think in those terms with regards to other demons. But I'd been here so long, and I had human friends. What if one of Haagenti's goons Owned Michelle or even Wyatt, and made them feel like they were starving, or itching all over with no relief, or slowly burning? I couldn't stand the thought of them suffering like that. They were my friends.

"It's what we do, Wyatt. That's part of being a demon. We spread plagues, create famine, start wars, and we Own. A lot of my Owned humans are willing."

"That doesn't matter. You're punishing innocent people."

Innocent was a kind of subjective term. I'm certain the worst mass murderer had people who thought he was innocent. I wasn't sure how to explain this whole thing to Wyatt, though. I didn't even want to look too closely at it myself at this point. I'd changed how I felt about humans over the last few months and now I found myself wondering about these things too.

"Most of the humans I Own are what you would consider bad. I don't have any nuns or charity workers. I daydream about Owning people like Hitler and John Wayne Gacy, not the last five winners of the Nobel Peace Prize."

People are more accepting of torture when they think someone had it coming.

"What if it were me, Sam? How would you feel if a demon Owned me?"

I went cold at the thought. I'd fucking kill anyone who hurt Wyatt. I couldn't think about all the humans I Owned, couldn't wrap my head around why it was okay for them, but not for the humans I'd come to care about. But I did want to reassure Wyatt that he was safe with me. I reached out to touch the side of his face.

"I would never Own you Wyatt," I told him. "I've resisted this long, and I'm confident I won't slip. I don't want to ever Own you."

"What if you slipped? Would you torture me? I know you said some are happy, but happy how?"

"I won't slip, Wyatt. I won't." The thought of Owning him made me feel ill. The thought of anyone Owning him made me ill.

"I heard your brother talking about Haagenti. It's escalating, and there's a good chance I'll be killed. Don't you ever think about Owning me? That way I'd be beyond Haagenti's reach. Tell me you haven't thought about it."

I honestly hadn't.

"Wyatt, I love you. And that's why I can't Own you. It would kill me to Own you. I'm absolutely terrified that one of Haagenti's demons will kill you, but never once did I think Owning you was an acceptable alternative. Never."

His eyes were sad. "How can you possibly say that about me, while you continue to Own and torture all those other humans? I'm no different than them, and if you can do it to them, you could do it to me."

"I won't do that to you Wyatt. I swear on all the beings I Own."

A ghost of a smile crossed his face. "And you have no idea how ironic that statement is." Shaking his head he pulled me close.

"I don't want this to end, Sam." I got an odd feeling that he wasn't just talking about Owning or dying by Haagenti's hands.

"Me either." I pressed my face against his shoulder. "Everything ends, though. Even angels and demons. Everything begins and everything ends." I lifted my head, pulled his face down to mine and kissed him, rubbing my thumb over his jaw. "But not today."

~12~

The Eastside Tavern was surprisingly full for lunch. We'd snagged a table toward the back, and Wyatt told me about his latest video game adventures while I doused our fries with vinegar.

"Okay," I said, waving a fry at Wyatt when he'd finished discussing his success in killing zombies. "What did you discover about the angels? Anything different than Dar?"

"I can't remember what Dar discovered," he admitted sheepishly. "I was too busy fantasizing about your rear end and what I hoped to do with it." He handed me some stapled packets.

I summarized the conversation for Wyatt.

"Which one are you?" he asked, amused. "I think Obedience is probably out of the question."

"Oh totally. Personally I'm hoping for Prosperity, but with my luck I'm probably something boring, like Wisdom."

Wyatt choked on a fry. "Wisdom? Not likely. I really can't see you as any of these, Sam. Maybe there should be one called 'Trouble', or 'Mayhem'."

I would seriously love to be the 'Trouble' angel.

Wyatt motioned to the stack of papers in front of me. "I put together summaries on each of them based on scripture as well as modern stories. I've got to say, there are a lot of fruitcakes on the Internet though."

I glanced though the papers, and paused at one, laughing. "Well, Gregory's probably not this Gabriel guy, or I'd be pregnant."

"What?" Wyatt grabbed the paper out of my hand.

"See?" I pointed. "He only assumes corporeal form to appear to women and tell them their pregnant. Isn't that just hysterical? He's got a stork fantasy going on."

"I think it's just Mary," Wyatt said, searching the paper. "And sometimes he announces John the Baptist's conception."

"Yeah, he's a stork," I laughed.

I froze, staring at one of the papers. "Holy shit on a stick, look at this." I thrust it at Wyatt.

"Yeah Samael, also called Samiel, sometimes the fifth archangel listed with the other four. He's only cited in a couple of places…." Wyatt's voice trailed off and he looked up at me in surprise. "But you said your name was an assumed identity from a human you Owned. Samantha Martin."

"Yes, but angels don't believe in coincidence. And Gregory vehemently refuses to call me Sam."

Could it be? Could Samael be the other brother, the younger one who died in the wars? How could he stand to be around me when my current name was a constant reminder of how much he'd lost?

"It doesn't mean anything. He only calls you cockroach because it's derogatory and it pisses you off."

"Still, I go by Sam here, among the humans."

"There is a Satan mentioned as one of seven archangels in a few documents," Wyatt commented. "Some identify Samael as this Satan."

"But Gregory's brother died in the war with the demons. If he was this Samael, the fifth brother, then he wouldn't have been the Ha-satan, the Iblis." Or would he?

"Are you sure, Sam? Did Gregory ever say which side his brother was on? We humans have wars that fracture families; it could have been the same with angels."

I thought back on my conversation with the gate guardian, and with Eloa. Did he die in the wars, or was he *lost*? And nobody had actually said the demons had killed him, or even which side he'd fought on. I'd just assumed that. I remembered playing with lightning, in a thunderstorm with Gregory last August. He'd told me I reminded him of his youngest brother, told me of his impish behavior. Perhaps I'd been wrong. It would explain a lot of Gregory's odd fascination with me.

"Maybe there was always an Adversary, an Iblis, on the Ruling Council and before the wars, this Samael held that office."

Wyatt nodded. "So Samael was part of the Ruling Council, as the Iblis, and when you all split, his place was held for him. Originally it was seven angels, and now it's six angels and Satan. Same players, just one got banished."

Wyatt's words filled me with a strange sadness. Gregory's younger brother … was he this Samael? Had he been the Ha-satan, the Iblis, then he would probably have been the leader of the revolt. His own brother, the Iblis. The one who'd nearly severed his wings. The one Gregory had almost cut in half. How could things have gone so wrong that two beloved brothers almost killed each other? Over what? What could have been so important? Millions of years and he was most likely dead, with me in possession of the sword and the title. The Iblis.

"So now it's my placeholder." I frowned. It made sense. I'd always assumed that the Iblis was a military title that came about during the war, but perhaps it had existed before then. Someone to test, to push back against the angels on the Ruling Council. But the spot had been vacant for over two million years. Why had they not replaced the Iblis with someone else, even temporarily? Why had that chair remained empty for so long?

"So what angel was supposedly the Iblis?" I asked Wyatt. "Was it always this Samael?"

"Some say so, while some say Morningstar, or Lucifer. In the Old Testament, he seems to be an angel, sort of like God's thug. In the New Testament and Christian lore, he's the archenemy. He's everything that's evil and nothing that's good."

I hated stereotypes. I'm sure the angels had had a hand in that portrayal of us.

"He tempted Eve in the garden of Eden, caused the fall of humanity."

"Oh that is such bullshit!" I interrupted. "The demon wars were fought and we were banished long before humans were given the gifts of Aaru. It's just like those asshole angels to blame that one on us. It was them. They fucked it all up, falling into the sins of the flesh."

"That story is here too, that it was the fault of angels who fell into sin." Wyatt assured me. "In modern times though, most humans hold Satan responsible for the fall of Adam and Eve."

I fumed. We always got blamed for everything.

"Tempting Christ, trying to steal Moses' corpse. . ." Wyatt trailed off, looking at me nervously.

"Forget it. I don't want to hear any more." I was so pissed. If Gregory had been here, I would have yanked my barrette off and sliced his wings to shreds. Jerks, all of them.

"Is he dead?" Wyatt asked. "I'm assuming the previous Iblis, this Lucifer or Samiel guy is dead if you have the sword."

"I don't know. It's not like I'd die if the sword left; I just wouldn't be the Iblis anymore." I wished that would happen. The previous Iblis must have been psyched to be relieved of his duties.

"Yeah, but you must know if he's dead or alive," Wyatt continued. "We know whether all of our ex-presidents are alive or not. Don't you guys keep track of each other?"

"Not really," I said with some hesitation. "There are some demons that were alive at the time of the wars. I know a few of their names, but I don't exactly move in their social circles. One of them may have been the previous Iblis, but I doubt it."

"Why? Do you think losing the war was just too much and he killed himself?"

"We didn't lose," I protested. All this misinformation was irritating. "It was a stalemate. I don't know, I just think he's dead." Nearly cutting off Gregory's wings, and being almost sliced in half in return—his own brother. A long, vicious war with no clear resolution; an eternal exile, never being able to return to Aaru. I can't imagine wanting to live after all that.

Wyatt reached over and grabbed my hand, squeezing it reassuringly. "Okay. Let's just move on and look at the rest of the angels who could be on the Ruling Council."

I stared at his hand, numb, trying to shake off the feeling of sadness that blanketed every emotion.

"Don't be upset, Sam. I don't believe this stuff. I know you're not like that, that you're not like this horrible Satan of our legends."

But I was. I took a deep breath and continued to look at the papers Wyatt had so helpfully compiled for me. Dar was right, there was a lot of overlap. All the angel's responsibilities and duties seemed to run together after a few moments. Then one of the papers caught my eye and I laughed again, my depression evaporating.

"Metatron? Seriously? That's not an angel; he's one of those Transformer guys."

"No, it's an angel—supposedly one of the greatest; the first and the last, the link between the human and the divine.

Some sources say he's the same as Michael, but others say he's above Michael."

"Nope. He's a Transformer. That leader of the Decepticons. He totally rocks."

"Megatron, Sam. It's a 'g' not a 't': big difference."

I looked up at Wyatt. "I think you're on to something here. The angels are secretly Transformers. Or maybe they're like Voltron. They all join together in a huge lump to defeat any threat to Aaru." I envisioned the Ruling Council leaping through the air to stack up into a giant robotic angel. I hoped I was the head.

"So we're done with the serious conversation now?" Wyatt asked, gathering the papers together in a stack. "Because I would like nothing more than to put all this angel stuff aside and talk about cartoons and action figures."

Me too. I was really sick of thinking about angels. But there was one more serious topic before we could relax and have fun.

"Wyatt, I hate to tell you this, but there's a possibility that elf woman didn't kill the hybrid. Dar revealed some information, and it may still be alive. I checked, and there are twelve-thousand-four-hundred-and-forty-two female live births within the geographic area and time parameters. I can't narrow it down any further than that. I need your help.

Wyatt's jaw clenched. "No. We've discussed this. I'm not going to assist you in finding and killing an innocent person."

"It's not a person; it's a demon hybrid."

"I don't care," Wyatt glared at me. "I'm not doing this."

"Don't you see? This creature is dead anyway. If not by my hands, then by some other demon the elves send over. This Taullian guy won't give up until he has proof, one way or another, that this hybrid is dead."

I could see him waver. "No. I've got to draw the line somewhere, and this is it. I won't assist you to hunt down some poor young woman and do her in."

I ran a hand through my hair. "It's not a person, I swear. This is a demon/elf hybrid. You know how we demons are, and you've already articulated how horrible you think the elves are. Can you imagine a cross? It would be like a tiger and a great white shark coming together. It's probably already killed several humans. It might be in jail on capital murder charges at this point. We could be stopping it before it goes on some kind of killing spree. This hybrid is a monster set loose on humanity."

Wyatt hesitated. Teetering on the edge.

"What if someone had stopped John Wayne Gacy? Or Ted Bundy?"

"Promise me you won't kill her unless you have proof that she's committed murder. I need your vow on this, otherwise, no go."

"I vow on every soul I Own that I won't kill the hybrid unless I have proof or confession of its committing murder."

Wyatt nodded. He didn't look happy though. "So nineteen years ago? Female births within a hundred mile radius of Leesburg, Virginia?

"Yes, that's the twelve thousand number I came up with. In addition to narrowing down the live births, I also need to find a human, Joseph Barakel. He's the one that accompanied the changeling over. Maybe he escaped the demon that was to kill him. If so, he can tell me for sure whether the hybrid was dead or alive at the changeling exchange and maybe point me to the family so I can find the grave or the hybrid."

Wyatt frowned thoughtfully. "If the child is nineteen or twenty by this point, she may be in college, or she may have moved. In fact, the family may have moved any time after the swap was made. So I'll look at historical records, but after that we may need to expand our geographic search on likely suspects."

Crap, I hadn't thought of that. Why couldn't humans just stay in one place? If the family had moved, this elf hybrid could be anywhere in the world. The key would be to finding Joseph Barakel and tracking from there.

"This is going to be impossible." My mood had turned uncharacteristically gloomy. "We'll never find this hybrid. Haagenti is never going to give up. I should just go home and take my lumps. At least then you'd be safe. You can meet a nice girl, get married, have kids. Coach Little League like a regular human man."

Not that it was possible to even do that. My "lumps" had been changed into a death sentence. I felt even more trapped, more desperate.

Wyatt's hand clamped down on my wrist. "I hate baseball. And I don't want kids. Have faith in me, Sam. And have some faith in yourself. If this hybrid thing doesn't work, we'll figure something else out. Don't give up."

He moved his hand down to intertwine his fingers with mine and gave them a squeeze. My mood lightened. "Okay. Let's see what we can find out in the next week or so. Maybe we'll get lucky."

~13~

I carved into the table with a dull butter knife. A stale Danish pastry sat off to the left, and a half empty cup of black coffee perched on top of a daunting stack of papers to my right. The table had a solid coat of polyurethane on it, so I'd had to dig deep to even make a dent. I would have made more progress with a claw, but the hotel staff kept popping in and out of the room on stupid errands they'd improvised to give them an excuse to gawk at the angels

I didn't blame them. I'd gawked for the first hour, too. Even without visible wings, they were awe-inspiring. I'd really only dealt with them one-on-one, except for that brief time when Gregory killed Althean. A group was a whole other thing. My confidence fled. It was abundantly clear I was a scared imp facing down six ancient, powerful beings.

They'd stared at me for all of two seconds after Gregory ported me into the room then proceeded to ignore me. It was probably for the best. I couldn't have said anything intelligent at that moment anyway. I'd plopped down at my designated seat and looked through the paperwork as if I were actually reading it while they made small talk with each other and took their seats. I was the only one with a coffee and Danish. It made me feel even more out of place.

I wasn't sure what they were discussing. A few moments after the meeting had begun I'd realized that about fifty percent of their conversation wasn't verbal. After an hour, they had all turned to look at me briefly, their expressions ranging from pity to condescension. From that point forward all their discussion was spoken. Not that it helped much. They all talked at the same time. It was like trying to listen to twenty conversations simultaneously. I wondered if Gregory had clued them in that I couldn't hear their mind-speech—probably not. He had ignored me since we arrived; hadn't even looked at me. I felt like I'd been tossed in the deep end of the lake and told to start swimming. I was drowning.

A chunk of the polyurethane popped off the table and I looked down at my drawing with satisfaction. I almost had the trunk of the tree done. This stupid meeting was probably going to take long enough to carve a whole forest into the table. With a sigh, I scraped the knife over the table again, wondering why it sounded so loud. That's when I realized the angels had stopped talking.

I peeked up and saw them all staring at me.

"What?"

The dark-haired angel exhaled dramatically. He had short, spiky, pitch-black hair and shocking blue eyes. He would have been really hot if he didn't scowl so much.

"Are you for or against?" he asked. I decided to call him Dopey.

"Are you all still discussing the dude who petitioned to change choirs?" I asked. "I didn't realize I needed to weigh in on that one. I mean, it's kind of an internal issue, isn't it?"

Dopey frowned. "*We* finished that topic four pages ago." He nodded at the stack of papers supporting my coffee cup. "We're on item one-twenty-eight."

Shit. We had three hundred and thirty three to cover. We'd never get done. I had a vision of us as skeletons, all fused to the hotel chairs, a foot of dust covering the table and papers. Moving my coffee cup, I leafed through the stack. One twenty eight—something to do with punishment for anyone harboring Nephilim.

"What Nephilim? I thought you guys hadn't decided on the werewolves."

The red-haired woman spoke up. She was the only woman in the room. There had been a few more when I had arrived, but they'd changed to male immediately after.

"We haven't decided on the werewolves, but there are other Nephilim. We've defined the term to mean any offspring of an angel with another species."

"So if an angel knocks me up, is our kid included?" They all stared at me in horror. "Because then I should probably recuse myself from this vote. I wouldn't want to condemn my own offspring."

The woman's face went just as crimson as her hair. I decided I'd call her Bashful. "Not that it would ever happen, but you are considered to be the same species as angels."

"Is this a possibility in your near future?" another angel asked, this one with longer, wavy, black hair that shone purple in the light. He had a rather wicked hint of a smile in his eyes. I'd call him Happy.

"Could be," I looked him over appreciatively. "I'll grab your number on our next break and add you to my list of candidates."

Dopey tapped a firm finger on the paperwork in front of him. "Fallen angels are sometimes redeemed. We want to ensure that once they repent, they are not protecting their vile offspring from a just fate."

"That seems kind of like an internal issue too. I'll be Switzerland on that one."

"It's not internal when it involves other species," Gregory interjected. I decided to call him Grumpy, not because he was particularly grumpy at the moment, but because it sounded too much like Gregory to belong to anyone else.

"Fine. What did everyone else vote?"

Grumpy started to protest, but Dopey interrupted. "Four in favor, two against."

"Well then, I'm against. Not that it makes any difference since more have voted the other way."

Grumpy shook his head. "We need a *quorum*, not a majority. Your vote means we do not have a quorum and the issue now needs to be sent back to committee."

Oops. Dopey looked pissed. So did Sleepy and Sneezy. I wondered which of the other three I'd just sided with. I continued to carve as they progressed onto item one-hundred-and-twenty-nine, this time trying my best to follow the conversation. It was a topic I didn't understand, regarding evolution and vibration levels.

"I thought you guys took care of the problem with the fallen choir and the Nephilim ages ago. Why are you still fussing over it?"

"We've moved on," Dopey said, his voice like an arctic breeze. "That issue has been sent back to committee."

"We weren't able to exterminate all the Nephilim," Bashful replied, ignoring the frosty glare Dopey sent her way. "Some still walk the earth. They are difficult to detect and some believe that their angel parents may be aware of their existence and assisting them to remain undetected."

"Item one-hundred-twenty-nine," Dopey said, waving a hand to cut her off. It was Bashful's turn to glare now. "Who is for and who is against?"

I shrugged and went back to my carving, figuring they'd let me know when they needed my vote again.

The day wore on this way until a little after lunch. I was the only one who ate, of course. The other angels disappeared. If they'd been human, I would have thought they all ran out to check their e-mail, or smoke cigarettes outside the front door. Maybe they couldn't stand to watch me eat? Too tempting?

They were only gone for a half an hour and popped back in altogether. It was really weird.

"Wasn't sure how long you all were going to be," I told them. "I was getting ready to run out and pick up some beer."

"We used the time to return to Aaru and give us a much needed break from this physical form," Happy told me. "It is very uncomfortable for us to be like this."

"Well, you could have had me up to Aaru for the meeting," I complained, hoping to embarrass them. It didn't work.

They sat down and Dopey rifled through the stack of papers before him. Pausing, he shot a quick smirk at me. "Item two-hundred-and-four. Annual kill summaries to date and impact analysis."

Everyone turned to that page. I did too because kill summaries sounded a lot more interesting than anything else we'd discussed so far.

I looked at the sheet, perplexed. I'd expected a list of names and a bunch of inexplicable codes on who was killed and the justifications; instead there was a lengthy analysis on each individual as to the possible impact their death would make on the evolution of humanity.

"Wait. Is this just angel and demon kills of humans? What's with the impact analysis?"

The conversation halted, and the silence made it clear I was a total idiot, not deserving a second of their attention.

"Angel, Demon, or an inter-dimensional creature who have killed a human," Bashful explained. "When humans kill humans, or other indigenous earth creatures, such as vampires, kill humans, it is considered to be part of their destiny and not worthy of our concern."

I shook my head. "Okay. So what's the impact thing? How do you measure that?"

"Each of us has some level of omnipotence," Gregory interjected. He had hardly spoken to me since we arrived, and

I was surprised to hear his voice. "We evaluate the probability of our projections, compare them and compile an impact analysis based on our joint input."

"Omnipotence? You're fucking joking me. You guys really can see the future?"

Gregory locked his black eyes with my brown ones, and suddenly he was the only one in the room. Everything else receded into a rush of static. *"We see lines of possibilities into the future. Some are more statistically probable than others. What we predict doesn't always happen, but we evaluate the impact as best we can."*

"Not really," Happy told me. "They're just estimates based on our experience and projections."

I focused my thoughts on Gregory. *"What's your success percentage?"*

Every now and then I saw these spider webs of interconnection. Ever since Gregory had bound me, the visions clicked in unexpectedly, but I never knew how to interpret them. There were too many lines, too many possibilities.

"Thirty percent," he thought. He seemed proud of this number. *"Humans are increasingly unpredictable, and their actions don't follow typical models. I have amended a higher prediction ratio, but the others refuse to use the algorithm."*

A surge of admiration, almost adoration went through me. He was so fucking impressive.

"So if a demon kills Joe Schmoe, you guys not only look at his direct actions and effect, but the cascading effect on potentially thousands of other people? How many levels of relationship do you go to? And for how far into the future?"

"Direct effect for a normal lifespan," Dopey said with a snap of impatience in his voice. "Three levels indirectly for a decade."

"Modeling shows that after a decade, impact predictions degrade," Sneezy spoke up.

I shook my head in amazement. Three levels of relationship, and ten years ... fuck, I couldn't even fathom how huge that number would be. And then deciding the probability? Yeah, I juggled over two hundred Owned humans, but this was far beyond my abilities. I glanced over at Gregory, feeling hopelessly outclassed. What was I doing here? Why, of all the demons, had this stupid sword picked me? I was an imp, almost a Low. Why me?

"You're just a baby. You'll be able to do this too in a million years or so. Crawl first, little cockroach, run later."

It helped.

"So why bother? I thought you guys didn't interfere. If you decide there was a good chance that the dead guy was going to solve world hunger, do you jump in and pick up the slack or something?"

"We monitor closely. Sometimes the desired result is delayed a few generations. Sometimes another human takes the deceased one's place and performs the action," Bashful said.

"Because of ... past events, human evolution is occurring too fast, and it's erratic. There is a good chance they will de-evolve, or destroy themselves. They are also liable to interfere with other species' evolution. We won't take direct action unless a series of events occur that leads us to believe positive evolutionary outcome is improbable." Happy had a grim look on his face. I had no doubt what their direct action would be, and there probably wouldn't be an ark offered for a lucky few.

"As independent and individualized as humans believe themselves to be, they actually behave in ways similar to a giant organism," Gregory said. "An imbalance in Peru is rectified within a few generations by balancing actions somewhere else. So far, this has allowed the human race to move forward more often than backward."

"Why don't you just leave them alone?" I asked. "It's really arrogant to presume to know what's good and bad for an entire race of beings."

They all exchanged looks and Bashful finally spoke. "We mostly leave them to their own devices in their interactions with each other, or among other indigenous species, but many of their difficulties are due to issues that occurred with the transfer of our gifts to them."

"We *do* know what's good and bad for an entire race of beings." Dopey made a slashing motion with his hand. "They bumble around like fools. The whole lot of them would have killed themselves off thousands of years ago if we hadn't been helping them along."

"This wouldn't be an issue if you guys would have kept your pants on. Sheesh, you can't even hand over a few gifts without fucking everything in sight."

Dopey slammed his fists on the table and jumped up, leaning forward as if he planned to lunge across the table at me. Power snapped from him with a sharp bite of cold. I leaned back, balancing my chair on the rear two legs, and smiled while he struggled for control. He'd pummel me to bits, but it would be worth it. He'd never live down the embarrassment of losing control and beating up an imp in the middle of a Ruling Council meeting.

"Bring it on, Gramps," I said softly, trying to push him over the edge. "You're just pissed because you missed out on the chance to shove your cock into some soft, warm, human pussy. You'll just have to imagine what it feels like while you whack one off in Aaru."

That did it. He leapt across the table toward me, too fast for the others to stop. I pushed, toppling my chair backward to the floor, and he sailed over, missing me by less than an inch to crash into the wall behind me. Damn, these guys were fast. He'd scraped himself off the wall and was halfway to me before Sneezy and Sleepy grabbed him, the blue stuff flowing thick as they tried to calm him. Feeling confident they had the situation under control, I got up and turned my back on him to grab my stale danish off the table. Whipping around, I pitched the pastry at him and was thrilled to see it smack him right on the forehead.

Baked goods in the face trumps calming blue stuff. Dopey roared, throwing Sneezy and Sleepy to the side like rag dolls before diving into me. I wasn't able to avoid him this time. He hit me hard, cracking my back against the conference table and bending me from the waist to lie on the table. Icy cold white crashed into me, through my flesh and into my personal energy. He hadn't completely lost control. He was careful to avoid the red purple branching throughout me, and clearly was going for pain and damage, not my death. I whacked him with my cup, breaking the mug on his head and drenching his black, spiky locks with coffee. It didn't have any effect, so I pivoted my hips to the side, grabbing his thigh and swinging my opposite leg around to wrap around his neck. I twisted, and we rolled. I was only briefly on top before he reached up and crossed his arms, grabbing my shirt collar to choke me as he kicked his legs and rolled me again. Hot damn! Finally, an angel who knew how to fight!

We kept rolling past the edge of the table and crashed to the floor along with a heap of papers. He kept hitting me with the icy blasts, but this was primarily a physical fight. Not what I expected from an angel. I actually got the feeling that this was rather cathartic for him. He got in a few solid punches to my face before the others managed to drag him off of me.

I propped myself up on my elbows, sniffing as blood poured from my nose and a split lip. Dopey wasn't as damaged, although some of the wet on his hair was blood and not just coffee. Four angels held him back as he struggled. Four? Staggering to my feet, I saw Gregory, still sitting at the end of the table looking at his papers as though nothing untoward had occurred.

"I think human ninety two might warrant some further attention," he said, frowning at the paper.

I grinned at Dopey. "Should we call the meeting? Give the old man a day or two to lick his wounds?"

"I'm fine," he muttered, shrugging off the four angels and resuming his seat.

The rest of us walked to our chairs, and the papers scattered on the floor flew back in neat piles on the table. Cool trick. Everything else was trashed though—smashed drywall where Dopey had hit, coffee and broken crockery all over the table, a danish upside down on the floor. I wondered briefly why the humans hadn't come running when they heard the mayhem.

"I sealed the door and blurred their minds," Gregory thought. He sounded ... amused? *"Didn't want them to barge in and interrupt your fun, little cockroach."* Yes, he was definitely amused. *"I haven't seen Gabe that angry in...."* I felt a wave of pain and sadness. *"In a long time."*

So there was a Gabriel. And I'd just whacked him in the face with a pastry. I wondered who was pregnant.

"Ninety two seems fine to me," Dopey said, still breathing heavy.

They discussed, and I looked down the list of humans killed—mostly by demons. The next page was an equally large list of demons who'd met their end. I was proud to see my designation on quite a few. Haagenti, kiss my ass.

"Why are there no elf kills on this list?" I pondered out loud. The angels fell silent and looked at me in surprise. "True, they don't pop over here and kill humans like we do, but they're always yanking humans to their lands. That's got to have an impact. I mean, what if they grab the next Gandhi or something?"

The angels stared.

"Plus that one asshole is always losing his sorcerers. What if one makes it across the gates? What would that do to your impact report to have a sorcerer running amok?"

"That's ridiculous!" Sleepy sputtered. "Elves don't do such things."

I glanced over at Gregory. I was sure he knew about these doings. He was busy looking through his papers and ignoring the conversation.

"Our gates all require activation." Happy explained. "There is no way humans are falling through by accident to Hel. The only way a human could get there is if a demon activated the gate and took them over. To our knowledge, that has never occurred."

"Yours *aren't* the only gates," I insisted. "The elf ones aren't as complicated as yours, but they do have them. One is fairly close to my house."

Gregory continued to ignore me.

"The only beings that can create gates are angels," Happy said.

Gregory glanced up at that, meeting my eyes. "And demons," he said.

"They've lost that ability," Sleepy said. "They've lost almost all their abilities by this point. Demons have devolved significantly since their exile."

I continued to look at Gregory. I knew he thought I'd made that crazy, suicidal gate in Waynesboro, that I also made the one I used to sneak into Aaru and leave little "gifts". I shook my head.

"I didn't make either of those gates. They are wild, naturally occurring. The one I use to get in to Aaru is a fluke."

"There are no wild gates." He thought at me. *"Before the wars, we all worked together to seal them off. There hasn't been a wild gate for three million years."*

They didn't believe me. They didn't believe me about the elves, and they didn't believe me about the wild gates. Idiots.

"Do we get in on this private conversation?" Sneezy asked Gregory. He seemed rather miffed to have caught us in a sidebar. "Does it pertain to the business at hand, or is it a matter between a bound demon and her master?"

"Or between a bound angel and his mistress," Dopey muttered, loud enough for everyone within a three block radius to hear. Gregory's eyes narrowed and the air crackled with heat and ice. Sleepy moved his chair back slightly and looked at the table, no doubt appraising its possible effectiveness as a shield. The others were on high alert, ready to break up yet another fight. I wondered if all the Ruling Council meetings were this contentious.

"Are you picking a fight with *me*?" Gregory asked softly. "Because you'll end up with far worse than a cut on your head, brother."

These Ruling Council meetings were more interesting than I thought. Yes, there were hours of boring agenda items, but all that would be worth it if I got to see two angels having a brawl in a Marriott. Tension hung in the air. Dopey was clearly spoiling for a fight, and didn't look likely to back down. Gregory was just waiting for the other angel to make a move before he launched into what I'm sure would be a vicious counter attack. My money was on Gregory. Dopey was a lot of fun, and was in a close race for my most-favorite-angel title, but Gregory had no qualms about fighting dirty when he needed to. Yeah. I think I was Team Gregory.

The angel in question shot me an irritated look, and relaxed. "In the interests of finishing the meeting, I suggest we continue. I'll deal with you later," he told Dopey.

His tone scared the crap out of me, but Dopey just shrugged. "Whatever," he replied, like a sullen teenager.

The others shifted in discomfort, paging through the kill report and making random comments about it to ease the tension. I looked down at the paperwork. I really didn't want to spend all afternoon talking about whether some dead doctor in Cleveland was going to herald in the end of the human race. Maybe if I picked another fight they'd kick me out. I looked around for a likely candidate and met Gregory's frown. I think his patience with my "fun" had come to an end.

"Shall we move on?" Bashful asked. "I don't see anything in these kill reports that warrants further discussion."

"Where's the four-nine-five report for that human a few months back?" Dopey suddenly asked, the fake surprise in his voice fooling no one, let alone me.

As one, they all turned and looked at me. I had no idea what they were talking about. I glanced at Gregory, but there was no guidance in his stern face.

"What?"

There was no reply. Just expectant looks.

"Seriously. I have no idea what the fuck a four nine five is. Was that something on my to-do list?"

Silence.

"Can't help you if I don't know what the fuck you're talking about."

Dopey sighed, as if the whole scenario pained him beyond belief. "You instructed your hellhound to kill a human a few months back. Normally, you wouldn't get to live after such an act, but since you are the Iblis, you are given an opportunity to justify the murder using a four-nine-five report."

Shit. Gregory had told me there was a report, but I'd forgotten. It was his fault for not reminding me, or doing it for me. I'm a demon, I can't be expected to remember these things.

"The report is due within forty-eight hours after the kill," the angel continued. "And reviewed at the next council meeting. You've had ample time. I don't see the report."

"Can I get an extension?"

The silence was uncomfortable, and all those eyes stared at me. I got a feeling the answer was "no".

"Why didn't you remind me?" I accused Gregory. He didn't respond. I tried to recall what he said the ramifications would be.

"Punishment," Dopey said. I hoped that was a spontaneous word on his part and he wasn't reading my mind or anything.

"Oh no, oh no," I interjected, suddenly remembering. "It's 'censure' or 'reprimand', or something like that. So just shake your fingers at me and look disappointed and we'll all continue with this ridiculously long agenda."

"Twenty-four hours. Or punishment."

Okay. I could do that. "Fine. Whatever. Let's keep moving forward here. I'd like to be done before all my human friends are dead and buried."

"Punishment for noncompliance will be 'naked and restrained for one rotation cycle,'" he said, that smirk back on his face. One by one the other angels nodded, mine included.

Naked and restrained? *That* was supposed to have me shaking in my boots? Stupid repressed angels. That punishment sounded like my idea of some really fun foreplay. In the interests of wrapping this council meeting up though, I thought it was best to play along.

"Oh *please*! Not *that*!" I said dramatically. "I'll have it to you by the deadline, I promise."

The angels nodded as one and proceeded on to the rest of the agenda item.

It was moving on toward happy hour, when I remembered something. Leafing back through the pages, I looked over the demon kill report. There were a few marked as "unidentified".

"Hey, which one of these is the head?"

Confused eyes turned toward me.

"That head you brought over the other day," I prompted Gregory. "The one you said was a demon, but we couldn't identify it. Where is it on the report?"

The other angels began paging back through their paperwork. Gregory looked at me with blank eyes. As if he had no idea what I was talking about.

"The head. You brought it over when we discussed the agenda for the meeting."

"We're done with the kill report," Dopey interrupted. "That was hours ago. Table it for the next meeting."

I ignored him. "I thought it was human but you said it was a demon. Remember?"

Gregory nodded. "You were right. It was a human. Killed by another human, so it's not on the report."

He was such a good liar. I was almost convinced, but I'd been there. He had been positive it was a demon. Why didn't he want the Ruling Council to know about it?

"You said the human died ninety years ago at the hand of a demon. The head was reasonably fresh. It hadn't been decomposing for ninety years."

No irritation, no significant looks, no kicking my leg under the table. Nothing from Gregory that would indicate I needed to shut up, that he was trying to keep this hush.

"It was an identical twin to the one who died ninety years ago. And human preservation techniques are more advanced. The human was murdered by another then cryogenically frozen. It was only recently removed and beginning to decompose."

I wavered. Maybe the cryogenic technique had given it that "snow" smell Candy had noted. Maybe that's why it felt so empty. I had never explored a flash frozen human corpse before. Maybe Gregory wasn't lying after all.

"So why bring it to me then?" I asked, still suspicious.

He shrugged. "A source told me it was a demon. I had my doubts, but thought I'd have you check it out. Turns out it was nothing at all."

"Humans kill each other all the time," Sneezy commented. "Sometimes they blame demons. Sometimes they even accuse each other of being demons. It's so irritating when we chase down a lead only to find out it was just a regular human matter."

The others nodded, satisfied, and returned to a discussion of the vibratory impact of human genetic manipulation. I couldn't shake the feeling there was something else going on, something Gregory wasn't telling me. Something Gregory wasn't telling the other angels. Maybe I was just paranoid. It was probably nothing, as my angel had said. I was discovering things were not always as they seemed when it came to angels, and I vowed to text Candy as soon as we had a break.

~14~

It was early the next morning when Gregory ported me back from the Marriott into my kitchen. I offered to make him coffee, knowing full well he didn't eat or drink, and that after spending almost twenty four hours in a room with me and five angels, he'd happily make up some excuse.

He accepted. And he attempted to assist in the coffee-making.

"Ground up, burnt beans, right?" he asked, sniffing the canister of Folgers. I hated to disappoint him, but I was too tired to do fresh ground beans in the French press.

"The machine runs hot water over the beans, then goes through a filter into the pot so you don't have the grounds floating around your drink and getting stuck in your teeth."

I put a filter in the coffee maker and handed him a tablespoon. "Here. Scoop out ten tablespoons of the coffee grounds and dump them into the filter."

While he was occupied with that, I texted Wyatt to let him know I was back. I also had to re-send the one to Candy. Something, or someone, had blocked cell phone reception in the Marriott, so not only did hers not go out, but I'd returned to five messages from Wyatt informing me of his progress on our project, and that he'd killed yet another demon while safely behind his spiffy new wall. Wyatt also expressed the hope that I was "having fun". Ha, ha, very funny.

There was also one from him letting me know Amber was in town from college and that he wanted her to meet me. Ugh. Family stuff. Wyatt's mother refused to see me, or even speak my name. I could understand. Her darling boy ensnared in the clutches of an older woman. Much older. And there was that whole demon/Satan thing too. I wasn't sure how thrilled Wyatt's younger sister was about our relationship. This was probably going to be a very short, awkward introduction. Which would be fine with me. Demons don't do family stuff.

I looked over and Gregory was still measuring out the coffee. Carefully and exactly measuring out the coffee. To the grain.

"Oh for fuck sake," I told him, snatching the tablespoon and shoveling approximately ten scoops of grounds into the filter. "We'll be here all week and I need coffee right now. That hotel stuff never got changed from yesterday morning. It was like a pile of sludge for the last half of our meeting."

"You clearly have more than ten tablespoons in there," Gregory said reprovingly. "How can you expect consistent and optimal results when you don't measure correctly?"

"It doesn't matter. It's coffee, not rocket science." I poured the water into the machine and hit the "brew" button.

"Ah. So there is a range of acceptable input and output?"

I shot a frustrated look at Gregory, and realized he was teasing. It was a bit of a shock.

"Are you actually going to drink any of this stuff?" I asked him. I was irritable. I hoped these Ruling Council meetings were once a century or something or I was going to go stark raving mad. Gregory had been vague when I'd tried to pin him down on the frequency.

"There's no need for me to consume food or beverage to sustain myself, and as angels, we ensure our purity and high level of vibration by denying ourselves corporeal sensory stimulation."

"No, thanks" would have been an acceptable answer. I didn't need a fucking lecture on angelic purity. Pricks.

"I know you enjoy intense sensory experiences, but you shouldn't *need* this drink." The lecture continued. "And when are you going to deal with this demon who is flouting your authority and threatening both you and your human toy? You've let this go on long enough."

"All right, *Dad*. I'll get right on it. Squeeze it in after the interminable Ruling Council meeting and my recovery nap."

"You shouldn't need to sleep either. If you applied yourself, you'd have ample time to get everything done."

I slammed a coffee cup down on the counter, breaking the handle in three pieces. "Would you get the fuck off my back? I'll take care of things my way, and in my own time. I don't need you chewing my ass out with your holier-than-thou attitude. Get out of my house. Go back to Aaru and meditate, or sing a hymn or something."

I glared at the angel. He looked back at me, inscrutable and silent. The coffee machine beeped

"Are you going to throw a breakfast food at me?" Gregory asked softly. The corner of his mouth twitched.

I envisioned wrestling around the floor with him and my spirit-self came alight. The danish-incited fight with Dopey had been fun, but with Gregory there would be all kinds of sexual undertones. I had not a doubt in my mind that we'd wind up angel fucking. I knew there was no way I'd be able to resist. "I'm too tired to start a food fight. Besides, I don't have any pastries. Or muffins. I'd need to throw bacon at you and it might not have the same effect."

He walked toward me, and I tensed expectantly, like a rabbit cornered. He brushed against me, and stretched his arm down toward mine. My breath caught in my throat. I wanted him to keep going, to grab me and yank me right out of this body to join with him. I was tired, grumpy, but all that would fall aside with just one touch.

Gregory's hand closed around the broken coffee cup and lifted it from my hand. "I believe humans put some kind of dairy product in their coffee?" he asked. The question sounded sexy, like a proposition.

"Not me. Black as midnight on a moonless night," I choked out.

Moving away, he poured the coffee in the handle-less cup and gave it to me. I grabbed it with both hands as if it were a lifesaver, and sipped the liquid gratefully. Undeterred, he moved in closer and picked up a strand of my hair, rubbing it between his thumb and fingers. He was so close, and the power he leaked burned hot against my skin. I was getting used to the feel of it. I was beginning to like it, to long for it.

"I admire how deeply you imbed yourself into your form, little cockroach," he murmured. "Such commitment, such dedication to experiencing sensation is what I would expect from an Iblis. However, you need to know how to distance yourself. You must develop the skills you need to quickly adapt to the particulars of your situation. You must be flexible in your vibration levels. This is important."

"I have distanced from my form," I told him proudly. "Two months ago, Wyatt shot me in the head and killed me. I pulled back and held myself inside the dead flesh a few moments before I recreated myself. Any other demon would have died, but I managed to exist inside a corpse."

I felt his approval. His personal energy, his spirit self, extended through his fingers to touch my own. The feel of him soared through me more than any physical caress would.

"Try for longer next time." His breath stirred my hair and I closed my eyes. "Or remove yourself from the human form and exist within something inanimate."

"Mmmm."

I wasn't paying attention anymore. All I heard was the throb of his voice. That sound, his breath, the heat of his power, the pulse of his energy, all overwhelmed me. I reached out to him, our spirit selves swirling into translucent white where we touched. We pressed against each other, tantalizingly slow.

The front door slammed closed. It was like a splash of cold water. I tried to jerk away from Gregory, but he grabbed me and crushed me against him.

"Thought I'd join you for coffee." Wyatt's voice was tense, full of sorrow. And that hurt me far more than if he'd been angry.

"Send your toy away," Gregory said against my hair, his energy still stroking along mine.

I couldn't physically pull away, but I did yank my spirit self back, pulling it away from the flesh and consolidating it deep within me as Gregory had been urging me to do.

"No," I told him, keeping my voice soft. "I'm sorry. I love Wyatt, and I don't want to hurt him."

The angel released me, both physically and spiritually, and I turned to see Wyatt, standing forlorn by the front door. Something inside me twisted.

"Absolutely." I smiled at him. "Sit down and I'll get you a cup. I know how you like it." That last bit was intentional, to help him feel a connection to me that the angel didn't have. These were things we shared, little exclusive, intimate moments of our lives.

Gregory watched as I filled a cup with coffee, poured in the cream from the fridge and added a spoonful of sugar, stirring it before handing it to Wyatt. I reached over and kissed his cheek as I pressed the mug into his hand.

"I'm glad you're here," I told him sincerely. "He was just leaving."

I turned and looked at the angel pointedly. For once, he cooperated.

"Since I'm not going to drink coffee, and I have no desire to watch you play with your toy, I'll leave." He grinned at me, and suddenly he looked very human. "Rain check on the bacon?"

I couldn't help laughing. "Yes. I'll try to keep some pastries on hand for the next time though."

"What's this about pastries and bacon?" Wyatt asked as Gregory gated away.

He was forcing his tone to sound casual, to try and be nonchalant about what he'd nearly walked in on. If he'd been thirty seconds later, we would have been out of our bodies, lost in a joining of energy. I wondered briefly what we'd look like, what a human would perceive, if anything.

"Kind of an inside joke," I told him. "I threw a Danish at Gabriel during the meeting, and we ended up in a brawl. Really livened things up."

Wyatt smiled, the tension in the room lightening. "So there is a Gabriel after all?"

"Yep. One of the hotel employees must have been pregnant. Otherwise I'm sure he wouldn't have bothered coming at all. He was amazing, Wyatt. A total jerk. Constantly sniping at everyone. He even baited Gregory. Can you imagine? For a second I thought the apocalypse was going to rain down on our heads."

Wyatt chuckled and the tension evaporated. Sitting on one of my dining room chairs, he pulled me onto his lap.

"Where's Leethu? I'm not feeling the uncontrollable urge to boink everything in sight, so she must be out?"

I rubbed myself against him, happy to feel his arms around me, smell his familiar, warm, human scent. "Nah. She's upstairs. She hides when Gregory is here and totally shuts down the pheromones so he doesn't get irritated and kill her."

"I, ah, figured that was the reason I walked in on you in such a compromising position? Leethu had been turning it on strong and overcoming both yours and an angel's restraint?"

It was a good excuse, but I'd vowed to be honest with him. "No. Gregory finds her really repulsive, and seems to be immune to her influence. I don't know what his game is with me, Wyatt. He really comes on strong, and it's difficult for me to resist him."

Instead of being angry, Wyatt seemed relieved. He buried my face against his shoulder and kissed the side of my head.

"Thank you for being honest with me, Sam."

I pulled my head up and kissed him, relishing the closeness, the trust we had in each other. Trust. I think I was the only demon ever to know trust.

Wyatt pulled away from our kiss, giving me a brief peck on the nose. "Go get your coffee and let's talk. I've had a busy night and I've got lots of information for you."

I grabbed my coffee and plopped back down on Wyatt's lap. Now that Gregory was gone, Leethu's influence was winding down the stairs in a seductive spiral. We'd need to make this conversation quick before we became focused on other things. Wyatt felt it too. He ran his hands through my hair and his lips along my jaw line as he spoke.

"You were right. Within the timeframe allotted, there were twelve-thousand-four-hundred-and-forty-two female live births within our geographic parameters. Deaths would be easier. Fifty eight female infants less than one year of age died in the hundred mile radius of Leesburg in that particular year."

"Mmmm." I was feeling like I wanted to take this conversation upstairs into my bedroom, but I resisted. "Over twelve thousand, huh? That's going to take forever for us to weed through. Damn."

Wyatt's hands crept up under my shirt and deftly unhooked my bra. "Joseph Barakel is a rather unusual name. I've got two individuals with that name currently living in the area we're targeting. I need to check back at the time of the baby exchange though, but I'm sure I'll only find a couple of people. I think that's going to be our best bet."

I peeled off my t-shirt and tossed my bra to the floor, giving Wyatt better access. "Good idea. I can interrogate any Joseph Barakel in the area at the time of the changeling swap, even if he's moved out of the area. That's probably our best way to find this hybrid."

Wyatt's fingers were exquisite torture on my breasts. "So, I did good?"

"Oh yes," I affirmed, breathless. "So good."

Screw Leethu. Well, not literally. Wyatt and I made love on the dining room table then headed to my bedroom for a long morning nap. Leethu remained discretely behind doors, although her presence was clearly felt. Twice during our nap, Wyatt rolled me over for sex, and at least one of those times I'm pretty sure he wasn't even awake.

~15~

After our nap, I'd woken to Candy texting me back to let me know she had no idea what a cryogenically frozen human smelled like, but that Gregory's explanation seemed valid. Well, that was a bust. I guess Gregory wasn't hiding something after all. I was kind of disappointed, but it was just as well. I had enough to do as it was. Starting with this list of over twelve thousand baby names.

Wyatt and I had relaxed all through the afternoon and evening while I recovered from the Ruling Council meeting after which we headed out to The Eastside Tavern for dinner. After we returned, Leethu got pushy with her pheromones. I'd brought her back some nachos and entertained her as non-sexually as I could while Wyatt returned to his demon-proof home for the night. Before he'd left, he printed out the huge list of names and locations for the baby births, and the details on the two Joseph Barakels.

The pile of paper was daunting. There had to be some way to whittle this down. I picked up the shorter list and looked at the information on the two Josephs. My best chance to find this hybrid, dead or alive, sometime in the next century, lay with one of these two people, hopefully. If this was a dead end, I was screwed.

There was a pop and Gregory stood before me. I hadn't expected him and was annoyed he'd just appear in my living room without any notice. I'd hoped to press Leethu into some kind of chaperone service whenever he was around, assuming he'd be too busy thinking murderous thoughts at her to try and put the moves on me. Leethu was upstairs, though, still sleeping probably.

"Hey. What's up?" I asked.

He had a kind, gentle look on his face that was far more alarming than either his murderous, angry one or his intense, sexy one. Why was he looking at me that way?

"You've missed the deadline."

I searched my memory. Oh fuck. That stupid kill report, whatever its number was.

"I've really had my hands full and haven't had a spare moment. Can I get another twenty-four-hour extension?"

"No."

"But it's not like I even know where to get a two-nine-four report! I searched the Internet. You guys really need to have it on pdf so I can download it. Get me the form and I'll sit down right now and do it. It shouldn't take me long.

"Four-nine-five. It's two-hundred pages long. And the answer is no."

"I'm supposed to join Wyatt's sister tomorrow afternoon for a lunch. I promise I'll do it right afterwards." Not that I really wanted to meet Wyatt's sister.

"No."

Crap. I didn't have time for this bullshit. How long had that snotty jerk said? One rotation cycle? Was that solar, lunar, or what? As much as I was looking forward to being 'naked and restrained' I really had stuff I needed to do.

"A rotation cycle in Aaru is about thirty six Earth hours," he told me, his voice soft and kind. He was scaring the piss out of me. "I'll oversee your punishment personally, and I'll let that worthless human toy of yours know, so he can make excuses for your absence at lunch, and any other engagement you have on your schedule."

Personally? Oh shit. Naked and restrained with this angel personally "punishing" me was going to be an exercise in self-control. And I'd never had any use for that particular virtue. Or any virtue.

"This is really a bad time," I protested. "See this stack of papers? I need to wade through this as soon as possible so I can get that demon, Haagenti off my back. Things got really ugly when I was over in Hel, and he now has a kill order out on me with a huge bounty."

"So *deal* with it," Gregory ground out. "And I don't mean with a bunch of papers either. Get yourself through the gate and face him."

"Just give me an extension on this nine-four-two form and I'll hot-foot it right over to Hel and face him."

"So you're saying if I give you an extension, you'll go right now?"

"Absolutely," I lied.

"Then I will transport us right now to the gate, and throw you through it myself," he said softly.

Fuck. Haagenti had demons guarding that gate, and he had a death sentence on my head. Naked and restrained was looking like the better option.

"Uh, I just have a few quick things to do first. Maybe I'll meet you there? In an hour or two? You can wait for me."

Gregory sighed and shook his head in disappointment. "Then punishment it is, little cockroach."

Reaching over, he pulled me to his chest and gated me into the nothingness of Aaru. I'd been there before, sneaking in through the wild gate in Sharpsburg to leave random little gifts for Gregory. I never managed to get used to the feeling though. My whole body itched, like a wool sweater that really needed to come off. None of my human senses worked. Everything was white, silence stretching on forever. Gregory stood before me, the only corporeal thing beside myself in the place.

"Okay, let's get this over with," I said grimly. "Do you want me to strip, or are you supposed to do it?" Part of me hoped it was him. Part of me hoped it wasn't.

"I'll restrain you first," he told me.

I wondered for a moment how he was going to manage removing my clothes with me hog-tied on the floor, or whatever passed for a floor in Aaru. Maybe he was going to rip them off. Heat stirred in me at the thought. He'd never indicated any interest in physical sex with me, but I still had my fantasies.

My fantasies took a detour when he reached into me and coated my stash of raw energy with the slippery, silicone stuff angels used to keep us from using it. He'd done this before when we'd first met and were both trying to kill each other. I'd still been able to grab little bits of energy here and there, and the effect had left when he'd stopped touching me, so I was surprised when he released me and the feeling remained. I prodded the boundaries, but this time they were tight. Evidently 'restrained' didn't involve ropes or chains. I could look forward to the next thirty-six hours having no access to my raw energy. I'd be defenseless, unable to convert my flesh and fix any injuries. The thought made me nervous, but I was in Aaru, and I was the Iblis. I should be safe. Right?

I looked down at my clothes with a disturbing premonition. If 'restrained' hadn't meant what I thought, I wondered what 'naked' meant.

"Dissolve," Gregory said.

My physical form disappeared and I panicked. Complete and total panic. Without a physical form to house ourselves in, we die. We break apart, and drift out into the universe. The instant of our formation, we are gifted a shape from our parent, and we spend our first hundred years there until we develop the skill to Own and convert into other physical beings. This wasn't just naked; it was death.

I thrashed about, trying in vain to grab enough of the slippery raw energy to create anything. Anything. An insect, an amoeba, a single-cell bacteria. The slippery coating blocked my every attempt. It was like drowning, like suffocating while frantically trying to take a breath with lungs that no longer worked. I was going to die.

"Hush. You're not going to die." I felt the soothing blue along with his soft words. I wasn't sure he'd intended to put out the lovely blue that had always calmed us demons as children. I'd always fought against it when he'd done it in the past. I didn't fight it now.

"There." His tone changed and became mocking, challenging. "Take your punishment with some dignity. You are the Iblis, after all."

I felt him leave and the panic returned. There was nothing to hold me together. I was defenseless, I couldn't protect myself or repair myself if I was attacked. I was going to die, dissolve into nothingness. I yanked on the red purple within me and commanded the angel to appear. Summoned him. Begged him. Evidently the binding between us didn't work in Aaru because I remained alone. Finally the panic overwhelmed me and I just suffered in crippling anxiety and fear. It was like going insane. I couldn't track the passage of time and when I finally felt his presence again I was confused. He removed the thick wall blocking my raw energy.

"Form."

I waited for something to occur, but nothing did. I still existed as a being of spirit. Was I broken?

"No, you need to do it. Create your form, so I can take you home. Otherwise you *will* die."

Oh. I popped into the Samantha Martin form that I'd been wearing for so long and again felt that itchy sensation. In a heartbeat we were back in my house, next to the couch. Instead of releasing me, Gregory picked me up and dumped me over the back of the sofa to sprawl naked on the cushions.

"Here." He came around the sofa and plopped down a stack of papers on the coffee table in front of me. "Twenty-four hours."

"You asshole," I smacked him with a cushion to emphasize my anger. "You are all assholes. I've got all this shit to do. I didn't want any of this, I didn't agree to any of this. I was near death. My spirit self-shredding from the edges. I'm permanently damaged, I'll never recover. It's a wonder I can still convert."

"You're fine," he puffed out, exasperated at my drama. "You were never in any danger. You're supposed to use that time to meditate, to reconnect with the purity of a spirit existence. It should have been relaxing."

"You're fucking joking! I'm a demon. I don't meditate. And we die without physical form."

"No you don't. You just can't exist like that outside Aaru, so you're not used to it."

"I was dying. You were torturing me, allowing me to slowly die in your own realm."

"You were *not* dying."

"I *was*. I was dying. You abandoned me, refused to come when I summoned you. I thought you said you were compelled to come, no matter what realm we were in. Clearly you fucked that one up, because you left me there. Left me to die, alone and afraid."

"I never left your side," he shouted at me.

I stared at him; feeling like the wind had been knocked out of me.

"I never left you. I sent another angel to relay the message to your stupid human toy, and remained there with you throughout your whole punishment. You were never in danger. You were *not* dying."

He looked at me, fury and something else in his gaze.

"Twenty-four hours," he told me, pointing at the stack of papers. Then he was gone.

I stared at the report. It was huge. Two hundred pages, he'd said. But even the prospect of that daunting task couldn't erase his words from my mind. *He'd never left my side.* A full rotation cycle, with me freaking out like a fool, and he'd never left me. I shook my head, too stunned to ponder in depth the implications of his actions. It was evening, and I had a lot to do. Starting with a call to Wyatt.

My phone was dead, since I'd been rudely yanked out of my living room a day and a half ago and not charged it. I put on a pot of coffee while it powered up. It was going to be a really long night and I needed the caffeine. It had just finished brewing when Wyatt called.

"Sam? I'm glad you're back. Some angel showed up at my house yesterday and told me you'd been dragged off for punishment. I was worried."

There was a strange banging noise in the background as Wyatt spoke.

"Yeah, I neglected to fill out a report and had to spend a day and a half in the angel pokey. What the hell is that noise? Are you building something?"

I heard various other noises, then another loud bang.

"Uh, it's a demon throwing rocks at my house," Wyatt said apologetically, like it was his fault. "Uh oh, he's setting the shrubbery on fire. I better let you go and try and shoot him before the house goes up in flames."

"Oh no," I told him. "I'm pissed off and seriously need to kill something. Let me."

It was terribly unsatisfying. One shot and the demon exploded into a shower of blood and guts. Wyatt came out and we stood for a moment, staring at the mess.

"Trip to Columbia or freezer?" he asked, nudging a largish chunk with his foot.

"I've got too much to do. I'm thinking of just letting Boomer clean up this one."

Like magic, the hound was by my side, floppy ears raised forward in anticipation. I scratched along his back, rubbing the velvety brindle fur. His eyes glowed golden as he looked up at me for permission. The hellhound ate anything as long as it was dead. Didn't matter what. Didn't matter how decomposed.

"Wait until after we leave, then you can have him," I told Boomer. I didn't want to watch him eat, and I was certain Wyatt wouldn't want to either.

"Want me to come over?" Wyatt asked hopefully. "I can cook something. We can drink wine and watch a movie."

Oh, it sounded lovely. "I can't. I've got a two hundred page report I need to do by tomorrow, or I'm going to wind up back in Aaru again."

"Think you'll be able to break for lunch tomorrow? I rescheduled with Amber."

Fuck. "Can we do the day after? Just to be on the safe side?"

Wyatt nodded. "I found out more of Joseph Barakel while you were gone. The guy in Falls Church was definitely around at the time of the baby exchange, and he's still living there. Same address. The other one was around too, but it looks like he died a few weeks back."

I hoped the dead one wasn't the one I was looking for. With the way things were going lately, I wouldn't be surprised. Still, that left one Joseph Barakel to check out. I crossed my fingers, hoping that somehow this would be the one.

"You are the best, Wyatt. I'll work on this report for the Ruling Council tonight, and maybe tomorrow we'll go down and interrogate Joseph Barakel."

Wyatt shook his head. "You need to do that one alone, Sam. I'm not sure I can watch you interrogate someone. Promise me you won't kill him? Or torture and maim him?"

What was with Wyatt and the torture thing lately?

"Okay, I promise. No killing or torture. No maiming." I kissed him. "I missed you. I can't wait for this all to be over, so we can spend some time together, get rid of this demon barrier and Leethu, and get back to our lives."

"Me too," he whispered, kissing me back. I got the feeling he didn't believe it—that our golden moment had passed and our lives would never be the same again. That our futures wouldn't be the idyllic ones we hoped for.

Back at my house, I threw together a stir-fry, sucked down coffee and looked at the volume of paper Gregory had left for me. I'd hoped it would be a series of boxes to check off, but no, it required a bunch of essays on the deceased human, my reasons and methods of extermination, and a lengthy background on him and his immediate family. Then there was an impact analysis with a bunch of numeric algorithms. That was going to be practically impossible to complete since I didn't have the angels' omnipotence. I thought about calling Wyatt and asking him to do the research on the guy's family, but I'd put so much on his shoulders lately that I hated to keep asking him to do things for me.

I'd just poured myself a fourth cup of coffee, and was walking back to the table when everything went black and tilted away in a wave of vertigo. I felt myself fall, hit something hard and cold with my side, and heard the coffee cup shatter. Warm liquid splashed against my arm, and my vision swam in a sea of grey with pinpoints of light. As my eyes began to focus, I realized the dots of light were candles in a dim, windowless room. Fighting off the dizziness, I pushed myself to hands and knees on a cold, concrete floor and looked up. Looked up into the faces of three shocked teenage boys.

"Jake, it worked!" One squeaked, rattling a piece of copier paper in his hands.

~16~

"What is going on here?" I demanded.

The three boys ignored me and scrutinized their papers. The one in the middle, I'm assuming Jake, frowned.

"She's a *girl*," he said

"And she doesn't look like a demon." The other's eyes pivoted back and forth between me and his paper.

"What is going on here?" I repeated with more force. That got the teenagers' attention, and they backed a few steps away, toward a washing machine with a basket of laundry on top. I looked around and realized I was in someone's basement. There was a wooden staircase, stacks of boxes, tools neatly arranged on a peg board. Why was I in someone's basement?

Jake cleared his throat. "I would like the answers to next Tuesday's algebra exam. Robbie would like the new Call of Duty game, Riley...."

"Dude, you're saying it all wrong," one of the other boys interrupted. "You've got to use the correct words or it won't work."

There was a slight tug of war over Jake's paper. "I command you as a southern demon to bring me the new Call of Duty game." Ah, this must be Robbie.

"It's not southern, it's summoned," Jake corrected, snatching back the paper.

Okay. I'd had enough. "Do I look like fucking Santa Claus?"

Jake looked indignant. "We summoned you into a circle. You have to give us what we want."

I knew how this worked, but I didn't feel particularly compelled to perform a service for these boys. And I had no fucking idea how I was supposed to get the answers to an algebra exam.

"Call of Duty?" I asked Robbie. "Seriously? You summon a demon and you want a video game? Why don't you just walk down to the store and buy the damned thing yourself?"

Robbie mumbled something and Jake elbowed him. "His mom won't let him have it. Says it too violent. The store won't sell it to him unless his mom signs for it."

I couldn't believe it. Teenagers everywhere were scoring booze from an obliging adult, and this poor kid couldn't even manage to talk someone into getting him a video game.

"And what is it you want?" I asked Riley, who was staring at me with huge eyes. I felt like I should invite him to sit on my lap. Maybe give him a candy cane when he was done.

"A blend whot dig its," he choked out. I looked at the other two for clarification, thinking Riley was a foreign exchange student.

"He wants a blond with big tits," Jake helpfully translated.

Now that was more my style. I wanted a blond with big tits too. Maybe we could share.

"Look," I told them. "I really admire your ingenuity here, but I'm busy right now. Just send me back home and I won't kill you. Deal?"

"No." Jake said with surprising firmness for his age. "We summoned you, and you need to give us what we want. No deal."

That was something I was curious about. "How did you summon me? You're young. You're clearly not sorcerers or even mages. Did you use a scroll or something?"

Robbie rustled his paper. "We looked it up on the Internet."

And how the fuck was a summoning spell on the Internet? One that worked, that is.

Riley turned his paper toward me. "We downloaded this from a museum website," he said, finally able to speak articulately. "It's a thirteenth century spell some dude had when they burned him for witchcraft."

Oh great. I stepped closer to the edge of the salt circle and peered at the paper. Riley extended his arms helpfully so I could read it. "Summoning a Devouring Spirit." I recognized that spell. It had been translated from the original Elvish, no doubt to be copied and sold to a human population. There were portions that had blurred and been destroyed over the years, but the basic framework of the scroll was there, along with Riley's notes about the well-endowed blond he wanted to request.

"This is for a devouring spirit. It isn't the right scroll."

"We command you to grant us the answers to the algebra exam, the new Call of Duty game, and…." Jake tried again.

"De-vour-ing spirit, you fucking morons," I interrupted. "Devouring. Not granting. There are specific demons that do these things. I'm not one of them."

"I want a blond with big tits," Riley chimed in.

"The only blond with big tits you're *ever* going to get is the kind you blow up with an air compressor. Now send me home. Read the part of the scroll that banishes me and I'll let you all live to fail your tests, and wank off in your bedrooms without video games."

Their eyes were blank. I could swear I heard crickets chirping in the background of the silence. "We command you...." Jake began again, no doubt figuring that if he repeated it enough, I'd get bored and just give him what he wanted.

"Don't tell me. You don't have the banishing part of the spell. You morons summoned a devouring spirit, and didn't think to make sure you had a way to send it away when you were done."

I glanced down at the salt circle. It looked funny—kind of chunky and an odd color.

"Command you to grant us the answers," Jake continued.

I reached down with a finger and swiped the salt. It didn't burn like it should have. Bringing my finger to my mouth I tasted the bluish crystals.

"Ice melt? You summoned me into a circle of ice melt?"

"We didn't have enough table salt," Riley explained.

"The new Call of Duty game and a blond," Jake went on.

I stepped out of the circle. Jake's voice tapered off into a squeak and he held his paper up in front of him like a shield.

"One circle? Of ice melt? Next time use two circles, of the purest salt, with a triangle inside. Summon the demon into the triangle, with the two circles to reinforce the parameter, and wear amulets of protection. Make sure you have the banish incantation ready to go, and an incantation of no-harm to the spellcaster."

I moved a few steps closer. "There won't be a next time, though. You will all die by my hands tonight."

"Does this mean I don't get my blond?" Riley asked.

I changed direction and walked over toward him. "Oh you'll get your blond. She'll tease you and tempt you. Then as you penetrate her, the teeth in her vagina will tear and shred your cock to a useless, bloody nub. You'll scream in pain, but you won't be able to help yourself from doing it over and over again. For all eternity."

I ripped the paper from his hands, grabbing his shoulders and sent tendrils of myself into him to Own. Then pain exploded in my head and everything went black again.

~17~

I woke in a garbage bag, tied up with electrical extension cords. I probably would have suffocated, but during transport, holes had formed in the cheap bag. Someone's parents bought the generic, bulk stuff, and for that I was eternally grateful. I wasn't sure that I would have been able to consolidate and pull back my spirit self to live inside a corpse while I was unconscious. Tearing my way out of the bag, I shrugged off the electrical cords. I had no idea where I was or how long I'd been out. I was under a bush, surrounded by woods with a steep slope in front of me. I could only assume I'd been driven somewhere in the country, then thrown down an embankment to decompose.

It was a tough climb to the top of the slope where I saw a two-lane road. Which way? And would there be enough traffic for me to hitch a ride, or would I be forced to walk miles before I found someone? I'd been summoned out of my home without a cell phone, without any identification, or money. I had no way to call Wyatt to come get me, and I wasn't even sure I was within driving distance. For all I knew, I was on the other coast of the country.

I walked for about thirty minutes before I gave up and called the only being I didn't need a cell phone to reach. It took a few seconds before Gregory appeared. He took in our surroundings in disbelief.

"What are you doing here?"

"I was summoned," I told him sullenly. "By three teenage boys who got a hold of some scroll out of a museum. I don't even know where 'here' is."

"And where are these teenage boys?" Gregory sounded amused. "Am I to be reading three more four-nine-five reports?"

"I don't know where they are." I kicked some gravel off the road and down the steep embankment. "They knocked me unconscious and dumped my body down a ravine a few miles back. Trust me, if I could get my hands on them, you would definitely be reading a stack of four-nine-five reports."

It had to have been evening. Yes, the sun was definitely lower in the sky than when I'd first crawled out of my garbage bag. I started walking, and Gregory fell in beside me.

"They thought I was going to give them stuff, like some kind of demonic Father Christmas. Me! One kid wanted a stupid video game. The other wanted answers to a school test. Because evidently it's easier to summon a demon than to actually study."

We walked along the deserted road. A cliff rose up on one side, and the ravine deepened on the other. Scrub poked out of the gaps in the guardrails along the ravine side, waving bare thorny branches in the chill breeze.

"What did the other human adolescent want?" Gregory asked.

"A blond with big tits. Now *that* I can actually understand. I mean, you should have seen this kid. No way was he ever going to get laid in his lifetime without otherworldly intervention. That dude had a legitimate reason to summon a demon."

Gregory made a sympathetic noise.

"Is this what it's come to?" I asked philosophically. "Satan? Demons? What happened to the terror, the screaming in the night? Young humans are now asking us to be personal shoppers and pimps. Adults ignore us, or emulate us. I've seen humans do things that would make the oldest demon cringe."

"I know. Terrible, aren't they?" Gregory had a note of fondness in his voice. I halted and faced him.

"Wait. I thought you hated humans—that you were just doing this Gregori thing out of duty, because you angels fucked things up so badly."

He looked at me for a long moment then turned his eyes west, toward the golden sun snared in the tree limbs. "I changed my mind. I've changed my mind about a lot of things."

Without further clarification, he continued walking. I scampered to catch up, and we walked, side by side, in a companionable silence. The sun sank lower into the tree line, sending out rays of orange that faded into pink and violet in the darkening sky. Long shadows spread across the empty road. I hadn't seen a car the entire time I'd been walking. Those teenagers had done a good job; this road was perfect for dumping bodies.

I glanced over at the angel beside me. He seemed peacefully lost in thought. I wondered why he hadn't asked me what I'd wanted when I summoned him. He was always harping on about how busy he was, how I was distracting him from important duties, yet here he was, just out for a stroll as if there was nothing more important than enjoying the evening sunset with me.

"What angel did you send to Wyatt the other day?" I asked, making small talk.

"Eloa. He's always happy to do stuff like that, and he gets along well with the humans."

"That ass-kisser." Eloa had appeared female last time I'd seen him, like a pouty Marilyn Monroe. "Of course he'd do anything for his *Tsith*," I added, uttering the disgustingly mushy term Eloa used to refer to Gregory.

Gregory shot me a look. "That's disturbing."

"Tell me about it. He probably has a little shrine to you in his choir. I'll bet he practices writing his name as Mrs. Eloa Tsith. Then he dreams of the pair of you with little fat baby angels at your feet."

"I doubt the last part," Gregory commented. "Angels can't interbreed."

"Seriously?" I asked.

"Angels can only have offspring with demons. There has been no creation since the split."

Wow. No angel babies for two and a half million years.

"But demons can interbreed. So you all really got the short end of the stick with the separation of our kind, didn't you? Why in the world would you have banished all of us and basically condemned your own race to extinction?"

"Sometimes painful things must be done to keep true to one's values. There was simply no compromise on either side of the issue; we chose the only morally acceptable path."

I shook my head in disbelief. The whole thing seemed so stupid and childish, but, of course, I hadn't been alive at the time of the war.

"And demons can interbreed, but they shouldn't," he added. "Their offspring continue to degrade in vibration pattern. Within another million years or so, demons will be nothing more than animals."

"So we're like the hillbillies of the spirit world?" I asked. "Inbred, ridiculed, made fun of?"

"You could be so much more than you are," Gregory said. "Some of that is because of sloth, some because of improper formation."

I walked along, feeling self-conscious. I tried to convince myself that this was all very subjective, that the way of the angels was not the only one of value. Still, I felt so puny, so weak next to this angel. An imp. Nothing but a cockroach.

I felt Gregory reach out to me, touching my energy with his own. "You show great promise, little cockroach," he said, reassuringly.

It helped. And it also reminded me that this welcome break, this stroll at sunset with an angel, was only postponing all the things I needed to do.

I sighed and turned to Gregory. "Give me a lift home?"

"No." There was a hint of humor in his voice, as though this was a ritual, a joke we shared between us.

"Seriously? Why did you think I summoned you?"

"Seriously?" he mocked me. "I am not your taxi service. Call your toy to come get you."

"I don't have a cell phone. Besides I don't even know where I am. I could be in California for all I know."

"Just outside of Bethlehem, Pennsylvania," he informed me.

"Well that doesn't do me any fucking good when I have no phone, no money, no ID, and I'm walking down a deserted road in the middle of stinking nowhere at nightfall."

"Figure something out, oh mighty Iblis."

"I did. I called you so you could give me a lift home."

"Nope."

I fumed in silence for a bit. "Fine. I'll just assume my winged form and fly home. Maybe I'll grab a few humans along the way for a snack."

"That's a long flight," he said thoughtfully. "And some human is liable to shoot you out of the sky. You'll wind up stuffed and mounted over a fireplace."

That was true. Humans were a lot like demons. We would be thrilled to shoot someone out of the sky and mount them over a fireplace. And from what I'd seen in the last forty years, humans truly loved taxidermy.

"Then I'll fly to the nearest city and hijack a greyhound bus to take me home. I'll make sure I run a bunch of cars off the road on my way. Maybe plow over some puppies and kittens too."

"Well, I can't allow that to happen, can I?" He was making fun of me, that little smile quirking up one side of his lips, his eyes dancing. "I guess I'll have to gate you home. That way, all the puppies and kittens are safe from your murderous intentions."

This seemed a little too easy, but I decided to take the offer at face value. I halted and turned, expecting him to grab me like he always did. Instead he remained where he was, arms open, waiting. Waiting for me to come to him. Feeling like this meant something far deeper, I stepped close, pressing myself against him as his arms wrapped around me. We stood there, on the deserted road at sunset, the heat from his power a force even the winter wind couldn't cut through.

"For this, you will owe me another favor," he said into my ear. The purr of his voice warmed me. The heat of him burned as he pressed himself against me, both flesh and spirit. I wanted to hold there for all eternity, wrapped up in him, feeling him surround me, feeling him inside me. But I couldn't let myself be enslaved by my desire for this angel.

"Another favor?" My voice was raw and shaky. "What the fuck? Are you trying to collect the set or something? How many favors does one angel need? And they call *me* greedy. Sheesh."

"A favor."

The seductive pull of him intensified. I needed to agree to this favor, or I'd be agreeing to something else in a few seconds. And I really wanted to. I closed my eyes and inhaled, rubbing myself along him, trying to fill every sense, corporeal and otherwise, with him. He pushed in for a brief, tantalizing second then pulled back, just outside of my reach.

"Do you grant me another favor?" he asked.

"Yes," I breathed. I'd agree to anything. Anything.

He gathered me in tighter, but instead of the delicious joining I was longing for, I felt an instant of vertigo and saw a flash of light from behind my eyelids. I opened my eyes and we were in my living room. There was a scream, and a bowl of pasta flew across the room as Leethu dove to safety behind the sofa. She peeked over the edge at us with huge eyes. I was relieved and disappointed. He'd hardly pursue angel sex with the annoying succubus watching us.

Wrong. Leethu's eyes grew impossibly big as he continued to hold me close, laying his energy right on top of mine and joining in a thin edge with mine. I was torn between the urge to reciprocate, and the need to regain control, to push him away.

"Leethu is watching," I warned him, pulling slightly back.

"Go away," he commanded. He didn't even look at her.

Leethu squeaked and darted for the stairs.

"Stop. As your Iblis and head of your household, I command you to stay."

Leethu froze halfway up the stairs, shooting pleading looks down at me.

"So now you want her to watch?" he teased. "Make up your mind here."

"No. I want you to leave so I can finish this stupid report of yours."

He leaned back and looked at me in surprise. "You're not done yet? What is taking so long?"

I pulled myself out of his arms and gained some much needed distance between us. "No, I'm not done yet. I got summoned, remember? I was just starting when those stupid boys yanked me out of my living room and into a circle. Before that I had to go over to Wyatt's and kill a demon that was trying to set his house on fire."

I glanced over at the clock. Eight at night. Fuck. Fuck, fuck, fuck.

"I'll give you until dawn," Gregory said, his eyes following mine. "Only because I've had such an enjoyable evening, and I'm feeling rather generous."

I glared at him.

"It's ample time. You should be energized after your long nap in that roadside ditch. A couple of hours on that report then pop over to Hel and take care of your demon issue then resolve the problem your sister has and get her out of your house. Everything wrapped up by dawn. I'll show up to collect the report, and make you a cup of coffee while you lob breakfast foods at me, or do whatever it is you do in the morning."

Still glaring.

He grinned and rubbed a piece of my hair between his fingers.

Nope. Still glaring.

"See you in," he looked at the clock. "Ten hours."

Then he was gone and I was glaring at the spot where he had been.

"Ni-ni, he really scares me," Leethu whined.

"I know, I know." I looked over at the daunting stack of papers on the table. "I've got a lot to do tonight, so can you try to stay quiet and out of sight?"

"He'll be back in the morning?" Leethu asked. She was clearly planning to be at the farthest end of the house.

"Yes, but hopefully after that we won't see as much of him for a while." It was a depressing thought—more depressing than the stack of papers calling me.

I worked all night on that stupid report. It was impossible. The amount of detail, and the questions were absolutely ridiculous. I took a brief break to make a pot of coffee and looked desperately at the hint of pink on the horizon. Fuck.

The sun was full up by the time I felt the burn of Gregory's presence. I was late. Damn it all, I was late.

"Deadline," he said. "Past deadline, actually, even with the reprieve I gave you for being summoned by a bunch of teenage boys."

I wouldn't have put it past him to arrogantly yank me out of the middle of something to meet an arbitrary angelic deadline. Still, it had been very generous of him to give me an extension.

"I'm almost done," I told him. "Just fifty more pages left, although I couldn't figure out section four. I kind of had to wing that one."

He sighed. "Let's go."

"Get yourself a cup of coffee and sit for a bit. Just a few moments more."

"No."

"I'm almost done! Just chill out for a bit and I'll race through these last few pages." I'd just scribble some shit down and hand it over. I doubted anyone would read this stupid report anyway. Well, that snotty Gabriel might, just to spite me.

He sighed again. "Let's go," he said, reaching for me.

"No, no." I felt the panic rise in me again. "I can't do that again. I can't. Please. I'm almost done."

There was the faint blue again. I think it might be an involuntary thing with him. Either way, it was a nice gesture.

"You won't die. I promise, and, unlike you, I keep my promises."

"No. I can't. I can't."

"I will stay by your side again. You won't die."

"No, please no."

He frowned, perplexed. "You don't react like this when we join, and that act requires us to be non-corporeal. We faced terrible risk doing that here, yet you were fine. Why do you panic in Aaru, but not here where there is a chance of death?"

I hadn't thought of that. When we'd angel-fucked, I'd been too occupied with the sensation to think about the risks. I hadn't even notice I'd left my body behind, never considered that we might die. I guess I just trusted him to take care of me. He'd been in me, around me, a part of me. I'd assumed I was safe in the embrace of his personal energy, of his spirit self.

"Uh, I uh." Shit, what should I say? I could hardly tell him this. Pride is not my sin, and normally I don't have any problem admitting weakness, but I just couldn't spit this one out.

He waited patiently.

"I'm a trespasser in Aaru. Even if I am the Iblis, the angels hate me and I don't trust them to honor my diplomatic immunity. Accidents happen, and it's easier to ask forgiveness then permission."

"I'm *right* there. I won't leave you. Just relax and enjoy it. Your kind used to live as beings of spirit before the exile. Back when you were angels."

"We're not angels anymore, we're demons. Please. Just a few more hours."

His face hardened. "No."

I was restrained and naked in Aaru in a flash, trying to push down that sick feeling of fear.

"Relax." He sounded irritated, but that blue continued to cover me, soothing and calming. And then he was gone.

I tried to remind myself that he was right next to me; that I wasn't dying. I kept thinking of all the demons who existed this way millions of years ago and reassure myself I'd be okay. I couldn't sense him anywhere near me. And I didn't feel okay. I felt ... naked—naked and defenseless.

"Oh for the love of the Creator," I heard him say. Then I felt him. Felt his spirit surrounding me with its red purple, his energy a furnace of fire against me. And I felt safe.

~18~

After Gregory returned me from my punishment, I pounded out the last few pages of my report, sent Wyatt an obligatory text telling him that I was, again, home and, again, sorry I'd missed the lunch with his sister. Then I went to bed and slept like the dead until the next afternoon. With the Ruling Council off my back, I could now turn my attention to finding the elf hybrid and hopefully getting Haagenti off my back then finding and retrieving my horse.

Dar's light was flashing on my mirror, but I didn't have time to deal with him. I grabbed a bite for the road and headed to Falls Church, hopefully to have an enlightening conversation with Joseph Barakel. I had a lot to think about on the ninety-minute drive to Virginia, but the angel dominated, pushing every other thought aside. He was being caring, protective even, towards me. Six months ago he'd wanted nothing more than to end my life. When had his attitude changed into … this? Wyatt was right, I thought with some guilt. It was more than just sex; there was a weird kind of friendship there, something that up until now, I'd only felt for Wyatt. Whatever it was, I wanted it to grow, to see where we'd end up.

I pulled up to the row of townhouses that my GPS indicated was my final destination, and parked the Corvette a few blocks down. The neighborhood was like a graveyard. Clearly everyone worked nine to five, and it was only four in the afternoon. No one answered the door at Joseph Barakel's house, so I rifled through his mail and peered in his windows. He definitely lived here, judging by his bills and junk mail, and the house looked occupied, so I let myself in and explored while I waited for him to come home.

According to Wyatt's research and my quick addition, the guy would have been about mid sixties in age. The clothes in the closet indicated he was around six feet tall, about two hundred pounds, and not a particularly snappy dresser. There were a lot of sweat pants, button down sweater vests, and slip on shoes. Healthy food sat in the fridge, and not a beer in sight. I rifled through some magazines about technology on the coffee table along with a crossword puzzle book. Boring. Until I got to the box under the bed, that is. That held a nice variety of porno mags—nothing unusual though.

I dug through a wooden box on his dresser that held spare keys, change, a pair of ancient cufflinks, and some golf tees stamped with the names of various clubs. The elves didn't golf. He must have picked up the sport when he'd returned to live with the humans. I'd almost put the box aside when I noticed another small one taped to the back. Prying it free, I removed the lid and pulled out a picture, a lock of hair, and a ribbon. The picture was of a young blond girl, about ten years old, smiling at the camera. Her hair matched the little scrap of blond that accompanied the photo. Flipping it over, I saw a name on the back and a date from ten years ago. Susannah Boschetto. She'd be about twenty years old now by my assessment—jackpot; maybe.

I slipped the picture, the hair and the ribbon into my pocket. Susannah didn't look much like an elf, but that wasn't surprising. Her demon half would have quickly adapted and allowed her to blend in with the other humans, to assume an appearance similar to her human parents or siblings. And she was blond, like the human changeling Nyalla. Everything matched, but there was still a niggle of doubt in my mind. What if Joseph Barakel had a child of his own? Yes, the last names didn't match, but sometimes unmarried women gave their own names to babies. He'd been over here nearly twenty years, and although he wasn't particularly young when he came through the gate, human males often had children in their mid and later years.

I scoured the townhouse, looking for signs of a previous romance as well as signs of a child. Even if they'd been estranged, he still might have childish drawings, pictures, holiday cards. It wasn't likely that his only possession would be one picture, a lock of hair and a ribbon, all tucked away in hiding.

There was nothing. Not one sign of feminine influence in the house—nothing to indicate that at any time, a female had bought him a gift, or had left something of her own there. No scented candles, decorative throw pillows, fashion magazines. The guy's towels didn't even match. Yes, twenty years was a long time, but men didn't just date once with enough passion to have a child, then never again. This man's house screamed eternal, virgin bachelor. Or at least guy-who-only-fucks-prostitutes.

There was nothing to indicate he had a child, either. No notes, letters from college, pictures on the fridge. Susannah Boschetto couldn't have been his daughter. She was someone else. Someone whose identity he needed to hide. Someone he didn't want others to connect to him. He cared enough to keep these small things, but was paranoid enough to hide them away so no one would ever know. I now had a picture, even though it was dated. And I had a name. A name I could match against Wyatt's list of births. A name I could use to pressure Joseph Barakel for information.

He came through the door about six in the evening, dropping his keys and turning a rather alarming shade of gray when he saw me.

"I know your secret, Joseph Barakel. I know about the girl."

He clutched his chest and staggered backward until his rear hit the door. "What girl?" he stammered. "I don't know anything about any girl."

Shit, this guy was a worse liar than I was. I let him have his space, gave him a moment to try and recover his wits.

"The girl, Joseph. Blond looks innocent and childlike, but we know different, don't we? I know all about her. And I know how important she is to you."

His eyes bulged. "I don't know any girl. I work, come home, play golf. I don't know any children at all. No girls."

"There's no need to lie," I said soothingly. The guy was going to stroke out if I wasn't careful. "I know you watched her, but it's all over now. The gig is up."

"I never touched her," he protested. "Never. I didn't do anything. Just talk to her that once. That's all."

"Tell me where she is, Joseph." I took a few slow steps toward him.

His eyes widened. "I don't know where she is."

I showed him the picture. "Susannah? Where is she Joseph? I need to bring her home."

He made a gurgling noise and slid to the floor in convulsions. I stared at him a moment in astonishment. These humans were so fragile. I hadn't even touched the guy. I raced over to him and crammed my energy through his body, trying to stabilize his heart.

"Where Joseph? Where is she?" I insisted.

It was no use. He was thrashing about too much and I was doing more damage than good. His heart beat furiously out of rhythm. Looking up at me, he croaked out "Garage," then went silent as his heart seized and refused to work, despite my intervention.

Fuck. Who knows what kind of weird death thoughts he'd been having. I was certain he wasn't keeping a twenty-year-old co-ed in his garage. He must have been hallucinating about power tools or car repair or something. At least I had a name to go on. That was more than I'd had this morning. A solid lead, at least.

Feeling rather sentimental toward the old guy who had served his elf mistress so well, I tossed a blanket over him, and arranged him in a more comfortable fashion before I left.

Susannah Boschetto. Very soon I'll be returning you to Hel.

~19~

Susannah Boschetto was definitely on Wyatt's list of births, but her parents appeared to have left the area a few years ago. Wyatt reluctantly checked local colleges trying to track down her records while I made us sandwiches.

"There's no A," he mentioned cryptically as he scrolled down a list on his laptop.

"Are you talking to yourself, or me?"

"You. Susannah Boschetto doesn't start with an 'A'—neither her first or second name. I thought you said there was a baby ring with the letter 'A' on it."

I shrugged. "Maybe it was an heirloom. Her grandmother's ring that her parents stuck on her finger. Don't worry about it."

"Remember, you *promised* you wouldn't hurt her unless you proved she was evil." Wyatt paused from his work to meet my eyes. It was the third time he'd said this.

"You said murder, not evil. I can only kill the hybrid if I've proven it has murdered, or if it confesses to murder."

"Or turn her over," Wyatt added. "If she's innocent, you're not going to turn her over to the elves either."

I wailed in frustration. "How the fuck am I supposed to get Haagenti off our backs with you adding all these amendments to our deal?"

"Do you want my help or not?"

"Yes. I'm sorry. I won't turn the hybrid over to the elves or kill it unless I have proof that it has committed murder."

"Can we have sex and get back to this afterward? I'm having trouble concentrating here."

Leethu was definitely contributing to his frustration. I wanted to help him out, but we had a job to do.

"Leethu! Turn it down. We're trying to work here," I shouted upstairs.

She was bored. I caught her in dog form, wiggling her rear end at an interested Boomer when I'd returned from Falls Church. Not that I minded, but it revealed Leethu's frustration. I needed to wrap this up and get her home, not just to get Haagenti off my back, but for her own sanity.

"Can we order pizza?" she shouted back down.

I dialed the number. She'd had sex with every delivery guy this week. We didn't even have to tip them anymore. Last time, the assistant manager had personally delivered our pizza. We had more leftover pizza at our house than I knew what to do with. I eyed the blinking red cabochon on my mirror frame as I placed the order. I hadn't had a chance to check Dar's message or get back to him. I needed to call him as soon as I was sure the pizza sexual relief was on his way.

"Couldn't you get more information out of this Joseph Barakel guy?" Wyatt grumbled. "Even with a name, this is worse than trying to find a needle in a haystack. It's like this girl just vanished. I can't find anything on her; sports mentions from high school, theater, community service, college announcements, engagement notices. Nothing."

I concentrated on putting the finishing touches on our sandwiches, although it seemed kind of silly to be making them with all the pizza in the house and more on the way.

"Unfortunately he didn't provide much information."

"So go back and get more."

"I can't. He stroked out and died before I could find any details on the hybrid's whereabouts."

There was a smack noise as Wyatt slammed shut the laptop lid. "You killed him. After you promised not to. Sam, how am I supposed to trust you! You lie to me, you kill everything that gets in your way. You're like the grim reaper. Like a steamroller of death. You promised me, and you still killed him."

"I didn't kill him. I swear to you Wyatt, he died of natural causes. It was a coincidence that I happened to be there."

"I don't believe you. It's just too convenient that he happens to die right when you're there interrogating him. Did you use your Mean? Scare him to death?"

A demon's Mean reflects our status in the hierarchy, it's kind of a presence—a bullying, intimidating, sort of presence. To humans, a demon's Mean is terrifying. Their instinct is to flee, or to comply with whatever we are demanding so they can then flee. But I hadn't used my Mean on Joseph Barakel. Not even a little.

"No, I didn't use my Mean. I'll admit, it was probably startling to find me in his house when he got home from work, but I wasn't threatening. I kept a well-modulated voice, presented my evidence and asked him where the hybrid was. He admitted to watching the girl, but dropped dead before he could tell me where she was. I swear to you, Wyatt, I didn't kill him."

Wyatt considered my words, his face grim. "All right. I believe you," he said, opening the laptop. He didn't sound like he believed me.

I plopped a sandwich and chips in front of him then answered the door, ushering the pizza delivery guy upstairs. He took the steps two at a time. Obviously he'd been here before.

"I'm going back farther, to see if maybe there was a divorce and a name change or adoption of the girl. That might be why I can't find any later records," Wyatt commented, ignoring the sandwich.

I took the pizza into the kitchen and sat it on the counter, grabbed my sandwich and went back over to sit next to Wyatt. He mumbled, typing while I ate. If he couldn't find any trace of this girl, I'd be shit out of luck. I wondered how much it would cost me to put a hit out on Haagenti. Probably more than I had. There weren't many people who would go up against him. I was so screwed.

"Oh no. No, no, no." Wyatt said, putting his face in his hands.

"What? Did you find her?"

He looked up, shock in his eyes and swiveled the laptop around. A news report from ten years ago about a missing girl, presumed dead. Susannah Boschetto. The picture on the screen was the same one I had in my pocket.

"Oh Sam," Wyatt said softly. "That poor little elf girl. Her mother sent her here to be safe, and she didn't make it past ten years."

"Maybe this is part of the cover-up. Maybe Joseph Barakel moved her from the parents' home to another, or maybe even raised her himself, to keep her safe." Maybe I was grasping at straws.

Wyatt shook his head sadly, and hit a button on the laptop. The screen flashed to another article. Joseph Barakel, suspected in the disappearance of ten-year-old Susannah Boschetto, questioned.

"He couldn't have raised her himself. The police would have found out. He was their main suspect."

"We need to find the corpse," I told Wyatt. "Did the police ever find the body? If not, Barakel said 'garage' before he died. I thought he was just rambling, but maybe the kid is buried in a garage somewhere?"

Wyatt nodded and turned his attention back to the laptop while I walked numbly over to my mirror to call Dar. Why did I feel so horrible? I should be elated. Wyatt could find the burial site, and I'd return the child's remains to Hel. Job completed, Haagenti dead, and all without violating Wyatt's increasingly strict ethical parameters. But I wasn't happy. I kept thinking of a ten-year-old child, murdered. Hybrids were considered the equivalent of animals, but I'd started thinking of her as a sister demon. A little girl who'd never discovered who she was, who never realized her abilities. Her life cut short. I mourned, and it was a weird feeling.

"Mal, I found the demon who has been delivering the messages, or rather, he found me," Dar announced proudly. "He wouldn't give me information on where to find Joseph Barakel, but I'm having him followed."

"It doesn't matter Dar. Joseph Barakel died today, and it looks like the elf baby died ten years ago."

"Mal, that can't be," Dar protested. "He's been sending regular notes about the girl. Why would he keep up the charade for ten years?"

"I don't know. Maybe he was scared the mother would have him killed or order him back?"

"Still, I've got something I need to deliver to you; something from the elf woman. That's how I found the demon who's been doing the back and forth. He contacted me to get this to you. It's a letter."

"Well, read it." I wasn't expecting it to tell me anything important.

"I can't. It's warded so only you can open it. I'll send a messenger over with it tomorrow."

"Sam, I've got it," Wyatt shouted.

"Dar, I've gotta go. I'll call you when I get your note."

I raced over to look at Wyatt's laptop. There was another newspaper article showing grim-faced police escorting a body shrouded in plastic on a gurney. Susannah Boschetto found in the garage bay of an abandoned service station. She'd been missing a week by the time they'd found her body. There was evidence of sexual assault and death by blunt trauma to the head.

"Sam, she's dead." Wyatt was furious. "She was a little girl, an innocent child. You said she would be an abomination, a hybrid monster who'd likely be killing humans right and left, and yet she was weak enough to be kidnapped, raped and killed by a human? At ten years old? How could she possibly have been a monster when she couldn't even defend herself against her attacker?"

"I don't know, Wyatt." I shook my head, perplexed. "She should have had basic skills. This shouldn't have happened. Maybe he surprised her and knocked her out first? Raped and killed her before she regained consciousness?"

I felt a twinge of unfamiliar grief and anger. If she'd known she was an elf, known her demon heritage, if she'd been schooled the slightest bit in any of her skills, she might have been able to defend herself. She wouldn't have died. I was sad, thinking of what she could have been. I wondered about the abilities she would have had. Just ten years old. A good percentage of demons made it to fifty, even with our high rate of childhood death. She hadn't even made it past a decade.

But she was dead, and there was nothing to be done about that.

"Can you find out where she was buried?" I asked Wyatt.

He hesitated and took a deep breath. "Yes. But that's it, Sam—the last thing I'm doing for you. I'm not looking up any more information on these births, no more on any Joseph Barakel. No more on any humans, or hybrids, or anything. I'm done. No more. There's just too much death in your wake, and I can't keep pretending it's justified."

I met his eyes, but something crashed inside me, aching like a wound in my chest. "Okay."

So there I was, at two in the morning, digging up a corpse. I'd brought Boomer to help, although I'd had to stress several times that he wasn't going to be eating this body. Hellhounds were amazing diggers, and Boomer would make short work of it. I was grateful for his help since I hadn't had much sleep in the last few days. It would have taken me a whole night to hand dig the grave solo. Thirty minutes and Boomer hit the lid of the liner.

Modern cemeteries insist on either a grave liner, or a vault for all burials. Their use makes landscaping much easier as the ground doesn't settle as much, the body decomposition is less likely to affect the ground cover, and the casket lid won't be crushed by the repetitive traffic of heavy grounds maintenance equipment. It made grave robbing much more difficult. In the olden days, the wooden casket lid would be rotted and splintered by the weight of the ground above. Dig, pry some spongy wood away, then grab the remains. Now, after all the digging, I'd have to blast off a sealed, heavy, concrete, metal-reinforced lid from a tightly confined space.

I'd been dreading we'd find the child buried deep in a vault. Although not guaranteed to be sealed off from all the natural elements, vaults were over two inches thick, wire reinforced, and often lined in plastic. They were built to last for centuries. They lids were sealed tight, usually with tar, requiring a jackhammer to smash through to the casket inside. Boomer could get through one, but the noise was deafening, and we'd both be covered in white dust within moments. A huge percentage of graves had the dreaded vault, so I was ecstatic to see a simple liner on this one.

I shimmied my way into the musty grave, and managed to wedge myself sideways enough to loop the metal cable I'd brought through the liner's top's ring. Thankfully they made these things with rings or handles attached so excavations wouldn't be impossibly difficult. People did relocate loved ones, and the occasional forensic investigation required an exhumation.

Boomer helped me out of the hole by dragging me out by my arms, soaking them in drool and grave dirt.

The Hellhound grabbed the end of the steel cable with both of his jaws and pulled, neck muscles corded and straining. There was a faint crack, and the liner top popped free from the grave in a shower of soil. I looked over the edge. The coffin was a beautiful thing, white, even after years in the ground, with barely faded pink roses carved along the top.

"Just lift the lid."

Easier said than done. Caskets are sealed before burial with a line of adhesive in the tight fitting groove that joins the lid to the base. The pretty brass latches along the side and matching hinges in the back were nothing to that adhesive. I swear at the end of times, when the world becomes a fiery ball of death, that adhesive will still be intact, strong as ever. I was glad I'd brought Boomer. The hellhound ran a fang around the edge of the casket lid, literally cutting through the top and bypassing the dreaded stuff. Within seconds, he'd pushed the lid up and out of the grave, revealing the remains within.

"I'll hop down and run a scan. I'll probably just take the head. It will be easier to transport."

Boomer looked at me with inquiring eyes before leaping out of the grave.

"No, you can't eat the rest of her. We may need to come back." Who knows if that crazy elf lord would want the whole thing.

I climbed in. I'm not squeamish, but I was glad to see the liner hadn't been one of those air-tight vaults that keep all the anaerobic nasties on the inside and the scavengers on the outside of the coffin. I didn't relish having to slosh around in a sea of liquid, smearing it all over the seats of my Suburban. At least I'd had the forethought to bring the SUV instead of my Corvette. Boomer always made a slobbery mess of my upholstery, and I had a feeling I'd be bringing a head back with me. Not something I wanted up close and personal in a little sports car.

There was a moderate musty-sweet smell of old decomposition, but the body wasn't as far along as I had expected. Skin stretched tight, blond hair still curled with ribbons. Such a waste. I reached down and sent tendrils of myself into the body, checking for demon energy and traces of elf genetic material. Frowning, I sent more of my energy in, but found nothing. This child was human: one-hundred percent human.

I pulled back and looked down at the body, perplexed. Had Joseph Barakel taken the identity of the elf baby to his grave? Or perhaps the other Joseph Barakel had been the correct one, the guy who had died a few weeks back. Either way, they were both beyond my questioning at this point. I was back to having to weed my way through over twelve thousand names. Unless Dar could manage to get something from the demon postman that would lead us to the child, I was screwed. I thought about going back and fighting Haagenti, like Gregory kept insisting. I didn't want to do it. But I might not have a choice.

~20~

Dar's messenger never made it to my house the next morning, but Gregory did. He actually rang the bell at my front door and handed me an envelope, pushing past me to walk into my living room.

"What's this?" I asked. It looked like a party invitation.

"A demon was killed while coming through the gate at Columbia Mall last night. He had this on him. It survived his transmutation, and it is warded to be opened only by you."

"You killed Dar's messenger?" I was pissed. "You let every piece of shit Haagenti sends to kill me through, but you kill a messenger sent by my own household?"

Gregory shrugged. "Demons are not allowed in this realm as stipulated by the treaty. We make every attempt to dispatch all who violate the law, but an occasional one does slip through."

"Occasional my ass. Wyatt killed one last night while I was out digging up a body, er, I mean, doing important Iblis duties. Your gate guardian couldn't catch that Low piece of shit, but Wyatt took him out with a forty-five?"

"We both have experienced firsthand what an excellent aim your human toy has. Oh, and I wanted to compliment you on the very effective barrier around his home. Eloa was quite impressed."

"Michelle's aunt did it," I admitted. "She's some kind of priestess. Unfortunately it doesn't keep demons from lobbing shit at Wyatt's house, or trying to set it on fire."

Gregory nodded. He'd picked up my report and was paging through it. "Hmmm, yes. That is a significant design flaw. I like how you addressed the deceased's lack of artistic sensibility in this report. Raphael will be particularly sympathetic to that point."

Oh good. At least someone on the Ruling Council would vote in my favor. I had no doubt where the others would stand.

"So I expect your next four-nine-five report tomorrow?"

What the fuck was he talking about? "Why would I do another one? That one is for the serial killer I had Boomer take out this fall. I didn't kill the teenagers in Pennsylvania. Do I need to do one because I fantasized about killing someone? I hope not, or I'll be doing these stupid reports every few hours."

The report vanished from his hands. No doubt it was already being delivered, in triplicate, to the other council members.

"They are only required for actual killings, not imagined ones. I'm referring to the human in Northern Virginia that you killed. I believe his name was Bagel or something."

"Joseph Barakel." I was sure Gregory knew his name. That angel knew everything, omnipotence aside. He was just fucking with me.

"Yes, yes. That's the one. Please have the four-nine-five report in my hands by tomorrow midnight. That should be more than enough time."

"I didn't kill him," I protested. "He stroked out in front of me. I never laid a hand on him. I didn't even get to serious threats. It wasn't my fault."

"Still, he died as a direct result of your presence. Tomorrow midnight is your deadline."

I tossed my party invitation on the table, and marched over to the angel. "Fuck you. I am not doing that fucking report for a guy I didn't fucking kill." I punctuated my words with a finger on his chest.

"Tomorrow. Midnight."

And he vanished. Asshole.

I picked up the note the dead messenger had been carrying and checked it out. Pretty, cream doeskin parchment with no name or address. The paper had been folded into thirds and sealed with a wax sigil that burned as I ran my finger over it. The characters in the wax danced with a spray of gold glitter, and the seal released. The writing inside was angelic script in gold. The elves had their own language, but the sender had kindly written in mine, no doubt in case I didn't read Elvish.

Greetings to the Distinguished Iblis from Tlia-Myea of the Glorious Kingdom of Cyelle,

I was most distraught at our meeting, and uncertain that I conveyed all the information I had regarding my shameful actions. When I saw that I had given birth to demon spawn, I had the baby killed and submitted as a changeling. I had the demon I sent to accompany my human kill him after he made the baby exchange, to avoid any future blackmail. I purposefully remained unaware of the demon spawn's destination, but recently, information has come to light that may help you support my claims.

I was certain the baby had been transferred to human foster parents alive. Otherwise she wouldn't need a demon to communicate back and forth. Why was she going to all this bother to send me a note re-iterating the lies she'd told me before?

There is a child buried in Mount Olivet cemetery, in Frederick, Maryland. That child is elf born. I'm positive with your skills you can find that baby. I'm certain that as the baby is presented to my Lordship, it will be discovered to have demon energy signatures. Although I am facing death, my family will be joyous that the deceased demon spawn has been found, and the matter put to rest forever.

I only longed for a child to love. A child I could protect with all the ferocity of motherhood. As a mother, I would have done anything for my child, given my life to protect her, cursed with my dying breath any who would do her harm.

I am grateful for your service to my Kingdom and my Family,
Tlia-Myea

I stared at the letter—a carrot and a stick, all embedded in the flowery language of the elves that led to so many misunderstandings among our kind. I'd learned to read between the lines though, and I could understand her need to be obscure, in case the message was intercepted and the ward broken. The baby was clearly alive. Hidden away somewhere, safe to live a human life. She'd offered me a way out. A dead elf changeling baby buried nearby that I could dig up and present, if I could somehow alter it to make it appear part demon. And in return for my participation in the deception, I'd earn the gratitude of her family. A dead woman could grant no favors, but elves would always honor a family member's request. And then there was the stick. The little paragraph at the end, basically letting me know that if I were to find her half-breed daughter, and lead her to harm, she would curse me. Elf curses were not something to be taken lightly. And a curse could not be lifted once the caster died. I'd just have to live with it forever.

"Leethu," I shouted up the stairs. "Can you come down a second?"

Leethu raced down the stairs like her pants were on fire. They probably were. I don't think there were enough pizza delivery guys in the tri-state area to satisfy her at this point.

"The elf maiden you fucked and impregnated, Tlia-Myea, who is she? What family connections does she have?" Leethu would know. Demons don't bother much with family history, but Succubi have always kept track of that sort of thing. They are master manipulators, and knowing family connections helps in blackmail.

"Oh she is well connected, Ni-ni. I would not have impregnated just any old elf, although I would have been happy to have sexual relations with any of them or their humans. Her mother was a half-sister to a previous Lord of Cyelle, and her father was a member of the court of Wythyn."

"A cross kingdom mating?" I was surprised. "But the kingdoms generally dislike each other and think that the others are beneath them. Why would they cross breed?"

"Oh it happens all the time," Leethu assured me. "It keeps the gene pool from becoming overly inbred. They do have diplomatic dealings with each other and invite notable individuals to social events. Even the lower-ranking elves will negotiate to do some skills exchanges with other kingdoms. There is no shame in having sexual relations with an elf from another kingdom, and the joy of birth overcomes all prejudices."

"She was clearly raised in Cyelle. Identifies herself as a member of that kingdom. Would she have pull with her father's family in Wythyn?" If so, maybe this connection could help me get my horse back.

"Oh yes. Elf children are raised in the highest-ranking parent's household, but they are still beloved by the other parent's family. This kind of thing helps solidify alliances between kingdoms and can prevent war if conflicts arise. No one wants to risk the chance of killing his or her offspring."

This was looking better and better. But there was one thorny problem to address.

"Say I want to make something dead look like a hybrid. A dog or something. Any ideas on how I might do that?"

That shrewd look flashed across Leethu's face, reminding me she was far more intelligent than she appeared. Succubi were always considered dim bulbs, beautiful, sexually appealing, fragile, with the mental abilities of a box of rocks. They worked that perception to their advantage.

"That would depend on who you need to convince," she replied. "Slap some horns on it and the humans will be calling in their exorcists. Drive a bit of your personal energy in it and it will pass a casual scan by demons, elves, vampires, and possibly werewolves, although they would be the most difficult to fool."

Her innocent eyes were contrasted by the smug smile. "Okay, what's the hitch?" I asked.

"A really good demon scan, really deep, will reveal the deception. Most demons are sloppy and lazy. They'll just take it on face value. You would notice, Ni-ni. You are curious and greedy for sensation and knowledge. You would sense it right away." She paused for effect, and I obligingly waited, hanging on her every breath. "Sorcerers would be a problem."

Sorcerers. Fuck.

"So, they have a spell that can reveal a body was altered after its death?" I asked.

"No. Not as far as I know, but they do have a spell that can tell if the composition is not according to natural law."

I was pretty sure this High Lord wouldn't take my word for it if I showed up with a dead baby. He'd have his own people check. And I had no idea how hybrids were composed, let alone anything about "natural law".

"Of course, human embalming and preservation techniques can interfere with spell results," Leethu continued. "Much of human technology and their medical treatments interferes with spell results. Demon energy is complimentary to human endeavors, but elf magic is not. It is a vexing problem for the elves. Their sorcerers are very useful in Hel, but, increasingly, the humans in this realm can disrupt their magic. That is one of the reasons the elves are partnering more and more with demons."

Holy shit. Leethu was a wealth of information.

"How do you know all this?"

Leethu smiled her enigmatic, Asian smile. "I have always enjoyed the company of elves."

I felt a chill creep across my skin. I was beginning to think Leethu was a good ally to have.

"I took the liberty of inviting a few of those delivery men over today. I hope you approve?"

"Yes, of course." Anything to keep Leethu occupied. An orgy in my guest bedroom was a small price to pay.

Leethu danced up the stairs to prepare for her visitors, while I pondered my situation. The succubus' assurances aside, I sincerely doubted either of us could stuff enough energy into a twenty-year-old elf corpse to make it appear half demon. And I seriously doubted either of us had the skill to do it in a way that the elves would believe. It might be worth a shot though. If we could pull off the deception, I'd get Haagenti off my back, ask a grateful elf family to assist in getting my horse back from Wythyn, and stave off a nasty curse.

My luck never went that way though. Chances were good the fake would be discovered. I'd have two enraged elf lords after my ass along with Haagenti. I'd still be minus my horse, and that fucking elf woman would probably still curse me.

I indulged in a moment of self-pity. My leads had all dried up. Wyatt refused to help me further, and there was no way I'd be able to sort through and check over twelve thousand young women for demon energy. This whole thing was a bust, and I was facing certain death at Haagenti's hands. Why was this happening to me? I'd been a good imp. I didn't deserve all this shit raining down on my head. Had my ever-present luck finally deserted me? Packed her bags and left for greener pastures? Everything I touched lately went wrong. If only the fates would shine on me once more. If only they'd send that elf-hybrid to my house like a present with a big bow on her head, I'd never ask for anything else in my entire life.

My doorbell rang, and I jumped, thinking for a moment the fates were delivering on my prayer. Then I laughed, remembering Leethu's posse of delivery men. Let the orgy begin! Smiling, I opened the door. Instead of a posse of delivery guys, I saw a young woman.

She had golden blond hair with cobalt blue eyes. Olive pants and a form fitting, button-down shirt highlighted her perfect figure. Her features were oddly symmetrical. She had a kind of aloof appeal, like a queen, or a big name movie-star. I could imagine people trailing around after her, wanting to please her, but remaining at a respectful distance. She smiled at me, and I felt the slight pull of attraction, a hint of pheromones.

"Ack." It was the only sound I could get out of my mouth. I just stood there, like an idiot, with the door half open. I couldn't think. I couldn't speak. I couldn't politely invite her into my house. I could only stand there and stare.

There was an elf at my door.

~21~

An elf *hybrid* at my door, that is. She didn't have a bow on her head, but clearly this was some kind of divine gift. The fates were taking pity on my plight and sending me a get-out-of jail-free-card. No digging up dead babies and trying to rig them up to look like hybrids. I had the real thing right in front of me. I could whack her on the head and have her delivered to that elf Lord lickety split.

"Hi, you must be Sam. I'm Wyatt's sister, Amber."

My thoughts came to a screeching halt. This could *not* be happening. I couldn't exactly brain Wyatt's sister and drag her carcass off to the elves. He'd never forgive me. Maybe she could meet with an unfortunate accident. One involving a truck. One where I had a convenient alibi.

Shit. I promised Wyatt. And this girl in front of me hardly looked like a murderer. There had to be something she'd done in her past. Maybe hit a deer with her car? Wasn't murder, but maybe it was close enough.

"Ack," I said again. I couldn't seem to communicate.

Amber smiled, apologetic and absolutely charming. "I'm so sorry to just show up like this. I know you've been very busy, but I'm returning to college tomorrow and I really wanted to meet you before I left."

Shit. She was leaving tomorrow. What the heck was I going to do? Here was my salvation, right in front of me, but she was Wyatt's *sister*. There was no way he would be on board with this, no way I could possibly convince him to turn her over to Taullian. He'd never believe her to be a murderer, a monster.

"Ack," I replied.

"Wyatt talks about you all the time. He's very fond of you. I've never seen him like this with someone before." Amber was graciously ignoring my rudeness and lack of verbal skills—clearly the elf part of her heritage.

I was debating the wisdom of inviting her in versus sending her away when I heard car tires on my gravel road. Crap. Leethu's orgy participants were arriving. I couldn't have them see Amber, couldn't risk that they'd tell Leethu, or that the Succubus herself would discover the elf hybrid. I wouldn't put it past her to just lop the girl's head clean off.

"Come in, come in." I grabbed her by the arm and practically dragged her into the house, slamming the door as the compact car full of horny young men pulled into my driveway.

I heard footsteps upstairs. "Is that my party?" Leethu called down.

Oh shit. Shit, shit.

"You … uh, you need to get into this closet and just stay really quiet for a bit."

I didn't wait for the inevitable protest. I grabbed Amber and shoved her in, slamming the door in her face. Leethu's footsteps danced down the stairs, full of eager anticipation.

"Stay there," I called to her. "I'll let them in and send them up."

Fuck, this was all starting to resemble a 70's sitcom. The doorbell rang and I opened it, fully expecting to see Mr. Furley at the door. Instead I saw four men, varying in age from eighteen to thirty, all with the biggest ear-splitting grins I'd ever seen. I hoped the one was eighteen. I wouldn't put it past

Leethu to be bonking a minor. It's not like human laws really applied to her anyway.

"Oh good, you're here," Leethu said. She was standing right behind me, clearly ignoring my edict to stay upstairs. I closed my eyes and prayed with all my might to whatever mythical deity listened to demons that Amber would stay quiet in the closet, and that Leethu and her harem would make a quick retreat up the stairs.

"Should I put on a pot of coffee and bring out a cheesecake?" Leethu asked. "Would anyone like a beer or a glass of wine? Perhaps some nachos?"

What the hell? She was a succubus, not Paula Deen. She was supposed to fuck these people, not play hostess.

The men crowded around Leethu eagerly. Of course, the underage one wanted a beer, and a couple seemed interested in nachos. How long could I keep Amber in the closet? I should have knocked her out first, just to make sure she didn't get impatient and come crashing out.

I raced into the kitchen and grabbed a roasting pan, filling it with beer, bags of chips, and plopping the cheesecake on top.

"Here," I thrust it at a surprised Leethu. "Take it upstairs. Have them eat it off you, drink beer out of your belly button or something. Hurry, hurry. Let's get this party started, folks."

Leethu seemed particularly intrigued by the food sex idea and made her way upstairs, a line of horny men trailing after. I waited until she was safely in the bedroom before I opened the closet door to let Amber out. She stared at me in shock, her hair a tangle of gold after being crushed in between the winter coats. It's pretty difficult to unnerve an elf. I'd need to remember that stuffing them in a closet usually works.

"Why am I in a closet?" She didn't sound angry, which I'd expected. Instead, she seemed curious and rather amused. No doubt her demon half coming through.

"My sister is here, visiting, and she's having a bunch of pizza delivery guys over for an orgy. Thought it was best if they didn't see you."

Her eyes got huge. They were very expressive. "Why? What would they do if they saw me?"

I shuddered dramatically. "You don't want to know. Let's go out to the barn and we can chat there." *I can figure out how I'm going to handle this impossible situation,* I thought.

I grabbed a six-pack of beer off the counter and led Amber out the French doors, past the winterized pool and patio, and into the barn. There, I invited her to sit on a hay bale, popped open a beer for her, and began looking around for a useful tool just in case she confessed to offing eight fraternity brothers and burying them under her crawl space. There had to be a sturdy shovel somewhere

Amber drank the beer. She clearly wasn't a stickler for the law, but then again, neither demons nor elves were particularly lawful races.

"So, Wyatt has told you about me? That I'm basically the devil?" I tried to make conversation as I looked around for an appropriate weapon and pondered how I'd get her to confess to something I could reasonably consider "murder".

Amber made an exasperated noise. "Why is it that assertive women, women who are successful in a male-dominated society are always labeled bitches, demons, and devils? If you were a man with a lucrative rental empire, a mid-life-crisis sports car, and a much younger piece of eye-candy on your arm, everyone would be congratulating you and patting you on the back. But because you're a woman, you're Satan?"

I halted in my search, wincing at her depiction. "Yes, but I really am. The Iblis. Ha-satan."

Amber waved her hand dismissively. "Every successful individual has had to make tough decisions. As much as we'd like the world to be filled with peace, love, and a cornucopia of plenty, it's not. You don't have to live with that label though."

"Yeah, actually I do. I don't want it, but I've got the title and all the stupid responsibilities that go along with it. Meetings with assholes, four-nine-five reports, people who want my head on a platter."

Boomer came into the barn and made a beeline for Amber, rubbing himself all over her and looking at her with adoring hound eyes. I wavered in my resolve, watching her as she petted the dog. She didn't seem like a demon hybrid. Maybe Leethu had done the impossible, maybe she truly would pass as an elf.

"You need a vacation," Amber said. She had noooo fucking idea how badly I needed a vacation.

"Does your brother know you're here?" I had a sudden thought, a worry that Wyatt would walk in on us as I killed her. If I killed her. She smiled at me and my heart sank. She'd probably never murdered even a mouse in her life.

"No. I stopped by to see him before I came to your place, but I can't seem to get in. It's weird. It's like he has some kind of invisible wall around his house."

I laughed. I couldn't help myself; the whole thing was so funny. Of course. She was half demon. She couldn't go through the barrier. Wyatt had inadvertently locked his own sister out of his house.

"Hey, did my house smell particularly good to you? Sort of sexy?" I grabbed a beer and sat down on another hay bale.

"Well, yeah. But I figured that was because you were having a sex party. Maybe incense? Or one of those pheromone sprays, like elk musk or something."

Amber fingered the top of her beer can awkwardly. "What does your sister look like? I mean, not that I swing that way or anything. Because I don't, you know. She just … her accent. Well, you know…." Her voice trailed off in embarrassment.

I laughed again. Didn't swing that way. Yeah, right. Liar.

"Leethu is gorgeous. She likes women as well as men." And dogs, and cats, and birds, and anything she can get her little paws on. But then again, so did I.

Amber's face turned crimson as she turned away. I took a swig of my beer and watched her—a demon/elf hybrid. There had never been one before her. What power did she have? Elf magic? Demon energy? All wasted inside someone who thought they were nothing but a human woman.

"Look, you're not who you think you are. Don't restrict yourself to the narrow confines of what defines humanity. Just go with it. Let that amazing, terrifying, powerful being inside you reveal itself." I had no idea why I was telling her all this.

She glanced at me and took a deep breath, as if she were making an important decision. "I can't. If I do, I'll kill someone."

"Yep," I agreed, taking a swig of my beer. "Some people need killing, though." Maybe she was more demon than I had originally thought.

"I'm not joking," she protested. "I'm responsible for my father's death. It would be so easy for me to do it again."

Ah yes. Wyatt's father had been electrocuted while putting in a line for a dryer. Amber had been a very young witness. She'd blamed herself for the death. Wait. Oh fuck no. No way.

"You shot a lightning bolt at your father." A statement. Because I knew very well what had happened, and it had nothing to do with household appliances.

She startled, looking at me as if I were a mind-reader then slowly nodded, her eyes wide with fear and grief. "He was always so mean to Wyatt. Wyatt adored him, and he treated my brother like dirt. That day, I just snapped. It came right out of me: a bolt of electricity. And I kept pouring it into him until I was sure he was dead."

"It's okay," I reassured her. "These things happen all the time. No big deal."

Holy shit! She *had* murdered—a human, too. And not just any human; Wyatt's father. She was just like every other hybrid, just like I expected. By Wyatt's rules, I'd be justified in killing her. Worry gnawed at me. Even with the confession, Wyatt might not agree, and Wyatt aside, I was conflicted myself. Part of me was elated, but another part didn't want to see her die. Lightning. What else could she do? What other skills did she have?

"You don't believe me." She rose to her feet, angry.

"Watch." She walked over to the barn door and raised her hand. Lightning streaked from her palm and blew a huge chunk off the elm in the pasture. Smoke and pulverized wood filled the air as the limb crashed to the ground. Piper and Vegas raced around the field in a panic, bucking frantically in their efforts to escape the killer tree limb.

"Damn. I rather liked that tree. Although I guess it did need pruning."

"Did you not see what I did?" Amber rounded on me. I half expected a bolt of lightning to come my way any second. "I just blew up a section of a tree."

"Sweetie, I've been doing that from the moment I was born. Do you want me to blow up the other half? Would that make you feel any better?"

She looked confused. "So, you're just like me?"

"Well, not exactly. You're only part demon."

She looked pale. "A demon? I'm a demon? Is Wyatt one too? Which one of my parents was?"

"Nope. Wyatt's human. He's not biologically your brother, but honestly, demons don't care about that sort of thing. He's still your brother as far as we're concerned. It's kind of complicated. You were placed with your human parents, swapped out for their human baby—kind of like foster care, only they weren't aware of it."

Amber shook her head in confusion. "So was my birth mother a demon? My father?"

"With hybrids, the father is always the demon. We are genderless, but we can impregnate a female of any species. So your sire was the demon."

"Why didn't my birth mother raise me?"

I patted her on the shoulder. "See, that's the problem. The demon part of you is no big deal. Lots of humans have demon somewhere in their ancestry. Hybrids don't have a lot of power, so the angels don't make too much of a fuss. Your mother is the problem. She's an elf."

Amber's eyebrows practically hit the ceiling. "Okay. Now I'm thinking you're crazy. There are no such things as elves. Not in the North Pole, not in hollow trees making shortbread. No elves."

"Right. There are no elves here. That's part of the issue. The elves live in Hel, side by side with the demons. They don't take kindly to mixing the gene pool. Your elf mother tucked you safely away over here so her friends and family wouldn't kill you."

We'd gone from "wow, I'm a demon," to "wow, my brother's girlfriend is insane." Amber was beginning to regard me like she needed to shoot me full of electricity and make a break for it.

"You know, it was really nice meeting you. Very enlightening. Look at the time. I really need to get going, and I'm sure you want to get back to your orgy."

Amber edged slowly toward the door. I'd found a shovel, and snatched it up, blocking her exit. I couldn't let her leave until I'd decided what to do.

"The circumstances of your birth leaked out, and your elf mother is now in prison. The elves want you dead, your body returned so they can cover it all up."

She halted, her eyes wary, hands twitching by her side. "You're crazy. Insane. Mother was right. I should have never come here."

I ran a hand through my hair. "You seem like a nice girl, and with you being Wyatt's sister and all . . . I really don't want to kill you, but it's better I kill you than take you back to the elves for them to do it."

"Don't do it," she begged, her voice soft and persuasive, the pheromones flowing. "Just let me go."

I wavered. I wanted to let her go, and it had nothing to do with the faint succubi-like essence. There was a reason I was staying my hand, and I just couldn't figure out why.

Amber took advantage of my moment of inattention and shot me with a bolt of electricity that would have killed a human. Instinctively I swung the shovel, but instead of hitting her it swooshed through the air throwing me off balance and numbing my arm as it rang against the barn wall. She was fast. Damned elves. As if that wasn't enough, she hit me with another huge blast of electricity.

"Ouch! Bitch! Cut it out!"

Amber flitted around the barn at a ridiculous speed. "Seriously? You want me to hold still while you bash my brains out? Not likely."

She continued to shoot painful volts into my flesh while I attempted to deflect them with the shovel. They wouldn't kill me, but it really fucking hurt. Finally I tossed the shovel aside and prepared to launch my own energy at her. I really didn't want to, but I wasn't about to run around with a shovel while she cooked my ass. Luckily I hit with the first strike, and she dropped down from the rafters with a shriek. Before she could recover, I was on her, trying to hold her steady.

"Just calm down and listen to me," I shouted as she struggled, continuing to send small sparks into my skin.

"No," she snarled, and I saw the demon behind the elf.

Amber was panicked, desperate. She'd murdered once, and I knew she'd do it again. There would come a time when she would lose control, and people would die. But when I looked into her eyes I saw the threads of her future before me, like a cobweb of possibilities. Spots glowed, highlighted, and I knew there were significant things this supposed abomination should do. If I killed her, all that would disappear, perhaps taken up by another, or perhaps lost forever.

I made my decision. I don't know what happened as I straddled her, but something bloomed up inside me. Killing her would be wrong. I couldn't do it even if she had murdered Wyatt's father, even if she were predisposed to kill again. I couldn't sacrifice this girl in order to avoid confronting Haagenti. Her life for mine? I couldn't do it.

With that realization came a surge of despair. Haagenti. I had no way out, no option left but to face him, and face what would certainly be my death. I knew what the probable outcome would be. It was time to say goodbye to my long vacation. Goodbye to Wyatt and my friends, and face the end of my life like a big girl.

I loosened my grip to let Amber go, only to feel something hard smash into my side, knocking me off her.

"Son of a bitch," I exclaimed, fixing the broken ribs as I looked up. It was Wyatt. And he was pissed.

"Sam, why are you pinning down my sister?"

I'd never seen Wyatt look this way at me. Cold, furious, suspicious. He held my discarded shovel, ready to smack me again. He'd always trusted me, supported me in all my demon weirdness. He'd helped me kill demons, broken all kinds of Internet security laws for me, shot an angel in the head to protect me. He was the one being I trusted to always back me up, no matter how crazy things got. But he'd found me struggling with his sister, and all that had fallen away.

"I wasn't," I stammered. "I mean, I thought about it, but I decided not to. I'm not Wyatt. I won't do it."

"Wyatt, she's trying to kill me," Amber wailed, jumping up and running to hide behind her brother. She was working the faint succubus pheromones as well for the helpless little sister angle.

"I can't kill her, Wyatt," I told him. I was miserable that he needed to know. "But you need to know that she's the hybrid. I realized it the moment I saw her."

Wyatt was stunned. He shook his head. "No. I was there when they brought her home from the hospital. I saw her grow up. You're wrong."

"Check the list, Wyatt. I'm sure she's on it. She can't get into your house. She can't get past the demon barrier. I had to hide her from Leethu. It's her."

"I won't let you kill her," Wyatt said, his voice firm with resolve. "She's my sister, and she's done nothing wrong. You promised me, Sam. You promised me you wouldn't kill the hybrid unless she'd murdered. How could you betray my trust like this?"

"She did kill, Wyatt. She murdered your father. Electricity. You've seen me create lightning. Well, your sister can too."

Wyatt shook his head again, and turned to look at his sister, who was still cowering behind him. "No. It was accident. Wasn't it Amber?"

She looked at the ground, squirming under his scrutiny. "I was just a child, Wyatt. He was mean. I haven't done it since."

I would have done anything to have spared Wyatt the pain that shot across his face. "He wasn't mean, Amber. Yes, he had his faults, but he was a wonderful father, and I loved him. How could you kill him? Our own father."

Tears glistened in the girl's beautiful eyes. "I was five, Wyatt. Five. You saw how devastated I was afterwards, how many years of counseling I went through."

He stared down at her, weighing her words. "I won't let you kill her, Sam. Or turn her over to the elves. No matter what she's done, she's still my sister. I'll live my whole life with that stupid barrier, killing off Haagenti's thugs. Tell them you couldn't find her. I don't care what you tell them, you're not taking my sister."

I ran my hands through my hair. There was no good way to say any of this.

"Wyatt, I swear to you I'm not going to kill her. I planned on it, but I'm not now. There's a bigger problem, though. Don't you see? The elves won't give up. Others will come to track her down, and it's a miracle no one has discovered her so far. Any demon that gets within twenty feet of her can tell. A werewolf a mile downwind can tell. And if she stumbles across a vampire? They'll be on her faster than a fat man on a Hot Pocket."

I took a few steps toward Wyatt, wanting to wrap my arms around him, wanting to rub my face against his chest and smell his warm, human smell. He backed up, brandishing the shovel, and something inside me broke. Oh please no. Not this.

Amber peeked out from behind her brother. "Is she telling the truth? Am I really some kind of elf/demon freak? I'll be walking down the street one day, minding my own business, and someone is going to jump me and rip me apart?"

"I'll protect you," Wyatt said desperately. "You'll be okay."

"How, Wyatt?" I asked. "She can't get in your house; she's half demon. Are you going to seal her up in a vault somewhere? Hidden away, safe from everyone? What kind of life is that? Death would be better."

"You're just saying that to save your own skin," Wyatt snapped. "I know how you are, Sam. I love you, but I'm not blind. Kill her, turn her over to the elves, and get Haagenti off your back. It's quick, it's easy, and you won't consider any other alternative that might actually take effort or possibly put your own self at risk."

"I'm not going to kill her! Not killing her. Not, not, not!" I yelled.

His accusations were really unfair. I'd put myself at risk over and over for him. I'd put my neck out for Candy, for Dar, and for a bunch of smelly homeless people that I didn't even know. But I understood. He'd discovered horrible truths about the little sister he loved, found me straddling her as she tried to fight me off. It was a shock, and right now I looked a lot like the villain. Heck, maybe I was.

"Then consider some alternatives. Help me think of a way to keep her safe. For me."

I'd do anything for Wyatt. Attack an ancient angel to protect him, fight off a hoard of assassin demons, kill my own brother if need be. I'd help him protect his sister, and then I would turn myself over to Haagenti for probable execution. Wyatt would finally be safe.

"I'm listening." I sat down on a hay bale and opened another beer. "Bring on the alternatives."

Wyatt looked bleak. "Maybe Candy can hide her with one of her werewolf packs. No one would think to look for her there. And they can defend her against any humans or demons the elves send."

"Would they risk violating their existence contract over this?" I asked him softly. "She's part succubus. How long could a young werewolf resist her? How long before she falls in love with one of them?"

Wyatt's face fell. He was clearly desperate, out of options.

"Stop discussing me as if I were a package or something," Amber said, stepping out from behind Wyatt. "I'm going back to college tomorrow, going on with my life. I'm not going to live cloistered away in a fortress, or foisted off on people I don't know."

"Sam's right," Wyatt told her. "You've been lucky so far, but you'll be in even more danger now that the elves know about your existence. They'll be looking for you."

I admired her gumption, and I got the feeling she was going to do whatever she wanted, regardless of what either Wyatt or I said.

"Sam, what can we do to convince the elves she's dead?"

I had only one option left, and if it worked, it might solve both our problems. "We need to check and make sure there isn't another Joseph Barakel," I told Wyatt. "If so, then I need to kill him. He's the real risk here, the link that someone can trace to Amber."

"No," Wyatt's voice was firm. "I'm not helping you find and kill another human. I'm not. No more killing humans, Sam."

I bit back my words. His sister's life was on the line, and he wouldn't let me kill this one guy to protect her? I'd never be able to find this guy on my own. I'd better just hope he was already dead of natural causes.

"Okay. I'll try and see if I can get the elves to think she's already dead. I'll dig up an elf baby changeling from the same time frame; try to fake a demon energy signature in the corpse. We might be able to convince the elves that the baby really was dead all along. They'll call off the hunt, and even if someone picks it up again, the trail will lead to a dead end."

Wyatt looked hopeful. "Amber will still need to stay clear of vampires, demons and werewolves, but that will be less of a risk once the elves no longer have a bounty on her head."

I nodded. "I'll give her some ideas on how she can bring her abilities out, so she can better defend herself." If I ever made it back alive from Hel, that is.

"Thank you, Sam," he said, but his words lacked the warmth they'd always had before.

I left them alone and walked back into the house. I'd lied. I was positive the dead elf baby wouldn't pass, that the whole ruse wouldn't work, but I'd give it a shot, do what I could to make sure Amber was safe. I'd do it for Wyatt. Then I'd walk right out into demon lands and face Haagenti. I'd never see Wyatt again, but I wasn't sure how he felt about me after tonight anyway.

~22~

I'd kicked Leethu's harem out the moment I walked through the door, threatening them with evisceration if they weren't gone by the time I counted to ten. I never saw humans move so fast. Leethu went to protest, but the words died on her lips when she saw my face. I locked my bedroom door and spent the entire sleepless night curled in a ball on my bed, missing arms and legs around me. Missing the feel of a heartbeat against my cheek, the tickle of warm breath in my hair. Around three in the morning, I just couldn't' take it anymore. I got up, made a pot of coffee and snuck down the road toward Wyatt's. Boomer had wrapped up his nightly excursions early and trailed after me. The hellhound was perplexed by the barrier around the house and kept bumping against it in an effort to get in. I just sat on the perimeter and stared at the house.

In the living room, pale blue light flashed out the window. Wyatt was awake and playing his video games. I felt better, knowing he was sleepless too. I wished I could go in, tell him I loved him, comfort him, but I knew that given what he'd walked in on in the barn, my presence wouldn't be welcome right now. The cold frost melted under my rear, soaking my jeans. I sat until sunrise. Finally, when the morning light obscured the flashes from the video game, I got up and stiffly made my way home to do the barn chores.

Wyatt must have come over earlier in the night and brought the horses in. I turned them out and mucked the stalls, filling them with fresh shavings and adding a flake of hay and clean water to each. Diablo's stall sat empty, and it added to the horrible sorrow eating through me. Gregory was right, the elves cherished horses and he'd come to no harm with them, but he'd be a prisoner, locked down and forced to comply as a regular horse. I needed to get him back, although once Haagenti was through with me, he'd be without a master. Maybe he was better off with the elves.

What I really needed to do was put the self-pity aside and get to work. I forced myself back into the house and sat my still damp butt down at my dining room table to pursue Wyatt's short-list—the list of babies who had died within the timeframe and area. Fifty-eight babies. Wyatt had listed the city and state of each, so I quickly identified three babies that might possibly have been close enough to have been buried in Mount Olivet. I sincerely hoped it was one of the babies on the list. I'd call the cemetery when they opened, and check out all three names. Everything was closing down on my head so fast, that I really needed this to go smoothly. If I had to search the entire cemetery for a hybrid infant, I'd run out of time. That done, I called Dar.

"Mal, they killed my messenger." Dar was subdued with shock. Demons got killed all the time going through the gate, but this cut close to home.

"I know. Next time I think you'll need to come through yourself. You're better at evading the guardian, and you can defend yourself pretty well."

"That's a problem too. Things here have gotten really bad. Haagenti has a careful watch on the gates and an order to take out anyone of your household. I had to send an unknown guy, someone unaffiliated with you. They'll kill me if I try to get through, and even if I make it, they'll be waiting for me when I return."

Shit. This put a wrinkle in things.

"I swear to you Dar; this is almost over. I just need one more thing, and it's urgent. I need you to contact that demon messenger, the one who has been the go-between from the elf woman and that human. Let him know I've found the dead hybrid baby, and am prepared to bring it back as proof to his Lordship, but I cannot do that unless I have the name and the address of the human servant who did the exchange." Wyatt had forbidden me from killing any more humans, but I really needed to do this to ensure his sister's safety. I'd make sure he never found out. It would be one last gift to him, and if he hated me for it, so be it.

"You found the baby?" Dar was excited. "But I thought she hadn't killed it, that you were looking for a young adult?"

"Baby," I emphasized. "Tell the demon that I verified Tlia-Myea's story and will return with the dead hybrid infant. Tell him that somehow the human escaped death, and is still living here."

"But why?"

"Totally hush, Dar. Tell no one but that demon—stress that I will not be able to bring the remains of the baby back unless I have the name and address of the human. Otherwise, it's not happening."

Dar remained silent.

"Just tell him, exactly like that. And I need the information by tonight. There is to be no negotiation on any of this. Clear?"

"Got it, Mal." Dar disconnected. He loved this kind of cloak and dagger stuff. I had no doubt I'd have my answer by tonight, if not earlier.

I mulled over my schedule. I needed to dispatch the human servant so Amber's existence would be virtually untraceable. Then dig up an elf baby tonight. Leethu and I could work all morning on the corpse, and with any luck I'd be back in the elf lands by tomorrow afternoon. *And dead by evening*, I though cynically. Which left me today to get my things in order.

I'd done this before. Made out power-of-attorneys, lists-of-assets. When I'd gone after Althean for the werewolves this past summer, the chance had been good that I would either be killed or in Hel for the rest of my life. I'd left everything to Wyatt, gave him instructions on where everything was, how to access the safe and the communication mirror. I didn't need to change anything, but with what happened last night, I was worried he wouldn't think to do anything. So I sat down to write.

Wyatt – If you're getting this note, then Haagenti has me and my return will be delayed far past your lifespan.

I didn't have the heart to tell him I'd be dead. Let him think and hope that I lived on.

Everything is still in place for you to assume all my possessions and business interests. Please feel free to enjoy them, or disburse them however you see fit.

Vegas is your horse. I bought him for you and have always considered him a gift. He's a good boy and a lot of my best memories are of us riding together. I hope you can bring yourself to keep him.

I know you doubt me right now, and you have every right. There are things about me that I've always tried to hide from you, things that I knew you couldn't accept. I'm sorry you've seen this part of me, sorry that I've hurt you. Yes, I had intended to kill the elf hybrid, but I just couldn't. She is a hybrid. Hybrids have the same value as an animal. They are often considered to be monsters. And she'd committed murder. Admitted to it.

But in spite of everything, I discovered I couldn't trade her life for mine. And not just her. I realized last night that I could no longer trade anyone's life for mine. Self-defense is one thing, but I can't bring myself to kill a relatively innocent person just to get myself out of trouble. I hope eventually you can believe what I'm telling you. Know that I'm sincere in this.

I love you. I think I'm the only demon that has ever felt that emotion, or maybe I'm just the first to admit it. I love you. You are my most favored human, a being so very precious to me. You are my best friend, my partner in crime. I will never, ever, forget you or what you have meant to me.

Sam

I blotted off the splotchy wet marks and put the letter in an envelope, sealing it and writing Wyatt's name on the front.

"Leethu!" I called.

She bolted down the stairs with surprising speed. I had a sneaking suspicion she had been following me around, watching me since last night. Her face was worried and scared as she searched mine. I handed her the envelope.

"I'm going to try and locate an elf changeling body tonight. If I do, I'll need your help to try and alter it somehow, so it appears to be the hybrid baby you sired."

Leethu's brow knitted. "I'll do my best, Ni-ni, but it may not pass."

"It needs to pass. If not, the elves will throw me out, and Haagenti will grab me. You do know what that means, don't you? I'll be killed. There will be no Iblis to protect you. If you stay here, the angels will kill you, if you go home, the elves. There's a substantial price on your head. This baby needs to pass, or you're dead."

Leethu paled. "I understand."

"If it doesn't work, and Haagenti grabs me, give this letter to Wyatt, and then do whatever you need to, to protect yourself."

"How do I know if it doesn't work; if Haagenti has killed you? How will I know when to give your human this message?"

I thought for a second. There might be no one in my household left to deliver the message. I strongly suspected Haagenti would take out his rage on every one of them. And this whole scheme was doomed to failure anyway.

"Actually, just give it to Wyatt as soon as I leave," I told her.

Leethu bit her trembling lip. "You'll contact me if it works? To let me know if it's safe to come home?"

I nodded. "Yes. But I need you to swear you'll give the letter to Wyatt."

There was a moment of silence as she looked at me. I felt rather like I was being dissected by her beautiful brown eyes. "I swear it upon all the beings I Own that I will give the letter to Wyatt."

"Thank you." I hugged her tight then I collected Boomer and headed to the cemetery.

~23~

I pulled my Suburban in through the massive iron gates of Mount Olivet cemetery and headed left around the prominent Francis Scott Key memorial. Boomer was beside himself with excitement, like a dog in a Snausages factory. He smeared drool all over my windows in a halfhearted attempt to push his head through the glass. I appreciated his restraint. He really could break through the SUV window if he truly put some effort into it.

"No snackies today, boy."

The one good thing about all the demons Wyatt and I had been killing was that Boomer had been less motivated to chow down on corpses from local graveyards. He was basically a lazy hellhound, and would take a meal of opportunity any day over one he'd actually have to work for. Demon corpses and road kill had been making up the majority of his diet lately. In fact, I really needed to put him on a diet. He was getting a little thick around the middle.

The man on the phone had been very cooperative when I told him I was researching some family history and wanted to know if any of the three names I had were interred there. One was, and he helpfully gave me the location of the grave and directions, which were useful given over thirty four thousand bodies had been laid to rest in this cemetery.

I circled to the right, along the fence line and past the seemingly endless line of markers from the Civil War—

soldiers, some of them unknown, lined in formation in death as in life. Young men, their contribution to the human race rewarded with death. I wondered why the angels didn't study the impact of their loss. So many lives. Perhaps it would have destroyed any faint hope in the evolution of humanity.

I was sure I'd become lost after so many turns in the labyrinth of the cemetery when I saw the marker. Finch. Infants were sometimes buried in an area of the cemetery known as Babyland then moved later after the family had time to purchase a section of plots, but the Finch family were long-time Frederick residents, and they had at one time purchased a large number of grave sites.

The standard sized plots were large enough to accommodate an infant at the foot of an adult grave. Leah Finch was buried at the end of the grave of her grandmother. I stopped and looked at the large stone, which listed the names of six family members buried around it. There were blank spots for two more names. With Boomer on a leash, we circled the large square monument, reading the smaller, embedded stones. There, at the foot of Martha Finch's grave, was Leah Finch. She'd been a week old.

I thought about her parents, their grief. Wyatt's family had it better. They'd been given a live baby in exchange. They'd got to see her grow up, love her as their own. This family had no such luck. They'd had their healthy child stolen from them in the night and replaced with a corpse. They'd mourned, wondered what had happened, if something could have been done to prevent the death of their baby, carried the scars of her loss with them forever. And all the while a human baby grew up a slave to the elves. Treated humanely, but denied the loving, normal childhood she should have had. It pissed me off. I'd always liked elves, admired them even. But now I was beginning to hate them.

"What do you think, Boomer?" I asked softly. "Is it an elf baby, or not."

He looked at me with a quizzical, angled head, and sniffed the ground around the stone. He did a thorough job, long strands of drool extending from his jowls to leave snail tracks of slime across the grave marker and the brown, frozen grass. He looked up, nodded, then poised a paw to dig, tilting his head in question.

"Not yet, boy. We need to come back at dark. And I'm sorry, but you won't be able to eat this one either."

Boomer looked disappointed. He'd had plenty to eat lately, so I refused to feel guilty, even as he fixed his big, sad hound eyes on me. Dogs have short attention spans though, even hellhounds. As soon as he got back to the Suburban with his massive rawhide stick in the back, he forgot all about the corpse and settled in.

I was shocked out of my mind to walk through my front door and see Wyatt sitting at my dining room table. Catching my breath, I steeled myself for the coming conversation. The one where he told me he never wanted to see me again. The one that confirmed I'd lost him forever.

"So have you made any progress on finding suitable corpse to pass off as Amber?" His voice was cracked, strained.

"I've located a changeling corpse from around the time of Amber's exchange. Boomer and I will retrieve it tonight." I told him, standing as if I were giving a military report.

Wyatt looked at me, his eyes demanding truth. "You said you'd fake a demon energy signature on the elf baby, to try and make it look like a hybrid. Will that convince the elves? What are the chances here?"

"It will work," I lied. "I'll imbed the demon energy as deep as I can. There's no way they'll know the difference."

Wyatt's eyes dissected me, digging past the lies to where I squirmed with doubt. "Sam, you've never even bred before. The one experience you had in practicing a formation, you killed the demon sire. How do you expect to make this look convincing?"

"Leethu is helping me. She formed your sister, she's formed many demons. She knows her life hinges on this. It'll work."

"So Leethu thinks this will work?" he asked.

"Yes, she's confident it will work," I snapped. I didn't mean to take my anger and frustration out on Wyatt, it wasn't his fault. This was the only option we had. Besides turning over his sister, that is.

"Funny, because that's not what Leethu told me."

Everything seized up inside me. When had he seen Leethu? Had he given in to her seductive pull? Sharp pain lanced through my chest. He was mine, and I didn't want to share that part of him with anyone. But how could I possibly feel at all possessive, at all jealous after my little speech about not needing sexual fidelity? Hypocrite.

Wyatt watched my face. "I spoke with her this morning, while you were at the cemetery."

I couldn't help myself. "Did you? She and you?" Quickly I gained my composure. "I mean, because I had hoped to join in on that. Did you take pictures? Because I really want to see them."

I was a horrible liar.

The silence stretched on as Wyatt and I stared at each other. I tried to look nonchalant.

"Leethu is very good at turning off the pheromone stuff when she wants to," he finally said.

That didn't exactly answer my question, but I really had no right to an answer anyway.

"Leethu has her doubts," I told him. "But I believe the plan is going to work. I promise you that. Amber will be as safe as she can be. And so will you, because the Haagenti issue is going to be resolved in the process. Problems solved, and we can all go on with our lives."

"Your plan is going to work?" His question sounded like an accusation.

"Yes."

Which plan, I didn't specify. Let him think the elf baby would pass, and the high lord would take out Haagenti. It was easier than him knowing I'd be dead. I thought this deception, this omission would work, but it didn't.

"The plan with the elf baby is going to work? Or the plan where you throw yourself at Haagenti like a virgin sacrifice?"

How did he know?

Wyatt waved an envelope at me and I froze. Leethu. That stupid bitch Leethu had given him the note. The one he wasn't supposed to get until after I'd gone back to Hel. I scrambled to explain it away.

"It's just standard stuff, Wyatt. Like this past summer with Althean and the werewolves? Just making sure things are in order, because something could happen. Everything will be okay."

He continued to wave the envelope at me, his voice choked. "Leethu says you're not coming back, Sam. That this elf baby isn't going to pass. That you're going to just hand yourself over to Haagenti. He'll kill you, Sam. He'll kill you."

I forced myself to walk over to the table and sit in a chair next to him. "I hope the elf baby passes, and they take care of Haagenti for me, but if not, I've got to face him. Gregory is right. I should have faced him before this. Instead I was a coward. I hid, and put you at risk. Put all my friends at risk. I'm not going to turn myself over to him; I'm going to fight him."

The end result would probably be the same as if I turned myself over to him, but hopefully I'd get in a few licks and save a bit of face before he killed me.

"And what do you think the chances of you beating Haagenti are?" Wyatt asked, his eyes looking suspiciously wet. "Significantly better than this elf baby passing as a hybrid?"

I shook my head. There was no sense in continuing to lie at this point. Wyatt knew how uneven this fight would be.

"So you were just going to sneak out? Head back to do this without even a word to me? You'd return to Hel, leaving me nothing beyond this note that I assume I wasn't supposed to get until after you were gone. With the distinct probability that you'd be killed?" He stood and took a step toward me before clenching his fists and turning away. "You'd do that to me? I'd have to live my whole life with this note, having never had the chance to say goodbye. Never having the chance to tell you one last time that I loved you. I'd have to live my whole life with that burden. I know you're selfish, Sam, but sheesh, that is really low. Even for a demon."

I put my head in my hands and stared at the table. Nothing I did was right. I was a lousy demon, a lousy girlfriend, a lousy Iblis. I even stank at trying to be a human. I wanted to hide. To crawl under a rock and let the world pass me by. *There will be no more rocks*, a voice said from my memory. Gregory. And he was right.

"I couldn't face you, Wyatt. Couldn't bear to see that look in your eyes, the one you had last night in the barn. I couldn't bear to have you back away from me. I may be selfish, but mostly I'm a coward." I raised my head and looked at him. "I'm not sure you can forgive me or feel the same way about me again. I just wanted to sneak away and pretend that last night didn't happen. I wanted to remember the good parts, the wonderful things we shared. I was afraid if I faced you, all I'd remember when I died was a look of hate in your eyes. I'm too much of a coward to go through that."

He made as if he were going to move toward me, but stopped. "I don't hate you, Sam. You are who you are, and I'm a fool for thinking otherwise. I'm like those animal handlers who imagine the lions are fuzzy kitties, with the same emotions and thought processes as a human, and then feel betrayed when they get bit."

Unable to hold back any longer, he walked toward me and put a hand on my arm, squeezing it gently. "I can't make that mistake again, Sam. If I'm going to have any sort of relationship with you, I can't keep pretending you're human. I can't keep ignoring that you're a dangerous predator, with a completely different set of ethics from me. I can't keep compromising my own ethics to suit yours."

"You don't hate me?" I tried hard to keep the waver out of my voice.

He moved behind me and wrapped his arms around my shoulders, snuggling his face in my hair. "I love you, Sam. I'll always love you. I don't know how to handle what happened. I want believe you when you say you weren't going to kill Amber, but I need to process it. I need space to think about things. But I'll always love you. Nothing will change that."

I closed my eyes and took a breath, feeling his arms around me and his face against my hair. For a second, I imagined that things were okay between us; that we were in love without a care in the world, that his sister was a human, that no demons were out to kill me and that the sword of the Iblis was back in the hands of the vampires. It was a brief indulgence, a fantasy of how things might have been. But there were no more rocks to hide under, and I had things to do. I gave Wyatt's hands a quick squeeze and got out of my chair.

His voice tense, Wyatt asked, "So how exactly do you plan on taking care of Haagenti?"

"No idea." I remembered Gregory's words. "I've been told I should go in with a 'mighty show of power'. Maybe I need to channel my inner Dirty Harry."

"So you're going to tell him to go ahead and make your day?" Wyatt smiled. It was a shaky, lopsided smile. I knew he was trying to cheer me up, pull me out of the doom and gloom slump I was in.

"I was thinking of asking him whether he thought I fired six shots or five."

Wyatt looked thoughtful. "Actually I see you more as Eastwood's character from *The Good the Bad and the Ugly*, than Dirty Harry."

"So I should go after Haagenti wearing a poncho with a six-shooter in a hip holster? The poncho might get in the way, although I guess I could throw it over his head and attempt to suffocate him."

"Okay, so the poncho is a bad idea. The attitude is right though. I can't see you doing a 'mighty show of power,' but I can see you as the lone gun, the stranger who walks into town and sets everything right. The one who sneaks in shots from the roof of a building, then walks the lonely road out of town while the gun smoke clears."

I liked that vision, especially without the poncho. Wyatt was probably right, but I didn't know how sneaky was going to work. Haagenti had people everywhere looking for me. I couldn't exactly creep around Hel, picking off the entire demon population one at a time. First things first. I needed to take care of things this side of the gates so Wyatt and his sister could be safe. Then deal with a probably enraged elf lord, or two. Then I'd worry about Haagenti.

~24~

Wyatt headed back to his house to kill some zombies and presumably have some alone time. He'd just left when Dar called. I hit the button, eager for his news.

"Mal, I need your help." His voice was strained, oddly quiet. "I have information for you, but it's not safe, and I need to give it to you in person. I'm trying to make it through the gate, but the guardian attacked me the second I got through. I had to jump back. Now I'm hiding because there is a shitload of Haagenti's men patrolling the gate."

I was pissed. That fucking guardian had let every Low through, but killed Dar's messenger? Attacked Dar with intent to kill? How the fuck was I supposed to get anything done?

"I can probably sneak through, but I'd need to be quick, and I need to make sure I don't get chopped to bits once I'm on the other side of the gate. There's no way I'll be able to jump back to this side again. Haagenti's guys will grab me. And they allegedly have orders to kill."

"Wait there. Give me fifty minutes." Thirty to get to Columbia Mall, twenty to find the gate and take care of the guardian. "After fifty minutes, take your best opportunity and get through the gate. Okay?"

"Got it. Thanks, Mal."

I drove down to the mall and anger built inside me with the passing of every mile. I felt cornered, with everything closing in on me. This was the final straw. I was going to smack-down this gate guardian. I was so pissed off by the time I arrived, I yanked the Corvette into a handicapped spot and jumped out, running into the mall and knocking aside several shoppers leaving Nordstroms. The mall was busy, but I strode purposefully through it, looking for the gate and that bitch guarding it.

I recognized her right away. Heck, I'd seen her every couple of days for the past few months when I lobbed demon heads through the gate to Hel. She was an elderly lady, impeding traffic as she hobbled, bent over a cane in front of the jewelry store. The gate was by the cell phone kiosk, but I ignored it and went right up to the guardian.

The humans gasped in alarm as I grabbed the elderly lady and slammed her up against the glass that held an array of engagement rings.

"A member of my household is going to come through the gate to meet with me," I said, trying to keep my voice low. "You will allow this."

"I cannot," she gasped. "I'm forbidden. None of your household is allowed to pass."

She really did look like a harmless old lady. At any moment I was going to have a helpful citizen attacking me. I needed to act fast.

"Tell your boss to meet me at my house and I will take this up with him. In the meantime, Dar is going to come through. If you do anything to stop him, make any move to harm him, I will tell the Ruling Council to replace you. I'll tell them you let a Low through last fall, that you continually leave your post, seduced by gluttony."

She paled. She'd told me once she couldn't wait to go back to Aaru, but I'd seen how she'd worshiped those containers of sweet and sour sauce. I knew she'd not be happy to leave that behind.

"No more sweet and sour pork for you," I whispered.

"Okay, okay," she squeaked.

I let her go and faced the hostile crowd.

"I caught her groping up my three year old son in the bathroom," I told them. "Sick pervert."

The gate guardian shot me a look of pure hate, and took off, much faster than an old lady with a cane should be able to go. As the crowd raced after her, I turned and saw Dar. He looked at me with a combination of surprise and admiration.

"Nice job. Think they'll catch her?"

"One can only hope."

Dar walked along beside me as we made our way back through the mall to my car. "I have the information on the human servant for you," he said, passing me another small card.

I broke the warded seal and looked at the name and address it held. Jacob Bara in Mount Airy, Maryland. Hopefully he'd be home tonight when I came calling. An easy kill, just to make sure no one could track Amber through him, and then I'd grab Boomer and head to the cemetery.

"I have the other information you wanted too," Dar added.

I drew a blank. Had I asked him for something else?

"About stripping a demon of their energy?" Dar reminded, seeing my confused look.

Oh yeah. The head Gregory brought. Not that I needed the info anymore since he insisted it hadn't been a demon after all. I hated to tell Dar that, after he'd gone to all this trouble, though. Besides, I still had that feeling that there was something going on that Gregory wasn't tell me, or the Ruling Council, about.

"Elves can interrupt a demon's ability to use their energy, but they can't drain a demon of stored energy," Dar said. "A powerful sorcerer can completely hamper a demon's abilities, blocking their use of energy or prohibiting conversion of energy to matter." Skilled humans, including sorcerers, had always been able to bind a demon, rendering them helpless, but draining them was something different. And binding was always a temporary state—unless the angels did it. Dar continued. "No one has ever been aware of a sorcerer who could actually drain stored energy from a demon, although it seems feasible."

So it was all conjecture at this point. Maybe they could, probably they couldn't. And it didn't really matter anyway, since the head had been human after all. I should have just dropped the topic, but my mind kept gnawing on it, exploring the possibilities.

"What about personal energy?" I asked Dar.

He held the Nordstroms' door open for me. I was happy to see my car hadn't received a citation for my illegal use of the handicapped spot.

"Our spirit self disburses when we die, you know that."

"Yeah, but there are traces, there's a signature that identifies the corpse as one that held a demon. What could wipe those away?"

Dar looked amused. "Who would care? The demon is dead. Who would care if some trace remained?"

I beeped the alarm off on my car. "Humor me, Dar. Let's say someone wanted to hide the fact that the corpse had been a demon, wanted to make it look like a human. Or someone was greedy and didn't want any energy whatsoever to remain."

Dar laughed. "Like you? A devouring spirit could probably suck every last trace of personal energy from a demon, leaving a shell behind."

I started. Me? "Are there a lot of devouring spirits around? I've never met another one."

"Thankfully no. So unless you've been running around draining demons, I doubt it's happening."

Dar gossiped about all the goings-on back in Hel as I drove home. All this conjecture about the head and energy draining was intriguing, but I had far too much on my plate right now. I shoved Dar's information into the back of my thoughts and returned to fuming over the issue with the gate.

I was still pissed. I'd taken my anger out on the gate guardian, but it was Gregory who was really at fault. I know he wanted me to return to Hel and deal with Haagenti, but I'd had enough of his interference. I couldn't keep track of everything I was supposed to be doing. I needed to be in contact with my household, with elves and demons to do my job as the Iblis. And sensitive information couldn't always be relayed over the mirror. I needed them to come and go freely. If some miracle happened and I managed to off Haagenti and make it back, I needed to be able to use this gate. As the Iblis, I should be allowed this privilege.

Gregory was waiting for me, messing with the TV remotes in my great room as I walked in. Dar froze in terror the moment he saw him.

"Don't worry about him," I told my brother. "He's here to see me. Why don't you go upstairs? Leethu is up there and she'll be thrilled to see you."

Dar brightened considerably at the prospect of a thrilled succubus waiting upstairs, and headed up to see her.

"Another stray cat, cockroach?" Gregory asked.

"A brother," I told him. Fuck, I was practically running a damned hotel, a safe house for demons.

"So I'm assuming you called me because you have the four-nine-five report done? You're early, little cockroach. How unexpected."

He knew damned well why I called him. I was positive the gate guardian told him. Still, mention of the report threw me off topic. "No, it's not done. I'm not doing it. I'm filing a protest, appealing to my union rep, or whatever. The guy died of natural causes."

He walked toward me. "Beginning to enjoy the punishment, my little cockroach?" Should I do away with all pretenses and just bring you up to Aaru with me permanently?"

I shuddered, but held my ground. "No punishment and no report. I'm filing an official protest here. What's the protocol for that?"

He stood well within my personal space, but thankfully didn't touch me, physically or otherwise. That welcome burn of his power flowed over my senses, and I struggled to keep my thoughts on how pissed off I was.

"I lodge your complaint. We schedule a meeting with the Ruling Council for you to present your case. Then we vote. If the vote is in your favor, then no report is necessary. If not, then you will have twenty four hours to present the four-nine-five report in person at a second meeting."

What a fucking pain in the ass. Still it bought me some time, and if Haagenti killed me, I'd at least die with the satisfaction of knowing that these angels would never get their fucking report.

"Okay, do it." I waved a hand at him. "Make it so."

"Good. And now I need to discuss a little matter with you about my gate guardian."

I felt my temper flare, but he held a finger up, to cut me off before I could say a word.

"Those gates belong to the angels. That gate guardian is under my direction. As my bound demon, I've allowed you limited passage to and from Hel, but I am under no such obligation to allow any of your friends, family, or pets through. Do not badger, threaten, or harass my gate guardian. Do I make myself clear?"

My temper exploded and I started stabbing him in the chest with my finger.

"You fucking asshole. You listen to me right now. You want to let a bunch of Lows through the gate to hassle me? Fine. I don't care. But you *will* allow members of my household and those doing business with me passage. I'm not putting up with your bullshit games. The next time you interfere with my business, hinder me in any way, I'm going to rip your fucking head off and stick it in your ass. Do I make *myself* clear?"

I was sure I imagined the ghost of a smile that flickered across his face.

"Very clear. However, none of this changes the fact that the angels own the gates. You have no rights to them beyond those we grant you."

I struggled, a mini war going on within myself. Part of me was on the verge of a tantrum, wanting to whip out the Barrette of the Iblis and proceed to cut his fucking wings off. Part of me reasoned that a logical approach would yield better results, and that angels were all about debate, rules, and loopholes. I just needed to find the loophole.

I fingered my barrette while he watched me placidly. For the first time in my life, logic won.

"So you all are now a democracy? The gates are owned by the angelic host as a whole and each angel has equal access and say when it comes to their usage?"

"No. Of course not. The gates are solely under the governance of the archangels."

"You mean the Ruling Council?"

Gregory shook his head. "A subset of the Ruling Council."

Ah. Like a committee. "So, if Sleepy is on the Ruling Council, but not an archangel, he has no say over who can come and go through the gates?"

Gregory looked enigmatic. "Why would he want to use the gates? This hypothetical Sleepy angel would never want to journey to Hel, and I can't see him wanting to allow a despised demon through to interfere with the precarious balance of evolution here. "

"What if he bound a demon?" I waved a hand as Gregory raised a skeptical eyebrow. "Could happen. You've started a fashion trend, and now everyone wants one. Sleepy binds a demon, and needs it to go through the gates. Can he do this?"

"Yes. He's on the Ruling Council. Not every angel would have that privilege. Of course, not every angel has the power to bind a demon."

"So, as the Iblis and a member of the Ruling Council, I insist that my demons be allowed safe passage." I sucked at this debating thing. I probably should have chopped off his wings instead.

Again, that ghost of a smile. "But little cockroach, you have not bound these demons to you. We are comparing dissimilar scenarios."

"They are bound as part of my household. Is not my household mark equivalent? They are mine in the same way as a bound demon would be."

"But they are not. They are not compelled to do your bidding, they still have free will."

"As do I," I told him, running a finger over the tattoo of his sword on the inside of my upper right arm.

He paused, considering my words. I'd never been under his compulsion, had always retained my free will. He'd made an exception to the definition of a bound being, and set a precedent.

His voice was calm. "I will alert the major gates that they should allow your household to pass unharmed. Please let everyone on your end know that they must adhere to behavior standards or they will lose their immunity."

"I will," I replied, still fighting the urge to rip off his wings.

"Is there anything else, Iblis?" he asked with no innuendo, no sarcasm. He was speaking to me as though I were a business associate. As though I were a peer.

"That is all," I told him, feeling suddenly regal.

He nodded and gated away. As soon as he was gone I realized that for the first time he'd addressed me as the Iblis, not as 'little cockroach'.

~25~

Jacob Bara lived in a small rancher on a cul-de-sac in downtown Mount Airy. I parked along Main Street and drank beer at the nearby sports bar until nightfall then made my way down his street. Luckily things were quiet, and no one besides a wandering dog noticed my presence. I knocked on the door, and a stout, bald man in his late sixties answered.

"Jacob Bara?" I asked.

He nodded, so I showed him the little embossed card Dar had given me with his name and address. He paled and ushered me in.

"What happened to the other demon?" he asked. "Are you taking his place?"

"No. I'm here because we've got a bit of a problem."

He was clearly comfortable around demons, ushering me to a comfy chair and getting me a beer. He plopped down on the couch across from me and twisted his hands together.

"Is the girl ok? She was fine a few days ago. I haven't checked on her since she went back to college. Nothing's happened to her I hope."

"She's fine, but someone has leaked rumors of her existence to the High Lord Taullian, and he's hired a demon to track her down and kill her."

I didn't tell him that demon was me. Still, he turned an alarming shade of gray and knotted his hands into a tight ball.

"I'll never give her up. Never. I don't care how much I'm tortured, what anyone does to me. I'll never betray my family."

"I'm confident that you're loyal." I handed him the other card, the one with the offer from the elf woman Tlia-Myea. "Do you read angelic script?"

He nodded and read the card slowly then looked up at me, the paper rattling slightly in his hand. "Have you found this elf baby?"

"Yes."

"Will it work?"

This guy was pretty quick on the uptake for a human. He could have been a sorcerer if not for Tlia-Myea's desperate desire for a substitute child.

I shrugged. "Probably not. But it's the only option where the girl stays alive."

He looked down at the card again. "If it doesn't work, they'll send more after her. Maybe find the demon who did the changeling exchange with me, or the one who has been delivering my notes, bribe either of them for my name and trace her that way." He looked up at me. "I'll do anything to keep her safe."

"You can't live." I told him, confirming what he already knew.

He nodded. "Tlia-Myea was wonderful. Like a mother to me. She treated me as if I really were her Elven child. And my step-sister has grown into an incredible woman. She's the equal of any full elf. Smart, beautiful, powerful. I've had a good life, better than any other changeling human. I'll accept my fate."

"So how do you want to do this?" I asked. "Are there things you need to do first? Arrangements you need to make? We're on a really tight timetable; we don't have more than a few hours."

"I have nothing to do. There will be no way to trace her from me. I've left nothing that can possibly hint of my time with the elves or my involvement in this."

He looked at me expectantly. I stared back, uncertain what the delay was. Didn't he need to go get a gun or some pills or something? A noose?

"I'm losing my nerve here," he told me.

"So what's the hold up?" Put your head in a plastic bag or something."

He looked rather frightened. "I thought you were going to do it."

Fuck. Not that I normally minded offing humans, but now I had to deal with paperwork. And this would definitely violate Wyatt's edict.

"There's a two-hundred page report I have to fill out if I do it, and I'm not sure the angels will consider the Dr. Kevorkian excuse to be adequate. You have no idea how horrible their idea of punishment is."

He stared at me, his eyes huge, his hands trembling. "I can't. I just can't."

Fine. Getting up, I took a quick drink of my beer before walking over to him. "Do you want me to Own you, or not?"

He looked horrified. "No. Oh please, no."

It might have been kind of cool to Own a human who had spent his life in service to the elves, but I'd respect his choice. I made it as quick and painless as possible. The other humans would think he'd just had a heart attack.

I finished my beer, rinsed the glass and put it in the dishwasher before letting myself out. One loose end tied up.

It was late evening by the time I parked on a side street a few blocks from Mount Olivet. After leaving Mount Airy, I looped around to my house to grab Boomer before heading to the cemetery. On my own, with just a shovel, it would take me the whole night to dig up a modern grave. I could do it faster with my special skills, but then the grave would clearly look disturbed and I'd learned to try and keep things as under the radar as possible with humans. They were really persistent when it came to investigations, and modern technology meant they could track me down a lot easier than they could seven hundred years ago. Getting caught wouldn't be a problem if I was already dead, but I had the faint hope I'd be able to defeat Haagenti and return. It would really suck to come back and find everything I owned confiscated and Wyatt behind bars as an accessory to a felony.

Second time in one week I was doing this. I may be a demon, but I'm not much on digging up corpses. Hopefully this would be my last for a long, long time. I carefully removed the baby's marker, and the sod covering the tiny grave, then let Boomer go to work. He skillfully moved dirt aside into neat piles with his two huge heads and massive paws. He wasn't normally so neat, but I'd asked him to be more careful with the dirt so I could replace it as easily as possible. Under regular circumstances, he'd fling chunks of ground half a block away, blast through the vault and casket, and be enjoying a late-night snack within minutes. About four feet down, Boomer hit the coffin lid. He jumped out for me to take a look.

This grave was tiny. Caskets this small were a combination of vault and casket, negating the need for a big concrete vault or grave liner.

"Can you pull it out?" The grave was so small we wouldn't have any room to maneuver. And although four feet wasn't particularly deep, it was too deep to stay up top and reach down to the remains. The whole process would be easier if Boomer could bring the coffin to the surface.

The hellhound cocked his head to the side and looked over the edge. Grabbing the steel cable I'd brought in one of his jaws, he jumped down, landing with his feet carefully poised on the dirt ledge he'd made surrounding the casket. Boomer weighed nearly three hundred pounds in his hellhound form. I appreciated his care, especially since I didn't know how sturdy the lid was after nearly twenty years in the ground.

He dug down to free a handle, looped the cable around it before leaping back to the surface. Grabbing the ends with both jaws, he pulled slowly and steadily, stirring the casket from the embrace of packed dirt. Slowly he edged backward, easing it out an inch at a time, but over the years, the ground had a tight hold on its prize, and, after a bare inch of movement, the pretty brass handle snapped off and flew through the air.

The devastated expression on Boomer's face was priceless. I almost laughed.

"It's okay, boy. Let's dig it loose a bit more, and try with the other handle."

He did just that, leaping back in and sending dirt flying with renewed enthusiasm. In no time at all, he was easing a much-loosened casket up and out of the grave. I brushed the dirt from the cream and gold, faux-marble lid and instructed Boomer to cut the top off. A few quick slices of fang, and the lid slid to the side, revealing pink satin.

The coffin was a vault casket, so it was solid with a tight seal. Normally decomposition would have mottled and stained the pink ruffled lining, but this was pristine. The tiny baby, nestled peacefully inside, looked as fresh as the day her grieving parents had laid her to rest. That alone clued me in to the baby's ancestry. Elf babies were magically preserved, held in stasis from the moment they died. An exchange might take place within days, or within years of a death. The elf baby needed to appear absolutely fresh at the time of the swap, and years in the ground had done nothing to diminish the power of Elven preservation techniques. Such a tiny little thing, with wisps of golden hair and a pale pink bow of a mouth, her ears an illusion to pass as human. I reached out with my energy, to scan her, and confirm what I already knew.

I couldn't bear to separate her head from her body; she was just too perfect. Gently lifting her from the satin enclosure, I wrapped her in a blanket, setting the little form inside a duffle bag. A twinge of guilt went through me, but I reminded myself this baby had died long ago and there was a young woman, very much alive, that necessitated my disturbing the rest of the dead.

I put the casket back together as best I could, then Boomer helped me lower it into the grave and return the dirt. After replacing the sod and marker, the grave looked much as we'd found it. With any luck, the site would have few visitors and the property maintenance people wouldn't be around until spring for mowing.

Slinging the duffle bag gently over one shoulder and the steel cable over the other, Boomer and I climbed over the high cemetery fence and mad our way to the Suburban.

~26~

Leethu twirled a lock of her silky black hair, her face a study in concentration.

"It's still not quite right," she mused, half to herself. Dar was upstairs "recovering" from an entertaining evening with the succubus. It was just as well. He'd be a serious distraction at this point. Especially all hopped up on hormones.

"How did you form the original child?" Perhaps if she remembered, she could duplicate her efforts here, on this corpse.

"Oh, that was a work of art," she said proudly. "I manipulated the elf portion so it was the majority of the formation. Just enough of me to provide defensive ability and the conversion skills to fix wounds and illness. I wanted her to appear to be a full elf, but be able to turn on the power if she were in danger."

Clever and thoughtful. I had no desire whatsoever to form an offspring, hybrid or otherwise, but I could appreciate the great care and skill that Leethu had put into her elf hybrid.

The succubus shot me a sly look under long, black lashes. "You've seen her, Ni-ni. Isn't she perfect? She looks like a full elf, like a clone of her mother. Didn't I do well?"

I felt cold. "Of course I haven't seen her," I lied. "If I had, do you think we'd be wasting time trying to cram demon energy into this thing?"

Leethu resumed her work, a little smirk on one corner of her sensuous mouth. "I have no wish to find my elf hybrid girl, Ni-ni. It would only prove my involvement in her creation. I hope she remains safely hidden away, out of the hands of those who might turn her, or her body, over to the elves. That way I can deny my part in this. It could have been any Incubus. Clearly the elf woman was mistaken in her accusation of me." Yes, Leethu was far more intelligent than any demon gave her credit for.

"Here," she said, nodding at her hands.

I reached over and sent my energy down in beside her to the spot she indicated, then burned a small trail along the cells, leaving traces of energy behind. We were purposely using raw energy instead of personal energy. It left a stronger marker and didn't readily identify a particular demon. If this passed their scrutiny, neither of us wanted the baby's parentage obviously linked to Leethu, or me, through our energy markers. Best to keep things vague and let them assume it had all dulled over time, that the Elven stasis had been compromised because of the demon genetic signature.

She pulled back and looked down at her work, disgusted. "This has got to be the stupidest thing I've ever done. We'd be better off using papier-mâché and wire hangers."

"A piñata hybrid?" I asked, always happy to find humor in the darkest of times. "Fill her with candy and cheap plastic toys?"

Leethu tittered, her laughter like wind chimes in the breeze. "Or a bottle of wine. Those elves love their wine. Maybe they'll get all drunk and forget how shitty this fake baby is."

I joined in. "Maybe if *we* drink the wine, the baby would be less shitty."

Dar came down to us bent over in a fit of giggles around the body laid out on my dining room table.

"Is that dinner?" he asked.

"Boomer hopes so." I couldn't help it. I'd probably be dead within twenty-four hours. Gallows humor was all I had left.

Dar looked over the beautiful elf child. "This would be crudités to Boomer. Better get a bigger corpse."

I wiped the tears from my eyes. "Can you do anything with it?" I asked, gesturing to the body. "It's shitty and Leethu and I are out of ideas."

He shooed Leethu out of the way and sent his energy into the baby. After a few disgusted noises, he glared up at me. "Seriously? Are you fucking kidding me?"

I wrinkled my nose. "I told you it was shitty."

He grumbled. "… Better off using papier-mâché and some wire hangers."

"That's what *I* said," Leethu laughed.

Dar glared up at me again. "Come take this out. Over here. Now. Come take this shit out and start over."

Fuck, he sounded like one of the teachers back when we were kids. I scurried over, just like I would have in school, and obediently removed the energy I'd placed in the baby.

"Leethu, yours is almost as bad. Get over here and take it out."

The succubus complied, rubbing her hip against Dar as she worked. Dar viewed her with interest.

"Oh no, you turn it off right now," I scolded Leethu. "We've got work to do here. You both can fuck all you want while I'm in Hel meeting my end at Haagenti's hands."

Dar looked guilty. He should. It was him that got me into this mess with Haagenti in the first place.

Leethu stepped back and Dar once again checked the baby before pulling away and standing, resolute, with his hands on his hips.

"Hybrids aren't like whole demons. It's not just the formation, it's the path the demon portion takes once they mature. Yes, their formation has some impact on how much demon they have and what their skills are, but where it resides is remarkably similar from one to the other."

"So now you're the expert on hybrids?" Sarcasm dripped from my every word. Dar was famous for going off on a convincing academic rant on subjects he knew absolutely nothing about. Many fools had died following his impressive-sounding advice. I wasn't about to be one of those fools.

Dar looked a bit embarrassed. "Well. I, uh … I have made some hybrids, for sale, and they brought a very good price."

The elf hybrid that Leethu had created was an anomaly. A forbidden, get-a-demon-killed kind of anomaly. Most hybrids were either human crosses, just for fun, or animals. Fucking animals wasn't exactly something a demon wanted to put on their resume. Creating offspring with them was almost as bad. Still, there was a good market for hybrids, and a demon that didn't mind the rather embarrassing reputation could make some serious cash. I wasn't aware of Dar having that reputation though. So either he was lying or he'd been paying another demon to take the heat for siring his various animals.

"So, let's hear some names here," I scoffed. "What hybrids have you bred and who owns them?"

Dar squirmed. "What, are you going to check references? Do we really have time for that?"

"You're lying. You sack of shit."

Leethu was watching this back and forth like a spectator at a tennis match. "That goblin hybrid of Macariel's is Dar's. Andros supposedly sired it, but I could tell."

Dar gurgled something unintelligible.

"A goblin? You fucked a *goblin*?" Oh, this was far worse than an animal. This was serious blackmail material. I wondered how he'd gotten Andros to take the rap for that one? Of course, I'd give just about anything to have a goblin hybrid. That would be epic.

"No. No." Dar gurgled something else. It was an entertaining noise. This was turning into the highlight of my day.

"Yes. Yes." Leethu fixed him with a forbidding eye. "Do you think I can't tell my own brother's creation? Then there was the troll hybrid last century."

Dar choked and I squealed in delight. A troll? Dar? And a troll? I would have paid good money to see that. How does one even fuck a troll? Their skin is like a sheet of granite. He'd break his dick off in that thing.

"We will never speak of this," Dar pleaded. "I'll help you with this baby, but we will never mention this again—among ourselves, or with anyone else. Agreed?"

"Agreed," I lied. This was way too juicy to keep to myself, and Dar knew it.

Leethu patted Dar on the arm then announced she was going to get us all beers before high-tailing it into the kitchen. Dar shifted his weight from foot to foot, staring down at the elf on the table.

"Does this mean you won't be accepting my breeding petition?" he asked, his voice deceptively casual.

"I don't know," I teased. "I figured you'd withdraw it. I don't think I can compete with goblins and trolls. That's pretty exotic."

He looked up, a rather silly smirk on his face. "Mal, fucking you is far more exciting and dangerous than anything I've done to date. And having you sire an offspring I form is pretty high on my wish list."

That was probably the nicest thing anyone had ever said to me. "I like fucking you too, Dar. And if I ever decide to breed, I'll definitely give you due consideration."

"Bitch," he said affectionately. "I'll use my energy to alter this elf body for you. Just so you can see how awesome I really am."

"Are you sure?" I asked, taking a swig of the beer Leethu handed to me. "What happens if the elves identify your energy signature? They might think you sired the hybrid and come after you."

Dar snorted. "They'd never believe it. Besides I'm not afraid of the elves; you're the only being alive I truly fear."

"And well you should." I walked near him to watch over his shoulder. I really was very fond of Dar. Fond enough to die protecting him.

"See? Here, just under the solar plexus. Then here at the lower part of the brain."

"One at the crown?" Leethu asked, also leaning over a shoulder.

"No, leave that for the base form. As well as the tip of the frontal lobe, and heart areas. If the sire resides there, the hybrid is unstable."

Dar moved his energy down the body. "A small amount here, just under the left ribcage next to the stomach, then a large amount just inside the tailbone. Let the tailbone serve as a cradle, as a seat for the demon energy. If there is a tailbone, that is. If not, well, you just have to make due."

I was impressed. "Do you do all this when you form?" I asked.

"No, the formation follows the standard procedure, the same as if you were doing a demon formation. With hybrids though, you need to consider whether the end result needs to pass as the maternal animal."

Leethu nodded. "I created the elf hybrid to seem to be one hundred percent elf."

"And that's the way most hybrids are formed," Dar confirmed. "Usually you want them to be discrete, to fit in visually and behaviorally with their non-demon family."

"Behaviorally is not really achievable," I commented, thinking of Boomer and Diablo.

"Yeah. And sometimes you really want more demon, just to create interest or added power." Dar finished and sat back, a satisfied look on his face.

I checked and discovered a newfound respect for Dar. He may fuck goblins and trolls, but he was damned cool in my book. Leethu must have been thinking the same thing. Her gaze roamed down Dar's form in admiration.

"Nice job. Wanna sixty-nine?"

Okay, maybe she wasn't thinking the same thing I was. Dar was definitely up for that proposal, and he followed Leethu up the stairs with a spring in his step, leaving me alone with the corpse.

"Come on, Sweetie," I told her as I wrapped her in a towel and put her back in the duffle bag. "Your journey is almost over."

It was done. Reluctant to rush things, I walked around my house, committing it to memory. The fireplace, the huge sectional couches that had seen lovemaking, naps, and late-night movies complete with popcorn. The enormous French doors leading out to my patio and pool. Ah, my beloved pool! I remembered summers when I sunned on a deckchair, hoping desperately to attract Wyatt's interest while he trimmed the grass. Boomer's face peered in at me, and I looked past him to the stables—the stables with Vegas and Piper. All the beautiful horseback rides with Wyatt by my side. I wandered around front where my Corvette was parked in the driveway. The Corvette that Wyatt was always pestering me to drive.

Wyatt. I hadn't seen him since late morning. He knew the schedule. He knew I'd be leaving. Why hadn't he returned to say goodbye? My heart shriveled. Maybe that was his goodbye. I had nothing more to wait for. I should have just left, but something held me back. I didn't want to watch television. I didn't want to get drunk. I didn't want to have sex with Leethu and Dar. But I didn't want to leave. Not just yet.

I curled up on the sofa with an afghan and must have dozed off because suddenly I was on the floor hearing a crash.

I sprang up and there was Wyatt, in my open doorway, holding a large box and a shotgun. He saw me, an expression of relief crossing his face.

"I thought I'd missed you. Sorry. This all took longer than I thought."

I barely heard what he said. I raced to him and threw my arms around his neck, jabbing myself painfully with a corner of the huge box and the stock of the shotgun. He was here. He'd come. Come to see me off, to say goodbye.

"Hey, whoa there."

He scooted over to the table, with me still clinging to him, and put down the shotgun. Pivoting around, he shoved the box on the table and wrapped his arms tightly around me. He'd come to see me one last time, and I wasn't going to squander the opportunity by holding back my feelings.

Wyatt held me for a long time, rocking slightly and smoothing my hair. Finally he pulled away and looked searchingly into my face.

"I brought you a present."

"And you brought a shotgun. Is that for your own personal protection? Just in case I decide to Own one last human before I go to Hel?" I tried for a teasing tone, but I honestly didn't know why he brought the shotgun.

"I have an idea," he said, ignoring my Own comment. "But first, the present."

He pulled away and handed me the huge box. I shook it. Something in tissue paper. Opening it, I pulled out a long, tan oilcloth duster.

"See? It's split up the back, for when you're on Diablo. You can even button it around your legs if you want. The oilcloth repels rain and makes it easier to clean."

Cool, but why would Wyatt buy me a full length jacket? It was stinking hot in Hel, and my chances of getting Diablo back were pretty slim. I frowned in confusion.

"It's cowboy attire. A kind of duster, but without the shoulder cape. It's sort of *High Plains Drifter* meets *The Good, The Bad, and The Ugly*—a more tough-guy choice than the poncho. I thought it would help with your mojo."

It was a sweet gesture, and one I didn't expect. A little spark of hope lit up inside my chest. Maybe, just maybe I'd make it out of this alive. "Thank you."

"That's not all." He looked mischievous as he pulled the tissue paper from the box and revealed a large, leather belt-like contraption. He held it up in one hand and slid the shotgun into it with the other.

"It has two loops here to fix to a saddle. Normally it goes on a Western saddle, but I'll modify it to work with your English one. I have no idea what saddle the elves have, or if you'll need to ride bareback, so this harness here is to convert it into a shoulder holster. The shotgun goes along your back, and you can pull it from the scabbard over your shoulder. Like this." He demonstrated.

I was confused again. "So this is for mojo too? Because you know how much I suck at shooting things with a gun. Especially this gun. I don't think Remington and I see eye to eye on things."

"This is where my idea comes in." Wyatt pulled his shotgun out of the scabbard and sat it on the table. "Take the barrette out of your hair."

"Huh?" Did he want my hair loose? Perhaps to run his hands through? But what did that have to do with his shotgun?

"The Barrette of the Iblis. Take it out and sit it next to my shotgun."

I did as he said, looking quizzically at the gold, feather-shaped hair ornament, so tiny next to the huge Remington.

"I can't think it's going to be any more useful to me as a gun rather than as a sword."

"Humor me," he said, gesturing to the barrette.

I concentrated, willing the sentient artifact to transform into a replica of the firearm beside it. With a flash, the barrette changed shape, and now two identical shotguns lay on the table. The only way I could tell the Shotgun of the Iblis from Wyatt's Remington was that strange pull of attraction I'd felt for the object from the moment I'd seen it.

"Well I guess I can club Haggenti with it," I commented. I was a terrible shot, and now I had to worry about carrying bullets and reloading. It did look cool though. Maybe the mojo factor would work. It certainly had more mojo in its current form than it had as a barrette.

Wyatt reached out tentatively and touched my firearm. Gently he picked it up and examined it.

"No safety," he said with a grimace. "Hopefully the sentient part will ensure you don't shoot yourself or one of your friends. Just in case your gun doesn't like me, let's take it outside." We walked out the front door, and Wyatt pointed the barrel toward the empty field while pulling back the action bar. "All clear," he announced, handing the gun gingerly to me. "Please don't point it at me. I'm a little nervous."

I was perplexed. "But you said it was clear? If there aren't any shells in the gun, how could I possibly shoot you?"

"I have a theory." Wyatt took his hand and gently turned the barrel further away from him. "Try and shoot something."

Ignoring every lesson Wyatt had ever given me, because the gun was *empty*, I held it with my arm extended and pulled the trigger. There was a roar and I promptly flew ass backwards onto my driveway as the gun clattered to the pavement.

"Sam!" Wyatt shouted, jumping out of the way. "You're gonna kill someone. Keep a hold of your gun, for crying out loud."

I stared at the shotgun in amazement. It had been empty. Wyatt had checked, and I trusted him implicitly when it came to guns. What the hell had just happened? Slowly I reached out and picked up the weapon, happy to see no scratches or dents. Wyatt ran a shaky hand through his hair.

"If that were a normal firearm, I'd insist on it being checked over before it was fired again, but I'm pretty sure since it's some kind of magical weapon, it didn't take any damage."

I looked at him in surprise. "So I don't need bullets? I don't need to re-load it or worry about running out of ammunition? What the fuck is this thing shooting?"

Wyatt shook his head. "No idea. I'm assuming that was just a regular slug, but with this thing, it might shoot different stuff depending on what you're up against."

I ran my hands over the gun in amazement, while Wyatt moved nervously out of the way, trying to keep the barrel as far away from him as possible. This fucking rocked! Badass mojo, and a useful weapon. Maybe this piece of crap antique I'd been saddled with wasn't so stupid after all.

"Let's go see how you look with the whole package," Wyatt said, his voice warm.

I got up, being very careful where I pointed my Iblis Shotgun, and followed Wyatt back into my house. A few moments later I had my favorite torn jeans and white wifebeater on, with the oilskin coat open in the front. The shotgun holster was actually comfortable, and held the coat snug to the back and sides of my body. The shotgun stock stood up past my shoulder, just within my peripheral vision. It would be easy to grab and pull from the holster, as long as I had some maneuvering room.

"How do I look?" I asked Wyatt, pivoting slowly around so he could see every angle. He smiled.

"A no-named stranger, riding in from the west, unconventional, and seemingly unthreatening. Doom will fall unto those who oppose her, who underestimate her, because she fights dirty."

"Yeah," I replied with a fist pump. "Haagenti is going down!"

Wyatt helped me take off the holster and sit it with my shotgun on the table. I carefully laid the coat beside it.

"Thank you." I'd never been more sincere in my life. "Thank you for this, Wyatt. After everything that happened you didn't have to do this. I appreciate everything you've done for me, and I'm not sure I can ever repay you."

I was talking about far more than just the coat and the shotgun holster. He knew.

Wyatt walked over and wrapped me up tight in his arms. "Come back to me, Sam. That's how you can repay me."

I wasn't sure what I was going to come back to. I had a feeling it wouldn't be quite what we'd had before, but as long as Wyatt wanted any kind of relationship with me, it would all be good.

"I will. I'll be back," I vowed, hoping I was telling the truth.

I snuggled my face into his chest, breathing in the scent I'd come to love. If I could just freeze this moment in time, hold still in his arms forever, life would be perfect. But nothing is forever. He pulled away slightly and I felt the coolness hit my skin that had been so warm against his. Looking up, I felt that last thing I'd expected to feel this evening, his lips on mine.

His kiss was gentle, poignant, and full of the sorrow of goodbye. I think he'd meant it to give closure, but something happened between us during that kiss. His lips grew more demanding, and I responded, digging my fingers in his hair and holding on as if I'd never let go. Hands traveled down my back to cup my ass and push me tight against his growing erection.

"Let me stay here tonight," he said, breaking free to whisper against my mouth.

"Is it Leethu?" I asked. I didn't want him doing something he'd regret later under the influence of Leethu's persuading scent.

"No. I need you." His voice was raw, as if he couldn't help himself. I know I should have pulled back, should have let him go, but I needed him too. Both of us feared deep in our hearts that we'd never see each other again, and that was enough to push away all the difficult logistics of our relationship and concentrate only on what we felt for each other.

So I gave him my answer, dipping my head to run my tongue from his chin up to his lower lip, teasing my way into his mouth as I dug my nails into the back of his neck. He shivered, returning my kiss and lifting me up by my rear. I obligingly wrapped my legs around his hips as he climbed the stairs, somehow managing to keep his mouth firmly attached to mine.

We were slow, meticulous, committing every inch of each other to memory with hands and mouths. Each time our bodies hovered over the edge, we held back, wanting this night to last as long as possible. I sent strands of my spirit self into him as he sank deep within me, timing our orgasms to coincide in perfect union. For a brief second, we were one, and all the doubts, anger, and fears faded away, unimportant in the firestorm of our love. No matter what the future held, we had this moment, and that was enough. It gave me a reason to live, gave me the strength to fight. I'd do this for him, because of all he'd given me during our time together.

I spent the night in that twilight space between sleep and awake, immobile in the straitjacket of Wyatt's arms and legs with his gentle snoring stirring my hair. There was nowhere I'd rather be.

~27~

Morning came too fast. Wyatt and I were subdued and somewhat distant as we had coffee and made small talk, avoiding the topic of my looming departure. The magic of our last night had faded away, fear and a strange awkwardness taking its place. I put on my mojo outfit. Leethu and Dar came downstairs for a last minute check on the body then discretely vanished upstairs. I knew they'd been deliberately giving Wyatt and me time alone, and I appreciated it. For demons, they were both pretty cool.

"Well, I guess this is it," I told Wyatt, adjusting my shotgun harness and picking up the duffle bag that held the carefully wrapped body.

"I'll be waiting," Wyatt said, clutching me tight and inhaling deeply against my hair. I knew what he meant. No matter what happened, he'd watch for me. As he grew old, ill, he'd watch for me. Even if he married and had kids, grandkids, he'd watch for me: because no matter what, some bonds last forever.

"I'll be back," I promised, knowing it wasn't likely I'd be keeping that vow.

Then we pulled apart, slowly, reluctantly, afraid to meet each other's eyes. I stepped back, fingering the elf button in one hand and hefting the duffle bag over my shoulder. Forcing myself to be brave, I looked into his blue gaze, at the human within, the human who loved his hybrid sister, who cared little for material things, who was loyal, caring, generous; the human who loved a demon, who loved an imp, who loved the Iblis, who loved me.

"Glah ham, shoceacan."

I stood in the Cyelle kingdom, deep in the Western Red Forest outside the Elven city. Tossing the used elf button into the sticker bush to my left, I adjusted the duffle bag on my shoulder.

Five, four, three, two, one.

"Welcome, Iblis. We are preparing a room for you right now. Please follow us to your accommodations."

Three elves. I'm always amazed at how fast these guys are. I remembered Amber, darting all over the barn, leaping on and off the stable stall dividers and smiled a small, private smile. Yes, she was very elf. Leethu had done a good job.

The elves led me through the stretch of meadow surrounding the Cyelle capital and through the main gates. Citizens politely ignored my presence, but snuck quick, curious glances at me when they thought I wasn't looking. I wondered how many demons were escorted into the city on their own power as opposed to strung up and incapacitated. *Or on a runaway horse*, I thought, remembering my last visit.

We walked for quite a while through cobblestone streets. None of the guards offered to carry my bag. They clearly knew what it contained through, from all the nervous looks they darted at it. I wondered what they thought about the odd item attached to my back. There were no firearms this side of the gates. I doubted any of them had ever heard of a shotgun before, let alone knew how one operated. I was tempted to blow something up just to demonstrate, but I figured I was going to have a hard enough time getting out of here alive.

The second set of gates opened before us, and we marched to the left down a path of fragrant pine needles, flanked on either side by twisted yew, and willow trees. This wasn't the main entrance used by dignitaries and persons of importance. No, I was being led around to the back door. And I'm sure this shameful entrance was all due to what I held in my blue duffle bag. A little side door opened in the wall, and I ascended, elves before and behind me. The narrow stairs rose several flights before a slim door hidden in the wall slid open, opening into a vacant hallway. It was a maze of twists, turns, and stairs to reach my "accommodations". I wasn't sure if the circuitous route was to delay me in time to prepare my room, or to avoid encountering other elves. Probably both.

The room looked almost the same as the one I'd had previously. I gently put the bag on the bed, noticing the horrified winces of the guards.

"So when can I expect to meet with his Lordship?"

"Unfortunately Lord Taullian is out of the city on business, but we have notified him and he will return by late this afternoon." The guards shifted, exchanging nervous glances. I wondered what that was all about.

"A sorcerer will be here shortly to relieve you of your, uh, your baggage," one of the guards said, looking at the baggage in question as if it held the most virulent plague in Hel.

"Not happening," I told him. No way I was handing this thing over to anyone but Taullian. I had a bad feeling it would disappear, or be replaced by a corpse other than the one I brought. "This will have to stay in my possession until his Lordship arrives."

They nodded, and bowed, making a quick exit and leaving me alone. I checked the door and wasn't surprised to find it locked. I'd been given a lot more freedom last time, but then I hadn't been carrying around the remains of a shameful abomination: demon spawn. Still, a bored demon isn't a good thing, and I *was* surprised they hadn't provided me with some sort of entertainment. I wasn't bored long. With a soft knock on my door, an elf arrived pushing a cart full of food. Another elf accompanied her, carrying what appeared to be a basket of rats. My entertainment had arrived.

There's only so much fun I can have with a basket of rats, and I wasn't particularly hungry. I occupied myself splatting various fruits and tarts against the walls. Lucky for them I was summoned before I set the curtains on fire or exploded myself an exit through the beautifully inlaid oak floor. Again it took us forever to reach our destination as we roamed the entire castle, weaving through halls and circling through rooms sometimes three times. At last we turned onto a wide, gilded hallway and paused before a set of indigo and gold doors. They opened and inside was … nothing—or rather, nobody. Empty chairs sat around a vast table.

"Please have a seat, Iblis. His Lordship will be here momentarily."

I certainly hoped so, because this was boring. I looked over at one of the guards remaining with me and resolved that if this asshole didn't show up in ten minutes I was going to pop the guard's head off. Keep me waiting, huh?

The guard was spared a nasty fate by the prompt and ceremonious arrival of Lord Taullian. He strode in like he owned the place and walked over to where I'd placed the duffle bag. Behind him, her arms held by two guards, was the elf woman Tlia-Myea, face pale with fear. Her eyes met mine, searching for reassurance.

Lord Taullian frowned down at the duffle bag. "It's rather small. Did you put both the incubus and the girl in there?"

"It's the baby."

His head shot up, eyes steely. "Baby? Not 'girl'? And where is the incubus? This Leethu?"

"Baby. The incubus in question denies involvement. As she is a member of my household, you will need to prove to me that she sired the child before we can even begin to negotiate punishment."

Taullian's eyes grew cold. "The mother says it was this Leethu, and I believe her."

"You believe her about the identity of the sire, but are convinced she lies about everything else?" I scoffed. "We all look the same, constantly change forms and share names. Succubi and incubi are particularly hard for non-demons to identify. What makes you so sure it was Leethu and not someone else?"

He was silent a moment, shaking his head in disapproval. "Fine. Where is the human?"

"The human is dead," I said in my best "duh" voice. "You didn't say you wanted his body, too." I was a terrible liar. This wasn't going to be easy.

"I *do* want the human." His eyes bore into mine, as if he could bend me to his will simply with his gaze. I'd been shrugging off an angel's compulsion for months now; this guy couldn't do anything to me.

"Oh *yes*, your Lordship," I gushed. "Shall I get you a partridge in a pear tree while I'm at it?"

He looked affronted, but I didn't care. "Do you want this fucking baby or not? Because I'm sure your buddy over in Wythyn would be ecstatic to have it."

"The human is dead?" He'd flinched slightly at the mention of Wythyn, but recovered in a blink.

I inclined my head toward the elf woman. "She said the human was dead, and I can assure you he is, in fact, dead. Dead, dead, dead. And if you want me digging up and hauling around more corpses, then we need to renegotiate."

"I don't think you're in any position to renegotiate. From what I've heard, you're in rather desperate circumstances." The elf lord waved his hand over the duffle bag. "I'm feeling generous though, so I'll accept the body of the demon spawn as fulfillment of our contract. Assuming that you've delivered me the actual body, and not some hacked up forgery."

I felt a bead of sweat roll down my back and hoped that Dar was as good as he said he was. Pushing the bag toward him, I gestured for him to take a look. Wisely, he took a quick step back and motioned for a guard and sorcerer to come closer to the table. The sorcerer murmured a string of incantations and the bag glowed faintly white.

"All clear, your Lordship," he announced.

At a slight motion from his liege, the guard stepped forward and unzipped the bag with shaking hands. I was never so tempted to scare the fuck out of everyone by screaming and jumping aside, but I restrained myself and stood quietly, with my hands clasped in front of me. With the bag unzipped, the slightly green guard stepped back and again to allow the sorcerer to do his work. Satisfied that the corpse wasn't going to explode or transform into a giant piranha, he stepped back.

"Well, go ahead," Taullian said to the reluctant guard, his voice full of irritation.

The guard took forever to edge his way to the table. With a deep breath, he reached in and removed the tiny bundle from within. He carefully laid it next to the duffle bag then began to unwrap the towel. And there she was. Looking just as she did in her grave. Perfect and beautiful. Returned to her homeland, her features changed slightly, shedding the human mask they'd held to fool the grieving parents. Features became impossibly symmetrical, ears elongated to delicate tips, cheekbones and chin sharpened slightly. The baby glowed and everyone in the room gasped, for a moment their prejudice slipped away and all they saw was the most precious thing in all of Elven existence, a baby.

"That's not a demon spawn," Taullian said, his voice full of reverence.

For a moment I thought we'd failed, that as good as Dar was, the baby hadn't even passed physical scrutiny. Then I looked over toward Tlia-Myea and realized that the other elves in the room were seeing what she'd seen when she looked down at her baby—a child, beautiful, even if only half an elf. It was a shame that the others wouldn't have been as forgiving of the demon under the exterior. She'd been right to send Amber away. The child's chances with the humans were far better than they would have been here, with only her mother to protect her against such bigotry.

"My Lord, hybrids can be very deceptive," the sorcerer spoke up. "Please allow me to check."

I tried to keep my breathing even. Now was the moment of truth.

The sorcerer stepped forward and took a green stone from his pocket, placing it on the baby's forehead between her sparse, blond eyebrows. The stone instantly lit up, green and pink. He nodded.

"There is demon energy in the baby," he announced.

"Of course there is," Taullian said impatiently. "Demons aren't idiots. She'd hardly present us with a true elf changeling baby and think we would believe her. Check the composition. I want to make sure this is really the demon spawn and not some doctored up fraud."

That was pretty insulting, but he hadn't exactly been friendly from the moment he'd seen the contents of the bag. He clearly had expected me to bring back a fully grown woman, dead or alive. He didn't believe Tlia-Myea, didn't believe that she'd killed the baby. And he wasn't about to take this corpse at face value.

The sorcerer cleared a space around the baby and pulled a piece of chalk from the pouch at his side. We stood, watching as he drew intricate symbols and flowing Elven text around the baby. He finished one circle then began another. This was going to take fucking forever. I didn't think my nerves would hold out. I snuck a peek at the elf woman. She was pale with a tearstained face, staring resolutely at the baby on the table. She wouldn't look directly at me, but I noticed she kept me within her peripheral vision. Her hand moved slightly, flicking an index finger. One? Or was I supposed to look in the direction of the finger. I fidgeted, moving side to side and released an enormous sigh.

"Is this going to take much longer? Cause I got things to do."

They ignored me. I turned slightly, looking around the room for something interesting and specifically looking to see where Tlia-Myea had been pointing. One of the guards. Was he someone important? Or maybe she'd meant something different. Maybe she just had a twitchy finger. Fuck, these damned elves were so impossible to understand. Nothing was clear and straightforward with them.

"It appears to be a hybrid," the sorcerer said. But there was something in his voice that told me I shouldn't be celebrating yet.

Taullian looked pissed. "But?" he asked.

"I don't know." The sorcerer scratched his balding head in a typically human gesture of puzzlement. "Everything is in the right place, it's the right amount. It just seems ... too right. It's not degraded at all. After almost twenty years in a grave, the demon energy should be a mere echo. It should have dissipated."

Fuck. Dar hadn't taken that into account. He probably hadn't studied any long-dead-and-buried hybrids to know. I was a terrible liar, but it was time to bluff like my life depended on it.

"For fuck sake! Don't you guys seal these babies in stasis?" I threw up my hands in dramatic exasperation. "How do you expect demon energy to 'dissipate' when you've got the corpse preserved like Joseph Stalin?"

Taullian frowned. I knew he didn't want to believe me, that he really wanted to prove that Tlia-Myea had been lying. He walked forward, overcoming his reluctance to be so close to demon spawn, and reached a finger tentatively down to touch the baby's skin.

"This preservation is very well done. Could it be possible the demon energy was sealed in stasis?"

The sorcerer was unmistakably in a tight spot. A lot was riding on his determination. Yes, Tlia-Myea would lose her life regardless, but her reputation in death hinged on this. If he confirmed this baby to be the hybrid, and he was wrong, an abomination was free to walk the world. If he declared it wasn't, and he was wrong, an elf woman's name would forever be smirched and countless resources would be wasted hunting a non-existent demon spawn. I'd wind up facing Haagenti's wrath too, but I doubted my fate weighed that heavily on his mind.

"My Lord," he stuttered. "I need to do further testing. In my lab."

Taullian nodded, and the guard came forward to carefully wrap the baby, glowing stone and all, back in the towel before gently placing it in the duffle bag. He followed the sorcerer from the room, carrying the bag.

"We've all seen that baby," I said to Taullian, waving my finger in what I hoped was a threatening manner. "That human of yours better not pull a switcharoo or anything."

He turned on me, fury and menace in his face. It was far more effective than my waving finger. "If you have lied, if that baby is a fake, then our deal is off."

I nodded. Yeah. I figured that.

But he wasn't done. He took a few steps toward me, standing closer than he normally would have if not overcome with anger. "That's not all. If that baby is a fake, then you have not only violated our deal, you've desecrated a precious Elven baby. That is an unforgivable act. It's an act of war."

It would be really nice if these elf fuckers would let us know these things ahead of time. That really upped the stakes. Not that I could do anything about it now. I could only hope Dar had done a good job and that all the shit I'd thrown up in the air landed in a beneficial manner. Still, I couldn't help but yank his chain.

"Shit, I had no idea. What about all those elf babies I've dug up over the centuries and let my hellhound have for dinner?"

Taullian dove at me, and before his guards could react, I'd thrown him aside to crash into a chair and roll across the floor. I was held flat against the table before I could do anything more.

"Keep your pants on elf boy," I said mockingly. "It's the real thing. Think I'd fake something this important with Haagenti breathing down my neck?"

He stood up, straightening his clothing and strange comb-over hairdo.

"Take her to her room," he announced.

The guards hauled me away, but not before I saw what his odd hairstyle had been hiding: a mangled ear, the top point completely missing.

~28~

After twenty-four hours trapped in my room, I was longing for Haagenti's torture. I no longer cared what the sorcerer determined, I just wanted out of this damned room. When a knock finally came, I raced to the door in joy. The face at the door wasn't a guard, but a human—a human mage. I stared at him blankly a moment before I realized this human was Kirby, the mage from the disastrous winter festival. He quickly slipped in the door, opening it little more than a crack and shutting it quietly behind him.

"I'm sure the guard outside saw you," I said wryly.

"He's one of Tlia's. A fourth cousin twice removed."

Ah, so maybe she *had* been pointing at him, identifying him as someone I could rely on when the shit hit the fan. I was perplexed though. How would a fourth cousin twice removed be loyal, when her own first cousin, Taullian, was determined to see her dead and dishonored? Was it the Wythyn blood in her veins? Elven politics were like a fucking soap opera.

"You need to get out of here."

No shit, Sherlock.

"No way," I told him. "I've got a business deal with the High Lord, and I'm not leaving before he delivers on his end of the contract."

Kirby looked around the room nervously. "I overheard one of the sorcerers. They can't validate your 'delivery' either way, and since His Lordship seems to desire a negative result, that's what they are going to proclaim."

Fuck. Dar *had* pulled it off, but it looked like it wouldn't matter. Taullian had his people so under his thumb, they'd bend anything to suit his whim. All that work, and I'd still be tossed out on my ass to face Haagenti. Or worse.

"What do they intend to do with me?" I asked.

Kirby shook his head, avoiding my eyes. "Normally, they'd just escort you to the border and forbid you to return. They'd spread the word that you weren't reliable to conduct elven business with and make sure all kingdoms were aware of your breach of contract. But His Lordship seems particularly emotional about you."

I thought back to our first meeting, his alternating moods of friendliness and fear. Had I met him before? Something nudged in the back of my mind, but I couldn't grasp it.

"He's ranting about having you imprisoned. Says he should have known better than to ever trust you again. That you continue to commit deliberate offence against the kingdom and the elven race."

Crap. It's not like *I* was the one who fucked an elf and impregnated her. And this was the first job I'd ever done for this guy, for his kingdom. At least that I could recall. I'd done a lot of work for elves though. Perhaps something pissed him off.

"He believes that the 'delivery' is a fake," I told Kirby. "Is desecration of an elven corpse enough of an offence for this kind of reaction?"

Kirby grimaced. "It's pretty bad. Probably. Especially combined with whatever you must have screwed up before."

"So I should make a run for it?" I asked.

"I don't know. It would be really hard for you to get out right now. Even with some of the guards helping, there are wards on the gates and alarms if you try to fly out. The fact that you're the Iblis might give him pause. I know his advisors will urge him not to act in haste against you. Still, you need to run for it if the opening presents itself."

The mighty Iblis, running for it. What a worthless title.

"Thank you, Kirby." I meant it. I'd only met him briefly, and here he was, risking his position and probably his life to warn me. "I owe you a favor. Is there something you would request of me?"

It would be in his best interest to call in the favor now. Human lives were very short, and it was a good possibility that he wouldn't see me again to collect before he aged and died. Kirby shyly handed a round object to me, wrapped in paper.

"It's the cats-eye marble I had with me when I fell through the trap. I carried it everywhere, even slept with it. The paper has my parents' names and address where I lived as a child, and also a note for them. Can you deliver it? I want them to know I lived and that I've had a good life. That I think of them all the time."

I put the package in the pocket of my jeans. "I will honor your request, as my favor to you."

He nodded, his eyes shining with unshed tears. I wondered as he walked out the door if he shed those tears every night.

Kirby had been gone a few hours when a more firm, authoritative knock came at my door. The guards, including the fourth cousin, escorted me with decreasing ceremony downstairs and back to the room with the long table. Again I waited until Taullian and his posse finally entered. Kirby was right. I could tell by the high lord's angry stride that all would not go well.

"You lied," he thundered, before he even reached the table. "Desecrated a perfect child, disturbed her eternal rest, and broke faith on our contract."

Yes, that was all true, but I wasn't going down without a fight.

"Bullshit. I busted my ass getting that baby for you. You know it's the real deal; you're just fabricating these lies because you're too weak to take out Haagenti as promised. You're reneging on our contract because you're too chicken shit to face him."

Taullian turned purple. I wondered briefly what the punishment would be for driving a high lord to aneurism. He muttered something unintelligible, then whirled around to face the elf woman who had been dragged in behind him.

"Where did you hide the baby? I know it's still alive. You're sheltering an abomination, a demon spawn you helped create. You're unworthy of the elven race, a disgrace to your family."

Tlia-Myea lifted her head proudly. "I told you. I killed the baby as soon as it was born. You have her corpse. Stop this insane witch-hunt now, before you have a war on your hands."

"You threaten me?" the elf choked out. "You threaten me with your Wythyn relatives?"

The woman nodded toward me. "Wythyn or the demons. You're making enemies left and right, my cousin."

"I am not your cousin," he sneered. "I am not related to anyone so weak as to fall for a demon's wiles, let alone one traitorous enough to shield a monstrous beast. You are not my cousin. You're not Cyellian. You're not an elf. You're dead to all."

I wasn't off the hook. He turned, walking toward me with a strange combination of bravado and fear.

"Give me the information on the child, and I'll let you live." There was something in his voice, a strange waver of indecision, as though he dreaded my execution just as much as he desired it.

"I already gave you the child."

I was a terrible liar, and I didn't even try with this one. It didn't matter if he believed me or not. Let him think I was definitely fucking him over. Let him wonder for the rest of his life where Amber was. He'd find her over my dead body. Which might be sooner rather than later.

"I'll have you put to death right beside her," he snarled.

"Really? Put the Iblis to death? How do you think you're going to accomplish that? You really want a war on your doorstep?"

"No one cares that you're the Iblis. It's a meaningless title. There isn't one being that would stop me from killing you."

But there was. I thought of Wyatt, Michelle and Candy, of Tlia-Myea and her family, Dar and Leethu, of Kirby. Not many, but there were some on my side. And there was one I was hoping would be particularly incensed at any threat to my person. Of course, he hadn't seemed to care about Haagenti possibly killing me, so maybe I was wrong. Either way, it was the only card I had left in my hand. Time to bluff.

Awkwardly sliding my arm out of the oilskin duster, I showed Taullian my brand. The tattoo of a sword with angel wings on the guard in red-purple that went beyond the skin to network deep within me.

"This being would stop you. Or perhaps you don't mind incurring his wrath?"

Taullian jumped back and the sorcerer behind him paled, his eyes wide with shock.

"She's bound. By an angel."

"You've been feeding the angels a load of Kool-aid about how pure and evolved you are for millions of years. What if they knew? Knew about the gates and the humans? I could call him to my side. Let him see how ugly the elves really are."

Silence stretched on. Finally Taullian clenched his fists in frustration.

"You will be escorted to the edge of our lands. Never return. If you ever fall in to Elven hands again, you will meet a punishment worse than death. Is that clear?"

"Absolutely." I smiled. "I think I prefer the company of humans to you anyway. At least they're honest."

Taullian choked. "Get out."

I was "escorted" at an extremely rapid pace through the palace, and the streets of the city, and out the gates. It was clear they weren't going to waste using an inter-realm gate on me by the mounted guards along the tree line. I wasn't exactly sure how far their borders were, but this was probably going to be a brutal death march.

It was six hours later and we were still tromping through the woods in silence.

"If you'd let me ride one of your horses, this wouldn't take so long," I complained.

Nothing.

"If you'd let me manifest wings and fly, this wouldn't take so long."

Nothing.

"If you'd gate me to the border, this wouldn't take so long."

"Lord Taullian said you are to walk," a guard finally replied.

I continued to complain about random things. Then I began to sing commercial jingles. When I'd run out of jingles, I sang all the tunes I could think of that Wyatt detested. Not that the elves had similar music tastes to Wyatt. They'd probably hate his dubstep just as much as the Carpenters' songs I was belting out.

"I can't take this," one guard said to another. "Can we just gate her to the border and say we walked."

The other guards looked uneasy. Taullian wasn't in a good mood. An infraction would likely result in an over-the-top, harsh punishment. Smiling, I began a new song. A song about the sweetness of love, about birds singing, flowers blooming, and sunshine shining.

"Can we gag her?" one of the elves asked hopefully. I'd like to see them try.

"Better not," another responded, seeing my maniacal grin.

I continued to sing the saccharine song, the elves cringing with every note. Encouraged by their reaction, I increased the volume and added some dramatic gestures. Faces twisted and several put their hands over their pointed ears. I swear I heard their teeth grind. Still we clomped through the forest, as I belted out the chorus, all about loved ones hurting each other and making each other cry.

"Let's just gate her out of here," one pleaded. "I don't think I can take three days of this."

Fuck. Three days? They intended to keep me walking, non-stop for three days? We'll see about that. I walked over to one of the elves and began serenading him personally with dramatic intonation and gestures.

"Nothing His Lordship would do to us could possibly be worse than this. Nothing. Where does she get these horrible songs?" A few of the other guards nodded.

I moved on to another elf, so he wouldn't feel neglected. I wouldn't have any problem keeping this up for three days. Who would break first? I was betting it would be the elves.

"Stop. Just stop already. You win."

I smiled.

"He'll kill us," another guard argued. "Just stuff pinecones in your ears or something."

"Can you take any more? If she's this bad now, imagine how much worse it's going to get by tomorrow," another argued back.

"I know a lot of songs," I assured them. I couldn't wait until I started singing Air Supply and they began voiding their bowels. Wyatt had told me their music had that effect. I was sure it was something subliminal.

"Let's strap her across one of the horses and ride as fast as we can. We could be there in twenty four hours."

They all looked at me nervously. I started to hum.

"I don't know about you, but I'm not about to risk offending the Iblis by strapping her across a horse like a deer carcass. His Lordship might be powerful enough for that sort of thing, but I'm not."

There were a few nods, then the original elf, the one who pleaded with the others to use the gate, spoke up.

"We use the gate, take our time getting back, and say we ended up hauling her there like cargo on a horse. Deal?"

None of them looked thrilled, but they finally agreed to the plan. We continued until we found a suitable spot in a clearing. The elves checked the trees, and one even climbed up to peer above the canopy. They were like monkeys, darting around and hopping from limb to limb. That done, they marked a circle of trees, setting up a perimeter to keep anyone from detecting the gate. With a wave of a hand and a flash, a haze appeared in the air before us, big enough for elf, demon, and horse to pass through two abreast. It was a big gate, no doubt to ensure I didn't escape in passage. No wonder they'd taken such precautions. The kind of energy blast it took to create a temporary gate this large would be felt for miles without their protective circle. The angels had a far more efficient means of moving about inside a realm, but even this overkill of an elven gate was beyond my abilities.

Two guards on horseback went through first, then I followed with a guard by my side and another leading my escort's horse at the rear. We appeared in a forest clearing that looked just like the one we'd left. My partner got back on his horse and within ten minutes, I saw the brightening light signaling the edge of the forest and the Elven lands. We stopped right inside the tree line, and I looked out upon the expanse of dry, dusty scrub. This wasn't the boundary of the Western Red Forest. Where had they taken me? I looked up at one of the guards quizzically, totally disoriented. He dismounted and taking my arm, walked me toward the border.

Trees thinned and I saw the swirls of red rise in dust devils around the thorny bushes. A hot shimmer hazed the horizon where large boulders stood. Suddenly I realized where we were. Dis. Haagenti's lands. They'd delivered me right to him. I jerked my arm away from the guard and halted.

"Fuckers," I hissed. "It's one thing to throw me out on my ass, but another to serve me up to my enemy."

The guard shot a quick look back at his companions and took my arm again. "It would have been far worse if you'd been tired and hungry after marching for days," he whispered.

I walked slowly, searching the haze for figures, for signs of demons coming to collect me. "Did that asshole of an elf tell them I would be here? Are they going to grab me the moment I step foot out of the forest?"

He shook his head, urging me forward. "We're here much earlier than we were supposed to be. One of us will signal him as we leave, but they're further away than they had intended. They'll be coming for you from the south. There is an angel gate into Seville about an hour to the east as the crow flies. Don't shelter in the edges of the Elven forests. All the kingdoms have been warned to shoot on sight. There is a price on your head. And the demons regularly patrol the borders now, too."

Bolt to the east, as fast and as stealthily as I could, and make it through the gate to Seville. Or I could just summon Gregory and have him yank me out of here. Or I could just get this all over with. The angel was right. It was way past time. Time to do what I needed to.

I paused at the forest edge, the front of my boot on the hard-packed red dirt with its light dusting of ultra-fine sand, the rest of my foot on lush, green, loamy moss. The elves did love their forests.

"Thank you," I told the guard. And I stepped out into the suffocating heat that stole my breath and burned my skin. It was time.

~29~

I headed due south, wishing this oilcloth coat didn't feel so damned hot, wishing I could change into my familiar reptile form that was better suited to this temperature. But I wasn't about to abandon Wyatt's gifts, or Kirby's marble and notes, and I needed this human form right now. This was who I'd become. This human shape was more than just a skin I wore. I'd been Samantha Martin in more than appearance for over forty years, and somehow that had changed me. If I went back to my old self, my old form, I'd be giving up all I'd become. Az the little imp could never hope to defeat Haagenti, but Az the Iblis had at least a snowflake's chance in Hel. And Az the Iblis was more than a demon; she was a demon who had somehow become slightly human. Samantha Martin, Wyatt, and all my friends had done this for me, and I wasn't about to disgrace what I had become by reverting to a common imp the moment the going got tough. So forward I went, sweating between the blistering sky and sand.

That guard wasn't kidding. We *were* early. I'd walked for over an hour before I saw figures far ahead in the haze. Some were large, some small, of all shapes and sizes. I counted nearly twenty, although it was difficult to be sure at this distance. Haagenti had brought a lot of back-up. It gave me a shot of confidence to think that I'd shaken him up so much at Taullian's party that he brought along twenty other demons, just in case. I tried to think of something that would help me hold onto my faltering mojo as we approached each other across the blur of red dust.

Gregory had urged me to do a "mighty show of power", which would work for an angel that had to be at least six billion years old. But how could an imp possibly pull it off? Yes, I was the Iblis, but it wasn't the powerful title the angels seemed to think it was. None of the demons cared. Being Ha-satan impressed no one. And I just didn't have the presence or the strength to intimidate demons many levels above me.

Wyatt saw me as the lone stranger, riding in to town and picking off my enemies from a rooftop in a stealthy, sneak attack. Like a demon sniper. That certainly appealed to the little imp who wanted desperately to hide under a rock, but I didn't see how it would work here in Dis, without even a decent sized cactus to shield me. Besides, the element of surprise had gone out the window long ago.

I had a shotgun I wasn't sure would even work in Hel, a really cool duster, and hopefully luck, that fickle mistress, would continue to walk by my side. But I was still an imp in human form, against a mighty demon. I'd just have to wing it. Rely on whatever mad skills happened to spring to mind.

"Haagenti. I'm gonna kick your ass!" I shouted. Or at the very least, bite it.

The approaching demons looked at me oddly. They'd never thought I was all together sane anyway, so none of them should have been surprised. We approached, imaginary spurs clinking like bells in the silence. The atmosphere was appropriate. Dis was vaguely desert-like with woody, brown spiked flora sparsely dotting the landscape, and a haze of crimson heat.

None of us launched an attack as we drew near. I hopped aside to avoid a thorny tumbleweed that would have done nothing to my reptile shape, but would have swollen my human skin like a balloon with one touch. The mojo from Wyatt's gifts was fleeting, vanishing along with the tumbleweed. What was I thinking, approaching Haagenti in such a vulnerable shape? There was no time to do anything different. I'd committed myself to this human form, and to assume another at this point would likely be seen as a sign of weakness. I stopped and awaited Haagenti's last few steps. I wanted him to make the first moves so I could react to his attack. It might not be the best fighting strategy, but it was one that had always worked for me.

The other demons held back, and Haagenti in his bullion form, sans wings, came insultingly close. That's when I realized that these other demons weren't here for back-up. They were witnesses. My resolve wavered. He was that confident. He'd brought a group along to watch me get pummeled, humiliated, and eventually killed. Plus I recognized two of Haagenti's household. Assalbi, no doubt still pissed from my smack-down at Taullian's party, and Progemon. They held back with the others, who seemed to be here strictly for the enjoyment of watching a fight. This battle was to be mano a mano, and Haagenti wasn't worried about any risk to himself. Of course, he didn't have much to worry about: soft human flesh against the might of his horns and claws.

"Oh good," I told him. "There weren't nearly enough demons to see me kick your ass, and send you running away at the elf festival. This will ensure you can't cover it up this time with excuses and lies."

He snorted, pawing the ground. "If it wasn't for Zalanes and those darned elves, I would have you in my dungeon right now."

It sounded like a Scooby Doo episode. "*I would have gotten away with it too, if it wasn't for those darned kids and their dog….*"

He eyed the stock of the shotgun rising above my shoulder. "No one recognizes you as the Iblis. You dare to carry a stolen weapon? A symbol of power you don't have?"

I smiled. "So you want me to put it down? Fight you without it? That's hardly fair, an unarmed demon in human form against your bull-lion shape. But then, you like to stack the odds in your favor, don't you?"

"There is no one stopping you from assuming a more defensive form. And besides," he gestured to the crowd behind him with a lion tail. "I'm giving you the respect of a one-on-one fight. Respect you don't deserve."

I rolled my eyes. Yeah, I was a thief, a liar, a deceiver—all reputable traits. What sins had he committed lately? Carefully I unbuckled the scabbard holding the Shotgun of the Iblis and sat it on the ground, edging it away with my foot. I wasn't worried about anyone stealing it. Even if they could, no one wanted the thing. No one but Haagenti, it seemed.

"I'll fight you in this form, with only my demon powers and my human flesh. I wouldn't want anyone to say I'd won a fight unfairly."

Haagenti laughed, a bellow of sound. "I'll remember that as I gut you."

It was a stupid, asinine decision, to fight Haagenti as a human. One of those impulse things. I should have taken the chance and assumed something with decent physical weapons, with a tough hide or even an exoskeleton. Maybe I figured death would be quicker, less painful this way. Who knows? I never really understood some of the things I did.

We carefully circled each other, watching. He wasn't a fool, wasn't rushing his attack. He'd probably not fought a human or had any direct contact with them beyond the Elven slaves for centuries. And I'm sure he wasn't sure what powers I'd managed to acquire during my time on earth. Finally he shot a short burst of energy at me, more to gauge my reaction than to actually harm me. As I'd done at Taullian's festival, I absorbed it instantly.

A bolt of lightning came my way next, but I'd played with lightning since I was in my crib, and I'd learned many things since then. I grabbed it, and split the blast into a thousand shards of light, sending them skyward in tiny sparks. The crowd made a gratifying "oooo" noise. Their appreciation snapped whatever control Haagenti had and he charged, swiftly impaling me on a horn. Before I could grab him, he'd tossed his head, ripping my abdomen and sending me flying over his back to land in the hard, red dust.

Damn, that hurt. I pulled back from the damaged area and quickly stuffed a dangling section of my guts back inside. I didn't care that anyone saw the extent of the wound, but I was concerned that the intestine would get hooked on Haagenti's horns and he'd completely disembowel me. I staggered to my feet, holding my side and watched Haagenti come in for a second attack. This time I succeeded in grabbing both horns and snapping them off with a burst of energy. Haagenti roared, swinging his head in pain, and I slashed with my new weapons, managing to rake one along his neck and jam the other into his shoulder.

For humans, injuries like ours would have been the death of us, but we were demons, and we were in Hel. With no threat from angels and plenty of energy to draw from this was almost foreplay. Haggenti staunched the bleeding, and recreated the horns in a flash while I rapidly repaired my gut wound. Within seconds, the only thing remaining was the horn in Haagenti's shoulder, annoyingly out of reach and impossible for him to remove without opposable thumbs. I knew it pissed him off to have it there, visible to everyone.

He rushed again and, this time, I stepped forward into him, too close for his horns and hooves to have any effect. I slammed him with a burst of raw energy as he raked one of his rear lion claws across my thigh. He grunted with pain from my blast, but his claw did far more damage on my human flesh. Falling to my knee, he seized the advantage and pushed me flat, pinning me with his weight. Now the fight began in earnest. Haagenti pounded me with blasts of energy while I took precious time to repair my leg. I absorbed as much of the energy as I could, pulling it inside my gigantic stash, but it was coming too fast for me to absorb it all, especially while trying to fix my injuries. Instinctively, I'd pulled back, withdrew from my human form as Gregory had taught me. That meant my physical body was taking immense amounts of damage, but my spirit self was not. I let him hammer away at me, let him think he was bringing me close to death. Little did he know I was probably the only demon who could live inside a dead physical form.

I had a choice. I could let him kill my physical body in a rage, play possum, and hope he just went away. But that wouldn't solve the problem and I was getting really tired of this feud. Knowing how much it would hurt, I extended my personal energy, my spirit being back into every cell of the flesh as I began to absorb and convert his attack. It hurt like fuck, but was worth the look of surprise on Haagenti's face. He increased his attack, energy pouring into me like a hot stream. I struggled, but I managed to convert it all. Furious, he began drawing directly from our environment, slamming me with the maximum he could.

"Why won't you fucking die?" he roared.

Because I'm a cockroach, I thought. *And we are really hard to kill.*

He was getting sloppy, desperate. I let some of his attack spill away from my control, burning and searing my spirit self with damage that would leave a permanent scar. His elation at this success was palpable. With another roar, he tried to increase the volume of the energy he was pounding into me, but he was at his maximum. Still, he pushed, and there, his own spirit self, right on the edge of his physical being, right within reach. Finally.

I seized him, and I pulled.

Mine.

He spooled out from his body like a line of thread into my grasp. Tearing, Shredding, Devouring. Before he could even register surprise, before he could make a sound, he was gone. The only remains an empty shell, a lion bull form collapsed on top of my prone body.

I took a ragged breath. The actual me, the spirit being, was injured, and that would never heal. I'd forever carry these scars, but at least no abilities or skills had been lost. My physical body was severely damaged, and although I could survive its death, I hadn't yet figured out how to move it around as a corpse. There was no time to repair it though. Haagenti was clearly dead, and I had to act fast. I shoved the heavy body aside, squirming and shuffling to wiggle myself free. Out of the corner of my eye, I saw Assalbi and Progemon run towards me, as if in slow motion. Their shouts rang out as I rolled to my scabbard. They were Haagenti's household, and with his death, they'd be mine to do with as I pleased. Clearly they wouldn't relish that fate, and I knew they'd try to finish me off before I had a chance to fix any damage.

Grabbing the stock of the shotgun, I yanked it free of its holster, thankful I hadn't bothered to snap it in tight. Wyatt had said the artifact wouldn't need loading, I sure as fuck hoped it didn't need to be racked either because I had no time left for that shit. I pointed the barrel in the general direction of the advancing demons and pulled the trigger. I suck at shooting. I couldn't hit an elephant if it were two inches in front of me. I just hoped the deafening noise of the shotgun blast, and the sight of an unknown and unfamiliar weapon would buy me some time. Imagine my surprise when Assalbi flew backwards in a spray of red. Progemon halted to look at the other demon in astonishment, so I took the opportunity and shot him too. Those two shots did more for my mojo than anything I'd done to date. I looked at the Shotgun of the Iblis in admiration and thought that I should have just blown Haagenti's head off when he was a hundred yards away, sort of a combo of Wyatt's plan and Gregory's "mighty show of power". It would have saved me a whole lot of trouble and hurt. Next time that would be my strategy.

I quickly fixed my physical body, which was beginning to go into convulsions, and stood up to observe my latest victims. They weren't dead, but watching them flop around in their own blood as they squealed was gratifying. It took them forever to repair themselves, making me wonder if the artifact had some effect beyond just physical damage, like the white stuff the angels attacked with. Finally Assalbi and Progemon rose to their feet, still bleeding and vomiting in the red dust. The crowd parted as they staggered back, rejecting them and making it clear to me they would not avenge Haagenti's death.

"Listen up, Bitches." I shouted, raising my shotgun to the sky. "I am the Iblis. I killed this worthless piece of crap as our blood feud warranted. There will be no weregeld."

The spectators nodded in agreement. Good. There would be no retaliation, but I knew many would discount this as a lucky break. Suddenly I realized what Gregory really meant. There were no more rocks to hide under. It had always been my habit to fly under the radar, to be underestimated in order to gain an advantage, but this was a time to show power: a time for others to fear what I really was.

"I am the Ha-satan, the Iblis. I ripped Haagenti out of his form and shredded him to bits. I consumed him. I am a devouring spirit. If any of you cross me, this will be your fate too."

There was an air of discomfort, but no one objected. Devouring wasn't an acceptable form of fighting. It wasn't an acceptable form of anything. What I'd done was icky, kind of psycho. But what revolts the sensibilities also terrifies.

I put on my scabbard, slipped the Shotgun of the Iblis into its holster, and turned around to leave—the lone stranger, striding off into the sunset. Wyatt would have been proud.

After a few steps, I realized I had no idea exactly where I was. I wasn't familiar with Cyelle enough to know where the elves had gated me, and I'd only been in Dis a few times. I had a feeling that heading to the city shimmering in the distance wouldn't put me anywhere near my destination. So much for my grand exit.

"Uh, hey," I called to the retreating crowd. "Can anyone tell me which way to Wythyn?"

One pointed to his left, never turning around. The others kept walking. Clearly I'd impressed them with my mighty show of power.

"Hey!" I shouted. This time I punctuated it with a shotgun blast and was gratified to see demons flinging themselves to the ground. "How do I get to Wythyn, and how far is it as the human walks?"

A tall, black, shadowy form with horns and red eyes approached me, eyeing my shotgun.

"Northeast." He pointed off into the endless sea of red dust. "About two days if you walk in your current form."

"Thanks," I told him, setting off.

I wasn't going home without my horse.

~30~

I walked for about four hours, my clothes plastered to me with sweat. Thirsty, hungry and tired, I realized there was no way I could walk all the way to Wythyn. The Elven forest was to my right, receding into the haze, but I was certain it was still Cyelle. I longed for the dewy coolness, but couldn't risk capture until I was sure it would be Wythyn elves hauling me away, not Taullian's.

Two days I plodded along, turning my head slightly to see if I were still being followed. A couple of the demons had left the group after I headed away and continued to trail behind me, close enough to keep me in sight, but far enough to be safe from a shotgun blast. I considered stripping off all my clothing, securing it into a bundle around the gun scabbard then transforming into something more suitable for the climate, something that could travel quicker than a slow human walk. My followers caused me some hesitation. I'd made a big deal about fighting Haagenti in a human form. Would changing into something more demonic decrease the effect of my statement? Would it be seen as a weakness that I couldn't travel the entire distance in the form I'd come to prefer? In the back of my mind I wondered if resuming my reptile shape here, in Hel, would cause me to fall back into the demon I was long ago. Would I shed my humanity as I shed the human form? I'd gotten used to walking that knife-edge between the two, come to enjoy the duality. I didn't want to lose that, didn't want to upset the balance.

I saw movement to my left and a flash of sun on scales, but it wasn't a demon. A sand serpent, surfacing from its tunnels deep below, tested the air for the scent of prey. Glancing quickly, I saw a figure in the distance behind me. One left. I wondered how long it would be until he gave up. Hopefully before I collapsed from dehydration. Another flash; this one closer. I pulled the shotgun from the holster and held it ready. Sand serpents didn't usually mess with demons, but they weren't particularly smart and often mistook us for an easy meal. In human form, I'm sure I smelled like an easy meal. Another flash. I stopped and waited, gun at the ready.

Ignoring the tickle of sweat rolling down my neck, I tapped my foot lightly on the hard-packed, red clay, just to let the serpent know where I was. The ground shifted slightly under my feet, softening into dusty sand. I jumped early, not wanting to rely too much on slow human reaction times, and shot the flash of red that rose from the ground where I'd been standing just a second before. Red flew apart in chunks, and the headless body vanished back underground. Sand Serpents didn't need their heads to survive, it's not like their brains were all that useful anyway. It would take him a few hours to form a vestigial head, a small nub, before he headed out in search of another meal. He wouldn't be back though. They weren't that stupid.

The demon following me had halted, watching from a distance. I kept him in my line of sight as I checked out the chunks of sand serpent scattered on the red desert floor. I'd lucked out. The lower jaw held a water bladder, and somehow it had managed to stay intact. This one was a good size, almost a gallon of liquid. I stuffed some of the salt-rimmed scales in my coat pockets, and grabbed a couple pieces of meat, brushing the desert dust from them. With my water tucked under my arm, munching on a piece of meat, I continued on.

Still, that fucking demon followed me. I wondered if he'd eaten the rest of the serpent's head. He must be in a form that didn't require much water or he would have turned back long ago. The sun was setting off to the east, tingeing the red landscape with lavender and brown. I'd finished my food and nearly all the water, and wasn't relishing another day and a half of this bullshit. I especially wasn't looking forward to tromping through Dis in the dark of night in human form. I was going to have to change shape. I thought about confronting the demon, but every time I stopped, he did. Every time I headed toward him, he retreated. The darker it got, the closer he came, and finally, as night fully descended, he was only about ten yards away.

I turned to get a good look at him and was surprised to see a Low.

"Why are you following me? What do you want?"

He looked respectfully at my feet, scaled claws by his sides. He was hunched over, as if he would have been more at home on all fours, and this added to the air of subservience.

"I offer myself to your household, Iblis," he said, bobbing his head to emphasize his deference.

Fuck. I already had one Low in my household. Were they all going to flock to me for protection and status? What was I going to do with them all?

"What skills do you have?" I asked with a sigh. Let's just get this over with, so he could leave and I could switch to a faster, more defensible shape.

"I can do the lightning," he said proudly. "And I can change color."

Any demon older than two seconds could do lightning. And what use would I possibly have for a demon that changed color? Maybe I could stand him in the corner at parties, like a festive color-changing lamp.

"Report to my Stewart and tell him you are to entertain others with your magnificent color changing abilities."

I was feeling generous, and tired. Honestly, I just wanted him to go away and this seemed like the quickest way to accomplish that.

"Yes," he squeaked. "Oh, thank you, Iblis. You will be most pleased with my color changes."

He scurried off Southwest, on all fours this time, and I watched until he vanished in the dark. Then I drained the last of my water and stripped, bundling all my clothing in a ball surrounded by my coat and held tight with the scabbard ties. I looped my belt through into a circle, then stepped back and transformed into my first form. It felt good: really good. The temperature was suddenly insignificant and the hard-packed ground felt softer under my claws. I shoved one of my three heads through the belt circle, sliding my little bundle down my neck to rest against the swell of my shoulder. With a flap of wings, I took to the sky.

What would have been a day and a half on foot took a mere hour. Hot thermals buoyed me upward, caressing my wings as I flew. The elven forests stretched out to my left, the bareness of Dis to my right. In the day, the contrast would have been more noticeable. The elven forests spread verdant with a clear line delineating the kingdom borders. Each kingdom had favored color schemes, plants and animals, and these changed abruptly, right at the territory line. Where the elven lands met demon ones, the difference was even more striking. We both manipulated our environments, but the elves had far greater skill. And demons really didn't care that much about botanical diversity.

I landed outside the Wythyn border at its south-eastern edge just as one moon glimmered at the horizon. The trees were identical to those in Cyelle. Even in the dark, I could see the moss and lush green stretching in a dense forest to the north. There was an addition of hanging moss on the trees here, and a slightly different bark texture, but these two kingdoms were visually similar.

I contemplated waiting until daybreak, but I was tired and just wanted to get this over with and go home, so I deposited my bundle and stepped back, transforming into my human, Samantha Martin, form. Dressing, I checked my pockets. Kirby's marble and notes were there, along with the salt-edged sand serpent scales. I strapped the Shotgun of the Iblis on my back and without further ado, stepped over the defined line that separated the red clay of Dis from the loamy green of the elven forest. Instantly, the birdsong stopped. Ah, the alarm. It wouldn't take them long now. I hoped they'd be quick about it because I really wanted a nap. I hadn't slept well the night I'd left, wanting to spend as much waking time as I could enjoying Wyatt's embrace, and I certainly didn't sleep while locked in my room in Cyelle. I strolled through the forest, but I didn't need to walk far. Less than twenty minutes later a net fell over me, dropping me to the ground and disabling my ability to use my energy. I felt myself dumped unceremoniously over the back of a horse and tied to the saddle. Finally, nap time.

~31~

"Look what we found."

Whatever net they'd thrown over me had blinded me, but unfortunately I could still feel pain as I was rudely dropped from about four feet and bounced down what must have been the hardest stairs ever. I couldn't fix myself, so I lay blind and bruised, in a heap on a cold floor.

"She came back? After last time? These demons are fools indeed."

I hadn't made it to the High Lord's presence. I'd get there eventually; since I'm sure he wanted a piece of me. Cursing him out, refusing to bend to his commands, then vanishing right out from under him. Yeah, I'd probably be seeing him real soon.

I felt something prodding my hip, like a stick. "She's got a price on her head."

"That demon guy? Hagen something?"

"Not just him. Cyelle would be very grateful if she somehow appeared in their dungeons."

I heard a laugh. "Cyelle can do their own dirty work. Although Lord Feille might swap her for one of their sorcerers."

"At the rate we go through them, maybe he should ask for two," a sarcastic voice said.

"Hush, you idiot. Do you want to be strung up for treason?"

Interesting. Seems I wasn't the only one who thought this lord was an asshole. They continued to discuss my probable fate in hushed voices, occasionally prodding me with a foot or some kind of stick object. Eventually, notice must have come of my summons, as conversation halted and I felt myself dragged along the floor. It wouldn't have been as bad if I didn't have a shotgun strapped to my back. The thing kept digging into me and catching on walls and doorways, twisting me in painful directions.

I bumped down another set of stairs, the shotgun jabbing into my back, my head and my arms, adding considerably to my bruises. I landed at the bottom feeling as though I'd been beaten repeatedly with a hammer.. Instead of setting me free, someone started beating me with another object.

"Az, Az. I am so happy to see you," came the voice of Feille, in time with the blows. I was really feeling the welcome.

"Let me out of this bag and we'll see how happy you are."

He laughed and kept whacking me. "I'll let you out in a minute. I'm just relieving a little frustration."

I twisted around so his next hit directly impacted my shotgun, and was thrilled to hear his stick crack and splinter.

"That was my favorite staff," Feille said, although he didn't seem terribly upset at the loss.

"Shall I get you another, My Lord?" a voice asked.

"No, I'm done anyway. Go ahead and let her out."

I heard footsteps and was rolled around as the net lifted off. As soon as I was free, I fixed my cracked rib and various bruises and straightened my clothing. My shirt was a bloody, shredded mess from the fight with Haagenti, but everything else was in good order. Feille had left my side and was sitting in a ridiculously ostentatious throne that rose nearly ten feet above his crowned head. A sorcerer stood beside him, hands at the ready in case I made an aggressive move. I noticed a circle of runes around the throne chair, no doubt to guard against demon attack. It pissed me off further. The guy was happy to beat the shit out of me while I was safely restrained in a net, and now he sat in his big, stupid chair, the very image of strength and bravery with protective runes all around and a sorcerer at his side. Bet he wouldn't be so cocky alone in a dark alley at night.

"Az, you dare to come back after the insult you delivered to me last time? And it seems you're making friends all over Hel. I'm deliberating which contract on you I'll take. Our neighboring kingdom, or that Haagenti creature."

"I think you'll have a hard time reaching Haagenti right now, unless you've got a medium on your staff. He's rather dead, you see."

A flicker of concern crossed Feille's face. Yeah, fucker. Wonder how he died. Wonder if I did it. Wonder how a little imp took Haagenti out. Go ahead and think about that.

"Well, that limits my options. Seems you'll be vacationing a while in Cyelle."

I knew those guys hated each other. Even if he had no other use for me, he'd dangle me tauntingly in front of Taullian's face before he'd turn me over, regardless of the reward, and I was positive he'd much rather get his sorcerer back. He had to be running low on them at this point.

"Oh, I love it there," I told him with a smile. "They fuck demons, you know. If I'm lucky, I may even be able to knock one of them up."

He looked properly horrified. So if the leak on Amber's existence came from his kingdom, it didn't come from him.

"Cyelle elves may be our enemies, but they would never stoop so low," he said, fuming over the insult.

"Doesn't matter," I told him, waving the subject away. "You needed my help; I told you I'd put you on the waiting list, and here I am. Now serving number forty-two."

He considered my statement, weighing the need to get his sorcerer back with the fun he'd have teasing Taullian with me. Of course, that would mean he would need to keep me here, properly restrained, under guard. I saw the realization flash in his eyes as he made his decision.

"Come on, dude," I prompted him. "I don't have all day. I've got things to do, places to be."

"The sorcerer's name is Gareth," he said grudgingly. "He and an apprentice ran off two months ago. Gareth was last seen in Eresh, but it is believed the apprentice has crossed twice through a gate."

Two months? He can't have been sitting on his thumbs for two months with a missing sorcerer.

"Did the apprentice cross through an elf gate or an angel one?"

"An angel gate. The first one was in Dis; this last time he left through Eresh."

There were two gates in Eresh. So he went to either Seattle or Milan, although he could have gone anywhere after he arrived. Use of an angel gate meant he'd had a demon helping him cross, and not an elf.

"There is a severe penalty for any of my elves or their humans caught assisting the runaways," Feille confirmed. "They would have been forced to use demon assistance."

"Does this Gareth have any magical item or scroll that I should be aware of?" Sometimes bringing back the sorcerer wasn't enough. If they had a scrying mirror, or a wand of regeneration, or something, the elves would want that returned too. And of course, I wanted to know if he had a weapon that might kill me before I could lay a claw on him.

"No."

Feille was lying. Which meant he didn't want whatever it was back badly enough to risk anyone knowing about it. If the magical item surfaced, he'd just deny any knowledge and claim Gareth did it on his own. Great.

"So you want the sorcerer and the apprentice? Or just the sorcerer?" It always helped to be specific about these things, especially after the little misunderstanding with Taullian.

"Both. Both alive. And both with their mental faculties intact." Ah, so the thing-which-would-not-be-named wasn't a thing after all, it was knowledge, or an ability held by either Gareth or his minion.

"So they have some ability then? Either the sorcerer, his apprentice, or both?"

"The sorcerer has significant ability." Feille admitted.

"So, why did it take you two months to decide to go after this guy?" Sorcerers were very valuable, and warrants for their capture were usually put out right away.

"We have had two other demons attempt to apprehend him," Feille said casually. "They did not succeed."

They gave up? Got distracted? Were still out there looking? I needed to know. I didn't want to be bumping heads with two other demons hunting the same quarry. "Can you be more specific? How exactly did they not succeed?"

Feille smiled serenely. "They were killed."

Yikes. So this sorcerer did have "significant ability".

"And their heads were returned to me in a box," he continued.

Oh, snap. So this sorcerer wasn't hiding, a desperate runaway trying to lie low. He was giving his former boss the middle finger. Significant ability seemed to be an understatement. Part of me thought long and hard about refusing this assignment, but the other part was intrigued. What was this Gareth's game plan? The elves would never give up looking for him. Did he intend to make a life with the demons and guard against capture for the rest of his life? Or did he perhaps intend to follow in his apprentice's footsteps and go through a gate? A few hundred years ago, it was common for mages and sorcerers to try and escape elven reach by going through a gate to live with the humans. It didn't always work out. Any show of magic would usually turn the humans against them, and many sorcerers either found themselves enslaved to powerful kings as they had been to their elven masters, or burned at the stake.

In modern times, humans would be more tolerant of their magic, but modern technology interfered with many of their workings, causing haywire results or no results at all. I didn't know of any sorcerer who had crossed in the last hundred years. Mages who had crossed, found themselves trying to sneak back to Hel, where their decades of training amounted to more than birthday party tricks and circus sideshow acts.

"And my payment would be?"

He smiled. It was a very unpleasant smile. "Well, you have already received some of your payment in two passages through our lands and gate. I would grant you free passage through our lands and gates for the next century, I would grant you safe harbor against Cyelle, and I will give you two transport buttons. If you don't use them in the commission of your contract, then you are free to keep them. I will even offer to have them recalibrated to the destination of your choice."

Not a bad offer normally, but given the nature of this sorcerer, it was a paltry deal. This was a really big dog, with an unknown magical skill that had already killed two demons. I wavered, wondering what I could ask for that would possibly be worth this suicide mission, and, as I thought, my hand hit something hard in my pocket: Kirby's marble. A twelve-year-old boy, snatched from his family. A man who was a virtual slave in Hel, but would never be able to adjust to human life if he somehow managed to escape. Something snapped inside me. Fuck these elves. I was team Gareth The Sorcerer. Anyone who ran off, evaded and took out two demon bounty-hunters, and rubbed the noses of his former masters in shit was someone I was rooting for.

"Nah. I think I'll pass."

I thought Feille's eyes were going to leave his skull. "You *will* do this."

Here we go again. "I don't have anything against this sorcerer. He sounds like a pretty cool guy, actually. We could be besties. Get off your lazy elven asses and get him yourself if you want him so bad."

He changed tactics. "The mighty Iblis is afraid of a human? The Ha-satan is too much of a coward to take on a simple retrieval job?"

Wrong tactic. Pride has never been my sin. "Yep. That's me, yellow through and through. Now we've agreed on that, I'll just be collecting my horse and heading on my way."

A shrewd look crossed Feille's face. "No job, no horse."

I let that hang in the air for a few moments, then casually removed my shotgun from the holster and held it down at my side. "You would steal my hybrid? You would steal from the Iblis?"

The atmosphere froze, and suddenly everyone in the room was tense and ready for action. I had their full attention. Feille shot a quick glance at his sorcerer then flicked a questioning nod at my shotgun.

"I don't know My Lord." The sorcerer was beet red, his hands white knuckled on his staff. Obviously *I don't know* wasn't something anyone should ever say to his lordship. "Perhaps a metal reinforced walking stick?"

I held it aloft. "This. . . is my boom stick."

They'd obviously never watched the movie, and the only word that registered in their arrogant elven brains was "stick". Feille relaxed slightly, thinking I'd try to rush him and beat him with it. He was confident his guards would take me down before I made two steps in his direction, and the sorcerer would block any energy attack, then throw a net on me in seconds.

"You abandoned your horse," he said, his voice full of disdain. "Left it here in my kingdom. It's my horse now."

I brought the shotgun up again in a smooth motion and shot off the top of his throne. Bits of wood, gold, and gems sprayed around the room. Everyone hit the floor, including the sorcerer who was too concerned about his own physical wellbeing to protect Feille.

"Give me my fucking horse, or I'll blow your head across the room." It was a bold move. No demon had ever publically attacked an elf before, and especially not a High Lord.

Feille screamed in an amusing combination of rage and fear, and his sorcerer recovered his wits enough to cast a net on me. I considered having Gregory yank me out again, but thought "what the hell" and pulled the trigger on the shotgun once more. With a deafening roar, the net exploded, sending chunks of bright blue fire all around the room. Once again, everyone hit the floor.

"My horse. Right now. Or I'll go find him myself and massacre everyone in my path."

The hate rolled off Feille in waves. He was backed into a corner, and that was obviously an unfamiliar feeling.

"Get the demon-spawn horse," he snapped at the guards.

Three took off, leaving their High Lord woefully unprotected. No doubt he'd punish them harshly later, but right now I'm sure they felt I was the bigger threat to their continued existence. Elves are fast. Within thirty seconds they were leading Diablo through the palace. He had a collar around his neck, no doubt to keep him from teleporting or shooting them with bolts of energy. I heard his welcoming neigh echo throughout the hall and he tossed his head, trying to shake off the three lead ropes attached to his halter.

"Where's my saddle? And my bridle?"

"He didn't have any when we found him," Feille lied.

The bastards stole my tack. I'd need to ride the horse bareback and without a bit. One wrong move and I'd be in the dirt. Stomping over, I snatched one of the lead ropes from a wary guard and looped it around the other side of the halter, creating a set of makeshift reins. The whole time I was careful to keep my shotgun at the ready. One moment of inattention and I was sure the elves would be all over me.

"Give me a leg up," I told the guard. He looked nervously at Feille then cupped his hands obligingly. I planted my foot in them and swung up on my horse, knocking him in the head with my knee on the way. It felt strange to be bareback on Diablo. He snorted his displeasure, and I pulled my legs more forward, careful to keep my heels out of his side.

"If you ever cross my lands again, ever use my gate, I'll kill you," Feille vowed.

I shrugged. "Are you going to have someone lead me out, or should I just ride my horse around your abode until I figure out where the exit is?"

He motioned to an unlucky guard, who led the way. I nudged Diablo forward, darting constant looks around and holding the shotgun aloft. Another guard followed at a safe distance, and we made a somber procession through the eerily silent palace and the empty streets of the town. Feille may be an ass, but he'd secured his people in case I changed my mind and started randomly shooting. The gates opened and the forest lay before me.

"Southwest will take you to Dis, although you'll need to go further south to avoid the tip of Cyelle before you turn westward," one of the guards advised. "Unless you're planning to head north to Eresh."

"I'm going toward Dis," I told him. From there I could head west toward the grasslands and Maugan Swamp, my old stomping grounds.

"May the Lady grant you her favor, Iblis," he added, smiling slightly. I wondered if he was one of Tlia's family or if he just admired my ballsy attack on his High Lord.

"You too," I told him, and headed southwest.

Diablo picked up speed once we made it out of Wythyn and into Dis. I'd also discovered that he could teleport me along with him, kind of like Gregory did. Any jealousy I felt at the fact that my horse could manage an inter-realm gate when I couldn't was squelched by the obvious usefulness of his talent. We made short work of the journey by teleporting through chunks. In mere hours we were thundering across the grasslands where I'd grown up. Cyelle lay to the north, just beyond a common land of woods, and wetlands dotted the northwest, eventually becoming the great Maugan Swamp. As a youth, I'd enjoyed snoozing in the swampy mud, hiding behind the rushes and cattails from siblings who loved to torment a little imp. I thought about stopping in to see my foster parents, Mere and Pere, or possibly the elderly dwarf, Oma, who had so often sheltered me from the attacks of the others, but I longed to get back, to see my friends, and Boomer. To hold Wyatt tight in my arms. To show that damned angel that I'd done it, that I was not the worthless cockroach he'd thought. So I turned north, into the swath of woods that served as a buffer between the demon lands and the forbidden Cyelle.

And there it stood: the angel gate that led to the Columbia Mall. A strange wave of nostalgia went through me. I'd used so many gates in my life, ones that led to places in Europe, Asia, South America. I'd started my long vacation, my forty years with the humans, through the gate in Seattle. But this gate, so close to where I'd grown up, I'd never traveled through this gate. I'd sent demon corpses through and activated it for a Low. Dar used it all the time, as did Leethu, but I'd never been through. Somehow this felt memorable, like it heralded a new stage in my life.

"Let' go boy," I told Diablo and he surged forward. I reached out and activated the gate as we plunged through.

~32~

We shot out of the other side of the gate in front of a children's shoe store and rode into instant chaos. People screamed and ran, terrified to have a woman on a charging horse appear from nowhere. They knocked each other aside in their haste, spilling packages and sliding across the polished floor. Diablo, thrilled to their panic, tore full speed down the center of the mall, vaulting a fake hair kiosk and knocking assorted ponytails and extensions everywhere. He wasn't so lucky with the cell phone kiosk, slamming into it and crushing electronics with determined hooves. I frantically held onto his mane with one hand, trying to remain seated, my other hand clutching the shotgun. I should have been more concerned with pulling myself upright, but Diablo's mood was infectious. I pulled the trigger, exploding lights and decorative ceiling panels.

"Woohoo!" I fired off a few more shots as I managed to right myself. I looked around at the humans shrieking and hiding behind huge cement planters, and saw Gregory.

"I fucking rock," I shouted at him.

"Yes, I see that." He didn't look particularly pissed at me, so I fired one more shot before holstering the shotgun and nudging Diablo over toward him. The horse danced sideways, wanting to continue his fun, but eventually complied.

"So, from your jubilant display, I'm to assume you finally took care of your problem back in Hel?" He rubbed Diablo on the nose, and the traitorous horse looked adoringly at him.

"Why yes. Yes I did." I didn't tell him that I now had a few other problems. I doubted the elves would be sending hitmen over to attack Wyatt and I, but the loss of their alliance would cause difficulties.

Gregory smiled. It was that unnerving, seductive smile that scared me as much as it turned me on. "So are you planning on riding your demon horse down I-70, or will you be begging me to give you a lift back to your house?"

Begging. His emphasis on the word sent all sorts of naughty thoughts into my head and a shiver down my spine. Though with an angel, begging might involve something far less pleasant than what I had in mind. Either way, there would be no begging from me today.

"None of the above," I told him. "Watch this."

I pulled Diablo back a few steps and informed Gregory that I would see him later. Ha. I wished I could see the look on that smug angel's face when we teleported away. I didn't need him anymore. I'd just use my horse to gate around from now on.

"Home, Diablo!" I waved my hand in a dramatic Lone Ranger gesture, and instantly found myself crashing to the floor on top of broken cell phones and fake hair. Fucking horse had left me behind.

"Very impressive, little cockroach." Gregory watched me scramble to my feet without even bothering to offer a hand. "Is he coming back for you eventually? Or perhaps you'd like to call your human toy for a ride?"

I hadn't exactly taken my cell phone to Hel with me. And I really didn't want to call Wyatt to come pick me up.

"Um. Can you please give me a lift back to my house."

He smiled again. "It's a bit out of my way. Quite inconvenient for me, you know."

"Please?" I begged.

The angel looked thoughtful. He even tapped his chin with his finger, giving my request careful consideration.

"Well, it *would* be nice to have another favor."

What the fuck was he going to do with all these favors? I was going to need to start a spreadsheet to keep track of them all. Maybe send him a monthly statement, showing favors owed, favors used, how many remaining ones he had left. Why did he need all these favors? It's not like I said "no" to him that often. Okay, maybe I said "no" a lot, but he usually convinced me to change my mind without the need to resort to favors.

"Fine. Another favor," I conceded.

He motioned me over toward him, and I willingly went into his arms. With a disorienting jolt, we were in my living room. Before I could even open my mouth to thank him, a piercing wail hit my ears.

Leethu quickly slapped her hand over her mouth as she recognized Gregory and I. She was a scant foot from us, and I could hardly blame her for being alarmed. Dar was on the other side of the couch, frozen in fear.

"I told you never to make that noise again," Gregory thundered. I wiggled an arm free of his tight grasp and punched his shoulder.

"Oh leave her alone. You appeared right in front of her. I would have screamed too."

"No, you would have blown my head off," he corrected. "Not screamed like some witless banshee."

True, but still, he really should give Leethu a break. "It's my house, and I say you can't kill her."

Leethu and Dar took the opportunity to dash upstairs where hopefully the angel would forget about their presence.

Gregory sighed dramatically. "Oh all right, little cockroach. I'll spare her life this once."

He was still holding me tight, and I wasn't sure what to do with the one free arm. Should I let it dangle awkwardly at my side? If he were Wyatt, I would have put it on his chest, but I didn't exactly want to encourage him. As it was, his spirit self was resting against mine in a comfortable intimacy, gently shifting in a caress. Damn, he felt good.

"Do you want to make coffee?" I asked stupidly, my arm extended at a ridiculous angle.

He rubbed along me, his power leak increasing and searing me with its heat. "No," he said, and I suddenly wondered what he wanted to do instead of make coffee. Oh, please, please, please.

"You have a lot of do." He released me. "I've submitted your protest on the four-five-nine report for that human in Virginia, but there is one due for the human in Mount Airy. Actually, I believe it's overdue."

Fuck! Oh holy crap. I did not want more "naked and restrained," especially after all I'd just been through in Hel.

"An extension?" I asked hopefully.

He smiled. "Twenty-four hours." And then he was gone.

That didn't leave much time, but there never seemed to be enough time. Which was an odd feeling for a near immortal to have. I picked up my cell phone from the dining room table. Wyatt answered on the first ring.

"I'm home," I told him.

Epilogue

I peered in the window, wracked with indecision. I should just leave the thing on their doorstep. Ring and run. But instead here I was, looking in at them—a man and a woman, in their late fifties. I was surprised they'd stayed together; so many couples get divorced after losing a child. Kirby's parents had moved from his childhood home in Wisconsin to North Carolina. His father worked some kind of tech job in Research Triangle, and his mom had gone back to school after his disappearance and received a degree in early childhood education. She taught pre-school and specialized in working with the learning disabled. They never had any more children, but they both were very active in their church's youth groups and Sunday school programs. Wyatt had found all this out for me. He had given this project his stamp of approval, encouraged me to give these poor people closure. But I wasn't sure it was the right thing.

I popped my head up again and observed the couple, eating together, plates on their laps as they watched some show on TV. They'd moved on. Managed to get through the pain of never knowing what happened to their son, eventually mourning him as dead. And here I was, to rip all that healing away and rub that pain raw once more. I couldn't reunite them with their son. They'd still never see him again. How could it possibly do any good to know he was alive, treated well but virtually enslaved in Hel? Wouldn't they be better off thinking him dead?

I felt the marble hard in my hand, smoothed the note Kirby had written to his parents. I'd granted him a favor, gave him my vow. How could I keep my word and not make life worse for his parents? There was no good way to do this. Fuck, I wasn't even sure they'd believe me. They might just think I was some wacko. This wasn't a job for a demon, this was a job for an angel. They'd believe an angel.

But there was no angel here. Just me.

I tried to be quiet as I tiptoed out of their flowerbed and made my way to the front door. I knocked. The barking of a little dog and footsteps sounded from inside. A bald man answered the door. His eyes looked like Kirby's.

"Hello, I'm Samantha Martin, the Iblis, Ha-satan. I have news to give you about your son, Kirby."

About The Author

Debra Dunbar primarily writes dark fantasy, but has been known to put her pen to paranormal romance, young adult fiction, and urban fantasy on occasion. She lives on a farm in the northeast section of the United States with her husband, three boys, and a Noah's ark of four legged family members. When she can sneak out, she likes to jog and ride her horse, Treasure. Treasure, on the other hand, would prefer Debra stay on the ground and feed him apples.

Connect with Debra Dunbar on Facebook at DebraDunbarAuthor, on Twitter @Debra_Dunbar, or at her website http://debradunbar.com/.

Sign up for New Release Alerts: http://debradunbar.com/subscribe-to-release-announcements/

Feeling impish? Join Debra's Demons at http://debradunbar.com/subscribe-to-release-announcements/, get cool swag, inside info, and special excerpts. I promise not to get you killed fighting a war against the elves.

Thank you for your purchase of this book. If you enjoyed it, please leave a review on Goodreads, or at the e-retailer site from which you purchased it. Readers and authors both rely on fair and honest reviews.

Books in the Imp Series:

The Imp Series
A DEMON BOUND (Book 1)
SATAN'S SWORD (Book 2)
ELVEN BLOOD (Book 3)
DEVIL'S PAW (Book 4)
IMP FORSAKEN (Book 5)
ANGEL OF CHAOS (Book 6)
IMP (prequel novella)
KINGDOM OF LIES (Book 7) Fall, 2015 release

Books in the Imp World
NO MAN'S LAND
STOLEN SOULS
THREE WISHES

Half-Breed Series
DEMONS OF DESIRE (Book 1)
SINS OF THE FLESH (Book 2) Summer, 2015 release
UNHOLY PLEASURES (Book 3) Spring, 2016 release

Printed in Great Britain
by Amazon